Selkies' Skins:
Castle and Well

BOOK ONE OF SELKIES' SKINS

BY
Teresa Garcia

THE STARDRAGON PUBLISHING

Selkies' Skins: Castle and Well
Book One of Selkies' Skins

Copyright © 2013 Teresa Garcia

THG StarDragon Publishing

ISBN-13: 978-0615947747
ISBN-10: 0615947743

First Edition

THG StarDragon Publishing
Attn: Teresa Garcia
PO Box 249
McCloud, CA 96057
USA

Story: Teresa Garcia

Cover Art: Samantha Buckley

Interior Art: Marantha Jenelle, Athena Garcia, and Teresa Garcia

Contents

Contents

Dedication

For my Vadise, with whom I always enjoy a good game and chat. Without you, Kirsty would most likely not have had a story to tell. You went and got me writing a whole story because of thinking up a character's back-story for our games and rekindled my inspiration. You ought to be proud of yourself considering how class was killing my writing. I just hope David is conveyed properly, and that my fried brain made enough sense on those days when all I wanted to do with our time was chat and recover instead of play...and that you didn't feel too neglected those days that writing, work, or school kept me quiet during the times you were able to be nearby.

This is also for my children, my greatest (and most exhausting) creative work. Once this is ready to read with you, I hope that you will enjoy it. Remember, even when Mommy is stressed past her limit and her hair is waving about all on its own like Goku's, and her eyes bug out, she still loves you.

Thank you to those readers who participated in the Kickstarter that helped provide the basic starting capital for this project. Your patience during the unexpected renovations and usual university studies that slowed my progress have been vastly appreciated.

In part I also dedicate this to Jan Parupia, who was also Marantha D. Jenelle and Amber Michelle. If not my biggest fan she was one of them, and I am very sad that you did not get to see this finished before your passing.

Finally, for my good friend, editor, and favorite earthbound angel, Faith. Simply for being my friend and my soul sister, because you deserve it. You and your family mean more to me than you know.

~Teresa

Section One
Whispered Tides

Excerpt from Marantha's fanart cover for the webnovel

CHAPTER ONE
LAND AND SEA

The waves washed over the rocks of Seal Point, steadily lapping their way up over the tide pools. The breeze had the characteristic bite of the Northern Ireland sea air, and was filled with the cries of gulls and seals. Blue eyes gazed back toward the half empty dock, her mother's vessel, the *Sea Witch*, a wooden fishing vessel that Kirsty had no idea how old it really was, had been gone since a couple days after David's visit. Her father's vessel, the *Cosantóir*, similar in style and just as weathered – probably in need of debarnacling again – bobbed forlornly alone, with its mate out to sea.

Her lips thinned and pressed together, and the wind worked more on teasing her dark hair out of the braids she wore. Kirsty whispered softly, in the Gaelic that her ancestress had taken such great pains to instill, invoking the sea to grant her mother's journey safety and fair winds. Though she was underage as far as the magical community was concerned, she often circumvented the rule in this manner, though she had yet to figure out why that worked. The more that she learned in school, the more she found that using that particular language instead worked better for her.

Kirsty's thoughts took on Marsali's voice as she remembered her ancestress' usual praise and echoed in her head, grimly satisfied. *"Rather difficult for the Ministry of Magic to regulate the magic of a Selkie, or other beast or being that has not submitted to their tyranny, isn't it, a chailín mo chroí?"* The Ministry was one of the few topics that always seemed to bring a bitter edge to the voice of the Selkie's painting, right along with detailed discussions about the loss of her sealskin, or the death of her human husband so long ago.

Hooves sounded behind her, striking rocks, and then muffled in the sand between, and several moments of picking their way down the beachfront resulted in Byron's whinny behind her.

"Kirstin, I've got the fire stoked up again, and the savory pie in the oven. I know you've got to be getting yourself into your school mindset, but the wounded Selkie needs your attention. Remember I'm bound and can no longer shift, or I'd do it myself to give you a bit more rest." The voice nagged, slightly more bitter than usual when recalling – as always – how he had been dealing with his constraints.

She turned around to stroke the Kelpie's nose, nesting her forehead against the wet, green, slightly tacky muzzle. Byron's tail lashed disconsolately at a fly on his flank, whether it was there or not, the sand beneath him absorbing the water ever dripping from him. His pointed teeth bared a bit, the urge to eat whatever was distressing the daughter of his current mistress strong.

"You'd be out there with mom right now, if not for me?"

"Aye, but you'll need a ride to London, I can catch up to her once you're safely off and ensconced next to your friends." He paused, and sighed. "One day you might be out there with her, especially if you end up trying to find new things from the sea for your potions. For now though, you can't help her on her missions. You'll go to school and get trained in human magic too, *then* you'll be ready if she needs you. And besides, you'll get to see David meanwhile, true, *a chroí*?"

Kirsty flushed at the mention of David. Byron chuckled a bit.

"Ah, I remember when your mother was this age. Etain was just as shy about all things Finnol." He nudged her up toward the stone house, a flowering vine currently working its way up to arch the doorway, a protective measure installed again before her mother's departure. "How about I tell you one of your mother's adventures while you work?"

"I'd like that..."

Meanwhile, older blue eyes cut their gaze over the stormy sea. The past month's sail had brought more storms than usual on her voyages, almost as if the sea itself wanted to push her limits. Mara had been in a strange mood all summer, and Etain had had to deal with it. Between Mara of the Sea and the Lady of the Well she was always busy enough... but a waterwitch often found herself dealing with far more than she was ever given credit for in the Magical world.

For the time being, at least, she was still on course. Though she could not see the stars currently, she could feel them. Etain wasn't fully sure where she was off to this time anyway. The letter the owl had brought had contained one small vial of water, and only the instructions that it was urgent that she track down the source of it. With instructions like this, perhaps it made sense that her daughter preferred the idea of potion making. It was safer seeming on the surface...

Yet, she still remembered the day that Tommy Tuckin had accidentally put too much pomegranate juice in his potion. To this day he still had no eyebrows, and she still had yet to figure out how he'd added that instead of toad blood when vials had been so clearly marked. She tried imagining the same sort of accident happening to Kirsty, but simply couldn't. Far too careful, and even more so was the young man that had become so close to her daughter.

Thunder boomed and rolled, the sky opening up shortly after, yet again pouring down cold rains to run off the deck.

"It couldn't have been a well spirit giving birth to a spring stuck the wrong way, or something else equally land bound..." Her gaze went to the vial of water clamped where she could check it near the helm, eyes widening as it began to glow a vivid blue. "At least I'm getting closer..."

Suddenly, something tingled at the edges of her senses. A chill ran down her spine, and the amulet hanging around her neck began to heat up, waking after several years of sleep.

Chapter Two
POCKET OF DEATH

The amulet on Etain's chest continued to heat, and the storm around her continued to thrash the sea into frothy mountains. Her ship continued to rise and fall, traveling several stories in what seemed like mere seconds, and it only seemed to be getting worse.

Unbidden, the prayer rose from her throat, a lone voice of song threading through the sound of waves and storm, drawn and mournful, slipping back and forth between English and Gaelic unconsciously.

"When the Storm is raging and the Thunder rolls, Oh Lady Mara, save my soul and deliver me from the storm. Carry me onward to fulfill my duty to you... and then to be reunited to my husband and daughter."

At her hip, in the plain and yet somehow oddly ornate leathern pouch strapped securely to the belt holding her skirts, a stirring answered. A pulse. She felt the odd coalescing of Power around her, quite different from the human magic, and different yet from the magic of the Merfolk she was a descendant of. Mara watched, the goddess of the bitter seas always watched the mariners that traversed her realm.

Etain couldn't remember a time that it comforted her less to be a Priestess of the Waters of Life and a waterwitch. Especially as the towering wave rose before her, obscuring the sky of the Northern Sea... Not that the sky was very visible except for when the lightning lit the clouds and took the form of dragons lancing across.

The wave before her began to crest, directly ahead, so without using her magic the boat was not going to pass safely over, as it would have if just 100 yards left or right. The closer the wall of water drove, the more that she could see through the white froth frosting the green 'glass' the phosphorescence of algae and the forms of fish and sharks caught too near the surface. Normally, the sea life would have gone further down... but she had no time to ponder how quickly the storm must have come to where she had found herself cast.

Clinging to her wheel, she banked hard right, toward the closer of the uncurled sides, murmuring commands in Gaelic to the boat. Unseen, due to focusing so hard on her course and willing the boat to move faster and the sails to finish adjusting themselves, strange glowing glyphs formed and vanished even though her wand lay in the sheath near her pouch. For her part, the old boat raced forward as eagerly as her Captain willed, skimming faster than should have been possible were it not for the old magics impregnating and enlivening her.

Eternity seemed to pass, then water crashed over the stern, yet her humble old 'fishing vessel' cleared well enough and began the rush down the backside. Even with sea legs, the rise of her guts was unsettling.

On the downward ride instead of the gulfing chasm before her Etain saw the face of her husband. Blue eyes bored into hers filled with worry and that *knowing* that he always had when he knew she was in danger. His dark hair was tousled, the way it usually was when stressed over paperwork or when *that reporter* would come too close to discovering the secret of those others also responsible for dealing with the water... from plumbing problems, to driving new wells, to... more dangerous and intricate things. Etain's own blue eyes bored determinedly back into his own, and every tiny bit of her soul screamed silently at him her resolution.

"I will return to you, even if I have to come back from my own drowning. Just keep the light going for me and do what you can at the Well, Finnol."

The downward momentum stopped, and the boat began to climb the next wave, the *Sea Witch* as resolute as the current captain. The crest of the wave was won, and then the gully and the next crest, till seven waves passed below and away. With each wave the amulet grew hotter, 'til it glowed with baleful green and blue lights, and the Devil's Fire played about the boat's bow and masts. And then, once that seventh wave was passed beyond, the Devil's Fire closed over the whole craft, and with a loud, rumbling *BOOM* that rolled away into untold dimensions and jostled the spaces between all things... The storm vanished.

The Devil's Fire crackled away.

Stars shone with a high, cold, light where before clouds had roiled and hid the skies, and far overhead hung the large pocked mirror of the moon, perfectly full and round. The amulet – that perfect disk of sea-worn stone on the same leather thong through the hole at dead center that her mother had hung round her neck the night of her very firstborn's birth – still seared her warningly. Cautiously, Etain released the wheel and undid the sticking charm keeping her feet secured to the floor, then flowed out onto the deck.

Over the side, the sea lay flat and smooth as glass, glowing a sickly green, mottled with blue. It wasn't the vibrant, beautiful glow that was known to amaze surfers, fishers, and divers. Somehow, it was more like an abomination of color, saturated with a menace that she rarely came across. A reek that could only be described as unholy wafted upward and filled her nose.

"Deadzone..." She observed, despite the lack of Finnol, Byron, or any members of the Finned Ones. Her hand rested protectively on her pouch, the shapes of two cloth wrapped vials at the top of all that lay within pressing back upon her fingers. "The storm must be a containment field the local water spirit is using. This is even worse than I thought..."

Plastic became apparent to her eyes next, floating and languishing, decomposing and slowly poisoning the waters even more than they already were. Etain pursed her lips, knowing well how it would be entering the food chain if anything happened to still be alive below the surface.

Now she drew her wand and pushed back her darkened,

reddish hair. Spell after spell she began to work through, and soon her hair, red cloak, and green skirts billowed around her, despite the severe lack of wind. And yet, spell after spell failed to do enough to clean the physical and magical taints that had somehow managed to be mingled together at the heart of this particular gyre...

Or what had been a small gyre...

Hours passed in this manner, and the moon slid beneath the waves while the stars faded, creating a silver bridge over the waters, for a short time, to the Land of the Faer. *"But... I am already here, aren't I?"* Cut the dry observation through her mind, with all the weight of anchor and chain. An even deeper part of herself acknowledged the passing of the moon, and cringed at the pain she knew would be and already had been felt that night by the boy she had come to think of as one of her own.

When the sun rose, still she had made little progress on the water. Even worse to see in the light, the water was a dead, decaying brown sludge. Even the red bloom algae taking advantage of the state of things seemed to be languishing.

"There is little else that I can think of for it..."

A sigh and a shiver passed from her at the same time, dread, and more than a little fear, weighing her down. Etain began to disrobe, unhitching the clasp of her cloak first and letting it puddle on the deck. Next, the outer layers, and the divided covers below her petticoat joined it. From her pouch, she pulled out a brown sealskin cloak and unfurled it, clasping it about her shoulders in preparation for use. Sheathing her wand and stowing the human magic, she murmured a plea to the Lady of the Sea and the Lady of the Well for their help and strength.

Her legs carried her to the top of the railing seemingly of their own accord. Several deep breaths she drew into her lungs, overventilating as best she could, anticipating that there would be no oxygen for her to draw on in the murky depths. Then she dove, knifing deep, and once more the green and blue flames licked around her, and the curdled magic and dying water burned her skin before the fur sprouted to cover her. Her legs joined to form a long, muscular seal tail to drive her even deeper.

Chapter Three
Waterhorse Worry

In the corner of the room, an eternally dripping green Waterhorse lay, looking toward the young witch at her bedroom desk. The thirteen year old peered into her cauldron glumly, the twin dark braids reminding him vaguely of cramped up fins. Byron had lost count of how many and what sort of potions she had been brewing for the household use, to tide them over till the next stretch of time that she could contribute. There always seemed to be something or someone brought to the area in need of fixing, despite the protective measures set up centuries ago when the fire and the forest deities had withdrawn and wandered on. So, the Makays, being rather soft-hearted toward those in need, tended to go through a lot of healing supplies. Every generation he had helped to raise so far seemed to have this tendency.

He was certain it was inherited from his Marsali.

"Only the stars know what on earth possessed that pair of wizards to test whether the River Folk had any magic, but they did. Every chance they got they were putting something into the water that they knew those Fishfolk weren't going to like. Maybe they were wanting the fish for themselves, or maybe they'd read too many of those stories saying that all Merfolk can't do magic. When we got there, the river was in one bad way though, and even the Merfolk were having to cling to trees to keep from being swept away by the water's rage. A couple villages just totally washed away; I remember running by a floating house and getting whacked on the head over a houseboat joke."

"I wonder how much of the story she is absorbing. Too full of worry for her mother. Each generation is the same way... If she's not careful, David's going to start feeling like something might be wrong, since he's got the ring..."

Kirsty sighed, stirring her potion and pulling her thoughts back to the image of her mother single-handedly saving an entire village from a freak flood brought on by mouthy young wizards and the ire of much put upon River Folk... Decidedly away from images of storm tossed seas and broken fishing vessels sinking as vicious Tritons speared a floundering seal.

"If it had been up to me, I'd have left them to swim and to learn their lesson. Cowans have an excuse, wizards don't."

Her potion merely continued to brew, not knowing what Kirsty was talking about, and not caring, though the water that formed the base half listened to the part Selkie mumbling during the pause in the Kelpie's story.

"Aye, the same here, but only because I am old and getting bitter as sea water. And the Cowans don't have an excuse either, but they pay worse when the Old Things wake."

"You aren't old... or bitter Byron."

"Ha, you should have known me before Marsali passed away. You wouldn't have known what to do."

"Go on, what happened next?"

"So, there she was, at the edge of the roaring water. First, she tried talking to the river. It talked back alright, and the wizards could only hear booms and grinds as it wore away at the ground. Told her where to look to unwind the knot that had been made, and where some different potions had been disposed of. Seriously, I thought proper disposal was taught in school... So she took care of all that, but then..."

Byron took a bite of the apple between his knees as he considered how best to describe what had come next. Kirsty laid her willow and Selkie hair wand down, checking her watch before turning to face him.

"There was more that wasn't so easy to tell her..."

Byron regarded her with his green eyes, a strange frisson running along the base of his mane and causing it to rise slightly, but not enough to show his frill.

"Yes... how...?"

"I did something a little odd when visiting David, at a spring." She trailed off, then continued. "Still don't quite fully get it... Go on... Maybe it'll help me understand."

"Well, the next part, we went in the water, and she used her sealskin... after we were under so they wouldn't see her change. She later told me that she could kind of see where she needed to go, to stabilize it and get it resting again. Water doesn't like to be in an agitated state long. I didn't see all that she did, but I could hear her singing, and I saw her glowing. And she made the water... move... a... sort of... molecular sort of thing. Time felt odd... And the water receded and slept again in its bed like it's supposed to."

"And the water was... warm... and new..." Kirsty's voice was dreamy, and her eyes were looking through him, not at him. As if he was not there.

Byron shook himself a bit, the gaze making him feel decidedly uncomfortable.

"Yes. It was. And it whispered so that even I could hear it. After she got on land again though, she slept for a long time. It took a lot out of her." Byron frowned. "I never did like that the Ladies chose Marsali's offspring... Such a great deal to ask of you lot, especially with how the Full-bloods tend to view you on either side." He sighed. "And one day it will be your turn. Hopefully, not anything as... large. There have been some generations where nothing was asked other than to watch the well and assist the full Selkies with their rites." The last brought a slightly hopeful tenor to his voice.

Kirsty's eyes cleared, coming back from whatever she was gazing at, locking properly with his.

"Are you sure Mum's going to be able to come back? Maybe you should go and catch up. I can find another way in to London to catch the train..."

"Of course she will. She's your Mum." He smiled, what he hoped was soothingly, given how ferocious and hungry his smiles always looked. "How could she do anything else?"

The cold block in his heart and his gut though, he couldn't help, and prayed to Mara and the Well his worry didn't show through his eyes.

Chapter Four
visions and vessels

Paperwork... mounds upon mounds of paperwork huddled together in the small office that somehow seemed to have never seen the light of day despite the sunlight streaming through the window... This is the sight that greeted tired and bored blue eyes after they lifted from the report, which he finished with the decisive scrawl of his name and title.

Finnol Makay, Deputy Director of the Order of Fisheries and Water Conservation

"Somehow, that signature just does not convey the 'we are all in a lot of crap, I've been warning you about this for years' vibe..." He thought, laying down the quill.

Finnol scowled, knowing that in order to have his report actually *read* by anyone at the Ministry, he was more than likely going to have to take a copy himself, and beat heads with it in Etain's absence. She didn't carry much clout either, since everyone that worked with the water health sort of dwelt on the edge of the Magical community, and ended up with nasty rumors circulated... and a particularly annoying reporter now and then trying to pry into places they oughtn't.

Nobody particularly liked being told they were polluting, whichever society they lived in. Whichever governmental office they took presentations to, they all received the same wary glares. He'd had a few curses tossed by Cowans as well, untrained and unknowing as they were. Worse, whichever of the governments they went to, *she* would be there with her acid smile and unbelievably keen ears.

Selkie blood was hard enough to hide as it was, without her snooping. He examined his fingernails, the charm disguising the unmistakable points and poison tracts showing the signs of beginning to wear off due to the combination of stress, annoyance, and worry. With a breathy word, the illusion strengthened, and once more his nails looked perfectly normal... if slightly sharp.

A knock on the office door broke the tedium, and a short, cheerful-faced blond in a strange lilac-pink skirted suit entered.

"The reports from the universities, and the head of the Ocean Studies department sends his regards to you and your wife, Mr. Makay. Also, the owl you've been expecting arrived and left a letter. There's a Cowan waiting for you in the meeting room, one of those fishing groups... the Marine Management Association?"

Finnol looked down at his robes doubtfully, a very distinct and dark Victorian air to his garb that day, though definitely still very clearly screaming something along the line of *oddball sorcerer* to the wider world. "Guess that means that I ought to change..."

"Your over-robe only, I think sir... What's under is fine for a meeting. At least you weren't in your seafaring clothes."

"Thank you Hyacinth... Though honestly I wish I *were*. Besides the fact that I hear it is totally and completely normal for them to wear those for a 'quick' stop at a company main office, then I'd be out there *doing something effective*. Really, when getting all those promotions after hiring on, I swear each one took me more and more from the sea..."

"As you say... But you and your wife also have the most experience in all areas... You can't have it all."

The lilac-pink clad receptionist withdrew after leaving the reports on his desk, and Finnol took off and hung up his comfortable old velvet over-robe. He ran a finger over one of the anchor clasps before straightening the trim black suit, hints of dark green and grey showing here and there about him, before heading out the door.

Placing his hand on the door frame, suddenly the world seemed to reel about him. The familiar rise and fall of the sea turned land legs to rubber, and the brine and spray surrounded him, along with the anticipatory zing that usually came before a sky shattering round of thunder. Yet, before him was the hallway.

Down the hall was another matter. Superimposed on the reception office, he saw the *Sea Witch*, fighting her way through the swells. Through the window, an eerie, sickly blue glow lit the cabin and the helm, as the familiar crackle of Devil's Fire swept over the boat.

"Dear Mara preserve us... please let that just be electrical and not magical..." He thought, while watching his wife's vessel plunge down the backside of the wave. And then, the angle came just so, and his wife's eyes locked with his.

A split moment of knowing that she saw him too across the miles and then the vision vanished. The small vials carefully hidden in his inner pockets cooled, and it was at that moment that he realized that the bottled waters bearing the essence of their family goddesses had even woken. Thoughtfully, he caressed them through the cloth in acknowledgment before continuing through to the meeting room.

"Don't make me a widower Etain..."

The meeting room was a very bland room, intentionally so, in order for the Cowans that he did meet to have no inkling of what they actually took part in by providing information and help. To them, he was just another researcher in another nongovernmental order concerned with water health, shipping safety, and fishery safety. Nothing special, nothing flashy, exceedingly and painfully mundane. Selkie and Merfolk conservation slipped right in very easily, and the occasional visit by various Merfolk easily went un-noticed. This position made it easy for him to know when Cowans were getting too close to one of the Merclans or colonies.

Covering up the occasional discovered remains of one of the several species of Merfolk was always a little odd though.

"Ah, Finnol! Nice to meet with you again chap. Family well? I hear your wife's out in the field doing some research."

Finnol slipped into a seat and shook the proffered hand of the somewhat rotund and sandy haired man. "They're doing well Marc. To what do I owe the pleasure?"

"Straight to the point, as usual, I see. Well then." Marc puffed a bit, leaning back. "I believe you had an interest in those shoals? It seems that somehow they've been creeping out a bit, getting closer to the shipping lanes. Been getting some rather strange reports about moving rocks, and *ghost fishes* of all things, being hauled up by a couple boats. Of course, no one *believes* them since the catches vanish from the holds by the time they get to dock... but I know how you take an interest in these odd paranormal sort of things. And one of them *did* have a seal sitting in the hold for some reason, but no seal could eat an entire hold full in just a few hours. Maybe something to look into for that book of sea tales you've got going on the side?"

Finnol leaned forward over the table, attention once more fully here and now. "Maybe... Got contacts for me?"

Etain smiled grimly as the transformation finished and held, the sleek white and brown-grey speckled fur and blubber layer over her muscles insulating her from the frigid northern waters. The powerful tail sent her further with each stroke than her birth legs could have managed. And yet, though she had transformed, the skin she had kept hidden about her had not sent her fully to a seal's form, not having been closed completely. After all, she needed her arms for the task she had to do, and she could not help the tentacle-like form her head hair had taken... her own subspecies being a god-magic-made combination of two Merfolk species by at least two deities, not that even most wizards would believe *that* one.

Etain continued down into the murk, propelled by strong flicks of her tail, and the light of the sun was blocked swifter than normal for her dives. Pulling out her wand, she lit the tip and held it in front of her. The hair of her ancestress listened as the human magic of her land-children passed through it, and refined it to its best focus.

She nearly threw up when the bloated body of a deceased shark floated by, slowly sinking to the further depths. Still, she kept on, following the strange feeling in her bones and tug of her gut. More and more bodies she began to find, of more and more creatures. At last, she found the location that she was being pulled to.

Nothing looked any different. Dead bodies continued floating with Cowan and Wizard refuse. She could see a barnacle covered boat suspended beneath the water, drifting in such a way that she half expected a ghost crew, or to be pulled down by Davy Jones himself. A flicker of magic still stirred within, the water sucking from that, and before it passed her by she thought she saw a pale and bloated hand at a porthole. A piece of waterlogged paper passed close by, and grabbing it she saw some incomprehensible Asian writing of some sort. She vanished the paper instead of releasing it back to the sea, and did the same with as much as she could of the garbage, causing the water to roil more than a bit as the atoms simply were put back to a more original state and sent to the land where they could be of more immediate use.

The deathly silence was broken by an approving sound from around her, and the sense of being watched intensified.

"Yes, you are being watched. So you're the waterwitch that answered? I was expecting something a bit different and more powerful. And a lot more pure."

"Area spirit?" She questioned in her mind, looking around. Her hair kept searching the water for some sign of movement, and her whiskers twitched, yet they could find no indication of anything moving bodily – that was living.

"Of sorts. One of Mara's and Arnamentia's 'children' I do believe? I feel their waters on your person."

There it came, the flicker at the edge of her consciousness, a stirring and vastness of deep currents and floating ice, and visions of the deities the ocean-being spoke of. The ethereal shark woman, tall, lean, and mean... clutching a spear that continually changed form. The wistful and translucent blue well and spring spirit that centered in the stone well up in the forest near Seal Point was the next image formed.

She turned the name over in her mind, memorizing it, in case it was the name that her patroness had lost, planning to ask later if it was the identity she sought to reclaim.

"Yes, their waters flow in my veins."

"Good, then you also contain the 'schematics' I require, for lack of a better term, from your mind and blood, halfling. Provide those for me, then we shall see what else I need, other than the humans to stop throwing their muck in me."

Half formed images of the crew on the last ship that had ventured into the waters followed. An enspelled item of some kind flew over the side, where it joined dumped potions – didn't they know how to divide and vanish – and it met with some leaking barrels of a glowing ooze with... the glyph for radioactive material?

A familiar sensation swept over her next, the deep need for sleep as pressure came on mind and body. Her lungs ached for air, despite the fact the breath she had taken should be able to last several more minutes. She could draw breath, when working the Ladies had made very sure that their Priestesses and Bearers could breath air, seawater, and freshwater... but she was afraid to here due to the evidence she saw of lack of oxygen. Pressure increased, or so it seemed, tearing apart her molecular structure, seeking the code she carried in her blood.

Chains, molecules, atoms. Things normally named only by Cowans, and some only spoken of by Cowan scientists, swept through her vision. She watch bonds form and break, watched the release and binding of pure energy into matter, felt the presence of an unnameable and untouchable *something* coalesce and grow stronger around her. The Devil's Fire flamed up again around her, electric discharge from some unknowable place. Her vision began to darken, the sheen of her furred body and face fading, and the sinking feeling of her life draining came next.

"Please don't take it all... I'm not ready to die."

"Nor am I. If I die, it spreads, and all the seas will decay faster. What is one halfbreed Selkie against the base of life itself? Especially as it seems you have already pupped. There are more of you."

She began to struggle. The pressure increased. Her wand flared now; not reacting of its own accord but also not hers either. The very definite pressure of two hands over her own came. Suddenly, the health of the water began to change. Deep inside, there was the thrum that came with *knowing*, and she took a deep breath. And then another. The garbage was still around. Things still decayed. Yet, oxygen had returned.

The breath had not come soon enough though.

"And if you take all her life force, how will she clean this mess here? Really you can be so unreasonable, don't we have enough trouble keeping them? I lost several of her pups to Finfolk and Taint already." The cold feminine blade of a voice cut through her consciousness, just as it escaped her. Something slid past her, powerful and sleek, bumping her toward the surface and out of the grip of the bitter spirit.

ᴄhapᴛᴇʀ ꜰive
lady oꜰ ᴛhe well

Kirsty sighed, repacking her trunk for at least the tenth time, pausing now and then to finger a book, or to unroll a parchment to rework her summer assignments. Looking around her room, she surveyed the warm colors and fretted over what extra things she needed to pack for her leisure time.

"Mistress? Is that enough blue yarn, and what about the purple? And did you remember your wool cards and spindle? Oh, here they are mistress. I shall wrap them safely... Now where did that bag go?"

A small form hopped about the room, passing in and out of visibility, and leaving a wet footprint here and there. Perhaps six inches, the little water imp rarely ever wore anything but leaves fashioned into crude clothing, save for special occasions when he preferred something that she had woven and sewn as a mark of honor.

"Yes Imp, I think I've packed what I will use of those colors, as well as the 'wool' from the furry hyppocampus herd in the North Sea. That ought to be interesting to work with."

The water imp, who had busily been doing exactly as he said he would, danced with glee.

"I had been hoping that you would get to that, mistress. Such strange stuff it is, Until Connor showed us a sample, I hadn't believed that they could actually appear *woolly* and not just... um..." The imp paused a moment and sat, pondering what descriptor he would be able to use without Kelpie ears overhearing and taking offense.

Kirsty chuckled quietly and patted the dark head lightly.

"Sea creatures so far north all have mechanisms to keep warm, like how what I do have of my pelt was so thick last winter. Also, different areas have different subspecies, like the plants I've been studying and experimenting with. Now, what's more interesting is the upsurge in trade between the Merclans, and how they are starting to be a little less harsh to those of us that are stuck on land for one reason or another."

The imp snorted. "Merchants and Traders definitely are your ancestors, mistress. I am only a simple water imp from the forest streams. I understand much more when you talk of fishing, sailing, and exploring waterways."

"Speaking of..." Kirsty got up, drifting out of her room and down the stairs then through the hall and to the mudroom with a curious Imp scampering along behind her. "Byron, I'm too restless, I'm heading out to the well and stream."

A muffled answer came from the kitchen, from around what sounded like a pot.

"Are you *sure* you don't want any help in there with the washing?"

An annoyed whinny issued, what she had learned to take as a "No, don't ask again."

"Alright."

From the living room, Kirsty heard the portrait of the full Selkie Marsali calling. "Don't forget your cloak little one. Convey my regards to her Ladyship if you speak to her." The voice – though not raised – carried well, conveying with it intimate knowledge of the depths of the seas, distant rivers, and loss, which gave it a strange, violin-like quality.

"Yes ma'am. Getting it even now."

"You have your wand?"

"Always."

She took her white lambskin cloak from the peg by the door. For the millionth time, she wondered why it seemed more like seal than lamb, then swept out into the late evening. Above her, the stars began to peek through the purple spreading over the sky.

The sound of sheep bleating in their field mixed with chirping crickets, the steady beat of the sea, calls of harbor seals on rocks, and, the closer she came, the trickling babble of the stream that danced down to the sea. She wandered idly up its banks to the source, breathing deeply the smell of the grasses and summer flowers that peeked through, and the way it mingled with the fresh and salt waters, and the trees that grew denser the farther out from the immediate precincts of the old village. Kirsty passed by an overgrown foundation thoughtfully, glancing at it only long enough to note that the fox family still used the den beneath.

Skirts swished around her legs, which she held out of the way when the path along the stream grew rougher. A quiet splash, and Kirsty knew that Imp had jumped in to swim upstream, though still nearby enough to come when called. Finally, she saw the rocks, exposed at the base of the hill, and the tiny pool left undisturbed for the animals of the area. In the growing darkness, the water bubbling up and filling the pool seemed to glow a light blue, though it lost that gradually on flowing out from the pool to form the stream. The water called to her, and she picked her way over to where the water came forth, slipping her hand into the pool.

Whispers of the depths below filled her senses, and she absorbed the information the water brought about the ground it had seeped through, and the current depth of the aquifer below. Kirsty noted with satisfaction and relief that the local water table, for now, was still untouched by the strange chemicals that she had felt in other waters, no laces of pain and illness to seep through her veins. Or at least, was so when this water had seeped up from it.

A soft splash – and the feeling of The Presence – drew her attention to the top of the hill, her heart rate speeding back up to normal from the slow rhythm it had taken. Gradually, her eyes saw the glowing form at the top, her inner vision seeing it long before her eyes themselves. Above the rim of the well, the top just glimpsed from her spot, rose the form of a long haired woman, translucent and emanating that same blue light, though much more powerfully than the water at the base. Long hair flowed in cascades as she stood watching the girl.

Kirsty stood, curtsying respectfully and with a slightly higher flourish than usual, an apology for being observed unaware.

"Greetings, my Lady."

"Greetings Kirstin... and apology accepted. You still need to work on being able to maintain awareness around you, in addition to that of the water system though."

"Yes, Lady..."

"You are still troubled. Do you need more of the water for healing the injured Selkie? Her wound takes so long with her being less than cooperative."

Kirsty shook her head, more hair working out from the braids she'd put it in. The well spirit sighed, and gestured, taking a seat on the edge of the ancient stone well. Kirsty climbed up the hill, sat at the indicated spot, then turned to gaze into the depths.

"Something doesn't feel right. It hasn't for a while."

The well spirit watched the young one quietly for a few moments, seemingly impassively, as the half Selkie undid her hair and began to run her fingers through, unconsciously trying to groom out her worries, as so many of her kind did.

"There are many things wrong in the world. It is not unusual for your precognition to have you so restless. The *Changeling*," here, she sniffed in annoyance, "is rising back to power. Meddlesome, soulless near-human that he is, poking into areas that should only be taught by deity to mortal in order to preserve the balance of things. May the Lord of the Hunt bring his wrath upon him at the end, for the hunt will be a grand one. Especially for the persecution he incites toward my hidden children."

Kirstin took her gaze from the deep waters, which rippled in reaction to the spirit, or more accurately, ancient deity, and her disgust. With surprise, she noticed a fierceness that was usually not apparent to her.

"This must be why the local Selkies all bring their spears here for blessing. It's not so much as to have her permission to hunt her waters, too. It's a far more complex connection, and they wish to draw on her power for more than that..." She thought, careful to do her best not to voice it aloud, and to guard her mind. In reply, she murmured to the ageless one, "No. Though that troubles me as well, it is not the chief of them for now. I have this feeling that something happened to Mum, or is going to soon."

"Your mother will ultimately be fine. I have not felt her death, and for now I can still feel her. My water is still in her veins with that of my sister, and she still carries my vial in her pouch."

Kirsty continued to fidget with her hair, openly regarding the deity.

"But, what if her boat was wrecked in a storm? The weather is getting odd, and there are still those clans that attack any half-blood they smell."

"And all the more reason for you to train hard, both in your classes in school, and for you to learn all you can from the Merfolk. You won't be a youth forever. This is the year you prepare for womanhood among the Merfolk. And due to current circumstances, I want tradition broken for your clan. You will train with the spears." The spirit regarded her, Kirsty having flinched back a bit at the blaze and roar that had accompanied the godly frustration, and gentled once more. "You are the last in the Makay line that carries a significant and awakened trace of Marsali's blood. No matter where in the world you settle, you *will* be head of this village and clan – what remains – when your parents die. And this village *will* be rebuilt, even if you link and reawaken my northern point of residence in order to be with the one you love."

"Don't worry Mistress Kirsty. Imp will help you! It is his honor to do whatever his mistress needs." A sudden pressure on her shoulder told her that the imp had leaped and climbed up to his favorite perch, and he patted her shoulder.

Kirsty's mood soured even more. "I am just a half-blood

Selkie, and not even that, perhaps. Ally would go on about fractions and dilutions. And the village of the past started as a human settlement, what good am I for those that grew in the sea?"

"Marsali once said the same, regarding her children, wondering what good she was to those that must grow on land." The well spirit carefully put her arms around Kirsty, pulling her close and stroking her hair once the much younger head was settled against her shoulder.

"Tonnes. Without her teaching, our mariners wouldn't have been so skilled in sailing. Boats and ships would have remained unbuilt and unenchanted, trading still in the Dark Ages in the open and closed societies, and our merchants would not have been so successful... Just as your and Mara's teachings contributed greatly. Marsali still teaches us to this day through the portrait. I wish I could be even half so wise, and my potions do as much good."

A bittersweet smile crossed the Lady's face. "Then train hard."

Chapter Six
Etain's Dilemma

The distant sound of voices swam into her consciousness, lapping like waves on a lake stroked by a breeze, breaking over her with the soothing hypnotic power that Etain always associated with water deities. Slowly, very slowly, the darkness retreated, the frigidity of the water registered, and the splinters of the plank below her dug into her bosom with all the comfort of embracing the fuzzy cactus that she had seen in Mrs. Kitsch's kitchen window whenever she went over to trade for her cheese and 'fix' her water pump. Yet, she had never given an embrace to the fuzzy looking cactus in the widow's window.

The fact that she was floating on a plank, partially in the water, began trickling through her mind, the cogs in her head began turning, and the brain fuzz began to clear. What were those things called, that would flit into ears and scramble thoughts? For half a moment, she wondered if she had somehow gotten a whole colony in her head. With the sorts of places she sometimes went, that explanation actually made perfect sense.

Etain pulled herself more fully onto the plank, thankful that it was at least a decently sized one. Unfortunately, she was cold, and currently only had her seal skin to wrap around herself to keep warm with, other than her own half-pelt.

The conversation carried on, and though she looked, she could not see who was speaking, nor could she make out what, exactly, was being said as she listened. To her normal eyes, she was the only thing on the face of the sea, riding the swells and drifting along on some unnamed current. To her inner eye, she was still too muddled to feel much clearly.

Current... before, there had been no current. No, she remembered instead dying water, choked with refuse, and the taste of poisons and potions mixing with the taint of oil, despite having been careful not to breathe, nor open her mouth. Rotting sea creatures floated, bloated, around her, and a hostile, sickened water spirit... And its pain, its anger, its disbelief had been a stone. She remembered the feel of her lungs burning, and there being no air to pull from the water, the tentacles of her hair screaming at her to get out, while her whiskers felt as if fire danced along them, that there was danger here, no matter what her deities and mistresses had charged her with, that it was beyond her power to work with and yet live.

And the brush of the shark in water where no shark would have lived long. The touch of Mara, Goddess of the Bitter Sea, mercurial as ever. She that claimed so many souls, and caused the frustrations of men and women to drive them to insanity.

Oh yes, she remembered now. Things began to take on less of a dreamlike quality, becoming more vibrant and immediate. Once more, she felt herself slipping from observer to participant.

Her eyes scanned again, taking in all that she could on the night waters, adrift. Finally, she saw her craft, mentally called out to it, and felt the reply shiver through her timbers.

"You're awake. Good."

The voice passed through her in the same way that the boat's reply had, marrow deep, thrumming in horrifying depth from within, to without. Etain's hair rose and her heart constricted, the ancient spirit gathering her attention to an almost painful focus.

"Yes M'lady. I am awake and awaiting your pleasure."

"My *pleasure*..." The voice trailed off thoughtfully, and a shark fin circled her plank slowly, before a woman in greys and whites broke the surface to stand on the waters. She clasped a spear, and where her skin showed beneath shell mail and cloth, it bore the sleek look of sharkskin, though the pattern ever changed.

Rows of teeth flashed as she spoke, lips curling back. "My *pleasure* is that these seas be returned to their original state. Yet those under my direct power are few now, and those favored with magic fewer yet. My *pleasure* is yet a long way to being fulfilled.

Just as my *pleasure*–"

The Ancient One took a breath, and the seas around them, which had begun to froth and steam, whitecaps just beginning to show, calmed again.

"You overwrote the taints here. That is what matters." Mara dipped her spearhead into the water, the blade alternating between clear quartz and wicked obsidian, stirring the water slowly. Spiraling outward, arms of power once more began to reach through the water as Etain watched.

Unbidden, Etain reached into her pouch, the straps miraculously having retained their hold, and drew out the small silver knife therein. White heat gave way to dark coolness and back into heat as the blade drew across her left palm, and the blood flowed from her hand, which she dipped into the water.

"Mistress Mother, accept my blood. Spare my kith and kin, howe're distant and thin the relation be. Fish, and mammal, and even further back. May my blood provide the spark that died."

"I accept the sacrifice. Life for life and death for death. Cycle ever flowing, the dreamer ever yet unknowing."

A baleful smile stole across Mara's face, cold, yet the gestures she made spoke of gentleness hidden deep within the paradox of salty brine and razor teeth. The water itself spoke, the spirit of the gyre slowly beginning to spin properly again.

"I acknowledge my death, I acknowledge my life."

Silent communication lapsed between the deity and the water, of which Etain was allowed no part, nor was it her place to pry. Coldness stole over her heart.

"*There is more than one. She needs me elsewhere. And here I'd hoped for a swift and easy mission. I should know better after these years, and those that have been taken.*"

"Indeed. Return to your craft, my favored one. The *Sea Witch* answers you eagerly yet."

Etain winced, looking up at the deity and withdrawing her

now healed hand from the waters, dismayed that her private thought had not been quite private enough.

The deity pointed toward the boat as it drew near, sea washed and storm battered, but intact. Etain frowned, noticing one of the cabin windows busted.

"Thank you, M'lady."

"I would be quick, if I were of flesh."

Sea spray brushed over her, dampening Etain even more, as the night was not allowing her to dry. Mara was gone, in presence and form, leaving Etain with the still sulky local spirit, as quickly as a tsunami recedes from the shore. Paddling carefully over, she reached her hand upward.

"Rope."

The boat answered, and the rope snaked down for her, wrapping around her body and hauling the Selkie quickly to the deck, forcing Etain to run up the side to keep from being scraped and gashed.

"Thank you..." She stroked the boat in word and deed, before walking to more closely inspect the damage the faithful craft had sustained, before even thinking of finding something warmer than the sealskin she held closed around herself.

As she expected, the cabin was dampened, and the lights would have been out if they were not magical. Once again, her hand reached without thought for the belt holding pouch and sling, and her fourteen inch acacia wood and Selkie hair cored companion quietly slipped out to swish subtly through the air, with a grandmotherly tune thrumming just beyond hearing. Just as quietly, the glass mended, and the cabin interior dried, all items that had been in disarray finding their proper places and states once more.

Descending below all looked clear other than a few items having been jogged loose, bindings having worn through during the storm. Deftly she re-secured and tidied, before finding dry clothing.

"If I'd been thinking clearly Byron, I would have left the others below. Am I getting so old that the water distracts me so much now? Think we can find our way back out of the pocket?"

Once dressed, she arranged the seal skin "cloak" back over her clothes, pouch, and wand-sling, looking around at no answer from her longtime companion and 'familiar.' Etain sighed, and sagged momentarily on remembering that he was back home still with the others. It was short lived though. She knew there was little time to spare with such dalliance.

A span of moments found her at the helm once more.

"Right then *Sea Witch*, heave ho. What other perils does the mistress lead us to?"

The boat creaked in reply and pushed eagerly forward, thrumming softly at her touch on the wheel.

From a distance, just beyond the range of her eldest living priestess above or below, Mara watched the witch and boat set sail once more.

"Yes little one. Perils indeed, but needful to draw your pup back to me and force her to reconcile the path she wishes, with the path I demand, not just the health of my own realm. I hope, for your sake, it is not your life I must take to keep the line doing as we created you all for. My sister is too soft, on those that are hers." Mara sighed, then allowed herself to disperse. Perhaps the Moon Lord would take her in his arms tonight and ease the ache.

Chapter Seven
SELKIE REFUGE

When Kirsty returned inside, a full-blooded Selkie was in the living room, leaning back in one of the heavily upholstered, winged armchairs that was drawn up to the fire. Dark hair spilled down over her shoulders and pooled around her, to spill out of the chair. In her arms covering the bandages around her midsection was a chubby toddler suckling hungrily at her breast. Like almost all Selkies she knew of, the baby seemed to have a large appetite.

"Mani." Kirsty nodded as she murmured the name, sweeping lightly over, and bending close so as to speak quieter. "Is there anything I can get you?"

The Selkie shook her head. "Not yet, Lady. When Banu finishes though I will be ready and allow you to check my wounds." She shivered slightly, and the toddler's complaint could be heard mumbled through the mouthful. Mani stilled herself, though the color still drained from her skin. Her eyes took on a distant, haunted look, empty windows gazing into a not so distant past.

"Alright. I'll heat the water and prep new bandages then, Mani." Kirsty repeated the name as often as she could work it into conversation, hoping that the bond of her name would help bond the selkie to her body better and speed the healing...instead of her soul following her husband and leaving the pup.

"I'll help." A rolling voice slipped in quietly. The voice was shy, as if the vocal cords it came from were trying not to shift their feet and toes the sand.

Turning her head, Kirsty saw movement in the corner, the form that had been sitting in the shadows rising, then making for the kitchen. When walking through the firelight, the orange glow made his skin *seem* a normal flesh-tone, though she knew in the sun it would have an odd green undertone. Though in human form, he was hairier than what she knew of the average human male, at least judging by the anatomy books. The hair was more akin to fur where the loincloth and the straps bearing pouches did not cover it. It was a fine, light brown furring running from the base of the neck to upper arm and mid thigh, somehow both thinner, and yet much denser than that of her own and her mother's, which was always so carefully hidden under cloth. The male chanced a short look at Mani, then shook his head sadly before continuing on.

Kirsty followed. If Connor had been in the corner, Olan, his brother, was as well.

"I'm glad there's another female here... less to worry about, even though she lost her husband." The thought slunk through the dark recesses of her mind before slipping to her consciousness, quickly suppressed again once realized.

Kirsty shuddered at the memory of how Mani had looked when David and Byron had brought her up from the shore. His sandy hair, usually neat, had that tossed and disheveled look she associated with stress and speed. In front of him lay, stuck to the Kelpie as firmly as David himself was, the bleeding Selkie mother as a sleek brown seal, a large arc of red indicating clearly her brush with the sharks that were becoming more common in the area. Held in David's arms, clinging tight, or as tight as any pup could with only fins, was a white seal pup, not yet bearing the darker speckles common to the local subspecies. The amount of blood to clean up had been far more distressing than the water, equally as distressing as the look in his eyes, and nowhere near as distressing as the wound itself had been.

Connor and Olan's advances toward her had fallen to a manageable level at Mani's arrival, possibly due to a combination of her sheer presence, and worry. This did not mean, however, that she trusted either of them with her fishing nets. She shuddered again, this time at the memory of having been entangled in her own net, and what could have happened if David hadn't been there visiting that day.

Kirsty walked over to the cabinets that housed the healing goods. On opening the door folded bandages rows of bottles and jars, and even various Cowan healer's instruments greeted her. They kept everything that a well stocked 'medicine cabinet' ought to due to their location and the nature of the wayward souls who tended to find their way through the various protections.

"Go slow Connor, you and Olan both. Give her grieving time."

She extracted the wash, healing ointment, and bandages, shut the door firmly, then took the items to the table and set up. As she worked, the cauldron she kept ready filled itself, and the water began to heat, long practice making it an automatic task.

"Lady Kirsty?" Eyebrows rose into his dark hair at the statement.

"You have no herd," she paused, trying to figure out the politest way to warn him without her distrust becoming too overbearing. "That's why you and Olan tried to capture me, you'd said. Now, you have one forming. With a pup in it already, no less." Kirsty's voice was tight, controlled, holding back the admonitions she still wanted to beat him with whenever getting too near.

She couldn't let herself. Mani needed others fully like herself near.

He made a noncommittal sound, fussing with one of the chairs to have it suitably located between kitchen fire and table, placing and plumping a cushion. A couple moments passed while processing his reply before he spoke. "She smells good to me, like you did. Takes good care of the pup. With no male to look over her, and not able to go back to the herd..." He worried again.

"It's already been told to you all that you can refuge here, so long as no trouble is started. Help out when it's needed." She began to roll some of the bandages, a final preparation.

"Well. That wasn't it. I mean... how..." He gestured toward the door separating kitchen and the living room, then back to her, and vaguely northward, furrows in his forehead, formulating how to ask but ending in blurting, "How did David catch your attention, and keep it?"

She blushed, and this time it was her eyes getting a far away look. "He helped me pick up my things, when I was knocked over by a prat that thinks he's something important just because of his family. Knocked over by that blonde upitty Pureblood right in front of everyone, then having to put up with him making a snide comment about waterwitches that I don't remember much of. That's quite the bother. I got the treatment fairly often actually since people think more about plumbing when it comes to water magic up here on land."

A pause, and Connor rested his hands on the back of the chair while listening.

Kirsty took a breath, then continued. "David helped me pick up my things even though he had helpers to get his own things for him. It was our first year we were getting ready for. I had no one with me, other than Byron – waiting where no one would see him since he can't change anymore – to take me home, because Mum and Da had been called away. Because he was kind to me," She paused and fought down the blush spreading further. "I was mildly interested, since so many of the 'good' families treat us so poorly, because our kind of magic and usual job isn't well respected when known."

Connor frowned, then went to help roll wrappings. By her scent he could gather that there was more that happened during that initial meeting than she wanted to say...or perhaps she just had no words for.

Kirsty continued working, moving from the bandages to adding into the cauldron appropriate herbs, placing her wand in and breathing a short spell in singsong Gaelic. The sanitizing water for the used bandages to began glowing brightly and a smile ghosted over her lips.

"I met him again on the train to school, and we sat and talked about who we were, what we are. He looked at my hands expecting webs..." She giggled at the memory. "He didn't do anything special to keep my interest, we just talked and found similarities. Differences too... The more I saw of him, in class and out, the more I liked him, because he was easy to get along with, and doesn't care that I'm not a full human..." Kirsty blushed deeper, "and he smells good to me. Like snow, and pine, fur and potion ingredients, and som–."

Connor raised his eyebrow and opened his mouth, having already smelled some of the potion ingredients that she used, but she cut him off, already knowing what he was going to say. With her eyes, she tossed daggers his way, pressing her lips together.

"The better smelling ones, not the ones that smell of decaying meat or ancient crusty socks!"

Connor couldn't help chuckling, and just let it roll through his chest. He paused a moment after her clarification. "So be nice, and helpful, and hope she doesn't think I smell incompatible."

"And don't push. Fishing nets are out."

"Never going to live that down, am I? Even though the two of you disarmed and subdued us."

Kirsty nodded. "That was the worst thought out courting ever in history. It really popped for me the whole idea lore tells about Selkie males being irresistibly charming. Weren't you ever taught to think with the head on your shoulders, not your hormones?"

The door opened, and Mani came in, wincing now and then and holding herself stiffly, somehow always seeming three steps farther back than she actually was. Connor went over to her quickly, escorting her to the chair he had set up. Kirsty glanced at the floor, expecting a dark haired toddler, or a waddling pup, but saw neither. Mani's dark eyes swept the table, warily looking over what was to be used, on her way. Finally, she sat and wound her long hair up, exposing her torso, which was covered only in the bandages and lightly dappled fur.

"No magic on me? Only your healer's tools, little seawitch?" The voice was quiet, and young, like it always was each time she had had to place herself in such a vulnerable position during her now months long sojourn.

"Only on the supplies, not on you Mani."

She nodded. "I will trust you again then."

Kirsty very carefully approached, making low, soothing noises unconsciously, and began the process of unwrapping manually, her eyes slowly able to survey her progress on the jumpy Selkie woman.

She smiled grimly at the progress, which would have been swifter had she been allowed the methods she would have preferred. Kirsty deposited the bandages in the sanitizing water, with another song, and started them to stir.

As she expected, the healing song calmed Mani, as it always did. Patiently, Kirsty cleaned out what remained of the shark bite, then applied the ointment that bore the healing and pain aids. Wrapping her in fresh bandages just as patiently, she was startled out of the dreamy state she often fell into, by the sound of her patient's voice.

"Lady..." there was a brief pause, and the swelling of the chest before a swallow, "I am willing to try one of your potions..."

Kirsty's hands hesitated a moment, then finished tucking the end. Without a word, she returned to the cabinet, fetching and carefully measuring the proper dose.

"If this doesn't work as well as I know it should, I'll have to find a formulation that will work optimally for them..." She thought.

Chapter Eight
here and gone

🖋irsty watched as Mani swallowed down the potion, hovering quietly nearby, and was gratified to see the healing process speeded on its way. Quietly she washed the old bandages and hung them to dry by the fire, disguising her sigh of relief. For her part, the Selkie tried not to make a face of disgust at the taste from the potion, choking it down with little relish.

Connor met her eyes and nodded, a silent acknowledgment of respect, for having finally gained the wild Selkie woman's trust enough. After a short period of observation, Kirsty released her charge to bed, and Mani drifted out of the kitchen and up the stairs to the bedrooms, guarded and guided by Connor. Retreating from his corner in the living room, Olan followed, carrying the now fast asleep Banu to the room at the end of the upper story that they shared. In short order, Kirsty herself followed, bound for her own room.

Ten o'clock came, heralded by the soft chiming of a clock on the mantle, the click of the doorknob opening, and the quiet swing of the front door. Finnol slipped quietly into the house.

"Late you are, my boy." Marsali spoke softly from her place on the mantle. Pulling herself onto her rock in her portrait, she arranged her tail carefully before continuing. "What happened at the office, then?"

"More shoals of ghost fish to investigate, moving shoals of rock, and a possible report of a captured Selkie to look into. I don't know if I'll be able to see off Kirsty at this rate. School's so close. Some of these I can put off, but I don't know about those shoals reaching for the shipping lanes..." Finnol yawned widely, sat down on the couch, kicked his feet up, summoned a mug of tea from the kitchen with a swish of aspen and Kelpie hair, then looked at the painting.

"It's an active time of year. If it's this bad now, think of what Samhain will be like." Marsali played with her hair thoughtfully, eying her descendant.

"Mmm." Finnol nodded. "Always busy when the Veil's thin."

He drank his tea down, before taking it to the kitchen and setting it to wash and stow itself, then ventured past the door to his study, up the darkened stairs, and turned into the upper hall. Quietly, he opened the one that was his daughter's, peeping in to see the usual mass of dark hair spilling in waves over her pillow. The water imp lay beside her as well, his head propped on the pillow beside hers, fingers tangled in her hair like a child, despite the pillow being too large for his diminutive body. On her desk, a final potion was left to brew, though he was unsure as to whether it was one of her experiments, or for use in the pantry. Quietly, he shut the door, then opened the one directly across.

Soft snoring greeted him from the portrait on the wall, and looking, an elderly woman in garb that suited a retired pirate leaned against a wall in her frame. He changed to his night clothes as quietly and quickly as he could, not wishing to wake Kara at this hour. Just as quietly, he slipped into bed.

At three in the morning, a klaxon sounded through the house. One of the elders from the family portraits, Stephen Makay, the grizzled former captain of the trading ship the *Tempest Queen*, ran from picture to picture, calling "All hands on deck," and waving his walking stick or poking other paintings awake as occasion dictated. Now and then he chucked things at statuary even though the objects did not physically leave whatever painting he was in. The targets hit though because the figurines did stir and listen.

Feet hit floors with resounding thumps, somewhat confused in the room of the full-blooded Selkies, and much more certain in Kirsty and Finnol's rooms. Kirsty managed to beat her father down the stairs to the study, her blue night robe open over her white nightgown, and skidded to a stop before the wall map. Red witch-fire blinked balefully at a point in the Atlantic. Below the dot, a label wrote itself.

"Oilspill." Kirsty's voice was dull and flat. "That's going to be a pain to clean."

Her father nodded, resting his hands on her shoulders from behind her, gazing at the glaring dot of fire. "You know what this means."

"That you definitely won't be going with me to the station."

He nodded again, then retrieved a quill and parchment from his desk, writing down the coordinates. "Be good for Byron, won't you?"

"Of course, Da."

Finnol nodded, then quietly left the study. Kirsty could hear him walking down the hall to the mudroom, and the squeak of rubber as he put on his response gear. Closing her eyes, she could picture him in the yellow suit easily, though it did not suit him. Perhaps a minute later, at the most, she heard the door open and shut, and she knew he was gone to the *Cosantóir.*

A gentle tap sounded on the doorjamb. When she turned around, she saw Olan, wild dark hair framing his face in bushy masses that eerily resembled seaweed, and onyx pupil-less eyes regarding her.

"What's the alarm about?"

It sank in that Banu's cries had joined the din, and continued after the painting's calls and the klaxon had subsided. She pointed to the map.

"Oil spill out in the Atlantic. So Da's gone to help deal with it."

"Alone?"

"Doubt Da will be alone. He'll likely meet up on the way with the Merrow family and the Andersens." She paused a moment, considering the likely trajectories of the others whose home ports she knew offhand without the need of looking up. "Possibly a few other seawitches. Then, of course, the Cowans will have their disaster response crews out. Let's have a look at the weather."

She went to one of the many shelves, tracing her finger over a small silver and gold globe, etched with an accurate map of the planet, then blew over it lightly. On removing her finger, it began to spin slowly, and clouds began to form and pass over the surface. Olan flinched back warily, then approached when nothing struck out at him.

He tapped warily, and Kirsty shook her head.

"It won't hurt you. It's just an enchanted item to show the current weather patterns. Handy thing when planning voyages, but not good for predicting weather."

With a tap of her wand, she planted the coordinates of the spill onto the globe, and it stopped spinning. She frowned at the size of one of the fronts in the northern sea, and sighed.

"At least the spill is on what looks like the trailing edge, and not the leading edge of a storm system. Biggest problem will be the Tritons, if I'm remembering Da's map of known locations rightly."

"So, Lady Kirsty... What do we do here?"

"Here?" She looked at him, and her voice dropped to a whisper and flattened. "'A dhath ar bith'... Nothing at all... Just fish from shore with the nets, help Byron tend his sheep, keep the Lady company and bring her anything she desires, see to any that wash up on the shore, or go fix Mrs. Kitsch's water problems if she sends word."

A tap of her wand, slightly harder than needed, wiped the globe of its clouds, and Olan winced at the contrast of the sharp sound with the silence that had followed her statement.

"Let's get back to bed Olan..."

He nodded, following quietly and shutting the door, making no comment on her clenching fists or her paleness. Instead, he slipped up the stairs and into the room he was sharing with the other Selkies.

"Well?" Connor whispered, after the door clicked.

Olan continued looking at the doorknob, not quite ready to raise his eyes to the tangle of limbs, discarded skins, blankets and pillows on the floor of their erstwhile lair. Banu had begun with his soft snores again, but the stirring next to Connor's voice told him that Mani had not gone back to sleep yet.

"In the morning. Hopefully she won't start having nightmares about this too." Olan whispered.

"Do... You think we should ask her if she wants to come and den with us tonight?" Mani whispered back.

"I think she might take offense right now, though she could use the contact."

Mani nodded and shifted in the selkie pile. "A strange child... I still don't understand why they sleep separate from their young."

"She's in a place that doesn't really exist with us though. Maybe that's why." Connor carefully put an arm over the pup, then looked to Mani for approval. "Sounds like not-adult-but-not-child lasts for years."

"Much stranger beings than I though just watching from a distance." Mani agreed as the three drifted back off to join Banu in slumber.

Chapter Nine
Soul Fish

Time stretched oddly here, and when the winds blew they held an odd touch, causing the fur of Etain's pelt to stand on end under her clothes, prickling and catching. Strange eddies and currents, contrary to the ones that she would have expected in the level of reality she was used to, sometimes pulled or pushed her boat off course during her periods of rest, despite the spells on the craft. The pocket had gone on for leagues so far, with no clue that she could find as to where the other end of it lay.

What bothered Etain most were the flying fish. Turning to look again, the silver fishes were still following. Above the water they skimmed, only submerging briefly enough to wet their scales, and then onward they would fly again, staring at her and her vessel with those strange, humanesque faces – calling out messages that they wanted relayed. Worse yet were the ones that looked like doomed clerics as they recited prayers in Latin, gaping with soulful eyes and warning her not to tarry or risk becoming one of them.

As she watched, one won its way onto the deck, sending a shiver up her spine, and her gut to turn. If it were an ordinary fish, she'd run out there in an instant, snatch it up, and eat it raw to help replenish her energy. The face and moaning instead made her use magic to sweep it off the deck and back to the sea, with another shudder as she imagined what it might be like to have to touch one – or what one could do given the right opportunity.

"Fish definitely shouldn't talk..." Etain shuddered. Ahead, she finally saw the flickering and shifting where one reality met another, hoping it truthfully was the one she sought, knowing the strangeness of the sea.

A hump in the water caught her attention, then winked out of existence. Shortly after, it came back to sight, much closer than she would have expected if it were mere flotsam, and repeated the pattern, heading her way at speed. Behind her, the fishes sent up a keening cry, lifting their slimy lips and exposing teeth that went unseen. Their morbid aura increased to one of malevolence, then they changed course, skittering away.

"Prepare defenses, my girl... Upper and lower." Etain muttered to her boat, gripping the wheel and turning hard to starboard, seeking to avoid the creature in front of her, whatever it would turn out to be. In reply, her boat strained, banking in eagerness as it leaned into the turn and cut through the sea. A shimmer ran over the boat, then spread out beyond, very different from the Devil's Fire that had encompassed it when entering the pocket reality.

This time, a giant head rose, grey and reptilian with fierce sword teeth. A neck followed next, carrying the head higher, smooth and muscular, bearing sleek silver scales. Beady black eyes glowered down at her before it struck, first with its head and then flipping itself around for a blow with its tail when the head met resistance.

Both times the magic field flared to life with a zapping, electric sound as it drove off the sea serpent, and bolts of blue flickered around the boat. Both times the shield held. The sea serpent hissed, then slipped below the water.

Etain continued watching for it. Sea serpents were rarely so easy, especially the larger ones such as this.

"Full sail, add emergency propulsion." she commanded her vessel, while conjuring a hard tail wind to aid the forward advance. It was with relief that she felt the winds respond.

Yet, the wind still responded too slow to her spell.

Her boat was pressed upward under her feet, not in the usual rhythm of the swells, and she gritted her teeth as the creature tried knocking her craft up out of the water, no doubt hoping to have her boat smash on the return. Running to the side, she was in time to see the head slide once again below the waves, and that the waves were now some fair distance below her keel. The shields were flared to life again where the head had impacted.

"Want te play do ye?" She loosed a blast with her wand toward where the beast would be, no sympathy, as it would have none for her.

The water churned upward violently where the red fireball had struck, leaving a crater that revealed a burned side, already being covered over again as the sea flowed back in. A moment later, gravity brought the boat down again.

Kirsty shook her head violently to clear the odd daydream, and scowled as she bent lower into Byron's mane frill. Once again, she scanned the waters with her eyes for things that might 'mistake' them for food, wand ready and feeling the waters as they swept deep into her lungs. Behind her rode her trunk, large enough to stow even her broom safely, secured firmly to the harness over the Kelpie's flanks by bindings and his own magic. She rode without saddle or blanket as they coursed through the frigid waters, her thighs locked on him as she shifted with him, stuck well by the same adhesive that had once pulled many a rider to a watery demise and tearing teeth. Her large brown owl would meet her at the platform, but the cage rode with her at speeds faster than one would expect of a 'horse.'

The remaining days before she was due to leave Seal Point for the train in London had passed slowly for Kirsty, the sands of her mental hourglass sticking together as wetly as beach sand sticks while a tide ebbs. The sheep really did not need all that much in the way of tending, under Byron's guardianship, despite her never knowing quite exactly how he managed. A 'stray' roan colored female of his kind had once nighted over in the barn with him. Other than that, Seal Point had been calm since Finnol's departure. Only so much excitement could be had in teaching the Selkie males how to fish from land like humans, since both boats were gone. Mani had developed a habit of watching from where she had begun to sit on the shore while Banu played.

And yet, her dreams had gotten worse, despite the peacefulness. Now, it seemed as if even while she was awake they came.

"Another?" Byron's gait did not break or slow as he spoke, his own eyes also keenly watching for dangers to himself and his charge. "You should speak to your Potions Master about those if they go on, or your Healer..."

"Glad he has stopped prodding about going to the Divination instructor..." Kirsty grumbled still, liking the school's Healer well enough. "I prefer the Potions Master. The Healer... she is good and knows my heritage, but he I can talk with about the latest discoveries or my own experiments. And he doesn't fuss."

A memory of waking in the hospital wing, and of the burn where poisoned claws and spear point left their mark, flashed into her mind. For a moment, she was back in that bed, looking down in horror at how much of her half pelt must have been exposed when the Healer had done the needed cleaning, and hoping that David had not seen if he had been present – despite how he always turned away as decorum called for. Now, it didn't matter as much, and her pelt was closer to an adult coloring than the childish brown she had been. Being fussed at to take potions to speed the knitting of her flesh while awake enough to do it on her own was something she'd rather avoid though, and even more the psychological discussion that might ensue if talking about disturbing dreams.

Byron snorted, creating a foam that rose upwards toward the surface after passing over her.

"You know when you're still wishy-washy and weak-kneed you need hounding to do anything that you should. I wager you don't complain about taste nor hounding if it's young David a-asking."

She grumbled again at his needling. "David has yet to fuss. Somehow he seems to get able to get me to go be looked at by just suggesting it."

This time, the Kelpie's snort was in amusement at her irritation. It passed quickly though, and as he avoided a particularly sticky patch of the silt bed below the sea, he frowned.

"So, what did you see, Kirsty?"

Kirsty shook her head, shifted against the Kelpie and drew another breath of the water. She let it release the oxygen into her lungs before breathing it out, grateful that Byron could prevent people from drowning as easily as he could kill them if he so chose. "This time I saw Mum's boat up in the air, like something had knocked her up out of the water. It was... weird. Disturbing. It wasn't designed to fly."

He frowned deeper and tossed his head, this time veering off course to avoid the shark he had scented in the water before it could scent him, not being in the mood to hunt. Despite how her news worried him, Byron did his best to not show it, since his goal was to keep her focused on school and training. "She's been knocked skyward by whales a time or two before, maybe that's what you saw."

The half-Selkie shook her head. "I don't know... I just hope these visions are just waking dreams and not actual visions."

Etain continued watching the water, and the air around herself, as her boat landed, thankfully still topside up. It was evidence that the protective spells on the craft still held. Water splashed up onto the deck and washed over, and as she was outside, soaked her. Her ears listened for any roar or call if the serpent breached behind her, and her nostrils flared while she scented the wind, despite how dulled that sense would still be in her human body.

Still her craft surged forward, which pleased her. If she had managed to stun the sea serpent, then she would be able to slip away without further trouble. Etain doubted that though, and she was right. This time, the serpent breached to the port, leaping over and clearly trying to land to the starboard, as if seeking to drive her down whether the shield zapped again or not. Another blast from her wand with a wordless spell – more intention than anything ever learned in her long ago classes – and a column of fire streaked through the magical membrane.

Her adversary creeled, and the stench of partially cooked meat and blackened scales filled the air, while the great sea snake flew backward. It wasn't a killing blow by any stretch of the imagination but she hoped that by the time the creature awoke it would once more be deep below and she would be many leagues away.

Etain took a deep breath, only now beginning to tremble as she turned back into the navigational cabin. "Soulfish and sea serpents. Let's hope there's not a mate involved with that serpent. You did well *Sea Witch*." She patted the nearest surface affectionately, while the vessel continued fleeing through the water.

An hour of quiet sea later, she finally let the shields go, then set about recharging them, in the likely chance they would be needed again. Etain paced the decks, placing her hands on the railings and singing the required songs, lingering especially on the poop deck and prow. Not for the first time, she leaned forward over the prow to gaze down forlornly where, in earlier times, she might have been able to have a small figurehead without attracting too much attention. Small was really all she needed permission to create and install. She drummed her fingers on the railing in consternation.

"Few ships have them these days, and if a Cowan sees it, even though small, they will look and likely see your figurehead glaring right back at them. Well you know that some of your tasks will require treating with the very creatures they are crafted to deter. The Sea Witch is to be no mere trading nor mere fishing vessel."

Mara's words rose fresh in her mind from that long ago time where she was granted her boat and given her place by the sea deity. Fresh now as they had been then, they still stung as sharply. The memory still possessed that high, cold, commanding rumble to the words, like the storm breaking over sea.

What looked to be the way out of the reality pocket came ever closer, Devil's Fire sparking up now and then on the crest of a swell. Etain breathed easier, looking eagerly to the border, though still unsmiling. Instead, she continued pacing the deck with her craft autopiloting, watching for anything else that might come up out of the revitalized waters.

Thirty minutes away from the border, the moans and cries began again, another school of the infernal fish approaching in their search for food and souls. She glowered, this school sounding larger, and indeed looking larger, than the last. The wind shifted, blowing in reverse now to give her a head wind, instead of the tail wind that had been holding. The fish came at preternatural speed from the starboard, as if they routinely patrolled the borderland.

Perhaps they did. She narrowed her eyes as she recalled everything that she could remember former Captains having written about the soulfish into the Makay Clan's logbook back home. A particularly haunting memory of the first of Stephen Makay's voyages, recorded in his handwriting and voice, floated up.

"Ever hungry, they devoured flesh and claimed the soul, rendering the victim into one of their kind, whether non-magical human, witch or wizard bearing no intention of ever becoming a ghost, or intelligent magical being. If a victim had both flesh and soul, these wanted it. I myself have seen how it happens, when a small party had gone out from mine Tempest Queen in one of the boats, collecting some ambergris the lookout had spied during this voyage."

"It was not when a single one managed to fly up onto our decks that we were in the most danger, though the danger inten-sifies naturally if you are in one of the lifeboats. That happens from time to time. It is when an entire school of them gets close enough and swarms. If there are no shields, or there have been reasons to have them down, as they do drain over time, they knock a victim off and drag him down. They latch on with teeth and attack through their numbers, gnawing, often as you yet live."

"The team that had gone out fought bravely, for the swarm had risen up seemingly from under them – sleeping perhaps. But there was not

enough time for us to respond and open fire. Even if we had, we were as likely to hit our men as these demon fish, that Mara herself must have created during a fit of rage some eons ago, no doubt when a lover had left herself or her sister due to a preference toward males. Neither Petrifying nor Blasting Michael, Angelo, or Miriam would have done my men any good, though in hindsight would have been the kinder fate. Both spells do have effect against the fish. Better would have been a storm to deter them, as then my men would have had more of a chance as soulfish hate them. Alas, I am no storm singer, and we have none in this crew."

"They have begun to pursue us with their new school. I will have a seawench perform a curse breaking for my crew and ship when we land. My family can ill afford the loss of the ship, and the families of my crew can ill afford the loss of husbands and wives. Mara have mercy on my soul, but I wonder what my clan has done to incur her wrath. Or are we being tested? If so, a cruel test."

Etain shuddered again, calling up the shields once more and this time singing up a storm. In Gaelic, and mixed with a bit of the older Irish, she began to whip up wind and wave, counting on the turbulence to send the fish down, or for lightning to form fast enough to frighten the fish away.

Plaintive voices rose up to her, some in elder languages and with syntax just as odd, others quieter and newer, more palatable to the ear.

"Mistress Witch, please, I beg thee bear me to my love. I left her in Bristol and vowed to return even if I died."

"Nay, Lady. Bear me out instead. Irish ye must be, an it be to Dún Laoghaire I had been headed!"

"Answer not these rapscallions! I was cast from the ship I had paid good gold to bear me up to convert the Finmen. And I was made an offering to pagan gods of the sea when the storm would have claimed every hand on that fell ship of secret heathens. My child, save your soul and the souls of that country, and carry me thence."

"No! Carry none of us, touch us naught!" called what surely must have been a newer soul, not yet twisted by the torment.

"Touch us with your living flesh and we will devour you, such is our anguish, or else seek to make an exchange of our soul for yours. Fly! Fly!"

And yet another voice, sinister. "You are older in years and have the bearing of a mother. Your man lies now with another, surely. How long have you been at sea? Why not leave that sorrow and join me, I'll not abandon you for another lass."

"Keep your pleas and lies! I stop my ears and harden my heart, knowing your kind! Back to your rest, or your hunts, you'll find no opening here, and no sanctuary. Look instead to your own deities, mine has not given me leave to free you. It lies within yourselves, a simple release of your sorrows and horrors." Etain called, the storm taking longer to form than she had hoped. Choppy seas seemed to do little for this school, and she looked again to the border, mentally urging her craft, already sailing at top speed, to somehow find a way to go just a little faster and leave that much sooner. She returned to singing again, to whip the storm faster.

The fish came closer. She could make out their dark eyes now, not yet having gone the red she knew was sure to come. As they came in range, she fired warning shots, petrifying those that her spell impacted, and those sank toward the bottom of the sea. Others continued skimming toward her though, wetting their scales briefly before lunging along. Several eyes had begun to go red, and she knew that now not only did they see her, but smelled her as well, tasted her on the air the way a shark tasted its food in the waters.

Fire this time she called forth from herself, keeping the school out of swarming distance. She conjured it on the surface of the waters and spread it like a vermilion and gold carpet of pain. A fair amount of them landed right in it, lighting up and burning as well as if spitted and thrust in. Guilt settled over her at the screams, though she was not extinguishing their existence. She added to their suffering in protecting herself. As the Devil's Fire began to crackle around her and cover her boat, she extinguished the fire she had created, heaving a sigh of relief to have escaped, even if only so narrowly.

"So many lost souls..."

CHAPTER TEN
PARTING

Byron emerged from a puddle, translucent and flowing up and out like water, despite having seemed so solid beneath the waters he had earlier traversed. His shape, and that of his cargo formed and solidified out of view of Cowans and non-Cowans alike. As Kirsty looked around, she saw the location her guardian had chosen for their exit from the water cycle and currents also had no hiding non-humans to see the materialization. Instead, it had the forgotten and disused look of a dumpster area or alleyway, stone walls, dust, and litter. The Kelpie grimaced and exposed his teeth in disgust, taking offense to the garbage defiling the puddle gate and kicking it out.

Vaguely Kirsty had hoped that perhaps the puddle would be near enough to luck out and see David's arrival with Urma, the dragon that she considered part of his family, and perhaps even his father...as terrified as she is of whatever he possibly thought of her. Such obviously was not the case. As she slid off Byron's back, once she felt his adhesive spell release its grip on her, she wondered if he had already arrived before her and boarded the train.

"Thank you Byron." She leaned lightly against him for a moment, slightly drained from how much of her own energy was used in the trip to simply ride. Her stomach grumbled, already demanding another stout fish meal, or at least some sort of meat.

Byron nuzzled the source of the noise softly, frowning softly. Through the generations long distance rides seemed to get harder and harder on the young as the blood concentration waned. *"How many more will I be able to do this with?"* he thought. "You're welcome."

The Kelpie waited on the young waterwitch to remove her things from his back, which she did with the thoroughness of practice. A final nod, and he watched her leave with her things. He stayed a moment, cautiously venturing to where he could peek at the platform. He smiled when he saw her going toward another young form, having arrived early enough after all to give them some time to meet before it filled with the usual bustle. She flung herself on the boy, who caught her and hugged as fierce as she was hugging him.

Byron sometimes wondered how he was able to withstand exuberant flying Selkie hugs. For a moment, he allowed himself the humorous image of what might happen if she succeeded in getting her sealskin, then happened to forget what form she was in if she were wearing it. David was quite able to catch her though, and if he stumbled backward it wasn't apparent from the angle of his view. He nodded firmly, satisfied, then turned around to step back into the puddle, becoming a literal waterhorse once more.

"Alright Mistress. I've delivered your daughter. Now to find you."

The Kelpie melded back into the puddle, then seeped into the ground to gallop his way down to the water table, ignoring the soiled passages beneath the city in favor of cleaner, purer, and more magic laden routes back to the sea. He began to move north once there, in the general direction he suspected Etain of heading to. He reached for her with his mind as he ran.

"Lady Mistress? Little Etain?"

Silence. He strained and listened with all his blood, but no ripple of acknowledgment came.

"Maybe I'm just too far away. Water! Have you felt the passing of any Waterwitches?"

A stirring of consciousness answered him. *"A few. Which interests?"*

"Lady Mara's, the female Selkie halfling, full grown, aboard one of Lady Mara's vessels the last I saw."

"The last Lady Makay passed these waters was two full moons ago,

alone. I have not seen her since."

The feeling of the direction and the path sailed filled him. Not for the first time, he was grateful that he had been granted the ability to understand some things the water said when pertaining to the whereabouts of his charges.

Yet, it was still no answer where she was.

"Thank you. I hope those beyond you can give me more."

Kirsty pushed her cart, laden with trunk and cage, along the platform while watching for her owl, or for David. Her brown owl had arrived ahead of her, having left last night, and was perched on a ledge watching for her. It threw itself into the air and swooped toward her, landing on the cage in a flurry of feathers. With a screech, it opened the door with a claw and flounced in to glare at her, as if accusing her of tardiness.

"We had a detour!"

The brown owl turned its back on her at the answer, and looked back toward the train, fluffing its feathers. She continued to push the cart along, toward the form she could now see, sweeping her eyes over the thin lad with the sandy hair and dark, well cared for, somewhat imposing, clothes. Since he didn't see her yet, she openly admired the sweep of his traveling cloak and his cool manner, while he looked the other way down the platform toward whatever had caught his interest.

"David!"

She left her cart and flung herself at him, intending to wrap her arms around him and demonstrate exactly how glad she was to see him. He looked toward the voice and smiled, opening his arms.

"Kirsty!"

She thudded against him and he stepped back a bit, but managed to hold firm. His arms closed in as fierce a hug, and her breath puffed a bit when she kissed his cheek.

"I missed you."

"I missed you too." He held tighter for a moment then let her go looking to see if anyone had accompanied her. She appeared to be alone without even Byron to watch over her. Then again, since she was here it was obvious he had brought her, and when they had first met she had been alone then as well.

Kirsty blushed a bit when she realized exactly how tight she'd been hugging, and how occupied she'd become by his ice blue eyes, and hoped she hadn't bruised him. Together they pushed their carts toward the train once the doors were finally opened and eyed a wan figure that that been napping against a lamppost.

"Think that's our new professor? I hope he's good."

David nodded, and turned his eyes back to his task, conscious of the figure's stirring and the weight of exhausted eyes.

They boarded the train, and he helped her with her things and getting them settled securely. They had not been settled long before there was a knock on their cabin door.

Both looked up, and moved away from each other, having previously been comfortably leaning against each other. Kirsty straightened her clothes surreptitiously, just in case anything had skewed. They saw blue eyes gazing out from a tired face, just as exhausted as he had seemed on the platform. Both of them recognized the look. It echoed David's, that came and went with the moon. He was lean, but would be more muscular if he were fleshed out a bit more, not in the stocky way of a body builder, but in the lithe way of some forest creature. Again, much like David's physique, but less well fed. Kirsty noticed what she thought were scars around his hands and wrist, but couldn't look for long without being rude.

"The two of you would be Mr. Valnarius and Miss Makay?"

The voice was soft and gentle, and Kirsty decided already that she liked him, if he were indeed the new professor. Both nodded and rose.

"Professor Hemming Gerwulf." He stooped down a bit to

their height, and shook their hands, smiling. "I've heard good things about you both from the Headmaster," he paused and nodded toward Kirsty, "and your aunt. It will be a pleasure to have you in my class this year. Mr. Valnarius, a private word in my cabin if you please?"

David and Kirsty looked at each other. Kirsty then curtsied and sat back down arranging herself again. David bowed slightly to her, then slid the door shut behind himself after stepping out into the hall behind the professor, following him to the very back.

Kirsty sighed and settled in her seat, watching out the window while waiting for the professor and David to be done talking about... whatever it was. She could guess it had something to do with David's condition, and if it was one that was shared, like she thought, that was one less nightmare. Imp slipped out from his hiding spot in her clothes, to find another spot in the cabin. She saw familiar faces moving around the platform, such as the blond back of Thomas' head, chased after by his parents in blue and green – with a lute?

She looked again. She had been right. Thomas was being pursued by lute wielding parents, and she wondered how he ever found the time to practice the instruments he accompanied the school choir with on top of all his pet projects. The red haired butcher's daughter, Ally, she saw being given bone-crushing hugs by both parents. Kirsty sighed, then yawned. The glass against her forehead was cool, and though she saw the Lilitu family through it as well, she was too tired to give a flying walrus.

"*Flying walruses,*" was exactly the last thought she had before drifting into an open eyed nap of indeterminate time. The sound of the door sliding open startled her awake, and she turned large, deeper blue, blinking eyes toward it. They stayed that way even after they had focused, and she relaxed on seeing it was only David, and not a trident-armed collywobble or whatever else her befuddled brain might have thrown at her.

David paused in the door a moment, and she inclined her head to the side shyly, feeling a tinge start to burn her cheeks. She hadn't been the only one blushing, however slight, and he slipped back into the seat next to her and got comfortable.

Once he was re-seated, she leaned against him comfortably and he put his arm around her.

"All well?"

"Well enough."

"What I think?"

He nodded, and she yawned, snuggling. Her own private talk would probably come later. She found herself hoping the professor was able to grab a decent nap. The silence stretched out, warm and heavy like a winter quilt on a stormy night.

"So, where are your parents?"

"Mum's out to sea again, and Da got called out to deal with an oil spill. Been having some nightmares about mum though, so if they get too bad, I'm supposed to talk to Professor Sevrin."

"I see..."

She yawned again, and curled into him.

He held her a little tighter. "Why don't you take a nap?"

Kirsty didn't fight the suggestion. Before the train whistle blew to sound the final boarding call, she was asleep, and when Ally and Thomas found the cabin, Diana the moon-faced girl and a couple others, she didn't wake.

Chapter Eleven
the moon extinguished

The storm raged with lightning splitting the sky and then the sea below like lances and crackling dragons hurled without a care of where they would land. Ozone and salt filled her nose, and she could feel yet more electricity in the air. She wasn't sure if she was walking or swimming but it was cold. Freezing actually, the rain that was being whipped around was turning swiftly to ice as the temperature continued to drop, and it would not have surprised her to see a Titanic-sinker bobbing about like a cork. She wished for a thicker pelt, a fuller pelt, or a blanket – better yet, to be back on shore. Wherever shore might be.

She tried to get her bearings, but all she saw were storm ravaged waves, and a single boat, or perhaps a small ship. Another flash of lightning, and something was pulling her closer then revealed that to be a more familiar outline than she had originally thought.

"The *Sea Witch*! Mum!"

The roof had been pulled off the top of steering room, leaving the wheel exposed to the elements, giving the boat an overall older look than it already had. It was more like the paintings she had seen of the family's smaller vessels, from back when they had possessed a fleet and the voyages were more often. Etain's cloak whipped around her, and her hair too, long snarled into a hopeless nest of tangles that would take a week's combing to be free of – a terrible fate for any Merwoman, Selkie or any other breed.

Faint strains of her mother's song drifted to her, but were snatched and bandied about easily. It didn't matter, Kirsty knew the words and she sang them herself praying that they would soothe the storm. There was the thrill-taste of magic in the air, and in the water when it splashed over her, both the rousing, and the calming varieties.

Someone, or thing, made this... But what?

She cast her eyes around, then felt a *something*, a tingle of magic, just like she did at school when other students were practicing, but much more like her own though. It was more like what she felt when singing with the Selkies in the loch and learning what spells they still retained. Yet, it was still not quite like theirs either. Following the direction it had been in she saw a swell wash over the face of a white haired, smooth faced, old man... trident glowing.

"Why couldn't it be a blasted collywobble? Does it have to be a Triton? Why do I even have to go to school with other students and not be taught both human and Selkie magic at home? I can only think of one reason, and it's silly. I'd know what to do if I'd be taken more often."

She took a breath, and extended her hand, biting her lip and summoning all the energy she could muster. She could only hope that if it were a dream, or if she was projecting, she could do something to loosen his grip on the storm. Kirsty sent all that she could into the spell, sending it flying toward him.

The cold was what woke her from where she slept warm and comfortable around David though he looked both as if she'd socked him somewhere soft that she oughtn't when coming back from her dream, or as if every single bad memory he ever had had decided to gang up and well up in his mind all at once with the vengeance of a hydra. Or at least, that was what she gathered from what little she *could* see.

It was dark, and she could feel her breath on her own face, the moisture freezing. None of the other students seemed to have turned the lights back on. Lightning flickered outside while winds howled and rocked the train on the track, and the rain beat every available surface. It sounded as if that rain was turning to hail. It felt so too according to her blood.

David had felt her move, and he rubbed her back soothingly. She'd not hit him, but neither had he gotten a pleasant feeling off of her as she woke, as if the *Thing*, whatever it was, that caused the lights to go out wasn't enough.

"Stay here. I'll go find out what's wrong. Thomas?"

"Help Nevin watch over the girls?"

"Yes."

Thomas nodded. "Like I'd do anything else. Can't leave any of these girls alone long without something happening." He put his gangly arm around Ally. "Poor us Nevin, we're more outnumbered."

Nevin gave a wry smile, blushing a bit at being noticed. "Like they're goddess touched."

Diana gave Nevin a sidelong look and elbowed him.

Kirsty was not keen on the idea of letting go of David, but she also knew through long experience he was not going to let her follow, and was not going to stay if he thought there was something that needed doing. He also more than likely was not going to make his way down the hall dragging her as she clung to his waist, though at any other time she might have tried for comedic effect. Or maybe just blushed and not done it...

She released him with a soft whuffing sound that she was sure he understood by now. Her blue eyes pinned him, as if, if she tried hard enough, she could impart some form of protection to him, like how a mermaid's kiss supposedly could keep a man from drowning.

There was a soft click between them as an ancient pattern began to unfold. Kirsty was unsure if he felt it, nor if it would matter if he had. This was a story her cells knew well without even being of age. It repeated in her blood so many times on both sides of the gender divide. Kirsty smiled weakly despite the dark.

He replied with a nod and a squeeze of her hand before he drew his wand and left their cabin. She looked at the others as well as she could after David had closed their door. The moon-faced girl's face was not the usual, dreaming serenity that it normally was, nor did it exude anything remotely like serenity. Curiously, her face and eyes still seemed to shine in this darkness, at least to her eyes. The boy that was with her, Nevin, held her close as they tried to keep each other warm. Thomas and Ally were doing the same, as the cold only seemed to be increasing.

"You'll freeze..." Ally opened an arm to Kirsty.

Kirsty went over to that side and slipped into the arm, now between Diana and Ally. They all huddled close together.

Thomas whispered. "Think you can do that warming song without being too loud? The one you're always humming when you knit."

Kirsty nodded and began humming the song, mentally knitting up some warmth though she never had any idea where it came from. There was a shifting sound up where the owl was as the bird moved closer to the source. Her friends pressed even closer, and the sense of dread only continued to grow and it reached bony fingers into her heart.

"Diana, cover your face. it's coming closer."

The moon-faced girl did so without question, though the others looked toward Kirsty's whisper questioningly. Diana closed in on herself, trembling. Kirsty tried to keep an eye on everything while pulling her wand from the sheath next to her pouch but flashes of memory distracted her.

Her mother's screams for her brother filled her ears momentarily. The feel of crumbling stone was below her feet as she tried, and nearly failed, to pull Etain from the cliff, and the rocks below during her mother's flashback during David's visit. A sickening feeling grew in her belly and heart as more memories, or more like fragments, assaulted her mind. She could see the green fish face, the serrated teeth of the Finmen above her own crib, and hear the scream as her mother drove them back, and her father's shouts. The scent of burned fish filled her nose.

The door opened, and another body squeezed in, pulling Kirsty from the jumbled memories. She looked to see who or what it was, then relaxed as she recognized one of her Housemates, before turning her face again toward Diana.

The light that she always saw inside Diana, soft and silver, was out. Kirsty swallowed.

"Nevin... Check Diana? She's not glowing anymore."

"Anymore? She never *glows*..."

"She does. Just check her." Kirsty ran her fingers through her hair. "Hop in the huddle, what's going on out there?"

The new person squeezed in closer.

"Some *Things* are searching the train. Not sure for what. I came to check on–" the girl, an underclassman, broke off and blushed, "someone, but couldn't go any further back. I'm just, so..." She shuddered, and everyone felt it and nodded. "I think they're looking for more than one person. I heard screams at one end, like someone was being pulled off."

Nevin adjusted Diana in his lap, after checking her pulse and vitals the best he could. "Wonder what made her pass out? I feel terrible, but not that bad."

"Pulled off?" Thomas rose, gripping his wand. "All our parents were assured the usual travel to school was going to be safe."

Kirsty waved him back down, stifling the urge to conjure a light.

"One of the Spiralis had hoped it was a suspected non-human." The girl continued. "Because they react a bit differently than us."

"Hogwash." Thomas spat, wishing he could use a harsher term, but refrained due to the presence of the ladies. "Everyone reacts the same. Scared. If there's any truth to it, it's because non-humans and part-humans get treated worse overall than someone from a non magic family. Almost puts me in a mind to try for

Minister when I'm old enough. Stop this blasted segregation nonsense."

Ally nodded. "I wish you would. I'd really like to see something bring the three communities together, instead of all the secrecy."

Kirsty wretched a bit. The feeling in her gut intensified, and her head began to throb as she tried to ignore or conquer the fear and bad memories. The cold also intensified, and she could feel her blood rebelling and fighting the unnaturalness. The pain flared, and she could feel something pulling on that source deep inside her. All she wanted right now was to be back at Seal Point in the water, or down the Lady's well again, or at least in the loch by the school. Even a bathtub would do, so long as it had water.

Imp's energy flared up around her own, she could feel his magic fighting to shield her from detection, but she could feel as it was pulling on him as well.

After the darkness and pain, there was the sound of voices. She felt, more than heard, the cabin door and David's voice. It was much sharper than usual and that made her want to fight her way closer. Strangely enough she heard the voice of the new Defense teacher. She felt someone hand her body to David, and could hear, as if through water, her and Diana's names mentioned.

When she came to again, she was in David's lap. The train was moving, and the lights were on. Looking up at him instead of the pulse in his neck, David looked both relieved, and more than a little ill. Kirsty reached up and stroked his cheek, smiling what she hoped was reassuringly. She turned to look toward the others, and breathed a sigh of relief to see the light was once again in Diana's face, even if she was the only one that ever seemed to see it.

"They're gone?"

David nodded and hugged her a bit tighter. "They're gone now."

Ally spoke. "We didn't lose anyone that David saw, Kirsty. Human nor not, in case worry about that's what made you and Diana faint."

Kirsty looked at David, and he nodded again, affirming what had just been said.

"I did not see anyone taken. Maybe there were on the other end, but no one that I know of. I'm sure we'll find out later if there was. I think we got rid of them fast enough." Kirsty pressed a bit closer, listening to the way his accent rendered the words.

"Oh *no*, I didn't pass out from the thought of someone being taken. One of the *Things* was close enough to take some of our life force. I'm alright now. I bet Kirsty could use a bath though. Baths fix everything." Diana smiled at them serenely, and not for the first time, Kirsty wondered exactly what blood was really running in that girl's veins. There was never the opportunity to ask her though.

Thomas sighed, looking first at David as he stiffened at Diana's comment, and then around the now packed cabin. He thought of a way to draw the others away from the hint, since he knew most in the cabin knew neither of their secrets. "So, how many students could we actually cram in here? Think we'd annoy the Prefects finding out?"

Ally looked at him incredulously before starting to laugh. "I think I'm a bad influence on you."

Kirsty started chuckling as the others' tension also broke. When they were firmly ensconced in their laughter, she shot David a look that, all too clearly, conveyed exactly how much she needed in some water soon. He squeezed her while no one would notice and nodded tiredly, looking out the window and upward to where the moon should have been.

"Are you ok?" She whispered in his ear, glad of the intimate position making that so easy.

"Will be." He held tighter.

CHAPTER TWELVE
DEN OF THE SEALION

They did not get to watch the castle rise before them during their approach as in previous years. Castle Carrick, which was built to incorporate the sacred three instead of the more usual sacred four, had a triumvirate look instead of the more usual foursquare layout. The storm was so thick they did not see the usually moonglow-white stones at all until they were nearly at the foot. They therefore did not get to see the statues of the three houses' heralds come to life and attention. Yet still, despite the tearing wind and rain, the black marble and white marble ravens of Bertramus hopped and glided from parapet to rampart eagerly from Bertramus' Tower, at the top of which was the Observatory. The fishtailed lions of Leomaris sported over the walls, coming from their tower, closest to the loch. The serpent of Spiralis awakened from where it coiled above the underground secrets of the subterranean House, and slipped up the walls to watch their approach.

As usual, a Spiralis serpent could not help trying to eat one of the Ravens of Bertramus, whilst the first students were filing in the main door once through the main gate. One of the Sealions of Leomaris put a stop to it, as usual, by a 'gentle' application of giant paw to stone head, bringing the usual titters (and huddled gasps from those whose first year in their hidden world it was) when Spiralis coughed the White Raven back up.

Kirsty paid the display no mind. Like the SeaLion of Leomaris, she was too busy helping to make sure that one of Bertramus' 'Ravens' could slip off unscathed. She planted a swift kiss on David, before he made his break away from the others to dash into the forest. Thomas was already busily bustling some of the females inside, using his own cloak to help shelter an unusually short first year that had lost their cape to the wind.

"An unusually tough initiation for the younger ones this year..." She

mused, whilst humming and distracting anyone that might have seen David slip away. If any had not already been distracted by the storm, they would easily forget or believe he had just been one of the storm shadows that were sighted often when the storms came. Indeed, those around her that were still out in the wet were already beginning to forget the chill cutting to their bones, hearing her as they all filed in.

Each time a first year student crossed the threshold they temporarily winked out of sight for their sorting and testing. Normally that would have been done through the trials of air, water, and earth between the station and the castle. Kirsty suspected the actual initiations were being altered because of the *Things* plaguing them.

Once across the threshold she dried herself and went strait for where the Choir was gathering. On a day like this, she knew their Director would be certain to make use of the magical voices he had selected and was always adding to. He was one of the suspected half breeds, and like her aunt, was involved deeply in some of the other students' 'special studies.'

The other members of the Choir had all known the same thing in their bones. When she met up with them, the tall form of the Director Elphen had just strode to the lines forming, his slightly pointed ears peeking out from his dark hair and slanted eyebrows hovering over smiling eyes. She stood in her place with her rank, and when Thomas arrived and took his place to the side with one of the school lutes, not his own, Kirsty listened to the soft rolling rumble of instruction given to them. As one, they marched into the Feasting Hall, up to the stage behind and above the Head Table, which looked over the three House tables forming the triangle the school was known for, and gave their performance. Though the storm still raged, fueled by a divinity's anger, none were able to hear it while the students sang and bones warmed and dried, nor after the Headmaster gave his speech, nor even during the following feasting.

Kirsty went up the stairs, her belly full from the welcoming feast, ahead of the others of her House. Here too the tempest still howled and tore at Castle Carrick's ramparts, far more noticeable than in the Feasting Hall, and whipped the loch below into froth. She wondered whether it was fierce enough to do anything to the loch-Selkies' village. The Lake called to her, she heard it whispering in her blood, just like the streams of water below the castle. She closed her eyes, trying to picture it, but was too distracted by knowing what night it was to focus well enough for any better water-knowing.

"When I can get into the Lake, I'll find out."

Instead of passing through the secret entrance like her Housemates would to their House common room she went instead to the door of her aunt's chambers. Not the office which everyone knew how to find, but where she lived during school months which hardly any of the students knew about.

When she got to the door, and hovered her hand over the trigger, the fishtailed lion emblazoned on the shield covering the entrance sprang to life and the marelion looked her over, no longer paint on steel and leather. It reared, rampant, and seemed as if it might leap right off the shield to devour her. Taking a deep breath she reached out a hand and placed it firmly on the muzzle even though she risked having her hand bitten off.

"Easy Leòmhann, it's just me. Kirsty."

The lion calmed, and nuzzled gently on hearing her whisper its name. After a polite request, again in Gaelic, though this time Scots Gaelic, it returned to being a golden ornament painted on an ancient shield. The shield swung open, a door appeared, and she opened that too. Kirsty went in and sat beside the fireplace, on the cushion beside the green velveteen wingbacked armchair.

On a table nearby was a tin of biscuits, and a small settee that matched the armchair was off to one side of the room with it. On the other, a bookcase dominated the wall, and around the room prowled a lion through the paintings. One portrait was empty, as it almost always was, due to Lady Bloomsworth being employed as she had been since her commissioning at the Founding with standing guard over the trigger entrance to the Leomaris' common room. Behind a desk, a dark wood door led to Professor MacLeòmhann's bedchamber.

She only had to wait a half hour or so longer for her aunt to finish eating and discharging the rest of her first-night duties, before the door opened again. Kirsty rose and curtsied before the tall woman with the severe dark bun and flashing eyes hugged her tight to green velvet robes, the scent of old books, magic, and the lake.

"I missed you auntie."

She nodded. "I missed you too."

Another bone crushing hug from the aging professor pressed the air from her lungs. Kirsty sat when requested, again on her cushion, while the professor sat in her armchair listening to what could not be sent by owls and gulls about her experiences back home since her visit for the Midsummer rituals.

"I am glad the Midsummer went well, but I must say I am not surprised by how busy your parents are and have been. There is far more afoot than I can tell you. All the worst sort of timing. Too much pressure on the clans." Professor MacLeòmhann sighed deeply, rubbing her forehead at the thoughts of other news her position made her privy to, then continued. "I am glad that it is still safe enough for you to board the train with the others instead of having to be brought directly by Byron. I fear that day may be coming though, no matter how much you like coming as a normal student."

Kirsty nodded. "I'm nervous. I don't know how I can balance school and what Mara and the Lady want me to be learning.

"You'll manage. Your mother did, and her mother beyond that. I daresay all of your ancestors on her side have balanced everything well enough. However, I want you to be particularly careful with these" she paused and wrinkled her nose, weighing her words, "*Things* on patrol this year." Her sharp green eyes pierced her niece. "You stay in your usual areas, or in the lake during your night studies when I am not able to be there. And no running around the forest hunting. That goes for both you AND David."

"But... not even a mouse? I've worked so hard to manage mousing."

"Not even a mouse unless it's inside. When you are with David for his transformations, you stay inside. Please. Helping him stay safe is the whole reason you are allowed to bend the rule regarding male and female students at night, and why I agreed to teach you how to be a Shifter on top of everything else on your docket."

"I know..." Kirsty sighed, chastened at the usual reminders, then nodded. "Yes auntie. I suppose I'd better go lay down and wait for the others to go to bed, so I can go keep him company without suspicion."

Her aunt nodded. "It would be wise."

Overhead, a particularly large clap of thunder rolled, and the rain beat harder on the tower window's glass. Kirsty got up, and gave her aunt one final hug for the night, before she would have to start referring to her as 'Professor' in front of the other students, then left for bed.

Kirsty sighed, looking up tiredly from her spot on the bed where she rested from the long, rather harrowing, train ride and the effects of the welcoming feast. Visions of darkness and storm continued to haunt her, which was not aided by the uncharacteristic tempest beating on the castle. That had blown in from the sea off beyond the loch and Kirsty could still feel some of Mara's rage in it, though she had no reason to understand why.

Crimson velvet hung around her and Imp sat watchfully beside her pillow, back from his ranging. She listened carefully to the sounds in her dorm room, the soft rise and fall of her dorm mates' sleep. Carefully and quietly she slipped out of bed, looking to see if they had left their drapes open. Several sleeping heads were peeking from crimson blankets trimmed in gold, but all eyes were shut in sleep. Ally was even snoring.

She slipped from the room, her blue night robe giving barely a whisper as she pulled it over her moon-white night gown. Down the steps she padded, the stone walls cool on her hand. Each wooden door gave forth the same heady silence on her way to the common room.

That room, she was pleased to discover, only had empty chairs, study tables, and the crackling fire. The boys of her House were at least in their rooms, if not asleep. Imp nodded a reply to her unasked question when she glanced at him. Kirsty sighed deeply, glad that she wasn't going to have to wait any longer on her self-imposed mission.

She made next for the portrait hole, and stepped out silently, with a nod of thanks to the guardian of the House where she hung upon the hidden door, stroking the fishtailed lion lounging on the painting of the shore. The lady in her rose dress and ancient blonde updo, threaded with pearls, nodded back in return, long since resigned to the fact that those under her care snuck out now and then for interhouse rendezvous, pet projects, illicit adventures, emergency toilet runs – and in Kirsty's case, specially approved classes, lengthy swims in the bath or lake, and monthly visits.

"Be careful... remember what's stationed outside the grounds."

"Don't worry, Lady Bloomsworth, no side trips."

"Good girl. I'll let your aunt know you've left. Everyone else is inside."

"Thank you."

She gave a formal curtsy to the lady, spreading her skirts with a rather provincial flourish. With a breath she willed the change she had been practicing at for years. Bones compacted and slid to new positions, and the disconcerting shrinking and changing of her skull and brain accompanied the unnerving momentary discomfort. Her vision and sense of smell sharpened more than it already was, and when she opened her eyes to verify her change as complete, she found her point of view much lower down.

Kirsty stretched, then examined sharp claws before making sure her fur lay in proper order. In less than a minute total a sleekly long-furred white cat with piercing intelligent blue eyes and black whiskers padded off. Lady Bloomsworth watched the cat as far as she could down the hall and stairs, before shaking her head and settling in for her rest.

Chapter Thirteen
out in the storm

Kirsty made her way through the halls, padding softly and avoiding the other cats that sometimes prowled the corridors, especially the one that belonged to the castle caretaker. She liked the night, how it gave a more mysterious and ancient aura to the already ancient and mysterious stone passages. The sense of height was intensified by the darkness and her ears twitched at every noise and the whispers of the ghosts going about their business. The scent of the old castle was very different from the scent of her home, though she knew both grew and shrank as need arose, and that her home predated this fortress. Once in a while, the light footfall of a student breaking curfew hit her ear, and she would take shelter in one of the standing suits or behind the ever rippling tapestries.

White blond hair and pale skin reflected the light of the flameless torch held by Morvan Lilitu, when she came across him making his way out of the dungeon unaccompanied and wearing the green and bronze of his house. She grinned to herself, leaping up onto one of the ledges above the nearest door, and waited, watching. As he stole closer to one of the cases featuring artifacts meant as motivational displays, black kid gloves clearly indicated that he desired something from it. She yowled as if something had stepped on her tail.

He spun around gasping, directing the light at her, and her blue eyes reflected a demonic red in the darkness. She puffed her fur and arched, taking full advantage of the height and surprise to be even more terrifying, and yowled again. A loud clang sounded in an adjoining passage, and there was a cackle as the castle gremlin hot footed for the disturbance. In response, Morvan spun again and tore away, Kirsty leaping after and following as close to his heels as possible.

She was passed by the gremlin. When she saw the raggedy

legs flash by, clothed in freshly stolen and mauled socks, she slowed to a more moderate pace and continued her trek to the door while flicking her tail side to side in satisfaction. At last the oaken doors soared in front of her and the castle heralds did not stir at her presence.

It took some ingenuity to actually get out of the castle, with the wind pressing in on all the doors, mostly in the form of timing her pushes just right after slipping back to her human form, in order to open the heavy doors enough to slip through.

Once out her travel was not any easier. The rain soaked her swiftly and the same winds that had locked her in the castle temporarily now thrashed the trees and threatened to scoop up her slight form and toss it around like a hailstone in a cloud. In truth, they did more than threaten to scoop her up, but actually did so on occasion.

The biggest gust carried her hissing and yowling all the way to the lake, where she landed with a splash. The storm exacerbated the lake's currents, to the point that in the normally placid swimming area there actually *was* a current. She would have never believed it possible if not for this current pulling her out, where normally she was winning swimming races and getting teased for her extremely conservative and old fashioned swimsuit.

The water pulled her under, and once again she took her birth form to better swim, giving up the idea of running around in her cat form, for the time being. She swam across the current, as she would a riptide, and angled herself back toward shore.

A net closed around her in the black waters while the current continued to pull. She struggled, then reached for the pouch at her waist, glad that her parents had taught her to always strap it on whenever leaving for anywhere. Willing the water to be breathable as air, she worked the silent magic that would allow her short periods of water breathability. Her lips and lungs tingled, and the burning from the inhaled water stopped. Kirsty reached inside the pouch for her silver dagger, and began sawing at the braided lake-weeds.

"Nightfish, over here. The alarm went off on this one."

She stopped sawing at the net, and turned toward the voice and the name. She saw the glint of silver scales in the green wisp-lights that the Hunters held by their sides, and the men-fish of the loch were by her in only a few thrusts of their powerful tails, despite the current. They looked more like shark-folk to her, than the fish-folk or seal-folk she could see around the Point at home.

"You caught an airbreathing 'fish,' Carin. Seaswimmer, no less." Nightfish untangled her from the net, then frowned, noticing the hole she had already managed to make. "I hope you feel like weaving a new net. My mate already has several to replace for the village."

"Not my fault, you're the one that picked this spot to set it." Carin crossed his muscular arms and looked Kirsty over. "We didn't expect you till tomorrow night, Seaswimmer."

"I got blown in by the wind."

"What do you expect on a night like this? That's why we're fishing this way, it's got everything stirred up and makes the fish run." Carin tugged on his green braid since he couldn't run his fingers through it. It's your own fault for being out of the land-dweller's castle. Even the wind knows the proper place for you is in the water. Why aren't you changed yet?"

"No skin yet. Next summer I get to go."

Nightfish finished dealing with the net, wrapping it up and securing it to his waist. "You should at least have taken a dose of the changing paste. I know our herbalists taught you how to make it."

She looked sheepish, and even in the greenish light her blush was evident. "I forgot it was in my pouch... and since it lasts an hour a dose... and I'm trying to get somewhere..."

Nightfish nodded knowingly. "You're out going someplace you shouldn't. As usual."

"NO!" She blushed deeper.

"Bah... adolescents. When you get to be our age, storm time courting is less important. Taking the opportunity for more food to feed the fry is far more appealing."

"Storm time... courting...?" She stared at the two mermen, who now looked at her with as much perplexion.

"Yes. Isn't that how it works with the land-dwellers too? While everything is stirred up, there is this energy that makes you just want to–"

Kirsty cut Carin off with a disturbed hand motion, and ah-ah-ahed like a pup, before resuming her swimming. The water temperature around her rose several degrees and her cheeks burned.

"They make me want to dance and sing, or knit, or put the Lilitu out in it. I have no idea what they do to you and am a little afraid now to find out." Nightfish chuckled as Kirsty continued. "As for humans, magic or not, most want to stay indoors during the storms. That's why we merfolk all get in so much trouble when a ship is downed in a storm."

"We know, but we're inland some so we don't get blamed for that as often." Carin shook his head at her harping yet again on differences. "Here... this is painful watching you, though the teasing is fun."

The pair grabbed her under the arms, then hauled her to shore and tossed her up. She landed in the shallows, and they surfaced laughingly.

Kirsty rubbed her rump. "Thank you. I'd rather not have to sit here and wait for the paste to wear off. I'll be in the water tomorrow night for my lessons. I assume they go on, under Lady Mara's rage against the land or not?"

"Always. What's a little wet to the people of the waters?" The mermen waved their spears, then dove back under to resume their net checking. Kirsty took a look around to get her bearings, making sure that she was still on the grounds, and not likely to attract the attention of anything dangerous, then sought the least windy path to the secret passageway that she could.

It took a bit to find a sufficiently sheltered path, and then she shifted again despite how unlikely it was for anyone to see her.

She slank, belly down as close to the ground as she could get. Despite the storm, the lake called for her, and the salty waters beyond the underground passage out to the sea. The older she got, the more tempting the song of the sea was, urging her to leave her lessons and claim her birthright first. Yet a skin wasn't a right for someone such as herself, as she always had to remind herself, but a privilege.

Kirsty continued for the sanctuary passage instead of answering the sea's calls. She had somewhere to be. There was not much that she could do to make what David had given her by protecting her so often anything close to equal footing. However, she could be there and hold him when he resumed the form that everyone knew and rest next to him in the meantime so that this part of him currently in its ascendancy would know that there were at least some that were not of his kind that accepted him simply as he was.

Kirsty smiled grimly once winning her way to the cave passage and then through the protective vines that led to where the rare students that were enrolled with his condition were generally sent. It always amazed her how much the humans, herself included truthfully, took for granted that their precious schools were all free of non-human students. While there was the whole, and as she understood it, usual 'my family is older than yours' and 'we're Pure Blooded human' nonsense out in the open, in her short years in the school system she had found several students outside the 'norm.' Some of those students knew, and hid, what they were. Others did not yet know, and though she could guess at their ancestry, it was not any of her business.

Thankfully for now there were those in power that would see to it that those with rights to more than one type of magic would be able to learn it. As much as she wished to be with her mother on the *Sea Witch*, she was also glad to be here.

Soon enough, she found herself doing more swimming down the passage than walking. When she had gone several meters paddling through the water, she gave up and slipped back to her birth shape. With a wave of her wand, she parted the water in the passage, which constantly was having more added to it, so that even though it was shallower, there was always going to be a bit of water where she walked even with Imp's help. Kirsty sighed and made a note to lay down some charms that would allow the both of them to pass dryly in the event of another deluge like this and hoisted the hems of her sopping nightclothes.

She held her breath when she pushed open the plank door at the end of the passage, remembering how the first time she had seen David's secret, fully and without the way he'd hidden it during the strange blood moon their first year of acquaintance, she had been forced to scramble all over the castle's post-room to escape. It was many months ago now, but she still rubbed her forehead where she'd plowed right into the door when she'd forgotten that a cat shape was not going to open the post-room doors with any sort of efficacy.

The wooden door at the end of the cave passage ended her reverie and when she opened it she was able to step up and out of the water. Warily, she drew her wand and mimicked the swirls her mother often used to temporarily stay water when doing some rerouting of waterways, just in case the level rose further than the base of the door. The Selkie hair at the core of the willow shaft sang and whispered wistfully, and she briefly saw glimpses of Germanic coasts and Scandinavian firths.

She heard a faint whoosh behind her. The warmth of the fire that inexplicably started up in the hearth whenever it was needed seeped into her bones, and she was aware of her scent beginning to fill the room. She sniffed delicately, making use of her sharper sense of smell. The smell of wolf hung in the air, stronger toward the stairs leading to the upper level of the structure built in the cave system, trapped by the rock.

No werewolf tore down the stairs of the refuge to rip her up for the crime of smelling human around him, despite how sure she was that her scent had reached him. She closed the door softly, then extracted as much water from her clothes as she could. Her pelt bristled at the idea of going and curling up next to a warm dry bundle of fur and robes as a sopping, stinky, most likely demonic looking drowned cat. Now, if she could finally go on her skinquest, then she wouldn't mind curling up next to him furry and wet, as a seal could at least be expected to be wet and thus be less of a shock.

"Though probably not an appreciated one in the middle of the night..." She smiled a bit at that ludicrous thought.

Still there was no sound of him coming, though she was still certain that by now he'd scented her and expected her. That could only mean, or so she thought, that he was either too tired to care, knew her smell enough to not automatically have the stereotyped reaction that folklore (and the increasingly common reports of attacks) would lead one to think... or that maybe she did not smell as human as she had just a year or two ago.

Kirsty shook her head in irritation at herself for so much dwelling. As far as scent went, maybe all that rain had just washed it all off, and it was silly to pick apart that riddle when she needed to rest before his change back. She slipped back to her cat shape, and padded up to the bed where there would be a warm furry body and a great big paw to lay over her back.

She hopped up on the bed, her claws sticking in the thin, musty blanket as she attempted to pick her way to her favorite spot. When she laid down she saw the thick white pelt beneath the too thin blanket and too large robes. An ice-blue eye opened when she curled up on his chest, and she kneaded at him, purring soothingly. She purred louder when he whuffed softly in reply, and put the expected paw over her, grumbling lightly from the awakening. It did not take either of them long to fall back to sleep, and the night passed by quickly.

His restlessness woke her shortly before the howl, and she sprang off of him as he bolted up in bed. David grabbed at himself and howled again, sometimes scratching, and often snapping his teeth, as the fur slid back into his skin, and bones cracked loudly to reform. Kirsty's stomach twisted at the sounds, but she stayed. She threaded around him and rubbed against him as soothingly as she could, purring and meowing loudly till he was sufficiently transformed that he wouldn't be able to bite and pass the infection on.

Though she wasn't so sure it was an infection in his case, no matter what all the books she had read on werewolves stated. Not given what she knew of his background and connection to a certain Lord of the Hunt that her goddesses had interest in.

Once he was transformed enough to not be too great a threat, she transformed and wrapped her arms around him from behind, careful to remain clear of his jaws while he continued his twisting, simply holding him and humming a healing song. She could feel the magic welling up from somewhere inside herself as she hummed, and the way her palms and skin tingled where it passed through to him. He clung once he had managed to turn enough in her tight grip, and though the whimpers broke her heart she kept holding and humming until his pain seemed gone, and he was simply resting in her arms, once more human, if more than slightly disheveled.

He took a shaky breath and looked up at her. Kirsty smiled at David and nodded, hoping he didn't notice how wet her eyes were. She waited on his breathing to even a bit more, laying her head on him, and relaxed when his hand moved on her back. When he was recovered enough, she told him of her aunt's warning, and the new rules for the year...

David eyed her. "So, what aren't you telling me?"

Kirsty blinked innocently. He sighed.

"The Mistress got put in the lake by the wind!" Imp piped up, popping into view and illustrating her flight with his hands. And she got caught in a net *again* Master. Imp wasn't quick enough, and the wind was too strong..."

David sighed again, and shifted uncomfortably, his bones still aching. "Again? Why didn't you stay inside? Especially with how those *Things* searched the train." He frowned, and gingerly extricated himself from the bed. "You weren't seen by one, were you?"

"No, I don't think so. I'm still here, and not whisked off to one of the reserves or in front of some tribunal. I would have at least had to fight one if I were seen."

David went to change into his normal robes, and Kirsty went down to the lower level while he changed, waiting. While she waited, she thought about the best charms to use in the passage, settling on one that would work only for those authorized to be in the sanctuary. By the time he was done, she had worked out the wording and the way the energy would need to flow, and again decided that using her wand would be the best focus in her lack of a spear. She was practicing the motions when he descended the stairs, books in hand and the twin ravens of his house emblazoned in silver and blue on his robing.

Kirsty blushed when she realized she was being watched. "I was just getting ready. I had to take this form to get through the passage, I wouldn't have been able to swim far enough as a cat. So I thought that if I added a bit of a charm to the passage the headmaster wouldn't be mad, since I'm taking care of something only a waterwitch can do properly..."

"Go on... I'd like to watch you work."

She nodded and entered the tunnel through the bedrock, making her way through and singing softly under her breath. Now and then, Kirsty paused to trace arcane spirals and sigils on the walls or floor, which glowed a brilliant sea green briefly before fading from sight. The entire passage thrummed, the echoes magnifying the song, causing it to reverberate like seals under ice or whales calling. As they moved through the knee-deep water, it parted around them, leaving the floor where they walked dry, but closing again behind them.

Finally she tapped the walls just shy of the vines, satisfied with her work and sealing it. The storm continued, but now it was a steady downpour instead of a tempest. The mood of the storm by then had also changed and Kirsty wondered what had changed the mood of the sea goddess that she had felt in it. She glanced over at David who smiled at her despite how tired he clearly was and she found herself blushing when he complimented her work. The blush held for quite some time as they left the dryness of the sheltered cave passage and pushed through the grasping vines to enter the rains.

Luck was with them. When they won their way through and then into the castle again the others still slept. The castle gremlin snoozed on a lintel smugly clasping Morvan's over-robe as she waited on one of the teachers to pass by. Quietly they passed by, careful not to wake her, and went to wash away the scent of the past night before students or staff would be stirring from their beds.

Chapter Fourteen
The Rig

Etain growled. "Would you LEAVE MY SHIELDS ALONE!" The Selkie woman shook her fist off the poopdeck toward the Triton that had hounded her the past week. One week of battle between the two over control of the weather, the current, even the tern that Etain had sent off with a letter to the Order had resulted in a strange bond forming between the adversaries.

Whether the tern reached the offices with her report as to her progress and experiences she could not be certain. All she was certain of was that she had caught a tern and that it had agreed to carry her report. He had even tried to wrest control of her craft's will while she had been distracted with the task. Communicating with the tern had not been easy in the first place.

As annoyed as she was at his interference, there was a part of her, likely the human blood given the generally more peaceful nature of the Selkie ilk, that enjoyed the challenge. The Triton broke the monotony of her sail now that they had at least agreed to leave the weather alone.

"Yer still in me territory, wench. Either get out, or have the decency to sink, halfbreed."

"I'm working on getting out of your territory. I can't teleport a whole boat! Though trust me... I would if I could!"

"Yer a seawitch. Work harder!"

He shook his trident at her, and it crackled irately, purple lightning playing over the black triple blades on the spar that formed the shaft. Water from the tips, propelled by the shaking, splashed her face while they glowered at each other through the shield. It landed harmlessly, stripped of any negative effects by the protections it passed through. Uncaring barnacles continued their slow, methodical takeover of the hull while the merfolk went at it yet again.

Etain narrowed her eyes further, paying attention to what the Triton looked like since he was close enough this time. Brown eyes glared back at her past crow's feet, set in a leathery face that had seen decades of sun. Long wild hair the color of sea weed bearing froth roiled around his head, the corona of hair and beard tamed only by a roughly wrought crown of beaten gold likely rescued from an ancient wreck. The body below the face was muscular, as one would expect of a being that lived always swimming. His arms were thick from shark wrestling, and every once in a while she saw the flash of a scaled tail, but could not tell if it was grey, or green.

"No seawitch that I've heard tell of ever successfully teleported a boat without a wreck." She continued, reining in her temper. "And I am not going to anger Mara by wrecking the boat she entrusted to my keeping for the sake of a cantankerous Triton baiting me, oh 'Lordship.'" Etain leaned on the rail, watching him while the sea bobbed her boat with the swells.

The Triton paused, sinking several inches before starting to tread again. "Yer Mara's own?"

"Aye, bred, bonded, and branded so." She displayed her wrist and the silver and gold bands where they twined each other, a third conspicuously missing, as it had been for generations. The bracelet's light pulsated with the beat of the sea.

He growled, grumbled, then huffed. "The Shark goddess is not one of my favorites right now."

"Why?" Etain kept her face schooled, waiting to finally find what was at the root she had suspected when first leaving behind the soulfish, and sailing into his own temper tantrum.

"The humans." He growled again, twirling his beard with a free finger. "She lets them press into our seas, and does nothing when they overfish. She is OUR goddess, yet she reduces her sharks along the coasts, and does nothing when the true seafolk are displaced, despite our prayers and offerings. Where do you think those sharks hunt?"

"They eat the local shoals of fish where they move to. And

where I come from, they eat the seals and Selkies just as we fish and eat them in return when possible." She replied carefully during the pause in his rant.

The Triton nodded. "They've been harassing the borders of our cities, and the humans forcing a move has not helped."

"She does send her sharks to other coasts as well..." Etain sighed, thinking of how reports of shark attacks were increasing in the warmer waters, in the Cowan's news and how ocean-ologists of all kinds discussed them more and more. Many of the reports Finnol would bring home with him had mentioned this. "You're in the middle of nowhere... How could you be found?"

"Oil close by." He crossed his arms and spat, wrinkling his brow, then pointed northward at her look, answering before she even asked, slowly easing into some level of comfort with the woman that smelled of seal. "We lost one of our cities to the drill recently."

"I sorrow with you." She bowed her head formally in sympathy, careful to use the more ancient wording. "Perhaps there is at least something that I can do still?"

"You offer help, even with me harrying you all this time?" He eyed her dubiously. "You're part human."

Etain drew herself up to her full height and glowered down. "It is my duty to my deities, just as yours is to patrol certain territories. Human or not."

He nodded, causing the waters to lift his large frame closer. As no malice was intended this time the shield let him pass. "I can take you there. We can't live there anymore, even after repairs, but the fish will still need to pass safely, seawitch."

"I will do my utmost, Triton." She grasped his hand gravely and squeezed the best she could, though her hand was positively dainty in all its callused glory in comparison to his textbook sized ones.

The Triton released his hold and began to swim, arrowing and leaping like a dolphin through the swells at the prow of the ship. Instead of due north, he took a tack 30 degrees to the west, and the *Sea Witch* followed gamely. Etain went to the prow, allowing her vessel to follow him on its own.

At last the ships and offshore platform could be seen. Mist in the air from the swells breached on the stays that dove down to the seabed far below. Though there was no oil slick evident yet, and it seemed to be running as clean as possible, she felt a dull ache through her body, and the queasiness of taint seeping into the water. The closer they came, the more she felt it, and when she got to a better angle, she could see buoys and floats containing the leak she could feel. The Triton slowed, the oil also effecting him adversely. When he halted, and turned to look at her, he was another few decades older.

"You see what I mean. There were many already cleaning, but this is since then."

Etain bit her lip and pushed her nausea and tears down. "I do. I'll try to sneak aboard first, and see what I can do there, before I go below."

Heart in her throat, Etain left her boat below, as securely as possible in such conditions, and climbed the ladder. As she rose, she hoped that there were no security cameras watching her ascent, and employed the basic cloaking spell that had served her in so many other instances of trespass. And trespassing she certainly was, in ways that the most active members of protests know and employ in their pursuits of defending their cause.

After what seemed like an endless ladder, she made the deck, and then picked her way across to the door. The scents of the place churned her stomach as much as the knowledge of what surely had once been below the waves here.

No security rushed her, and carefully she unlocked the door. As the spell worked, she could feel each step completed, and she opened the door softly as possible. An empty hall greeted her, and she slipped in. In the corner, the expected camera stared toward the door with a fixed lens, and Etain drew her cloak more fully over her head, despite the spell she had placed on herself.

The air had the peculiar taste that temperature controlled air tended toward, and her footsteps fell quietly after she muffled her feet. Her invisibility had not been countered, which meant it unlikely that any of the old charms that rendered magic void had been placed. The lack of 'superstition' worked in her favor and she held hope that the Ministry of Magi had no involvement, as the Ministry of Magic would certainly steer clear of anything Cowan when possible. The Ministry of Magi would not.

Peeking around a corner she held her breath to ensure it was clear before proceeding, and in this fashion she slowly made her way to the control room, praying to any deity that cared to listen that none of the crew would learn of her presence. If she could just find out what stage of operation the rig truly was at, then she could determine what the correct course of action would be. It would do no good to decommission the rig, if there were no cap that could be fashioned. That mistake had been made by others, in other operations that had opposed deep sea drilling in sensitive areas, that she was aware of, and each time it had resulted in a mess.

The man in the room monitoring the readouts was not impressive by any form of the imagination. A warm worksuit swathed his average build in grey-blue to counter the effects of the temperature swings out here when the heating failed. Blonde hair could be seen under the workman's cap, wispy and fine, and his facial scruff was far beyond five o'clock shadow. Slightly more impressive was the company logo though it displeased Etain greatly to recognize it. The futuristic red letters imposed on a racing white oval was one she had encountered several times since her graduation from the traditional school and beginning of her true career.

He was alone here, this was in her favor. Etain stole her way behind him, where she too could see the monitors and gauges properly. Images and numbers stared at her, and as she did her best to read them, she wished for a team of her own, to more quickly hamper the progress and enact a more permanent solution. She thought briefly of the triton, but he was forever seabound, and likely to simply chuck the offending humans into the brine and be done with it, bringing yet more out.

While she was deciphering the displays, the door to the room opened again and another man walked in speaking in a gravelly voice a question in a harsh sounding language. She thought it Scandinavian, or perhaps German. She grated at the fact that she had not learned these nor did she have Marsali's ability to understand languages she had not learned. Etain held her breath and posture, praying her spell continued to hold.

The conversation was done quickly, the one passing the other a large mug of strong coffee, black by the smell of it. The other then left just as her stomach began to growl, the sound masked by the door for the one leaving. However, the man at the monitor heard and looked around for the source. She retreated to a further spot in the room and stifled a sigh when he muttered to himself, as if deciding perhaps it had been his own stomach.

Etain watched as he took a sip, winced and grimaced, then set the mug down. She drew close again, touching the back of his neck lightly with her fingers and bending over him. A sighed word into his ear, and he was asleep in his chair, slumping down. Quickly, she drank what was left of the coffee, to quell her stomach since it threatened another growl, and discovered why he'd set it down so soon, after scalding her lips and tongue. When she set it down, exactly as it had been, the mug was half empty.

A few strokes on a keyboard, and a few buttons of varied colors and shapes began the process she needed. She closed her eyes and reached out with her awareness, heading down, searching out the pipe and the black substance within, feeling the water within the oil. With effort, she forced it to begin downward. The temporary cap began to slide into place.

Her cloak swirled as she turned, and slipped out of the door again, moving quickly. She only paused at a few valves to turn them to the proper positions and then made her way toward the exit. Hurried footsteps sounded in corridors, the crew moving for some purpose she could not be sure of but likely summoned by changes of workstations, and she moved faster. Her breath came in gasps, partly because of the speed she moved at, partly from the effort of sustaining the invisibility spell. She could feel it flickering and slipping.

The footfalls came closer, and a surprised shout behind her alerted her to the fact that her invisibility spell had completely failed. Desperation made her feet even fleeter than before, and she knew her hood had fallen back, revealing the spill of hair, but hopefully not her facial features. She heard more, could feel them coming, as whoever that was called for help on his radio in that strange language. Hearing it again she was more certain it was not German.

She unleashed her cry, hoping to use the sound to deafen or stun, not wanting to use an offensive spell unless she needed to. Her keen filled the small hallway, hurting her own ears even, and she heard the person drop to the floor. Turning around, she could see him clasping his ears but still looking toward her. An outstretched hand, and a desperate pulse of energy, and she flicked out the lamps by exploding all of them that were in her range. Etain's hair and cloak whipped around her in the magical current, and lightning crackled and danced around her, the water held in Mara's vial within her pouch drawing the electricity to it greedily.

The man managed to gain his feet again, running away from the apparition and screaming about the sea ghost. Once an unbeliever in the paranormal, he now would have his own tale to tell about his brush with the sea's mysteries, and how he had to run from an attacking 'ghost' on the haunted oil rig he'd worked. It would not be long before he would meet up with others, hopefully with torches so that he would no longer be in the dark with her visage etched into his eyes.

The lights around Etain died. She felt, more than heard, Mara's voice in her blood. That part of her that was Selkie quailed at the rage normally hidden in the sea. *"Go down now, before I kill them all for what they do to my children."*

"Yes Mistress."

Etain continued her run, shooting back out the door, pounding down metal pathways and stairs, scurrying down ladders, knowing full well that if the cameras were not on the same circuit as the lights, she was likely being recorded with infrared technology. Once her feet landed on the deck of the *Sea Witch*, she cast off moorings, then pulled her skin about herself and dove into the sea without removing her human coverings. Behind her, the boat rode the swells obediently away to where she wished it to wait. She hoped the *Sea Witch* would go beyond where they were likely to board it.

She continued downward, and the triton was at her side within the moment, bubbles from her entry still floating upward. Etain only went through half the change, leaving her as half humanoid as he was.

"Well?"

"I slowed and reversed the process, though I doubt it will take them long to reinstate full functions as their company intends. Probably didn't even know you were here and thought the buildings just odd formations, at least by the look of their monitors."

He snorted as they flipped and drove further down, thinking that these 'monitors' were just more of one of the human brands of magic.

"Aye, formations that take a lot of intelligent work to make serviceable."

Etain nodded in agreement. "Young race in a very different world, that denies what it is capable of on the one hand, while the other has reasons to hide itself from that majority."

Her attention drifted off to the water's health again, now that she was fully submersed and inundated with its information, causing her to miss the Triton's reply. Her whiskers and fur spoke of the way the current was running, and the direction the closest fish were in. Her blood sang of the way the currents ought to be running, the pH the water should be, and a host of other things.

Her movements stilled as she let the water take over and compress her.

They finished the swim to the bottom in silence, the structures of the now abandoned city coming into view around the base of the pipeline. Weedbeds lay unattended, deep sea sea stars and other things without names now beginning to run wild. The further in, banners waved and began to tatter, the magic of the city's king no longer keeping these fresh. Here and there a forgotten gem, carved shell brush, or pearl lay where dropped during evacuation.

Etain's tears mingled with the salt sea when they registered that the drill had plunged right into the center of the palace. The throne room, when she gained the floor, was exactly as it had been left though now damaged by the stress. The throne, or where it had been, was now occupied by the oil well and statuary was broken, still bearing their gem eyes and crowns of beaten gold and pearl.

"I taste old blood. It shouldn't be in the water anymore." She looked at the Triton questioningly, her voice unable to rise above more than a whisper.

Chapter Fifteen
Temple of Mara

Etain stifled her disgust at the taste and smell of old blood in the waters of the demolished throne-room.

"Father refused to leave. He entrusted the kingdom and people of it to my elder brother. Father remained behind on his throne crownless as the drill came to the floor, trying to mitigate the damage that would come."

The Triton's voice was more gravelly and deep than it had been, and when she looked to him, his expression was strained and gazing back at some scene that she could only imagine.

"I doubt they even saw him, or this, though there should have been probes. Perhaps all they'd seen was a large, noble fish." She trailed off thoughtfully, before continuing. "They see so little with their technology, even when something is right there. Part of the way the ancient magic of our kind's creation works, I suppose."

Etain's use of the term noble had not gone unappreciated. He nodded and drew a deep breath, even as he discarded her defense of her own kind.

"The most noble. I only hope my brothers and I can live up to the Neptunes of our past. We've already had to move so far and establish new territories, little halfling. Now we start yet again."

Etain swam to and touched the remains of the throne where some of it lay and then the piping where it plunged into the floor and bedrock below. The magic still contained in the shards licked at her, responding to her, seeking direction since the mind behind it was now gone. She closed her eyes and teased it out under the watchful eyes of the Triton. He said nothing while she worked, yet she heard whispers of the past Neptune-kings that had ruled the city from the throne.

"A new throne needs building when the new city is sited...

And to be linked into the seaplain matrix with those of the other sea-kings."

"It will be done. We will find an artisan of skill enough to represent all the people and kinds in the kingdom. I suspect you will be sent for at one point in its construction."

She nodded in reply, weaving the magic now into new patterns, and casting it outwards like a net to contain the damage. What oil she could she pulled together and worked back into the ground, breaking it up as much as possible trying to protect the burrowing creatures. It was then that she became fully aware of what the dark pall over the city had been. Oil, a vast, settling cloud of it, that she had swum through to get down and the thing most responsible for her feeling of heaviness and illness.

The Triton continued to watch her, noting the way the currents swirled and the way her hair lit and fur glowed. Another form superimposed itself over her as he watched, adding her own power. Soft seal lines were overlain by the fiercer and sleeker shark people lines, fins becoming slashes in the water. A second set of arms, spectral, wielded the wicked obsidian and crystal bladed spear and trident so familiar to devotees of the sea goddess that visited her undersea temples. The blades even glowed with residual fire from undersea volcanic origins.

Mara's eyes locked with his while Etain was wrapped in her duties and he felt the usual dangerous and unpredictable chill. His blood froze when she smiled at him, and though the Etain/Mara set was too far to reach normally, the tips of her trident rested on his shoulder in blessing. When a small burst issued into him his worry deepened as to what it boded.

When Etain had done all that she could and set the spell to work in perpetuity she felt Mara's rage die down... somewhat. When she looked toward the Triton again, it was to meet iced and distant eyes with a touch of what she thought was fear. She turned around, just to ascertain that he wasn't staring at something behind her, perhaps a crazed kraken deciding already to take over the abandoned room despite the drillpipe. There was nothing that would cause him concern though.

"Why... are you looking at me like that...?"

He shook his head, then looked away. "Is there more that you need to do here?"

Etain tilted her head to regard him, nibbling her lower lip lightly in thought. "No. I've done what I can for this place. I should get back to my ship soon, but–" She bit her lip thoughtfully, framing in her mind carefully what she would say, not wishing to offend him now that she was somewhat on his better side. "I would like to see the city before I go, to pay my respects to what once was."

The Triton crossed his arms, still with the same icy regard, though his eyes were beginning to thaw a bit. "Very well. Thank you for your help, I'll escort you then, halfling."

They made their way back out of the throne-room, and through the deserted city once she had said a quiet prayer for the soul of the Neptune-king that had given his life for his people and to make her job slightly easier.

The pennants still waved in the currents, and here and there wild fish swam. The water seemed healthier than when she had arrived, but now the city had more of a forlorn and abandoned feel. At the edges of her vision at times she thought she saw a swimming form, perhaps a Selkie, a Triton, maybe a Siren. Each time it would turn out to simply be a trick of the lighting and terrain, or so it would seem after inspection. It was as possible that she was seeing ghosts that would not be able to leave until a new home was found. The heavy pall of grief settled more heavily than the oil had.

Etain explored the city thoroughly, looking up often at the rocks piled into towers and how the coral was trained to grow over these to hold the whole together. Red, pink, and yellow specimens cemented the walls well, but were beginning to pale around the edges, already bleaching. Small fish moved here and there but not as energetically as they would have before. Starfish still moved over the rocks after their next meal. With architecture like this it was very easy to see how human technology would miss the buildings.

This habit of blending in did not apply to lintels and window frames. Here, these were carved of hewn stone with a strange mingling of Nordic and Celtic knotwork depicting scenes of the family's history, according to her Triton escort. Now and then, when venturing inside to get somewhat of a feel for how the people had lived, she would see the interiors carved with the forms of ancestors and was able to pick out here and there where Greco-Roman influence intersected with those confirming the Triton's statement about having had to move far.

At the northern edge of the city, she found the mate to the Neptune's castle. Where his castle had been decorated with banners, pearls, corals, and other bright living things, Mara's temple blended stone, coral, volcanic columns, natural tables, giant teeth, and spears. Above the entrance a stained glass depicted the softer side she once had shown more frequently, and she tied together the hands of a couple while collecting their blood in a cup. Guarding the entrance to the temple were two figures, both female. One, a stern shark woman in what looked to be Viking inspired armor wielded an obsidian trident and glared disinterestedly at those that approached. The other, a rounded though still quite muscular Selkie held a crystal tipped spear wearing similar armor. In contrast to the guardian on the other side of the entrance her hand was outstretched in a wary welcome, or perhaps warning.

Etain and the Triton slipped between the pair and through the open Temple doors. Inside, representatives of each of the sea-dwelling merfolk species waited in alcoves, forever carved in granite. A Samebito, Triton, Merrow, Selkie, Undine, 'Classical Mermaid,' Octopid, Naga, and a half-human, half sea dragon – that she vaguely remembered from her long ago Defense classes calling a Ryujin – along with several others each in their respective nooks, proffered books. These detailed the histories and creation of each of the races in Atlantean, Lemurian, and one other ancient script that she could not decipher that reminded her of Ogham and Runes mixed together.

She looked at the Triton, her hair flaring around her in interest. "The priests left these?"

"Mara wouldn't allow them to take these." He gestured to the statue, or at least she hoped it was just a statue, of a prehistoric shark of monstrous proportion. Over sixty feet in length and dwarfing the human formed version (despite its own larger than life size where she struck a commanding and threatening pose near the shark's nose) the shark lay in the focal point, as if merely resting. Etain's imagination gave movement to the vast gills and lengthy hair. One vast eye glared at them and at the world with cool contempt. Somehow, that onyx eye conveyed the sense of awareness, though she wasn't sure how. "She said that when her new Temple is built, she herself will move all of these, and that meantime she would transfer them 'elsewhere.'"

The onyx eye, larger than she herself was, continued to bore into her challengingly.

"Is that so?" Dreaminess poured over her the longer she gazed into the eye. "I wonder where the Lady plans to keep all this safe from the oil and the men in the meanwhile? It will take a long time to rebuild her Temple, yes?"

"Indeed."

He crossed his arms and huffed gruffly. Once more the Selkie's attention seemed to be drifting. It seemed that she was held by the eye's gaze. Surely she knew better than to look into Mara's eye? Yet, it seemed not, to him. She continued looking into it, and one band of her bracelet he could see reacting. He could even feel it in the water, an electric thrum, high and low at once, and a stirring.

Did he see the statue move? He narrowed his eyes, then checked the other statues.

Try as he might, he could not be sure if he really had seen Mara's statue stir. It stayed where it was, and the representatives of all her many children likewise continued to proffer their histories without movement.

The half Selkie that was the goddess' land-walking priestess swam up to the eye of the great statue, running a hand over the eye-ridge in awe. The statue felt warm to her touch and Etain reached out in mental quest trying to decide just what was going on. Though she felt something, knew it to be Mara's energy, it waited just out of her reach.

After receiving no answer, she instead went to investigate the Selkie statue. Carefully, she searched the shape and form of it. Though firmly in unchanging stone it seemed somehow as if it looked distinctly like each of the many sub-breeds including the freshwater-dwelling ones, depending on the angle, and changed slightly with each blink.

Etain carefully opened the book of Selkie History, reading what she could then sighing when she realized how much more she would have to read. The book alone was three times the size of the Makay Logbook back at Seal Point, which itself was at times nearly 1 foot thick. Yet, the book drew her and she looked pleadingly back at the statues of Mara, then to the Selkie, then back to the book. Experimentally she tried lifting the tome hoping that she had the clearance to take it with her for study.

The shark blinked. Etain did not see, but the Triton did, and he placed himself between the two while the curious Selkie attempted lifting the book. A shiver passed over the body of the shark, and the human version below it moved her head and lowered her spear to look at the Selkie. The pair continued watching as Etain continued testing the weight of it.

"I don't think you ought to be doing that."

The Triton's tone was firm, as if speaking to someone younger and slower, while trying to catch and hold her attention.

"I don't think I can." Etain panted, finally giving up her straining with a disappointed whimper. "It's too heavy, I'll never get it home or anywhere without Her help. I was hoping that my daughter could read some of this, and see for herself how important our family's function really is."

The shark turned itself, more directly facing the pair.

"We have something more important to worry about than any desire for knowledge." He placed a hand on her shoulder and spun her roughly to view the now living and moving statues.

She started, her eyes going larger and rounder than they normally were, and the blue of her eyes shooting to a panicked yellow at the size of the shark, now that it was moving.

"Why do you linger?" The humanesque statue gestured slowly, and shifted her trident. "You have restored what balance can be done here, and your craft bobs on the waves like a buoy waiting. You have more elsewhere."

The shark continued to loom behind the seemingly mild-mannered statue. Etain curtsied the best that she could in the water, as she had been taught on land, and though graceful was not quite what she had aimed for.

"When I was a girl, you promised that I would be able to read one of the tomes... and I thought, Lady, if you would allow, when the Winter Break comes for Kirstin and she returns for Winter Rites, if she read then she would understand too."

"And so now you have read. I can consider the possibility of your pup reading, but it will not be this winter. Summer, when she will have the time, moving the books will be part of her challenge perhaps. Or perhaps not, if she proves unworthy of the line."

Etain blanched. "She will prove worthy, Lady Mara. She is already overcoming the problem of most merfolk despising halfbreed blood that she carries."

"Through exposure though. A different route, and not the one I was looking for. This year and the next should help solve that problem though. Now that she's old enough, I expect her to get a proper education in the ways of the wild and the seas." The shark shifted and eyed Etain and the Triton hungrily, gliding closer. The human version of the goddess formed herself a shark's tail, assuming a more comfortable pose and height, floating now in the water despite her weight and a malicious smile ferally spreading. "At any rate, I do hope she survives to full adulthood, that werewolf boy she thinks so highly of has certainly prompted some interesting changes, and there will be more tests after my own that I wish to see how she weathers. I like the idea of another circle back if he's strong enough."

The Triton kept his eyes on Mara's manifestations warily, though he wondered about the child that goddess and the half-Selkie were discussing. In his lifetime, he had been witness to some arguments and discussions between her Priests, the Priestesses, and even had a few of his own. To date though he had never seen a smile unleashed quite as dangerous as was being so 'lovingly' bestowed on the half-breed by the goddess who either ate or broke her own as she made the lines stronger.

"What do you mean, Lady?"

"I mean that her sins will make her weak, if she does not walk carefully, and now that my sister and I are not the only deities involved in the family fortunes..." The goddess trailed off.

"What sins has my daughter committed against you? Will her blood four times yearly not be enough?"

"What sin!" The goddess railed. The shark snapped and the sharkwoman flung an electric bolt at the fins of the Selkie statue, which hit the mark and sent pains through every living seal-person no matter the blood dilution nor type. "Your daughter made an oath that she would bear no pups for anyone save that young potioneer, when the time came. I felt the ripple. What sin indeed! After you and your mate, she is the last of this line that combines all, the last bearing both my blood and my sister's, as well as the wood-hunt lord. It doesn't matter that so far he meets my approval! None of you have permission to make a decision that could end the line."

The Triton had no idea who the particular god was that Mara referenced or how his blood ran in their family line, but the loss and anger radiating made even his scales feel as if they were about to drop. How long had the separation been? Was this part of why her mood always changed so swiftly? Etain was thinking along similar lines, and though each drop of information always improved her understanding of the one her fortunes rested on, in this mood new knowledge was too dangerous.

"Let me take on the transgression then, Great Mother. Place the anger on me instead." Etain held herself firm, keeping her voice carefully modulated, though she trembled and knew the water had to taste heavily of her roiling emotions.

The shark held the pair framed with its jaws. One twitch and both Triton and Selkie would be food for her prehistoric self, yet the Triton held his guard firm unknowing as to precisely why he continued to shield her while the priestess and her goddess faced off. The twitch did not come and they stared together into the dark maw.

"I will stand witness. It sounds as though the child is young by our standards, so there is time yet Lady, and you will not have to worry about the preservation of your literal line." He'd done it, said something and fully gotten himself involved in the struggle. He could feel the bonds of the oath tightening around him even now as witness, the magic requiring the witness for the sealing of the transfer. All it required, was Mara's acceptance.

The jaws closed, and the darkness was absolute.

Chapter Sixteen
Flat Note

Kirsty smiled in her place as the music swelled in and around her during choir practice, and light spilled through the stained glass images, which looked different to every person. For her they showed merchant ships under full sail, red sunsets, rocky shores perfect to fish around if she could just get her own sealskin, and the occasional storm. These were offset on the other side of the room with images of waterfalls and the Well. Each rank was placed slightly higher than the previous, and the sound of their voices reverberated thanks to the stone walls. The room was built specifically for this purpose, long back when Choir was involved with weekly worship in the Chapel. As the religions of those coming to the school grew more diverse once more, Worship fell out of favor. Choir remained, and even grew stronger.

At the front their Director kept time, gesturing to each section for their cue as they practiced a song new to the younger years. Thomas, to the side as always, plucked the tune on a lute. It was his own this time and not the school's. Each note was like silver and gold, and as he played, an image formed in their minds as they sang the song. Kirsty regretted that David was too busy with his studies, and that Ally was too busy trying to catch the eye of her latest crush, wishing that they could be present to hear their progress. In front of the Director as the energy raised an image began to form. The story that they were singing of finally beginning to become visible after their long practice.

When her solo came, she rose up to meet the notes, closing her eyes and letting them fill her, becoming them. Satisfaction ran through her blood when she realized she was finally getting everything blended perfectly.

Then came the searing pain in her feet and legs, as if someone had hurled a fireball at them. The velvet of her voice cracked and instead of the next word, a squeal issued from her mouth as she fell, legs unable to support her and feeling as if she had gained a tail, instead of the legs she knew now folded beneath her. The suddenness of the fall and surprised flail pulled down others, some that had tried to catch her as they felt or saw the crumple begin. The image that they had collectively crafted shattered, and both Thomas and the director surged forward as one to get up to her rank.

"Miss Makay, What happened?"

"Kirsty, are you alright?"

The two spoke as one, while hands pulled her up, and she winced and whimpered when her weight was once more on her feet. It was taking concentration to remain upright, and suddenly she was very glad that David was not there to see.

"I... I'm fine. I don't know what happened." She looked at the Director and swallowed, as his keen eyes searched for the cause of her fall. She flushed, realizing that the entire choir surely had to be staring at her, possibly judging for all she knew.

"Really, you *are such a clutz* Makay." Glancing away and around she saw a few irritated looks though she pointedly refused to look in the direction of *that* voice.

"More than enough, Maldein."

"But sir, you saw her pull down everyone around her. Probably just looking for attention.

"Maldein, demerit. Leave now."

Morgana scowled, and swept with a huff from the room in a flurry of dragonsblood and ocher to go find Morvan, though not before casting a sneer her way and mouthing "sea trash."

She pushed her way up and fantasized about Morgana's next bath suddenly being filled with piranhas, or dashing her against the sides of the carved tub till she ran screaming down the halls claiming the gremlin jinxed her bath. *It would be so easy just to do it. Would Mara and the Lady mind?* "Maybe just a muscle twinge. I'll be fine sir." *"Oh no, where's Imp? Is he ok?"*

It was probably the wrong thing to say. His eyebrows shot up, possibly believing that her late night classes in the loch may have been partly responsible. He was aware of what her special classes entailed, she remembered, and mentally kicked herself.

"Can you go on?"

"Yes Director, I think so."

Thomas eyed her warily before returning to his spot at the Director's signal, and continued to do so after.

"Please, don't tell David. Not till I know for sure what happened. Please don't tel—"

"From the top, everyone. One, and two, and three." The Director said, and Kirsty heaved an internal sigh of relief.

The wand was a baton again, keeping the beat, and Thomas started at the beginning of the score. She lost herself in the music again, hiding in it this time. It was with relief that she got through her solo without another interruption and then the solo was a duo when the answer came from the next, and then a third voice rose. Opening her eyes, the three Founders were pictured in front of them, acting out the story of the building of the school, and why.

Headmaster Delphine Leomaris, voiced by the seventh year at the top left, stoutly defended the rights of the students from the sea to learn to control their gifts. The way his part was worded, she wasn't positive if he were secretly from the sea himself, or had loved someone that was, and she made a note to look in the library to see if she could dig anything up. Irritatingly, she couldn't make out details on what they looked like other than generalizations of hair and clothing.

A fifth year boy from Spiralis gave voice to Aemilius Spiralis, and the argument began in earnest, quickly spreading from trying to restrict the shapeshifting merfolk from entering, to all non-humans, as well as those whose magic "sprang from nowhere like the desert spring that harbors scorpions at the brink." Kirsty found her voice again, and Adalwufa Bertramus spread her arms between the pair, her blue and silver robes flying, trying to make the two listen to reason and stop fighting long enough to teach, complaining of how not finding some compromise would only hurt the students.

Mid note, the pain came back, but worse. This time it ran all over her body and she felt teeth around her midsection. She hit the expected note, now against the backdrop of the chorus, but something was thrashing her back and forth. Students looked up at her in confusion and cleared out from underneath her as she was lifted high. She couldn't see the shark that had her, shouldn't even be able to get at her here, but she felt around and jabbed for an eye anyway hoping to luck out and find it. Kirsty soon found herself flying toward one of the stone wall sections but not because she found the invisible eye. Instead, it was more like whatever had decided to attack had just decided to let go as quickly.

Just before she impacted with the wall she felt another force stop her. In her mind it felt somewhat like what being a ball and landing in a wicket keeper's glove in a game of cricket, or possibly more like those baseball mitts that she saw now and then if someone had some odd obsession with that American game. Kirsty was lowered to the ground but the world was still spinning. If her top wasn't severed from her bottom, it felt like it should be. Worse, she could feel her pelt spreading, and the itch on her face that heralded that whiskers might soon be on their way. Her very blood burned as if someone very powerful was currently blowing up at her, or something about her was being ripped out, possibly burned away.

Whatever it was, it hurt more than she cared to dwell on.

"Enough for today. Don't forget your daily practices, and we'll meet again next week. Dismissed. Harper, you stay please."

The other students filed out, the usual thundering bustle and swishing of robes now accompanied by whisperings about what might have caused Kirsty to have had such an unusual hap-pening. Rumors were already starting that it was because she either might not be as pureblooded as she led people to believe, or that it was because she was singing a part that normally someone from Bertramus took on. Kirsty sat on the floor, still processing and clutching herself, staring around for the source of her attack in a mixture of fear, wariness, and determination.

"Whatever that was, it won't get the chance to do it again."

Both Thomas and the Director thought that the way she looked around and tried to get back to her feet signaled too many times of being attacked. Neither dared say anything about their thought in case the other was unaware of her strange characteristics.

"Nothing. Oh Tempest and Swell, Mara, don't force a change now! If that's what's going on my Lady, please not now. I've nowhere to hide, Thomas hasn't seen."

Still no attack, and she shielded her face behind her hair. When Mara decided to use her control, it was always for very different and harsher reasons than her sister, and she never cared if Kirsty were where she could hide in water. The Lady, on the other hand, always made certain she was in a 'safe' place and that she knew why the change had been forced.

"Miss Makay, can you walk?" The Director asked calmly, though his silver eyes poured over her as carefully as if grading charmswork or an amulet attempt, and no doubt as carefully as the matron in the healing wing was going to be if he could herd her there.

"Please don't send me where I think you are planning..." She tried to stand again, this time with Thomas helping her. "I think so..." She peeked from under her hair at the Director, who pushed her hair back out of her face when he leaned closer to examine her. "My legs don't feel right though, Professor."

"Well, we'll take you to the healing wing and have Madam look you over. I can't see any reason any of that should have happened. It's an old song, no one's cursed it, and no one's ever had that happen to them. Have you been into anything *unusual* lately?"

"Is anything about my life usual?" She thought, then replied, "No sir..."

Thomas stifled a snort as the Director took up position on her other side.

"I haven't." Kirsty tossed a quick glare at Thomas.

"Very well then. If you do think of anything though, then don't be afraid to talk to me about it. Once we get you there, I'll go tell your head of house and the headmaster."

She groaned, imagining her aunt's reaction. "Can we maybe, not tell her, sir? Please?"

The Director shook his head. "You know she'll need to know."

Kirsty sighed and nodded. While making her way to the healing wing, Thomas and the Director caught her whenever her legs would give out. Luckily most of the students were either in classes or preferred spending their free time out on the grounds, so by now there were fewer students in the halls. Unfortunately, both Morgana and Morvan were 'recreating' near the foot of the stairs she needed, by 'practicing bird calls.' Cuckoo calls followed her as she mounted the steps, holding her head high and pretending she could not hear, since the Director was there.

"Just you wait... I'll show you who's the cuckoo, Lilitu..."

She growled when trying to get up the stairs and her knees buckled, but she knew better than to argue against anything the Director said.

"I hope I don't miss too much of Potions. I really wanted to be there for the start of how to do the race null-effect workarounds."

After navigating the passages, and the castle gremlin dropping the portable hole that he was repositioning in favor of following the trio to find out what was happening they finally made it to the large oak doors. Emblazoned here was the caduceus in red, overlaid on a triskele in white, and the whole encircled by a red circle. The doors swung open on their own to reveal a hall of beds, each curtained off from the others, and the odor of menthol and other healing herbs seared their noses.

At the far end, the Matron looked up from where she was tending to a broken leg. On seeing the gremlin floating 'innocently' behind Kirsty, she leveled her wand, revealing the spoon tip, which glowed irritably.

"YOU! What else did you do?"

Kirsty flinched, believing at first that the wand and the ire was aimed at her.

"Not you child. HIM." She pointed. "Portable hole and a broken leg. Who knows what other mischief he's been up to, and Lord have Mercy when the poltergeist breaks her seal again so they both can 'play' again. What did that nasty thing do to you child?"

"Him? The gremlin always seemed female to me..."

"Laryna... He didn't do anything to her." The Director glanced around, and the Matron indicated to them where she wanted Kirsty.

As they seated her on the closest bed, he recounted how twice their practice had been interrupted, and how the last time she had been flung about and needed Catching.

"Odd indeed. Step out a moment gentlemen, please. I need to check for bruising."

Thomas and the Director complied, and she shut the curtain.

"Harper has class, I'll send a note with him explaining that Makay will be a little late, and I should be going myself to have a word with the Headmaster and Professor MacLeòmhann."

"Very well. I will let you know my findings then."

Kirsty opened her robes and lifted her shirt glumly, exposing her half-pelt to the Healer and allowing those thin hands to sift through the fur and prod at her. She could hear the withdrawing footsteps, and wished that she was going too. Each gentle poke brought a wince as the Healer examined the places Kirsty had, so she thought, been surreptitiously clutching.

"You've been bitten, girl. Very large mouth. The Director said he didn't see anything, but did you?"

"No ma'am. Not a thing. One moment we had finally gotten the Founding Song's story to visualize, and the next I'm being thrashed around like by a shark at feed."

"Your studies haven't stirred up anything, not found any ancient artifacts in your dives lately?"

"Not that I'm aware of, no. But whatever it was, felt so *angry*. Frustrated... Oh!"

She jumped as something cold was worked into her pelt and skin, and became aware of a sting at each place the ointment was applied. Looking down, she could see where the Healer had discovered slow oozes of blood. Next came bandages wrapped around her chest to hold ribs in place, standard practice whether they were just bruised, or broken. When she was finished, she dropped her shirt again, and lifted her skirts even more grudgingly for her legs to be checked over.

By the time that the Healer had finished fussing over her, and forcing a very large dose of Bruise-mend on her to heal bone and muscle from the inside as well, the doors to the Healer's Hall were swinging open again. She tried to clear the taste of licorice and ground shell, and some less savory flavors from her tongue as footsteps hurried over the marble floor.

Kirsty lost that battle, and the flavor settled more firmly on her tongue as the warmth spread through her body, over nerves and everywhere the spectral teeth had abused. By the time her aunt was crushing her with a hug, and dripping saltwater on her shoulder, she was very glad of it as it protected her from any further damage.

"Auntie... you squishing me..." The vice-like grip loosened, and Kirsty drew breath properly. *"Must stop scaring Auntie. She'll break me one of these days."*

As brusquely as the Healer had, Professor MacLeòmhann was checking her over for damages. Dark eyes appeared behind her, framed by white hair, and draping robes incorporating all of the house colors flowed around him, from beneath the flatboard Doctoral hat.

"What do you think, Headmaster? Jinxed?"

"Quite possibly, but who here would be creative enough to come up with such an unusual style?" The warm voice washed over them both, making Kirsty remember quiet nights by the hearth.

"What could be be otherwise though? We've never had the song give anyone problems like this." Her aunt asked.

"I didn't say that she wasn't jinxed, just that if she is, it is not by anyone here, Belara." The Headmaster stroked his beard in thought.

"Who then, Artair?"

The Headmaster shook his head and removed from around his neck a medallion set with round polished agate and etched deeply with arcane symbols that were unrecognizable to her. He very carefully set this around her own neck and tucked it under her robe, patting her head after.

"This should do while you finish the process of repairing your grandmother's wardstone, Miss Makay. Now, I have heard some concerns that you've been having nightmares that wake your dormmates?"

"Thank you, Professor Guirmean..." She fingered it through the cloth. "I keep seeing Mum's boat, and things keep happening to her, Headmaster. Not bad enough to request any Dreamkill from the Potionsmaster, but... I keep seeing her boat sinking, and bits of it all over the waves, shortly before I wake. Nevermind the others, or the flashes I get while awake."

"It is natural to worry when our loved ones are so far away, and your mother's calling is not the safest."

"Yeah, and even in this community, not many believe in deities being involved with anyone."

She nodded, and rubbed where she had been bisected. "Yes, I'm used to Mum and Da having to be gone. Even if the fishing trips were just actual fishing trips, there'd be times it would still just be me and Byron–"

"-Byron and I."

Kirsty nodded and sighed, used to her aunt's grammar corrections. "Byron and I."

"Are you keeping a record of them?"

Kirsty winced. "Yes sir, even though I'm not looking forward to presenting the diary to the Divinations Mistress since she wants a record for class."

Did she detect the hint of a smile on his lips, in answer to the irritation?

"I would suggest making it a little more than a dream diary. I want you to keep track of any news you get from home as well, so that we can see if anything correlates, and also any little signs that you see."

She nodded.

"Can I get to class now?"

The headmaster nodded.

"Thank you!"

Kirsty curtsied to the adults, before scampering off.

"Your niece loves classes just as much as you did, Belara." The Headmaster gazed at the door with a small smile.

"I think in this case, she was simply more afraid that we might pry, or make her hold still for another dose of medication, Artair... Though I'm sure Potions does call rather loudly."

"Do you think that Finnol is still in port, or if we sent a

summons, we'd only rouse Byron?"

"Finnol will likely still be out. Byron was the one bringing her. All we can do is try and see if anyone answers."

The gremlin slipped after Kirsty having given the girl time enough to forget, hopefully, that she was still in range. The adults were still deeply embroiled in their discussion and the Healer was busy prepping the now empty unit for the next student.

"Meri..."

Shi paused, and slowly turned her head around one hundred and eighty degrees to stare back at the warning tone, blinking hir eyes innocently.

"Leave young Makay alone. I do think she's had enough excitement today."

"Yes, sir..." The gremlin continued on, ears drooping a bit, until the door closed behind her. *Didn't say not to go pick at that seal though, did he?* Hir ears perked back up as hir feet sped her toward the Observation Tower.

Chapter Seventeen
POTIONRY AND WATER MAGIC

He checked his pocket watch again, which sternly ticked away the time with all the precision of the best of German watches. The Schneiengert crest impassively stared up at him, a sapphire wolf eye on the right side and an argent bear eye on the left, with a crossed spear and sword framing the eyes, an upright wand dividing the eyes all on a field Kürsch purpure. It was one of the few insignia of any of the other schools that was ever seen among the students. Not quite accusatory, but certainly a bit out of place, it seemed a lone bit of flotsam in the usual sea of symbols.

The books in his arm he was looking forward to putting down though he could hold them much longer if needed. The copper ring on his finger, next to the wolf ring, that likewise always stayed on his hand, had been very hot not too long ago and he had heard what he swore was Kirsty's scream. As worrisome as it was to him, it had not been a valid excuse to be excused from the last class, and since he had known she was in choir... he had simply chosen to wait. After all, what could possibly happen to her while *singing?* Gaining a cracked voice box from going too far out of her range perhaps, and he had no idea how much that might hurt, but that was the most plausible thing he could think of to explain it.

With a sigh he stowed his father's watch again and leaned against the wall waiting either for the classroom door to open or for one of the others to come down the hallway. Preferably Kirsty, though Thomas would do too if something truly had gone wrong. The clicking of a measured stride echoed down the hall in the same metronomic cadence as the watch, and a man resembling a swooping raven in his button-down damask doctoral robe and the way his secondary robe billowed calmly walked up to the door, the hood down as always. The man paused before opening it, framing his words carefully, each falling clipped to the floor as evenly as if they were working on a finicky and explosive brew.

"You seem to be lacking your companion, Valnarius. Usually the both of you are here waiting to pounce into my classroom. Miss Makay didn't end up held after class for retaliation again I hope."

"I don't know, Professor. She had Choir."

"Ah yes." He frowned. "Your head of house has a way of getting them to sing their heads off."

He opened the door and swept in with David following and trying not to imagine Kirsty doing that literally, knowing full well that if she knew how she would – simply to spook someone. He thought it would most likely be Lilitu, with how much she despised Morvan. David could just see her chasing after him shouting about taking his head and eating his brains since Morvan was afraid of zombies.

"I hope she never decides to find out how..."

Ok, so maybe part of him did just to see Lilitu's initial reaction and the way Kirsty smiled when she was actually pleased with herself. He could deal without seeing her 'headless' though. The scraping of chalk on the chalkboard accompanied the scrape of his chair while he settled and the Potionsmaster prepared himself. The Silent Lady glided into the room, held aloft a dusty tome, and deposited it on a bookshelf next to a skull chalice and powdered sea-unicorn horn once the Professor had met her eye. She nodded with a wan, sad smile, and a meaningful look to David, then glided away again leaving the already chill room even colder in her wake. Minutes dragged by, extended by the time warping effect of one of the Departed, and then other students began to trickle in with taught faces and darting eyes.

The Professor took the skull chalice and placed it directly on his lecture podium, and those faces drained of yet more color as they too slid into their seats.

"Still not here."

Thomas finally came in, and shook his head when David looked at him questioningly, replying by doing the weird finger gesture he always made whenever trying to indicate '*tell you later,*' then made his way up to the Professor. Discretely as possible, Thomas relayed the message from the Choir Director, and the Potionsmaster's face darkened for a moment before he made a check in his roll sheet. With a bow, Thomas went to his seat in front of David, then leaned back, opening his mouth and preparing to speak. A loud shrill voice came from the hall overriding what he had attempted to whisper.

"And there she was, way up in the air and being shaken like a dogbone. So much for 'best voice!' The Director looked like he sprung a – what's that springy thing that makes the clock go?"

"Mainspring."

"Yeah, one of those things. Sent us all out early."

Titters and howls of laughter, erupting while the two cadres of Spiralis students caught up on gossip, were cut off abruptly by a spell from the Potionsmaster. He then hauled the offenders into the room with another spell and deposited them painfully in their seats, Muting them next, all within the space between a tick and a tock. From the storage came the sound of two separate pops as volatile potions popped their corks and the smell of ginger and greymold spread. His eyes sparked and teeth bared while the more involved students winced trying to think of which those might have been.

"How many times have I said to maintain a proper level of volume in and near my classroom?"

The eight students stared at him in shock, never expecting that they too would experience such treatment despite being from his House.

"One more incident like this, and you will all receive the lowest marks and ejection from this school, permanently influential parents or not. Am I understood?"

The green robed students all mutely nodded unable to answer

verbally even had they wanted to. Unappeased, he slashed at the roll sheet with his quill, a quiet ripping sound filling the air when his force actually punctured the paper. The lecture that followed was similarly full of violence.

"As advanced students, you have heard before about Bloodwork, and that the grey area here is so wide that it is generally avoided. Just as with Waterwork, it is very easy to abuse."

Murmurs and nodding heads answered as he eyed each student, beginning without further preamble. The skull continued to stare.

"Several reasons make blood such a powerful ingredient. It can be used in philters, pastes, brews... but how it is prepared and used is the key. If you add blood in a potion brewing at high heat, it will be useless, since you will cook out what makes it valuable. If using human blood, it is important to use a clean specimen. There is no cure magic or mundane for AIDS, so it does no good to be sloppy and give yourself or your client a disease... and that is not the only one that spreads by bodily fluid. However, done correctly, you can also temporarily and sometimes permanently transfer Tendencies..."

Quills scratched while students took notes, some trying to keep from wretching. It was this atmosphere that Kirsty meekly slipped into roughly a quarter of the way through, flashing an apologetic smile and curtsy as she came. She slunk into her seat at his nod.

"Nice of you to join us after all, Makay. I didn't expect it. Don't let it happen again though. Valnarius... you will explain what she missed after class and share your notes with Miss Makay."

Both nodded, neither responding to the titters from the few Spiralis students that were not Muted. The lecture resumed, turning to the use of other human parts in potionry, and the skull began passing around the classroom as he explained its use –

bordering on Dark Magic, but never quite slipping fully in. Bloodwork in Potionry took even longer once he returned to it, and as expected they were saddled with essays on what other body parts could be used to change how a non-human would react to species-specific concoctions... and *why*.

When the lecture was over, most of the students left as swiftly as they could, little birds flushed out of the grass by the hunter's dog. David, as instructed by the professor, explained what Kirsty had missed, casting worried looks over her while she copied his notes and made notes of her own of things to investigate later as well. By the time they were done Kirsty was rubbing her head.

"Do you want to go down to the Lake? You look like you need to."

"Yeah... I think I should. Water..."

David helped her up and gathered both her things and his own, offering his arm. Kirsty took it, smiling tiredly. Her blue eyes took a phosphorescent sheen, a brief flash of night-shining algae or witch-fire. Just as quickly, it was gone.

"Where do you want to try? Somewhere quiet where you can tell me what happened to keep you?"

"A bit later. I'm fine now, so maybe the dock, so I can show Thomas I really am fine."

"Alright..."

Kirsty and David made their way through the halls, and past the Great Hall's din, where students still lingered over meals. She glanced at the doors briefly, worrying her lower lip and sucking slightly. David faltered in his steps when she did, looking toward her.

"We could pick some sandwiches."

She shook her head in reply, smiling and flushing slightly.

"No. Not today. Sooner I've got my feet in the loch the better I'll be."

He nodded and they continued past, out into the courtyard

where they stepped from stone and then to sod. Students that had already finished lounged around, some on benches, a pair at the fountain. The pops, bangs, zaps, and curses of the gremlin attempting to break the seal trapping the castle's poltergeist carried down.

Kirsty inhaled deeply, savoring the lush wet scent of growing grass, slightly damp earth, and the water calling from the loch. It sparkled deceptively under the sun, lapping lightly onto the shore and beckoning the more adventurous in. She sighed loudly while the fresh air circulated and cleared out the weight of centuries, intrigues, and negative energy remaining from her odd experience. David smiled at her smile.

As good as the sun and wind felt, and the light touch of the moisture in the air, and the feel of her hand on the expensive fabric of his sleeve, a strange sense of lack nagged at her.

"Hey Squeaky, surprised you can walk. Going to go sob it all out to your boyfriend?"

Her hand tightened on David's arm, and she looked down to the ground slightly, pretending not to hear.

"Did you really almost get slammed into a wall during choir, Makay? I knew you were bad at singing, but that takes talent to be that bad."

"I hope the next time they use the toilet, it fights back." Kirsty thought.

David barely spared Morvan and Morgana his most disinterested gaze, continuing walking. Still, he patted her hand where her fingers dug into him.

"Not even going to defend her singing, Valnarius?" Morvan smirked where he leaned against one of the trees.

Kirsty's grip dug tighter. *"Don't react. Just jealous. Just more of that 'I'm better because we don't have to work' malarkey. Wouldn't last a day doing anything my family has done."*

"I don't need to Lilitu. I am quite pleased by her singing, and

I seem to remember a certain unicorn that would have gored you if she had not sung to it."

"Should've let it. He baited him... except then–"

David had continued walking, head held high and drawing her with him and breaking off the thought. As difficult as it was, she tried not to dwell and to hold her head high as well. David sighted Thomas and the others first and turned their steps to the docks.

Kirsty gazed into the distance kicking her feet a bit and processing what she had caught of the class. Part of her still tried to figure out what had really happened during choir and why so that she could actually even begin to answer the questions that she kept seeing in David's and Thomas' eyes.

Sunlight streamed around her and glinted on the loch while the laughter of the others rose up during their playing in the waters. They lapped at her feet soothingly, and her blood was calmer. This was fresh water though, so the traces of the sea goddess were faint, which was fine since she felt a stronger connection to the well goddess. Still, she felt Mara's whispers and promptings, the restlessness having stilled somewhat, and hopefully in the next week would be Byron's arrival after his *mission* to work on parts of her training he knew. The nightmares were not lessening, but other dreams had begun to come as well.

"Maybe if I delve more into her mysteries, she'll calm more. But... Mara scares me, no matter how necessary she is."

A murmur, or so it sounded, at her side drew her somewhat from her thoughts and the underground passages and deep seas that her mind swam through. She made a soft reply, only a sound to show that she was listening. Well, part of her was, but most of her divided between the sun and the water, and those far off musings. She changed her song slightly, though it turned out to be yet another song wishing a loved one's ship safe passage, and did make an attempt at being fully present, but her preoccupation still devoured her.

Morvan and Morgana had continued trying to bait her, wandering down to the loch behind them and making the usual snide comments. For the most part, so far, she had even kept herself from retaliating against the Lilitu boy when he had talked loudly with his Spiralis cadre (thankfully not his whole House) about how superior humans were to non-human magical beings. She had easily heard them standing by the trees just far enough away that if she did do anything they could claim innocence.

Currently though she could let that irritation go. Instead she sat on the dock dangling her feet in the water and leaning against David during this respite where the three houses could inter-mingle. The way that younger students eagerly swam with the loch's Selkies was a balm to her soul even if some of them had some strange views of what the Selkies did when not being watched, or how many types there were of just Selkies alone, or whether they really were Beings.

The sun still rode in the sky so though she could swim she and the Selkies had to be careful of how they acted when near each other. She ran the comb through her hair again while looking into the water, now watching Ally attempting to play tag with one of the young ones that had come to the swimming area. Kirsty ached for night to fall so that she could come back without others around, magicfolk or not. She still considered most to be Cowan, or outsider. Thinking on how different she was, both as a waterwitch and as a Selkie, made her restless once again, and she tucked her comb back into her pouch, leaning away from David.

"Maybe I think entirely too much. Need to shut my brain up." Kirsty thought, then said, "I'm going for a walk."

Thomas looked up from where he was attempting to stalk Ally. "Another?" He then exchanged a look with David, as if asking a question.

Kirsty nodded and got up, not bothering to explain why, as Thomas had more than likely had time to ask David what about her mother was bothering that she'd not shared, probably in their own common room. She could hear the rustling of David's clothes as he got up quicker, then took his hand when he offered it. The young Selkie in the water surfaced, and watched the pair walk off, noting which direction the pair followed along the shore. She eventually wandered back toward the underwater village, a flash of silver briefly streaking for the deeps.

Kirsty and David walked until they were nearly off of the castle's grounds till she found a cove that suited her needs. The pool was deep enough to allow her to come close to shore easily, and there were rocks to hide behind, as well as a decent wall of greenery curtaining the cove off. There were even willows that helped shield the cove itself from view at the castle, yet she could see what was going on in that direction and others. She whuffed in satisfaction, then plunged into the thickest bushes she could find assured that she was well sheltered enough from anyone that didn't know her secret.

"And just what are you doing?"

"Changing for a proper swim, what's it sound like? We've got what? An hour left before next class? I am definitely liking this schedule. Potions, lunch and swim time, and then on to Defense?"

David blushed and turned away from the bushes as she rambled and rattled, even though they were thick enough he had no risk of seeing anything. He pulled out his watch and checked it. "About that." He shook his head.

"Good. I want to see the village during the daytime. I only get to see it at night, and I'm tired of being held back by worrying about what people think. So–" She emerged from the bushes in her red bathing suit, covered carefully from thigh to mid-arm and lower neck so that none of her half-pelt would be visible, re-securing her pouch about her waist. "Still have that crystal the Lady gave you?"

She didn't wait for him to answer, but instead knelt beside the water, pulled out a white clam shell, opened it, and placed a dose of the green paste on her tongue. She grimaced at the taste, wishing she already had her own skin so she'd never have to eat it again. *Ever.*

"Yes, but I don't have anything appropriate to swim in, in that form."

Kirsty's change took place quickly and painlessly, as what was locked away in her blood activated from the ingredients and magic in the bitter paste. Her legs fused together, and she lengthened. White and silver speckled fur spread from the pelt below her suit to cover her from face to tail tip. Her hair kept its color, but it became thicker, almost tendril-like, and her face became curiously seal-like, including some black whiskers – despite maintaining obvious links to humanity.

The suit felt tight over her fur and caught a bit but it was a small price to pay to maintain some dignity and to be able to speak to David without having his back to her all the time. She slipped headfirst into the water and slid out several body lengths, before breaking the surface and fluttering her now much larger blue eyes at him.

"Too bad. I wish you'd get something and start keeping it in your bag like I do. It was nice to swim with you like that."

"I wasn't very good."

Kirsty made a dismissive sound. "I don't care how good you are. I just like being with you." She rolled her eyes as if this were obvious by now.

"Well... I will swim today, but not like that." He then began hiding his belongings to keep them dry, just in case anyone happened this way.

Kirsty grinned, and splashed her tail. "Good! Try and catch me."

They swam to where the waters turned green, and deeper, to where the waters turned so green they were black, and the light above them was wan and dim. Kirsty glanced often at David to be sure his air was still holding though she knew he would be monitoring the spell he used. She was prepared to experiment with the lore though, if his airspell failed, to see how truthful the tales were about their kisses.

They slipped into a forest of nearly kelp-like proportions, which cut off more of the filtered twilight that was the sun. Kirsty conjured a light in her hand, and held it before them as she flipped and slipped her way through till they could finally see the large rocks at the bottom breaking the surface of the shorter lakeweed beds of the central clearing.

David was falling behind due to her excitement propelling her faster so she grabbed his hand and pulled him behind, managing not to break the spell somehow. Or if she did, then he remedied the situation before she had a chance to notice.

The villagers were out of their caves, using the light that filtered down from the surface in great green bars to ply their various tasks. The weavers wove the fishing nets and twisted their ropes, singing songs of strengthening. Spear makers and knife makers chipped at stones to form new blades, or affixed blades that had been gained from the sea clans. In the center of the village, the cooks prepared the village food, and even they had their own songs to sing. The effect was rather like whale song, especially from the seal-folk that had made their trading visit that day and threaded about the groups. Male and female both seemed occupied with the tasks and from the opposite side a fishing party made their way in with nets of longish fish from the deep waters by the seaside passage. Water Imps, clearer and greener than Imp, swam with silvery fish-folk fry and pale Selkie-pups in the blended village of the reserve. Waterdogs patrolled the edges with long-fingered grundylows on the lookout for predators.

"There's so much more activity... Come on, I want to go see what their herbalists are up to, maybe I can finally see some of the preparations they only make by day." Kirsty slowed her pace and let go of David, kicking circles around him in glee, before taking off for one of the larger caves below the rocks. Her laughter mingled with the various songs complementing each other.

David shook his head, then followed after the best he could though feeling self-conscious. Some of the non-local merfolk that were trading looked toward him curiously, while others waved, recognizing him. The brown harbor seal Selkies from the sea simply stared.

He shook his head and kicked along after the capering Selkie-maid as best he could with two human legs. Before he could catch up, a tiny silver streak plowed into his side, wrapping its arms around his middle gleefully. Looking down in the region of his waist a little fry was looking up at him eagerly, her facial scales glinting slightly in the eerie light.

"What?"

Kirsty paused at his voice, thinking he was speaking to her, and looked.

"Shell! What on Earth?"

Swimming back, she helped David with extricating himself from the wiggly fry's clutches.

"I'm sorry, I was just excited to see him this far out. He's the only other Landwalker this far in, besides the Head Master and Head Mistress." The child spoke far more gravely than one might expect when trying to wrap her tongue around the strange titles. "I still don't understand what's so big about Mastering heads. I have a head... it minds..."

Kirsty giggled and looked at David, enjoying his reaction, which seemed a mix of resignation and confusion. She giggled harder when he gave her his usual unamused look. She *truly* did try not to giggle, but there were times, such as this, that she thought he was probably too cute for his own good. Shell scowled and crossed her arms.

"Stop laughing at me Seaswimmer. You Landwalkers have funny words and I'm just a little fry."

"Must stop giggling. Oh gods I'm doomed. Must stop."

She managed to control herself, studiously avoiding the little mental stormclouds that her imagination kept putting over them both. *"I'd like to Master my own head sometimes..."*

"No, you're right. It's not funny, but I'm not meaning to be mean. And yes we've got some weird terms. Where's your parents Shell? You were one of the ones up at shore... did you sneak off again?" Kirsty leaned closer and put her hands on where her knees would have been.

"Only a little..." Shell looked down and twisted in the water.

Kirsty raised her eyebrow and shot a look at David, who had finished straightening his clothes as much as was possible when trying to swim in them. She sighed.

"Come on then. Maybe we'll find one of them on the way to watch the herbalists."

Shell latched onto Kirsty's waist obediently.

It took a little time to get to where the herbalists had gathered, near the mercheiftaness' 'cave.' They studiously ground and mixed shells and weeds, and some of the harder to obtain mistletoe berries from trading with centaurian herbalists. The singing here was different than the rest of the village, somber and meticulous. These faces did not smile. Each flick of fin, curl of finger, or stroke with heavy, smoothed rock was more of an extension of some darker undercurrent.

Shell didn't like it here, staying close as possible. Kirsty could feel the fry squeezing her waist, her innards giving way slightly. She curtsied the best one can with only a furry seal tail, fitted skirt, and a shiny fry trying to become a belt, then knelt beside the white haired elder in charge.

Pupil-less silver eyes looked up from their task from behind a headdress of dangling shells and painted markings that flowed over her scales, slowly pouring over them before flowing back to her task, never quite focused on any of them. A voice like worn sails flapped through the water and broke into shreds.

"The boy comes a long way for a Landwalker with a fragile little bubble on his head. I hope you remembered to kiss him beforehand to prevent any unfortunate breaths for him Seaswimmer."

"I hope I am not intruding, I was asked to follow." David bowed.

"We have seen you harvesting before. You may watch. I do not know how much of today's you will find of use to you, Boy."

The elder indicated a rock next to her with the flick of a fin, out of the light. With another careful movement, she placed more of what they ground, her paste more of a bloody slime that she gathered each time she had generated enough.

"What is it, Elder?" Kirsty leaned forward slightly to examine the elder's handiwork.

"Bloodberry Preparation we make today. For them." Her tail flicked to the visiting group. "It needs to be prepared and taken to Mara's Temple, but their herbalist recently was Netted. So, they come here. One more thing to trade with."

"And what is it for?" David asked, watching.

"They use it to clean wounds, usually from shark bite. Sometimes it is acceptable substitute for... certain demands on her priests and priestesses. It must be Activated first, before that. At a Temple. We have no Priestess."

"Like the difference between a Cowan 'potion,' and a proper potion, Elder?"

"Yes Child. Just like the difference between their potions and a real potion."

She grabbed each by the hand, pulling them forward. Kirsty, being used to such treatment and demonstration, allowed it without question or reaction while opening the sensory center on her hand instead and closing her eyes to note the feeling of what was likely Unactivated. David tensed, but even if he would have drawn back, the elder herbalist was not as weak as her age made her seem, nor quite as blind as her eyes looked, and he too had his hand drawn over.

But unlike Kirsty, or so he thought, he felt nothing. "I feel nothing." He stated quietly.

The elder turned her silver eyes to him again as she let them go. "And why do you sound so shamed? At this moment, there is nothing to feel. There will be later."

She placed the gathered slime into a tarnished container of what looked to have been bronze at one point in its life if the color of the coating was anything to go by. The other herbalists, some old, some young apprentices, brought their various ingredients, each adding in order and watching David curiously a moment before returning to their tasks. The elder, when the first few were placed in, changed her song and pulled from the pouch slung at her waist a red stone, placing both container and stone carefully in what looked to be a form of heating rack.

A word, and a flash of heat, and then the stone glowed, heating the contents of the ancient and dangerous looking cauldron, flickering like flame... yet leaving the water itself untouched. Kirsty tilted her head.

"So *that's* how you make heat here to brew."

"Of course. This clan isn't completely devoid of all magic just yet. We still have these tools, just no more memory of how they are made."

The herbalists continued with what they were doing, measuring carefully. Kirsty watched, committing everything to memory that she could. When the mixture was rendered down, the elder looked to Kirsty. "A test. Do you remember the last chant I taught you?"

Kirsty nodded, and repeated it, blushing. More of a series of sounds and tones than words, her hair stood on end as she concentrated on hitting each exactly, and David's hair rose in response. The elder grabbed her hands and placed them on either side of the still hot container. This time she flinched, unprepared for the heat. Intuiting what her tutor desired, she began again, unfocusing her eyes as she chanted and toned, her blood boiling.

As she worked, some of the visitors gathered to watch, attracted by the chant that they associated with the finishing of their order, and then drifting away again with sniffs at seeing who and what was the one Activating. She ignored them, taking her hands off only when allowed.

"Can you feel it now?"

The elder looked to David, and he nodded.

"Now, we are done, and better than asked. Seaswimmer's stance feels as if there is something troubling. Tell this old lady what ails the spirit?"

Kirsty sighed, shooting a sidelong glance to David and adjusting the nonexistent school skirt, catching herself and covering by brushing what would have been her thigh were her legs not currently a tail. The other healers, finished with their work for the time being, watched her. Some leaned forward while others pulled combs from their pouches and ran them through their hair, listening patiently. After collecting her thoughts she related to them what had recently happened.

The Elder healer nodded gravely, not interrupting. Kirsty shrank back a bit on seeing the cold steel in David's eyes when she related the pain of the unseen teeth, knowing that behind those was still one of the Lord of the Hunt's hounds... human as he seemed. Whatever it was that she had experienced, she knew she did not want it happening to him. Nor did she want him finding trouble on her account.

"An unusual happening indeed. Have you done anything to anger any of the deities?"

"Nothing more than usual, that I am aware of."

"More than usual..." The elder sighed, shifting her position and eyed her pupil. "That at least will be solved soon enough. They see farther than we. *You should listen to what they say Seaswimmer.*"

Kirsty picked at her fur and scowled.

They did not spend much longer at the healer's circle, instead taking one more swim past where Shell's cave was. Humming, low and discordant, could be heard from within. The voice was coarse as new gravel, with an immediate edge that raised eyebrows and gritted teeth.

"Hello?"

"We have Shell..."

The humming stopped, and after a breath, a withered green hand pulled back the curtain of woven lakeweeds. Two glittering silver eyes peered from the darkness.

"Granmere!"

Shell bolted for a point below the eyes, plowing into the area beneath with the same zeal she had waylaid David earlier. David and Kirsty both sighed, and swam off after the elder's thank you.

Both were aware of the passage of time, swimming quickly.

Section Two
FAREWELL SEA WITCH

Seastacks by Teresa Garcia (AmehanaRainStarDrago)

Chapter Eighteen
End of the Trail

Byron had continued his northward trek as swiftly and thoroughly as he was able. The Kelpie had not kept track of how far he had gone. Time did not have much meaning when he was traveling as part of the water to go through it, nor would it matter to him until he was back at his mistress' side discharging his duties. Food he had taken only when coming across it, not wishing to waste any time if he could help it. Travelling alone did have one rather undesired benefit. He was swifter without any humans, only half-human or not, on his back. There was also the advantage of not having to be careful with his poison spines in his mane.

Still, it had been a long search through what were empty seas as far as he was concerned. He was quite positive that Kirsty would be well into this year's training in finishing her readiness for her skinquest, by now. Surely those hormone-laden distant cousins of hers were decent enough fighters to train her in the way it was done in the sea... As long as she had a firm understanding of all the worlds she was going to be required to walk in, she should succeed. So for now, his only worry was Etain, unless he had lost track of more time than he had thought.

Maybe more technically that worry was Etain *and* the nameless *Things* that the Ministry used to keep track of non-human magical beings and anyone else that they wished. He was well versed in how they worked, had encountered them so many times since the Ministry had wormed their binding onto him and stolen his other form centuries ago. As he thought of the Ministry of Myths his lips peeled back off of his fangs. He could never be certain which of the competing 'governments' were worse.

The question was, why were so many of the *Things* ranging so far from the prisons and the 'reserves?' Who had revolted hard enough to have them unleashed? Was it one of the merclans not yet forced into the reserves? One of the reserves pushing back and refusing to give up traditional grounds? An escapee? A product of one of the wars always boiling just below the surface of one of the many intermingled and intersecting worlds? Perhaps a natural imbalance making them breed?

"Maybe the gods will hurry and make a grand return and scare some sense into all those pompous windbags. Probably too much to ask, be my luck Mara would decide to ride her clergy for that. Or Herne's Hunting Dogs would chase them through their silly "secure" government buildings... Hmm... I rather like that thought. Right into where they've trapped the wild magic."

A tickle of coldness passed him by, and he sneered to think that even below the waves they were hungrily on the prowl for new beings to mark, or old ones to feed from. And so *many*. None of them seemed to behave the way the Cailleach's servant children did. He changed his heading to avoid the one that he could feel ahead. A Seafolk city came slowly into his view as he galloped, and his heart leapt, hoping that perhaps they would have some news of where his mistress had gone.

The outer buildings were empty. Weedy yards waved in the current, and nary any sort of pet nor guardian was to be seen. The fields between had the unkempt look of untended seaweed beds developing, and even the oyster-beds between the outcroppings had an almost haunted feel. It was not unheard of, especially if there were threats in the area, for those on the outskirts to retreat into the cities and citadels proper. So Byron pressed on with froth and foam rising, though marking that the outskirts were abandoned and oil still seemed to linger. Yet the oil was changed somehow, bearing a fey energy that seemed to be...waiting.

Byron passed through the gate in the walls of coral and pearl and into the city proper but here too silence greeted him. He slowed his pace just in case he was what had sent everyone to hiding or if there were still occupants as he hoped. Yet the streets remained empty, the markets abandoned, and the pennants on the undersea towers were all that seemed to move in the current. He paced slowly through the city hoping for an Octopid, a Deepsea Selkie, one of the Sharkmen... even a Triton, contentious as they were, would have been a welcome sight.

There was none.

He pressed on to the citadel in the heart of the city, and here too no living, speaking thing greeted him. Into the castle he went, to the throne-room. Here, all that greeted him was the pipeline for the oil rig plunging through the roof and the remnants of the splintered throne, drained of its magic. Which of the capitals was he in? He searched the walls for a pennant that bore a crest, but all that still remained were blank. The name had been taken just as surely as this half of the twin hearts was dead.

With a sigh he bowed low, paying respects when a final look around revealed part of a decaying hand before his tangled mane fell into his eye. The Kelpie then left, making his way through the city toward the spires of the temple. The guardian statues gazed at him hollowly, the Samebito woman and the Selkie woman armored and holding spears.

"Mara's militarist aspect. Explains the overtones of Viking and Grecian architectural elements."

Going past the external guardians, he came to the room of the representative Ancestors, each presenting their Histories stone-faced. Here at least magic still lingered, dormant. Waiting. The taste of his mistress still lingered in these waters, fresh and emotion laden, joined with the suppressed fear of–

"A Triton? But where are they then?"

The dead eyes of the stone Megalodon watched from where the body lay, and the spear points of Mara's more humanoid form gleamed momentarily. Catching sight of this a chill swept over him, shaking him to his very marrow.

"What within or beyond the seven waves is bloody going on?"

He circled and paced the room. Byron tasted the water and sniffed, and reached with his inner senses, but try as he might the track ended here. Wherever Marsali's blood had gone with Etain he could not hope to follow.

"Mara. What have you done? What are you playing at?"

The eyes of the Megalodon continued to stare, as did the sharkwoman. Byron studied the eyes of those statues carefully, hoping that there might be some clue left in the temporary bodies. For a moment he saw a flash of whirling waters fighting themselves, and a great unsteadiness.

Chapter Nineteen
Name Exchange

Etain opened her eyes only to discover that she was still encased within the darkness. Mara held her within herself, though whether it was stomach or womb – or for how long – Etain was not sure. Nor did it matter. She was out of phase with the rest of all that was. Meaning, quite simply, for now she was basically nowhere.

"Never did like this feeling." She ran her hands over herself, sighing when they told her what her nerves sang. She was alive, and whole. No missing pieces. And no blood on the water.

"If this is what happens when witnessing for a priestess, I am never doing this again. For *anyone*, halfling."

At least she wasn't alone. With company, she could handle this. Even if it were a once again grumpy Triton.

"Well, this didn't happen the last time I made any deals with Her. Then again, none of my children taken by the Finmen have ever been found. So I've not exactly ever had the opportunity for anyone to witness an *Intervening*."

There still was no light, but she was aware of the Triton's movement beside her, and Etain gentled her speech. "She won't have taken anything. You'd be screaming, writhing, and likely beating me with your tail fins or impaling me on your trident if She had. When she takes though she also gives in return." Briefly she remembered a similar conversation was Kirstin was but a pup and had asked after the scars and wild fur of her half-pelt during bathtime.

Etain still moved further out of his reach as he finished his check. By that time there was dim light and she could vaguely see him, a black form against a darker darkness. It was warm, and the feeling of languid suspension calmed her just as much as her caution of a panicking Triton warred with her shaky trust.

"You speak like it is a routine thing to be devoured by a goddess whose favorite and oldest guise is a shark that can swallow a boat whole. Where are we?"

"For her, it is. Be still now children." Mara's voice was just as hard as before. A note of preoccupation was present this time, and perhaps some fatigue.

The pair did as ordered, held still and waited for whatever would come next as their eyes continued to learn to see in the strange dim light. The sense of swift movement pulled their stomachs from their usual resting place, and without further warning, the sea goddess vomited them forth. As they left her mouth, seeing starlight shining off the deadly, deeply serrated teeth, time seized them again. The disorientation increased with the leap.

Etain's head contacted the side of the *Sea Witch* with a dull thud, at the very moment that her eyes seized on the stars. She did not have time to register the extra stars before the blow knocked her out. The Triton narrowly missed the same fate, instead his shoulder absorbing most of the blow. Etain, still wearing her skin, floated amongst her cloak and the skirts of her peasant-styled dress that had never been shucked before her dive whilst he got his bearings.

Mara groaned deeply before once more retreating from the physical world into her separate realm. The groan rippled around them as if the depths of the seas called out for succor and companionship. The whiteness of her skin beneath the moon and droop of her dorsal fin did not go unnoticed, nor the wretching sound that followed or the stench thereof.

"Illness? No time for that." At the same time as his thought he called, "Mara!"

No reply came. She was gone, leaving them beside the boat that waited patiently for them, drifting in the ocean's current. He called for her only once more before sighing and tossing his trident up to the deck of the boat. It clattered, and he could feel the *Sea Witch* watching and listening, waiting to defend itself and its mistress if he tried any harm.

"Aye boat, it is wise to be wary." He snorted and gathered the unconscious halfling woman in his arms, commanded the water to rise enough that he could jump out and onto the deck with her. Laying her down carefully, he checked her skull after.

He found no obvious cracks or soft places that did not belong. He sat beside her, debating whether or not to remove the woman's skin. He knew the Selkies usually took off their skins on land if they were going to be there longer than to bask in the sun since they liked the feel of moon or sun on skin. Seal-bloods were not at risk of drying out, yet this one... did seem to have some traces of Fish-blood, if his senses were correct. Erring on the side of caution, he pulled at the seam and removed it from her carefully while praying to all the deities and all the pantheons he knew of that his choice was the correct one – or at least was the most likely to be correct. He laid it over her to preserve some of her heat since it was a cold night.

No bolt came from the sky to strike him down. No shark leaped up to snap him up, nor was there any kraken pulling him to a beaky maw and noble death of heroic struggles.

"That was quite anticlimatic."

A scream overhead caused him to look up, just in time to see a white tern pass over head. It let loose a bomb faster than he could dodge since he did not see the release. Something warm, gooey, and stinky splatted on his tail, and looking down, he was dismayed to see the white guano running over his scales, reaching out from a brown pellet of an epicenter.

"Which of them have I angered? The ignobility!"

His tail became uncomfortably tight and dry as he sat next to the unconscious halfling, waiting, watching. He was contemplating slipping off the deck and back to the water to re-wet himself when her eyes opened. He frowned, pausing in his half begun movement to observe. The eyes of Mara's priestess at first had a glazed, unfocused look that he associated with whales and dolphins that had been stunned during human sonic naval testing. Then she groaned, reached for her head with one hand, and rolled to push herself up with the other.

"Wait. I was in the water. How?" She looked around, her eyes focusing on him as the pieces fell into place. He could see them fall, in fact. "Thank you."

He nodded at her gravely. "It would not have been proper to leave you alone in such a state."

She wrapped her sealskin around herself loosely, thankful that despite the discomfort of having kept her clothes on before leaping into the sea Mara had not destroyed them as sacrilegious. Etain was careful not to close the skin fully though to initiate any part of the change.

"And now what will you do?"

"The same as any other Triton in my position. Mara must have a purpose for depositing me with you. Surely she could have returned me to those of my former city, wherever they currently are."

Etain smiled grimly. "Yes, she would have been able to place you any place in her sea she wished. This is what worries me most."

He shifted, the skin of his tail becoming steadily drier and tighter. His scales itched as they dried, and as he had no desire to feel himself split open, he slid himself back into the sea with as much dignity as he could muster.

Etain got up and went to the cabin, working out their position. She could have asked the Triton, and did think about it briefly. Yet, she held back as he had already done so much and she was uncertain who currently had the heavier end of the debts accrued over the last span. The *Sea Witch* waited patiently for her instructions. By the time he hauled himself back out, to better speak with her while she performed her checks, he dragged himself to the door just in time to hear her mutters.

"This can't be right..."

"What can't be right?"

"My calculations. The location spell..." She turned to some instruments, checking them over and grumbling about being reduced to Cowan technology in her exhaustion. Said equipment refused to operate, and protested against the fluctuating fields the best it knew how.

"You could ask..." He crossed his arms, unsure whether to be amused or annoyed at her dismay and confusion.

"Well... the star readings state we're somewhere near the Bermuda Triangle. The location spell confirms it. And this..." she jabbed a finger accusingly at the equipment. "This refuses to work at all, and say's we're actually below the surface by 20 *fathoms*. But, 'tis preposterous."

"Did whatever magic reader object perhaps fall overboard and sink during the storm earlier? Or perhaps it is just broken."

Etain sighed and poured over her charts. "It's non-magical, there for if I get boarded by the Coast Guard or any other agency that doesn't acknowledge our existence, or some pirate manages to sneak aboard. And the sensor's just fine location-wise."

"Well, my blood thinks the location might be right. Where shall we go? To find a permanent site for the new city that I can direct my elder brother to? It should be in similar conditions to prevent too much shock living there long term."

Etain looked at the water vial that was still in its mount. The water no longer glowed, so she knew that at least that particular objective was met for the time being.

"Yes, we'll do that. First, I need to try sending my co-ordinates, or the *Order* may send out search parties depending on how long I've been gone."

"So many divisions in how you land-dwellers operate. I'm surprised you don't have a Department of Myths."

Etain smiled a bit, wryly. "That's where our Shifters are

supposed to register. They'd probably love to get their hands on you and quantify you."

She touched a few points around her charts, then traced the sending sigil before tapping her location. A green light flared up, and a dot lit up briefly. Normally, she could have expected a washback feeling as corresponding points lit up on the map in the study back at Seal Point, and in a corresponding map in the *Order's* office. No such washback confirmation came. She repeated the process using a human variation of the spell and utilized her wand as pointer.

Still nothing happened. Her point glowed on the map, but that was all.

"Something's blocking me... Shouldn't be anything here to do so though. So that just leaves—"

"A Someone." The Triton finished the thought.

Etain nodded, staring at the map a moment. "I'll have to catch one of the seabirds later on and convince them to carry a letter or bottle. First let's see if we can even get out of here. I should have figured I suppose, what with all the stories."

"I'll lead you on the safest way."

With that he took himself back to the water, slipped in without a splash, then stroked powerfully forward. The *Sea Witch* hesitated, letting him take a good lead, then a bit longer.

"Yes, follow my girl. He's not sunk us yet, has he?"

Grudgingly, the boat followed the Triton, creaking loudly so as to voice its thoughts at least somewhat. After all, her mistress *had* been gone to the sea for quite some time. The *Sea Witch* had had to answer Mara's summons and sailed through one of the gateways without her captain just to be there for Etain's release. The ghost pirates trapped in Between had even come far too close to grappling her port bow on the trip. The *Sea Witch* projected her protests as loudly as she could about the voyage.

"Yet you got away, didnae you? We're together again and

hopefully won't be parted quite like that again."

The *Sea Witch* creaked loudly under Etain's feet and shuddered.

They continued that way, the Triton leading and the boat reluctantly following with phosphorescence in their wake until the dawn beset them. Etain with a hand on the helm watched the sun rise anxiously, judging the local weather by the color of the sky. Golden with hints of red the colors spread like ink dropped onto fine grain rice paper and she heaved a sigh when she did not see the fiery blood-red that she had been braced to see.

Assured her vessel would stay its course and not veer off in protest at having gone so far and so long on the lead of another she walked to the bow. The water was a Caribbean green, and she wondered if this was the shade that had been meant when mariners had tried to describe it in the Makay Logs during their clan's world travels.

Midday came and the Triton was still keeping the same swift pace. Etain tapped her throat with her wand then cupped her hands and Projected as loudly as possible.

"Shouldn't we take a break so you can rest? Ye've been swimming roughly 25 knots ever since we set out."

A few beats passed until he turned his head to reply, slowing slightly. She eyed him, noting that indeed there did seem to be signs of fatigue. The set of his face and dullness of eye spoke one word, while his voice carried another.

"I'm fine wench, I just want out of here."

"Wench? Well, can't expect a Triton to stay civil to me for very long. Wondered when he'd slip back." She mused, leaning forward over the bow. "I would feel better if you rested. Can you really withstand such long fast swims?"

"I am second eldest son of Merisson! Tritons train for just such as this since we are birthed, before we even leave our Nurseries."

"Yes, and I know well of your strengths as a Triton but wouldn't it be wise to also be rested if we encounter anything large and hungry? I can find a way to keep you hydrated while you rest aboardship. Then you can both rest and eat, and we could still continue on." She kept her tone light and reasonable, as if they were discussing a mail chess move together against another team. *"I hope Finnol's having an easy time in the office. This one reminds me of Andersen on one of his stubborn days."*

He cast an impatient look at her, and continued on. Another league passed behind them before he indicated that he was finally ready for a rest. Etain heaved a long sigh when he brought himself aboard.

"I suppose this is far enough, and we can go with your plan for a bit. You mentioned food, halfing?"

"My name is Etain Makay or Brinetreader. Not halfling, half selkie, wench, sea witch, or any permutation." His way was beginning to grate on her again, but she kept her smile fixed and tone amiable. "But yes... and I said I'd think of a way for you to be able to rest without drying out."

Reluctantly, he moved to the place she indicated for him to wait, and sighed when she conjured a tub of water, which he pulled himself into. "I expected maybe a bubble of water so that I could move freely."

"I thought about it, but that could be too problematic for balancing ballast with how heavy water can be." She answered softly. *"And I don't want him going below deck and deciding to poke a hole in my hull if I'm busy."*

The ship held its course while the Triton stayed where he was watching the water for any hazards and listening for any hints that they moved closer to danger. Meanwhile, Etain went and got the food she had promised and handed him a sandwich prepared from her stores.

Curiously, he peeled back the bread, looking at the vegetables and the tuna salad. He sniffed, a look of puzzlement. "I've never had human food, are you sure this strange preparation will sit well?" He closed the sandwich and took a bite at her nod, savoring at as he chewed. "I like this way of eating fish. My given name is Mimir."

She curtsied while he ate. "Honored to be given your name, Mimir, second son of Merisson."

"Yes, well... Perhaps I have been a bit harsh with you at times."

Etain held up her hand. "You have your reasons to be wary, and to lash."

She left him to concentrate on his food, so that he did not feel obliged to make conversation, and to forestall a possible slip back into his gruffness. Instead, she walked to the bow, shading her eyes and leaning forward. When she could not make out what she was wanting to focus on, she went back to the cabin and retrieved a pair of binoculars, straining forward again.

"Mimir, what sort of kelp is this ahead?"

"Kelp?"

"Aye, looks so. I certainly hope it's not more sea-trash. I've seen enough of that before we crossed."

He had finished his sandwich and dusted his fingers, dragging himself from the water to where she was. Hauling himself up to sit on the rail, he grunted, then stared in as much wonder as she. "Purple kelp? Never seen the like of this... Not these shades. Red, brown, green... but not purple."

"I'd like to look better at that, and it's in our way. Maybe take some samples for my daughter."

"'Samples for your daughter?' Why would she need 'samples' perchance?"

"She makes potions, it's what she wants to do when she's grown. She's quite good at it, and maybe she'd find it helpful for her classes."

"Let's not get your boat stuck... I do not want to be pushing it through."

The *Sea Witch* creaked irritably in acknowledgment. It was bad enough she was carrying a grumpy Triton, whose fault it probably was that her captain had smashed her head into her side.

"No, we'll just get close enough to look and get some samples, then find a way around. Looks too thick from here to risk going through."

Mimir nodded. "I'll swim ahead again. Make sure to warn you where it's safe."

Chapter Twenty
Finnol's Hunt

He scratched hastily at his personal logbook, the pocket-sized spiral-bound black notebook he always kept with him. In his study back at Seal Point the usually green quill had turned deep red as it zoomed across the pages of his section of the Makay Logbook to copy what he wrote. The much less flashy clear V8 self-inking ballpoint in his hand jotted down the notes of the day so far, his position, and the thoughts currently plaguing him. Thoughts that, though embarrassing and he knew full well his family would read it later, may mean comfort for some grandchild at some point. That was the way of it. One never knew what a descendant would need to know of later.

The water lapped around the pilings, and the familiar smell of salt, fish, and old nets filled his nose along with the diesel of the various engines of the boats around him. The cries of seagulls mingled with those of the seals of the port, loud in the mist of the morning. A seagull flew overhead and dropped a bomb but it fell harmlessly on the wood of the pier instead of on Finnol's long waterproofed green velvet duster.

"Captain Makay?"

"Aye? You'd be the young Murphy?" Finnol looked up, a few new white hairs showing in his nut-dark hair. His dark blue eyes swept over the lad in front of him.

The boy had light hair that he had stuffed under the usual wool cap that protected the ears of those that spent their time out on the fishing boats. He looked less than twenty, so he would have been very surprised if the lad had seen more than three years on the sea.

"Aye. My Da's onboard, we weren't expecting you for another half hour."

"Ah, I'm a bit of an earlybird because of the tide. Don't want to miss it do we?"

"Because of the tide?" The boy repeated, his eyebrows raising. "We have a motor, we could still get out of port without the tide, though it does make it easier."

"Travelling with the tide is still better. When you've been plying the sea a few more years you'll understand why."

The boy nodded, humoring the man, who he found just as nutty as he found his father. But in this economy a job was a job after all. He gestured to the gangplank, smiling a bit. Finnol smiled back and walked on board, murmuring a thanks and feeling glad that he wasn't a vampire, given how a boat could slip between vehicle and home with only momentary notice.

He found the captain in the cabin performing checks, in the usual heavy and warm attire favored by seafarers. Wellingtons gripped the deck, with bluejeans rising up to a thick wool sweater, with a blue wool cap that looked rather like the ones sold in local markets made from Byron's wool.

A brief exchange of pleasantries ensued, each referring to the other by title and surname, shaking hands.

"You look a mite scrawnier than I expected from your voice." Captain Murphy's voice was deep and harsh from years of shouting, but jovial.

"My wife says the same. Still up for showing me those moving shoals and ghost fish?" Finnol replied.

"Surely, if they be there again."

It was short work betwixt the three to have the boat out to sea and beyond the arms of the port. They chugged along the rocky coast to the Murphy's usual fishing haunt.

"The rocks moved again, lookie there." Captain Murphy pointed after idling the engine a safe distance away. "That group used to be some 20 meters in. That first day, they'd moved a bit but I couldn't tell how much. Chalked it up to an early morning and tricks o' the tide we did."

"And the fishing that day?" Finnol asked, scanning the waters for any evidence of merpeople, Selkies or not.

"Was decent enough. The next time was better though, seemed like they was a-jumping for the net."

"Net fishing here, Captain? Seems a mite close."

"Casting nets now. Too tricky for the others with things shifting about. Like the sea doesn't know her own mind. Anyway, I had Mac and Duggan with me that day. Was a great haul, filled the hold quite well. But they all just went... puff."

The lad sighed at his father's conversation, hurling his net and pulling it in again as the 'old salts' traded tales.

"Puff?"

"Puff." Captain Murphy nodded at Finnol gravely. "I kind of wonders if I was Selkie tricked. 'Course, my boy." He nodded toward his son now. "My boy thinks I'm a crazy old codger for entertaining thoughts o' the like. But I tells him, 'the sea's her own land, full of mysteries. No telling what she's got under 'er skirts till it's too late, no matter how much we men thinks we knows.'" He nodded again and lit his pipe, looking around as if he thought something might suddenly materialize.

"A good philosophy." Finnol agreed. He tried not to wrinkle his nose when the smoke was blown toward him, but it burned. He turned and coughed to clear it from his lungs.

"Didn't realize ye were a sensitive to the smoke. Sorry there." Captain Murphy moved downwind obligingly. "So, what do you reckon? Scientific explanation for it, or proof o what ever' good sailor ought ter know?"

"Not too sure. I'll have to observe a while, and see a catch."

"Plenty of nets here. Always glad to help with a bit o' scientific research."

Several hours passed, and the hold was filled, replicating previous trips that Captain Murphy had had in the area. Nothing seemed to be out of the ordinary. The fish all seemed normal enough. While the other two were busy with their tasks, Finnol took out his wand and managed to test the fish with various charms meant to dispel Apparitions, in case they were ghosts like one of the fishers' theories had been.

The fish still remained, so they were either real, or really good illusions.

"One theory down." He thought.

It wasn't until nearly sundown that he noticed anything unusual in the area. By the rocks, down low where the waters broke and sprayed over the sort of outcrop that Etain had liked to drape herself over when they were younger, he saw movement. A sleek brown head bobbed beside it, followed by a body that heaved itself up onto it with the next swell. Wide black eyes stared back at him for a moment.

Finnol stayed still, scented the air though it blew away from him.

"Da', want to watch out. Looks like a seal over there."

"Don't want to catch one of those" Captain Murphy agreed with his son. "Might be one of those recently drowned souls from that ship sinking in that last big storm."

"Da', don't you think that's stretching the old stories a bit? I'm no lad naemore."

The so-called seal continued to watch them. It twitched now and then and lifted itself to curl its tail off to the side in a mermaid-like fashion now and then when neither of the full-humans were watching.

"Rather have a soul wind up a selkie than a soulfish lad."

Finnol flinched a bit at Captain Murphy's comment, then tore his gaze from the seal – certain that it was in truth a selkie by its actions – to check the humans.

"Soulfish?"

"Ah Lawd. Don't ask, you'll get Da' started on those too now." The lad complained through the strain of muscles, pulling in his net, now filled with silver fish.

"They're real. I saws 'em once." The Captain commented around his pipe. "Like flyin' fish, but with red eyes and human faces. Moaning and crying about what they were going to do whilst alive, to get yer pity. Then they eat you and turn you into one of them. Those be the Devil's work, I'm sure."

The sun set, and the other two were too busy with their bickering about what was and was not real or possible to notice the seal slip her skin off. Nor did they notice the lightly furred dark brown haired woman stand up on the rock and begin to sing.

Quietly at first, then steadily louder, her song rose and wove with the changing tide. The side closer to the boat began to rise, the rock seeming to grow... or perhaps be thrust up. Once it was loud enough to catch the human's ears, their movements slowed. A face came up on the side the lad was on, another woman opening her arms to him from in the water. She giggled and displayed herself, flashing large brown eyes and a gleaming smile from under her reddish-blonde hair. A similar form broke surface near the Captain, this one slightly older, and redder haired, but still young and winning. The Selkie women worked together, trying to sing the men into the water, one way or the other.

Finnol whipped his wand from the hidden sheath in his sleeve, Stunned both men without uttering the Word, then floated them swiftly into the cabin. The selkies sulked momentarily, then tried to turn their charms on him.

"Sorry ladies, I'm well mated and satisfied. This isn't a traditional clanground, so why don't you tell me what has you in such a frequented area?"

The eldest frowned up at him, bothered that he had no scent spike from any of them. "Why would we be talking to the likes of a halfling like yourself? We can take you out other ways."

"You could." He agreed carefully, nodding a bit as he chose his words. "But I might be able to help on the other hand. I'm with the Order of Fisheries and Water Conservation." He continued over her snort and sneer. "The *other one*, not the one with the Crown."

"Maybe then, but I doubt it." The eldest tucked a stray hair behind her ear.

"Our fishing ground got taken over. Most of our men were taken by trawl nets. We could get some of them out before hauled in or drowned. Not all. Not our husbands." Interjected the youngest. She twisted a strand of reddish blonde hair around her finger as she looked at him.

"Trawler nets?" He thought, trying to remember the lay of known Selkie fishing grounds and the areas approved for trawlers. Eventually he gave up and conjured a crude map of just the approved human fishing grounds and types. "Show me?"

"Just here." The eldest gestured after picking up a piece of driftwood that had floated into reach. The boat drifted closer to the sprouted rock, but still was not close enough to be a danger unless he dropped his vigilance.

The area indeed was squarely inside the boundaries granted as unfishable by treaty by human entities, according to the map.

"Why didn't you send word?"

"We don't know where to send it to. Our Emissary was one of them that we couldn't rescue. Not that our herd or our clan have much use for human ways of doing things." The eyes of the Selkies were wet, especially the brown one that had been on the rock and since put her skin back on to join them.

"What about asking a gull or a tern, or some other Messenger?"

"Too saddened to be able. They can't understand us still."

"Yet you can plot ways to torment men. Was it one of these?"

The nut brown seal glared up at him accusingly now while the eldest scowled.

"No." She replied. "But they are human, they use nets, and they are taking the food from where we had to move to."

"How about you let these two go, I do what I can about taking care of those poachers, and for the time being you frequent the sea around my home. Seal Point is kept safe from the two so-called ministries and the Crown. It'll be iffy enough if you stay here with what I had to do to them to have this talk and protect you."

The youngest snorted while the nutbrown one sneered. "Protect us? From what? Being drowned in nets ourselves?"

"Scientists are still wanting to prove the existence of sea people, for good or ill. Do you really want to risk what sort of tests you'd be put through? Have your skins stolen? Allow *men* to put their hands on you and have no way to fend them off or run away?"

"The half-blood is right. We can't know what they'd do if we were Netted and survived." She spoke to her sisters, seemingly the leader of them. "We'll take you up on your offer of refuge, for now." The eldest replied. "But we would like a say in what happened to the men that killed our husbands."

"Fair enough ladies..." He sighed, then pointed to a spot on the map, changing it a bit so that they could see. "That is where Seal Point is. If you have any trouble with the herds around there, go to the house above the docks and talk to those inside. They're family, and will help you if I'm not currently there."

The three nodded, the younger two more reluctantly than the eldest, then pulled the heads of their skins over their heads. For a moment, the sealskin faces sat over their human ones like masks before settling and melding. Soon, there were three brown harbour seals, one a reddish-blonde, one more of a certain red, and one regular dark brown... all swimming away in the direction of safe refuge.

Finnol rubbed his head and leaned on the railing a moment more. "Mara, what is going on? If this keeps up, the merfolk will be known publicly again within the generation... And then more humans will know about magic, and we'll have countries and religions fighting over who's got the strongest magic all over again. What do you want me to do?"

The ocean continued with her regular waves, and no tingle of Mara's attention touched him. He expected none, yet since he never knew when she or any other listened... he had no problem with voicing his thoughts to the Winds.

He was just about ready to turn and Revive the men he'd knocked out, when he felt the chill of one of the Ministry's *Things* prickle the edge of his senses. He could feel the licking tongues of dread, and rather than wake them, instead he sought to drive the boat away and back to port.

Finnol collapsed into the booth after ensuring that the boat was safely docked and the Murphys were able to go home, his vaguely Victorian era ship's captain attire blending in perfectly now with the pirate air of the favored reenactor's hangout. In the pocket of his doublet lurked the letter from Kirsty's school on her progress mundane, magical, and 'merstudies.' It had joined the small notebook crammed impossibly full of the notes from his recent adventures and the tales that had been brought to his attention otherwise.

The rotund and sandy Marc slipped into the booth on the other side, the largest flagon of ale he could get in each hand. One he slid in front of the man that looked rather like a piece of wilted seaweed. Marc drank from the other himself, then kept his voice carefully jovial.

"This is unusual. What's going on that you're calling me? On a phone no less, instead of by carrier pigeon."

He normally would have finished with "Who died?" but did not, given the usual sadness in Finnol's eyes being more pronounced than usual.

"Needed a friendly face outside the Office."

"Etain's still out then? I've not seen you looking so out of sorts since that fight you had when she left."

Finnol waved his hand and took a drink from his own flagon. Marc let the observation go, waiting companionably. After a long pull, he continued.

"How's your girl then?"

"Well enough, though Aunt Belara is rather concerned about her nightmares getting worse. She's a Sensitive you know."

"Aye, crack shot with knowing where a pipe's leaking. I remember her finding that without a set of dowsing rods and saving me a thousand pounds since I didn't have to have all the plumbing redone."

"Well, she's got other gifts than waterwitching. She's got the Sight too, now and then."

"Ghosts? Or you mean like clairvoyance and such."

"Foresight. So those nightmares bother me."

Marc took a pull from his flagon, not disturbed in the least about the thought of 'little Kirsty' being able to do more than point out leaky pipes, though he himself had no special powers. He'd always wanted them, and always loved the mage characters in the fantasy books... particularly Gandalf and Harry Potter. This was probably part of why he loved helping gather modern, supposedly true, sea and ghost stories for Finnol's book... and often found many other odd happenings for him.

"She loves her Mum, hopefully it's just worry dreams."

"Maybe, maybe not. She gets involved with quite a lot."

"Where are you headed with this Sailor?"

Finnol quirked his lips a bit in a smile at that, while a large bead of condensation coursed down the side of his flagon. "Crazy with longing most like."

Marc watched him a while longer, pulling slowly at his ale. "You got some bad news somewhere. Out with it boy. What's eating at you really? Other than no Etain."

"Do you believe in the gods?"

"In what way? Metaphor, literal?" Finnol gave no further indication of what he was meaning. "I do I guess, plenty of strange things to point that they might exist. Probably not as all powerful as they say in the old myths, probably quite a few of them too. Maybe I just need more ale though." He took another drink, disconcerted about his friend's unusual turn to the world of religion.

"And psychic powers I know you believe in."

"Everyone's got 'em." Marc agreed amicably, far more comfortable with that thought. *"Whew, thought he was going to go looney and say the gods are going to destroy mankind or something."*

"So... what about some of these mythological beings you bring me stories about, in your professional opinion?" Finnol fished while tracing a finger over the outside of his mug.

"I believe in them. And I think they've got as much right to exist, if they're real, as you and I do. In a proper habitat for them too, not some lab. How great would it be to be friends with a mermaid and hear about what it's like on the seafloor where we can't go except in a sub?"

"And if you saw one, or found some proof, would you keep it quiet?"

"Are you nuts? Of course! Well, maybe not a boat eating kraken... but if it talks, definitely." Marc scrunched his brows together and scowled.

Finnol took a drink and pondered his friend's answers. Was he doing the right thing? Was revealing this really what the turmoil in his blood was telling him to do? By telling these secrets would he be cursing Marc to the kind of existence he'd grown up in? *"Mara, forgive me if I'm doing wrong."* He put his mug down again and took a deep breath. "Fancy a little cloak and dagger in your life?"

Marc leaned forward, forgetting what was left of his ale. There was a spark in Finnol's eye that he'd seen now and then, usually when catching the very end of a broken off conversation between he and his wife. He'd seen it in the eyes of people at the *Fisheries* Office too, when even those who were paper jockeys seemed to have the determined step of someone set on changing the world. "You've got my interest."

Finnol leaned forward with a whispered incantation and time changed, the sounds around them becoming cloaked and removed. "You have to make a solemn oath not to reveal what I'm about to tell you. Horrible things will happen to my family if you betray us, and not just my own family." His hand extended over the table.

"Finnol, on my granddad's grave, you can trust me and I'll keep your secrets." Marc took his hand and a weight settled over Marc as he gave his word while water came out from Finnol's palm and wound in ribbons up his arm.

While the waters climbed his friend's arm Finnol began to tell of his adventures and thoughts, and the fears he had for his women.

Chapter Twenty One
Hunt

Kirsty sighed, getting up once more and moving as quietly as she could through House quarters. Imp had just let her know the last of the students from the upper year Astronomy class had not only returned, but gone to sleep. He had ensured it, in fact, by using various methods of getting her housemates to pass out just as he had done every night she needed to go to the Loch.

She sometimes thought that perhaps he was a bit too eager to please, as one student had once come to breakfast with a giant swelling on the back of his head but couldn't remember having fallen out of bed. At least the mystery had been short lived for her though the poor boy had earned the moniker Bed Head Boy.

She crept out of their quarters, transforming into the white cat that she had studied so hard to become and then ghosted to the Loch. Kirsty paused only in the courtyard where she could see the shining round of the moon, sighing that it had come on a night that her night classes fell on. When she transformed back to human form at the water's edge she shivered at the chill night air and discarded all but the swimming clothes under her nightclothes. Short work was made of hiding them. Shorter work was made of taking the paste that aided her training in this aspect. Fur and blubber would be welcome things.

Kirsty then slipped into the water, still gasping a bit as she adjusted to its temperature, and then kicked and wove her way to where she was supposed to be meeting with the Hunters. A shudder passed over her as she suppressed a yawn. Her tentacle-like hair looked even more frazzled and bedraggled, and static danced over her facial whiskers. She draped herself on a rock to wait, closing her eyes and trying to use her ears, hair, and whiskers to 'see' the waters around her the way Nightfish had been trying to teach her during his lessons.

Her nose twitched in irritation and her attention promptly splintered into a thousand panes. She could feel the currents and the slight movement of the fish two rocks over. Kirsty could feel the gentle beat of the moon since she was close enough that those reflected rays carried some power. The myriad streams that fed into the loch called her next, and the waters beneath the lock itself in deep passages that went to places she could never quite figure out. Loudest and strongest of all though were two pulls.

The loudest were the nightmare visions. The quieter was the ever present need for her own skin. Kirsty stretched, attempting to wrest her attention away from the calls to her quest and to her mother, to instead focus on the training that would prepare her. When she felt the movement of something large, she pointed off to her right and behind, thickening the water between to be an impediment.

"You're there."

"Good, but slow. You need to feel us sooner if you're going to go into Her Realm this summer and live. Why didn't you?"

"Too many calls... that way..." She pointed to her left, toward the sea. "And the new spring forming there," her hand pointed this time to the shore and beyond, eyes still closed. "And down below. I'm too far out still.."

"Too new. Must be from your position. Priestesses usually have trouble paying attention to close things at first, or so I hear. That's why they're to be protected if they survive."

Kirsty opened her eyes and looked back toward her male mentor, only yards away, and indeed far closer than acceptable though at least he was farther away than the last lesson. Nightfish floated in place, no spear of his own, his hunter-warrior's spear still just an obsidian trident head on a braided thong about his neck. Instead, he held two wooden youth's spears.

"What is tonight's lesson Nightfish?"

"More with tracking and spearwork. First we'll drill. Show me what you remember."

He tossed the youth's spear at her, then came at her with the other, and she caught hers hastily and parried, slipping back and off the rock, hoping for him to slip past. He made an approving noise, but as he slid by his muscular tail thwacked into her, sending her reeling and forcing her to concentrate on regaining her own stability.

"Not far enough back if you're going to try that Seaswimmer."

She got herself under control and struck at him, fixing in her mind that he was either large game that would fight back, or one of the Finmen that might come after any future children, or an attacker from another clan. They went back and forth till she had grown frustrated at her lack of competency and the wooden spear had begun to spark and her hairs to flail.

"No magic! You must be strong in both!"

Nightfish rapped her hands soundly with his spear after that demand and she cried out but did not release. Instead, she struck with her tail at him and the tendrils of her hair reached for him. This time, the discharge from her was not magic, but the sting of the electric eel and venom of jellyfish. He gave way.

"Yes, that! That's what you were supposed to be doing last meeting." He stuck the spear in the mud, and pulled out from the pouch at his waist a shell. From that, he extracted an ointment that he rubbed over the burn on his arms. "She was right... a bit of every creature in your blood... Makes me wonder if the old legends are true..."

He sighed when the sting in his arms and the flashes in his vision faded. "Alright, let's see if we can bring in anything significant for the fry and pups. No magic tonight remember, unless you're practicing with the congealing shield She insists you learn."

The night passed in tracking the scent of gamefish, searching for the particular breed that the village was low on for the children. Oddly, she discovered that she enjoyed these lessons, felt things stirring within her breast she'd not expected, and for once a quietening of her mind. At last, they found an appropriate food to bring the cooks.

The fish needed by the cooks to fill their current lack were large, unlike the smaller schooling breeds that were usually netted. These bore blue scales that flashed randomly with their own light where they gathered near to the underwater sea passage, though she only dimly registered where they were. Kirsty waited till she was sure of their demeanor, staying behind the rocks and weeds, picking out which were the most likely to be felled. The fish remained unaware of them while they skulked the edges, and Nightfish made no move to take one, instead seeing how much of her hunt she would be able to take by instinct. Despite the welcome stillness of her mind unnoticed she had a prayer filling her being and burning for fulfillment.

"I've never been after something this big with just a sharp stick." The prayer flowed through her blood far below and behind her mind. *"Please let me succeed, for the pups and fry if not myself."*

Unnoticed, she had more eyes watching than Nightfish's.

A smaller fish, though still fully half her size and with sharp teeth jutting out from blunt jaws, separated itself as the loose herd came in range. She erupted then, before they could separate too much or pass out of range again, chasing after the closest. At first some scattered while others ran with the main. When she was close enough she brought her spear to bear, taking her mark in the side and fully a foot behind where she had intended. The fish continued to swim, dragging her with it, her spear embedded in its side and the wound widening with each flick of its tail and beating of Kirsty's tail against him as she tried to drive it far enough in to hit something vital. It would not be as clean a kill as she had hoped.

Then the scent of the fish's blood brought the others back around to bear.

Her eyes widened when they turned and charged past her, enough of them to churn the water and hurt her ears, much the same effect as when Byron's sheep herd would stampede. These snapped and gnashed on their way, and the injured one she clung to tried to wheel and join its compatriots in getting at her. Terrified at the thought of being taken back into that snapping pack, some of which were fully as large as herself, she tried biting behind the neck while her hair released an electric charge. She tried to wrench her spear back out but it held firm.

A warcry came from Nightfish's direction, and he was out among the fish himself. Things were happening too quickly for her to keep track of time or order. She only knew there was cacophony around her, and released a cry herself after releasing her prey. This threw the fish off a bit, but she could still feel them coming. Her spear finally gave way with a sickening squelch and once it was released her prey floated downward with dim eyes.

She whirled round to protect her back in time to find Nightfish driving and striking, and the spearhead suspended around his neck sparked with a cloud of darkness misting, but unheeded and uncalled on. Then others were on her as well, and there was no further time to take note of anything. Her world narrowed once more to fending off the fishes' group mind, striking and blocking with the blade, the thrust of her tail to propel her force or change the angle, and employing her shield spell when she could manage.

Eventually, their cries stunned the fish enough to produce a good haul, and the others disengaged, outmatched. With heaving breath Kirsty made sure that the fishes they had brought down truly were dead, and not just stunned. Of the herd they'd attacked, three were brought down, hers naturally the least clean. She sucked her lip and scraped at it with her teeth while surveying her own kill and its raggedness, comparing it to the neatness Nightfish had managed during her defense.

"Not as bad as some first times have gone with this quarry." His hand fell on her shoulder.

"Still, I think I have a long way to go. I really am better with a net."

"And nets take time to weave. A spear is a quick make in tight spots. You'll get better."

She smiled a bit, ruefully. "I hope so. So... how are we getting these back?"

"A net..." He smiled innocently and pulled one from the pouch at his waist. "We'll suspend it between us and pull them home."

Her jaw dropped before she closed it again and glowered.

Taking the catch back went easily enough, even though the net was a bit heavier than she was used to carrying underwater. The farther they carried the net between them, the more she found the urge to have a skin to fully pull on and be done with the in between stage. The whispers in her blood demanded the abandoning of hands, to feel the waters pass over flippers like air must with a bird's wing. She wished to use teeth to rip flesh, perhaps from the shark that had taken Mani's husband, and to nurse little ones after several years had passed – or stranger yet, and something that she could not remember seeing done for the pups – regurgitate for them. Where that urge came from she had no idea. Kirsty suspected all this as part of her training, likely preparing her for long swims and building muscle, or perhaps it was a remnant of ancestral seal's needs that she did not yet understand. The more time she spent in the water, the more she felt her body changing to accommodate that and the more restless she became.

The preparation lessons she had been spared, as it was much the same as smaller fish, if a bit more of a process due to the size. Without either Nightfish or herself having sustained any injuries significant enough to warrant the Healers and their attentions, there was nothing new cropping up for her to learn on that subject either. However, one of the cooks who also happened to hold Healer status did give her an oral list of parts that were retained for use in medicines and their purpose. Kirsty dutifully memorized for trial of their veracity:

Liver and gall, or intestinal wall
When suffering Lack and vision falls.

Eye for eating and eye for treating
When scales suffer dimming pall.

Heart is courage and to incite
Whilst in a paste, sluggish appetite.
Eggs, if present there be inside
Fertility treatments several abide.

Glowing skin prepared just right
When needing to encourage might,
With brakenweed and scallson sting
Mixed with the stingmanta's wing...

There was much more of the song to memorize, every part having some purpose. The skin she was allowed samples of as well as several other parts that aroused her curiosity as to potions applications she wished to test. Finally, they released her to return to the castle, after having passed below for a total of three doses of the changing paste to hold her form.

Kirsty swam slower than usual, and laid on the shore longer than was her wont once she regained her legs, shivering and looking up at the colder stars. Her limbs were heavy, and simply laying there she felt as if she were washing back and forth on soft waves, pulled between the land and sea. With great effort she finally got into the bushes where she'd hidden her nightclothes, pulled the water out of her hair and swimsuit, threw that to the lake, and pulled on the gown and robe.

Once warmly clothed she promptly threw up, as was beginning to be a pattern with too little sleep and higher levels of activity. Unknown to her gold eyes watched her process. These eyes sat in a dark, fur covered face, perched above a long snout with the requisite sharp fangs that usually went with muzzles. His fur was matted and unkempt, smelling of musk and long months of lurking about the forest unwashed save by rain. His skin beneath that thickly matted fur hung loose, not yet anywhere near beginning to fill out from the scraps that he got in one way or another from kindly students taking pity on skulking canines.

Kirsty hunkered a bit longer, her weight on one hand while the other clutched her belly, recovering and occasionally dry heaving. The air grew colder where she was, though she was too focused on conquering her stomach and riding through the changing sugar levels in her blood, which provided an excellent mask. Finally she stabilized and stood again, feeling the unusual level of cold at last. She looked around suspiciously for the cause of what was beginning to fray at where bad memories were locked, and the movement of a sheet of darkness and cobweb further in the forest caught her eyes.

The sheet and webs trailed over the ground toward her, zeroing in quicker than she thought anything would be able to fly without boosts, sucking all the light into it. Something clamped over her mind the moment that she realized what she was looking at, and her muscles froze.

The growl in the bushes unfroze her muscles, just before the mangy black dog erupted from them toward the *Thing,* and she was running for the castle, still operating in a thoughtless space where terror was the only thing that existed. Too terrified to change to a cat, she risked being seen by any wandering student out of bed after hours, ghosts, or prowling teachers, but she did not care. She only knew that, given the proximity to the water, and the scent that clung to her, the *Thing* would take her if it caught her – provided that it didn't suck her dry before presenting her to the Ministry's Board of Half-human Affairs, or perhaps some worse Board or Department, Mara and the Lord of the Hunt forbid. The cold continued to chase, while cobwebs wormed further into her mind and teased out flashes of Finmen raids.

Then something furry knocked her feet out from under her. The darkness of the *Thing* whizzed over her head, her breath freezing on the grass she lay on. Something dark and mangy placed itself between herself and the *Thing*, though not as dark and mangy as what had been down by the loch.

"IMP!" She screeched in her mind while summoning her familiars winged and watery, with blood and thought. There was the answering push back from her brown owl, but he was too far away to arrive in time. Her tern likewise was too far distant to answer the call. Simultaneously came the press from Imp, scurrying from his post in the Leomaris housing, likely on his way to rouse her aunt.

"BYRON! DAVID! AUNTIE! A THING!" Each mental call for help was not so much a separate thought, as they were all at once and jumbled together, one yarn in the knit of thought. A pulse went through her, reaching out, and if she could have focused enough, would have felt it traveling through the water.

The water that was part of her blood and within the vials reacted with pulses of their own. The dark, mangy, smelly thing loomed between herself and the cobwebbed sheet of malicious ruin that was now between herself and Castle Carrick. The fall had provided an opportunity for thought to truly begin again. Kirsty took stock of where she could go, found the *Thing* to not only be blocking her way to the castle, but also the way to the Sanctuary. The other cave she knew of she knew she could not hope to get to in time and that it would provide no protection anyway, not from this.

She heard more growling, felt something unlocking inside of herself, heard a spectral horn and the baying of hounds from some nearby hunt that had been ongoing, and the shifting of the gaze of the moon toward them. With surprise, she then realized that some of the growling was coming from herself. The *Thing* faltered for a moment, unused to prey fighting back or making any indication that it would. The dark canine in front of her howled.

On instinct she screamed as loud and high as she could, stepping forward, raising her arm and feeling the sea rising inside. The canine's ears laid back trying to protect them from the sonic blast, springing forward at the same moment. Kirsty wasn't sure how the wand with Marsali's hair got to her hand, or when, but when she stepped forward her hand and the wand had slashed out as if with a sword, and a blade of magma-hot saltwater erupted above the springing furred animal and toward the *Thing*.

Wolf? Part of herself processed what she was seeing. Most was too focused on surviving to take note. Another howl answered the first from the direction of the Sanctuary, moving fast if she judged right. There were no further sounds of hounds nor horns, the specters perhaps having vanished, or perhaps only heard with the mind. Or perhaps it had only been a brief crossing of worlds.

The *Thing* fell back, avoiding the blow, but only barely. The wolf pursued it, pressing it away from her path back to the castle. Kirsty watched, breathing heavily, unused to unleashing and channeling such a large and desperate burst.

"What are you waiting on Girl? That werewolf is giving you a chance to get inside. The other will be here soon. Change so it won't be able to feed, or go inside, but you don't have time to catch your breath!"

Kirsty jumped at the unfamiliar growls and voice in her mind, raising her wand again and looking for the source. Gold eyes peered out from a nearby bush, a bit of black matted fur visible. Another howl came from the direction of the Sanctuary, answering the most recent call from the wolf pursuing the *Thing*, and sounding more angry than curious now. She knew that the coming wolf could smell her fear on the air. What the black mangy canine was doing here was a problem for another time. Maybe the forest god or the fire god had not totally abandoned the water goddesses she was bound to after all, or maybe it was the stray dog that Thomas had commented about befriending before Magical Mathematics. Or maybe it was all a distraction from her true purpose orchestrated by some rival she wasn't aware of.

She put her wand away and changed, becoming a white streak of fur and unnaturally large blue eyes blazing her way for the door. If that angry howl was David as she suspected it to be she wanted to give him no cause to attack her on accident or design.

She saw another white streak loping from the trees toward her and could smell him on the air. Kirsty yowled as loud as she could, still heading for the door and not about to change track.

The castle door was flung open and a woman in green tartan nightrobes came out, wand raised and glaring around with crackles of electricity literally dancing around her. Then the scent of books, pine, ginger biscuits and lemon tea came to her. If Kirsty were nearer she would have leaped into her arms, likely spouting hair all over. She was not though. Professor MacLeòmhann spared both of the white animals a glance as the door slammed shut behind her, and then she was off in the direction of the howls.

"Take her back with you and stay inside." Was all her aunt had to say to either of them as she sped out of earshot.

Kirsty ran past the castle entrance then toward the white wolf, meeting him and leaping onto him instead. He flinched and growled at her claws but did not snap at or throw her off. Her shivering form pressed close to him, still hissing and spitting, and he grumbled as he began back for the Sanctuary, his hunt interrupted.

If anyone had been there to hear them, their discussion would have sounded very strange indeed, cat sounds answering grumbles and whuffs, each with the occasional sneeze of distaste while Kirsty tried to relate what had happened, whether he would remember it or not in the morning.

The moon deity watched the whole with interest. Shi played with the idea of taking a form for closer inspection. Shi was far better placed to watch all by remaining non-corporeal and non-aspected for the time being though, so shi remained thus. Hir time for a better examination was coming, and it was not as if shi could not and did not enter their dreams. For now, shi would not meddle too much. Shi risked enough notice by Mara by tampering with Etain's voyage. To meddle too much with Kirstin would overplay hir hand, and any affect on the Hound she was so close to would certainly bring the Huntsman and his ire. It was too soon to be talking with the Hunstsman.

Hir little Mara would find out far too early what shi was up to if young David's master got wind of hir. Mara, shi knew, would then throw a fit as bad as when she had lost her last lover, and likely would forbid her selkies from dancing in the full moon's light, and the loss of the energy from that would affect magic poorly in other worlds where it combined with others and fell to worshipers of hir own. Diana would only be able to mask her closeness to hir for so long.

Chapter Twenty Two
About That Thing...

The werewolf ran as fast as he could and ignored as well as he could the claws of the bedraggled white cat that were digging painfully into his flesh. She was still shivering, and she stank of fear and the loch, but most heavily of fear. He would have preferred Kirsty to have gone into the castle with the humans he avoided but he obeyed his professor's orders. The professor wasn't part of his Pack, but he did retain enough presence of humanity to remember she was to be obeyed. She surely had her reasons whether or not she shared them.

He did not stop until he got to the Sanctuary, and then only to figure out how to slip past the whipping vines that obscured the passage with his cargo. In his human form it was simple. All he needed to do was stun the plant guardian. In this form however it was more a matter of timing. David grumbled to Kirsty, glancing back at her over his shoulder. Her claws retracted a bit, though the scent of normal wolves was in her nose as well as his own. Although the palaver sounded more like growling and muttering rather than speech, she understood it and felt a bit calmer.

"Are you going to stun them so you can get through safely? I don't want to risk you getting hit..."

Kirsty sank her claws again at the thought of letting go, then pulled them further out. She shook her head vehemently and sneezed before replying, sounding like a cat but speaking to him through the strange manner that she had discovered after her first successes with this shape.

"I... don't think that if I transformed again that I could turn back to this shape. Not right now. I don't want getting chased again, especially by you."

David grumbled and snuffed. "Alright, but be careful."

The vines seemed especially irritated tonight, and it took a bit for them to figure out the timing with neither of them being able to stun currently. They both managed to make it through and trotted along the passage, Kirsty having to hurry in order to keep up with David's much longer strides. When they were inside he relaxed a bit but not enough to fully untense his muscles and allow all his fur to lay down.

"So, what happened?"

Kirsty bounded a few steps to catch up and he stopped to scoop her up at her mew of frustration. Now that speed was not an issue he could revert back to a more bipedal gait. Her eyes were a lighter blue than their usual as he gazed into them.

"I was getting ready to go inside after my loch lessons... then a *Thing* came after me. But, I was still on the school's grounds so I don't know *how* it got on." She shuddered in his arms. "I had to fight it, managed not to pass out this time. If I had it would have taken me."

He stepped up into the main room and shuffled to the chair beside the fire. Kirsty sneezed when he sat down, then burrowed into his fur. David sighed deeply. The two sat like that until all her tremors passed, his paw stroking her fur.

He said nothing, nor grumbled anything. No growl, nor huff escaped him. Yet Kirsty could feel him thinking. She wasn't sure how to interpret the smell coming off of him, and she tentatively licked at him once stretching up for his muzzle.

He nuzzled back and sighed before tiredly standing up and shambling up the stairs for the bed, taking her with him. He took her under the cover with him and she snuggled in, very quickly falling asleep. The only thing that disturbed her was much later in the night, when heavier and slower steps than David's came up the stairs, then plodded their way past David's door and into the room next to his on the upper level.

A thud let her know that whoever it was had fallen into the other bed and the lingering scent from the hall told her that it was Professor Gerwulf. The kitty laid her head back down on David's chest and snuggled again, falling into dreams of swimming through the seas clothed in fur and frolicking with the special sort of narwhals that Mara held so dear, enjoying the respite from dreams of storm-tossed seas and floating debris.

Kirsty's rest was interrupted again by the howls of the two werewolves undergoing their change back. She was off David and beside him before he was even up, slipping behind him and once again morphing to her birth form, holding him as soon as it was safe. Soon enough, he was clinging back and resting from the ordeal, and she wondered why if all shapeshifters had the blessing of Herne, it was the involuntary shifters that had to feel such pain.

She doubted that she would have the courage to ask if she were to ever come face to face with the Lord of the Hunt. Mara was scary enough and the short time that she had encountered Brigit–

The screaming in the next room had also subsided, and she looked in the direction of what she knew was the professor's monthly room of refuge. It was a bit before there was any further sound of movement as their elder rested, but after a few moments there was rustling as he donned his clothing.

A light knock on the door came next, and the voice was as tired and thin as a banshee's winding sheet.

"Rise and shine children, moonset is too close to sunrise this month. We need to wash before anyone gets up for breakfast. Miss Makay's not been nibbled on I trust?"

"We're coming professor.." David called, brushing Kirsty's hair a moment before they started getting up.

Professor Gerwulf was still at the door by the time Kirsty opened the door, revealing him to be much paler and more bedraggled looking than usual. The beginnings of a silver streak had started above his right temple, when just the day before it hadn't been there.

"Professor...?" David wrinkled his nose in distaste of what-ever he had gone through, having no memory of how Kirsty had come to be snuggled against him.

"What happened?" The professor finished his pupil's question, putting his weight on the doorjamb. "That is your guess as well as mine David, for the same reasons. By how cold, tired, and incredibly saddened I feel... I may have had a run in with one of the *Things*." He shuddered at the thought of something too horrendous even for a proper name. "I'm thinking that hot chocolate with breakfast would be in order today, instead of the pumpkin cider..."

"You and Professor MacLeòmhann went after one last night sir, after one somehow managed to get onto the grounds. It attacked me on my way back from the Loch." She flicked her eyes toward David when she heard his indrawn breath, then back to the professor to continue. "Auntie wanted me with David for some reason. I just wanted away."

"Did it touch you?"

"No sir, but it came close. There was also this black dog, looked a bit like an Angus, but too scrawny to be one. It knocked me down and probably saved me from a Snatching."

"I see." The Professor sighed as she stepped out to allow David to change in private. "Then I shall make certain that the Headmaster, your aunt, and I are able to confer before the day progresses far. We will find a safer way for you to continue your studies. I also think we should find this stray dog if possible as well. Even though you think it isn't an Angus, there are other sorts of spirit dogs."

"Thank you sir..." She went down to the lower level and waited for David beside the table, only now noting the fact that the table was free of the past night's dinner scraps.

"Hm. Maybe that's why they came so fast. They'd taken the leftovers out to the regular wolves once done." Then the memory of that spectral horn came. *"Or maybe not. Maybe He was here."*

The walk back was slower than usual, but not due to the

young pair dawdling and trying to have a bit more time together. The professor's step was slower than usual, a slight drag noticeable in his step, and his students preferred to match their pace to his. When the three of them got to the castle entrance and stepped inside, they discovered the thin form of Professor MacLeòmhann wringing her hands from where she waited in the shadows.

The elderly professor was on her young niece almost faster than David could step out of the way or Kirsty could react. Her slim form trembled as Kirsty gasped for breath and blushed at the unaccustomed force.

"Och, Kirstine... Dunnae scare me like that again child." She sighed, mashing Kirsty's nose into her shoulder and stroking her hair, accent thick and on the verge of slipping into the Gaelic.

David and Professor Gerwulf stood nearby, exchanging looks of discomfort and surprise at the usually stoic professor's silent tears and slightly hitched breath. After a moment she released Kirsty and pulled David into a hug as well, which he returned awkwardly, unused to the intimate touch. Soon she released him as well and looked at her colleague, her speech a little stiffer than normal.

"Thank goodness you're alright as well, Hemming. I am glad."

He nodded and bowed lightly, the hint of a wan smile twitching the corners of his lips. "As I am of you. It seems that we had a little tryst last night. I hope I was well behaved and kept my teeth from yourself."

Professor MacLeòmhann smiled slightly. "Well enough behaved for a slightly hairy charmer. Still the same as a schoolboy..." She tutted at him. "Quite intent on driving the interloper off."

"It seems we have much to talk about then. Perhaps over a bit of chocolate?"

"Normally I would turn you down, but it sounds like a very

good idea."

Kirsty nearly choked and looked at David wide eyed. He shrugged in reply and inclined his head. She nodded in reply, and the two of them slipped off to tend their morning needs, leaving Professor Gerwulf using his humor to help dispel the effects of the night on Professor MacLeòmhann, and for her to be able to tell him of what he would not otherwise remember.

Chapter Twenty Three
PAY BETTER ATTENTION KIRSTY

Ally caught the paper roll that one of the school ravens had just tried to bomb her with, then tossed up a bite of her sausage. The raven caught and devoured it easily, then swooped on the girl to catch some of that red hair it had been trying to get at for weeks. Using the paper, she fended it off and tossed a coin of indeterminate value at it.

With her luck it would be her largest coin in her pocket. The raven caught this and obliged the human, letting her keep that hair with a derisive caw.

Kirsty noticed none of the ruckus next to her, instead staring into her cup. Her nose inched closer and closer, but never seemed to actually end up in the liquid. Ally pulled her up and pinched her side again to make sure her friend was really awake and had not been pulled off into the strange staring fits shiny surfaces produced in her lately. Once satisfied that Kirsty wasn't in Seer mode or about to fall asleep Ally finally opened the paper her father had sent.

Ally sighed in exasperation at the headlines.

North Korea denies nuclear testing.
Plastic pollution of oceans hoax.
Disappearances on the rise! Is your closet a portal?
Ghosts, are they real?
Newest oil rig in North Sea haunted, says worker.

"Got a copy of Enquiring Rogers and some printout off the internet that looks like dad thought you'd like. My dad must be off his rocker to send me the scandal sheets." Ally obligingly stuck the stapled sheaf of medical newsletters in Kirsty's bag when her eyes wouldn't focus on it. "Really, it's like you stay up all night when the moon is around full."

Ally then returned to picking through the news rag, still reading the headlines aloud.

Ghost fish responsible for off course liner.
Aliens control the U.N.
U.S. President really a Doppelganger.
Witchcraft... religion, folklore, or what that lady next door does?
Mermaids, Selkies, and Merrows – Oh My!

"Sounds like one of *our* papers. Are you sure that's really a *Cowan* paper?" Nevin leaned closer to Ally to read with her. His breakfast was already half gone.

"Yes, it's one from *my* world." Ally glared at Nevin, but turned the paper so he could see a bit better. "Not like one of *your* papers pays much attention to national events."

"But it's talking about real things like ghosts, selkies, and closet portals."

"It's a scandal rag. People read these for entertainment and to keep up on the gossip about movie stars and the Queen's family. I had a pen pal from America once that sent me a copy of their equivalent. Rife with Bigfoot and Batboy. To most, these aren't real... well, it has a few 'real' things like the North Korea thing."

"Closet portals are real, come off it. And what about those C.S. Lewis *Narnia* stories?"

"Just stories Nevin."

"Oh yeah? Merlin is real and *he* has stories told about him... Let's see how you feel next time you're cleaning your closet and you find yourself in a forest."

"Nevin... If you find a forest when cleaning your closet, then you really have problems. You should clean more often." Ally quipped and turned the page.

Kirsty yawned, half listening to the discussion and half wishing to go back to bed, preferably to reclaim her spot on David's chest and hope she didn't shed up his nose. Her mind churned over the plastic headline, oil rigs, disappearances, and selkies. With headlines like this either someone was doing their job really well to hide what was really happening, or doing really poorly at keeping things hidden. All she hoped for was that her mother wasn't one of those disappearances.

Ally thumbed by the selkie story again and toward the oil rig blurb. There were pictures of the rig, a very distant security camera shot of an older wooden fishing boat with some modern fittings, and an artist's rendition of the 'ghost' that haunted the oil rig. If Kirsty had been looking, she might have recognized the outline, the cloak color, and the way the 'ghost's' hair writhed, caught forever in inked pencil strokes.

Several more birds of various breeds and sizes came in, more packages for other students that would filter in for the rest of the morning. Instead of looking at the garish paper next to her, which Nevin was pouring over eagerly and sometimes giggling about, she gazed into her cup and tried to look for her mother. The sporadic and loud flapping would not let her concentrate, and Kirsty kept jumping every time she had nearly reached the proper meditative state. With a sigh she gave up and turned attention to her breakfast.

Kirsty yawned yet again and pushed her pastie around the plate, smelling a bit more of sea lily and lavender essence than normal to Ally. Ally watched her friend with concern, and noted the dark circles becoming apparent and the haunted way her friend randomly looked skyward, got lost in her cup again like some pub denizen, or jumped up eagerly at the rustling of wings. Each time one of the winged deliveries came for someone else Kirsty sat back down in disappointment mumbling "Even an addled tern or half drowned owl would do... Just to KNOW..." too low for any of the others but herself to hear.

Morvan Lilitu smirked more than usual at breakfast as he lifted his eggs to his mouth, directing his gaze across the dining hall. The eagle owl sitting on his shoulder flapped its wings loudly, catching his prey's attention for him. Kirsty did her best to ignore his triumphant gaze while Ally dumped seemingly a half cauldron of salsa on her salmon omelet.

"Earth to Kirsty! Back to shore from whatever little boat your brain sailed out on this time! You *never* eat so little. Are you sick?"

Kirsty re-affixed her eyes to the barely touched plate instead of the swirling waves of the oak table grain where it met the red and gold waves of the table runner. Several other students at the Leomaris table were beginning to pass silvers and whispers as she attempted another bite. More eyes from the Spiralis table began watching them, the whispers and hisses there coiling and waiting to strike.

Morvan leaned across his table, head over the green and bronze scales of their table runner, whispering to Morgana. A half concealed gesture caused titters among his cadre which Kirsty continued to ignore.

"Oh, there you are, that's a lot better. We don't want you deciding to fish in class in Professor Gerwulf's tanks..."

"Ally, honestly! Have you ever seen me that hungry?"

"Remember that time your Da' had you brought by for the lunch visit while he was at work this summer?" Ally paused a moment, waiting for the cautious nod. "Mum's goldfish jumped out of his tank when your stomach growled before lunch. No fish is obviously safe when you're around."

"Yer a right scunner ye are..." Kirsty kicked her ankle under the table and took a large bite, glaring at her friend and not even bothering to try dampening her accent.

Ally howled in almost mock pain, taking the reprimand in good nature, and intent on being as silly as possible to further keep her friend from her morose thoughts. Meanwhile, Kirsty jumped up, reaching for her mouth due to the searing fire now dancing on her tongue, the flames licking the air around her face, shrieking and yowling herself, before that cut off abruptly. She quickly extinguished that fire with conjured water, which promptly also drenched her entire frontside.

"Gods and Spirits!" Ally exclaimed when the water splashed her as well. The smoke still curled from Kirsty's mouth and wreathed her head, leaving only two large watery blue pools gazing out at her now in silence. "I'm so sorry. That HAD been the mild when I picked it up. I swear! Look, it's marked!" Ally pointed frantically toward the table, tears threatening to spill.

At the Bertramus table David looked up from his book and put both that and his tea down at the unexpected uproar. When seeing why he immediately sprang up and extricated himself from the table, which was not designed to be left speedily. "I'm checking on Kirsty..."

"Let us know how she is, I'll see to Ally in a bit, once she's calm enough to even hear me." Thomas looked up at David as he took the first step away from the bench.

David nodded and left quickly, blue and silver robes flowing and swirling with each quickened step.

At the table Thomas pushed the little cauldron of spicy salsa farther away from himself.

Diana leaned toward Thomas, frowning at his plate. "Thomas, did you put on the spicy or the mild?"

"Don't remember." He promptly scraped the bulk of his salsa off of his food. "Not giving Spiralis anything more to laugh at though. Poor Kirsty."

"Lilitu is not going to enjoy when this comes back to him..." Diana mused, turning now to look at the source of the loudest laughter.

Professor MacLeòmhann had already risen, and was sweeping toward Kirsty like a vast curling wave of ancient forest trees, eyes sparking and the air seeming to crackle around her. Students shrank into their meals as she passed, not wishing to bring that ire on themselves and the detention that would likely follow.

"I'm not so sure about that Rule of Three from Ethics, Diana..." Thomas sighed. "I'm quite sure his family has had a rivalry with hers for generations. If it existed, I'd think that it would be *her* family with more influence."

David frowned and finally cleared the end of the tables as Kirsty was being walked from the great hall by her aunt, trailed by a still profusely apologizing Ally, who was in tears. Still no further sound came from Kirsty. The focus was so intense on Kirsty and Ally that no one noticed the occasional item being knocked over by an invisible something that was making its way for Lilitu, Imp not even bothering to avoid any implements in his way.

The silence from Kirsty only seemed to be making Ally louder and louder, her words now reverberating in the hall with the same volume as an angered deity, though considerably more desperate. "I'm so sorry! Why aren't you saying anything? You're so angry with me you won't even yell?"

As he left the great hall to follow out the doors and into the hallway, Lilitu's laughter behind him grew in volume as well.

Diana narrowed her eyes at the laughing boy, speaking toward Thomas.

"Sometimes, that rule needs an agent. That's something I've heard from the White Lady... I had another dream about Her last night..."

Thomas looked at her. "Considering what I know of the myths about her, I don't think that is a deity I would like to be on the bad side of. Much less talk to."

"No. You wouldn't. In some ways she's a little like Cerridwen on a bad day..." Diana drifted off, still eying Lilitu. "Samhain's ritual will probably be interesting for her this year. I wonder if she'll be doing her own again, or if she'll take part in the Mythological Society Moot this year?"

Thomas shrugged, hiding a shudder at the memory of the stories of Cerridwen and Taliesin, and mentally edging as far away as he could from the mere thought of the White Lady too, as if the very mention of that cognomen would summon some aspect of a lunar – or perhaps madness – deity.

"No idea Diana... Hard to judge with how withdrawn she's getting... Then again, since we don't share a common room, maybe we don't get to see 'normal' anymore?"

Ally could no longer be heard through the closed door of the hall. The Headmaster was sternly gazing over the other denizens while the Headmistress was occupied, and each student went still momentarily if his gaze met even the corner of their own – as he had been since the start of the ruckus in his search for the culprit.

"She'll be calm enough now. Going to catch up."

Diana nodded, still eying Lilitu. As she watched, Lilitu went still under the Headmaster's eye. "Alright. I will keep watch a bit. I may learn something interesting... Like if Lilitu's behind this as I think."

"Don't do anything too crazy."

Diana only smiled. She knew that her definition of crazy did not match that of her friends, not even Kirsty.

While events continued to unfold behind her in the great hall, Kirsty found herself swept yet again to the medical wing. She did not complain though. Kirsty found that even though she wished to, she couldn't. Desperately she tried to remember what flavors she had tasted before the fire had broken out in her mouth, in case something had overshadowed the salsa, perhaps some additive easily Sent. No one had ever had such a violent reaction when salsa was offered with anything, nor had anyone's mouth been burned so badly. Smoking ears were routine, and as the weather got colder it was more often eaten to ward off colds and flu.

Try as she might, she could remember no off flavor.

"Be quiet Allison. If you do not stop the caterwauling we cannot hear when Kirstin does try to speak." Her aunt's clipped notes fell with the usual martial march, softened by the use of their given names instead of family names but received just as harshly.

"Yes ma'am." Ally sniffled, attempting to rein herself back in.

Their footfalls had not lost any speed, and after taking one glance at the icy deputy Headmistress the gremlin jumped back as they came into the hall she – or perhaps the gremlin was a he once more – had been setting a trap in. Hir hat, knitted of stolen left socks, fell off as it pushed through the wall.

"Kirstin, can you make any noise?" Professor MacLeòmhann asked, turning her head to check behind them when hurried footfalls sought to catch up.

In response, she tried, but her vocal chords refused to cooperate. She tried toning, wondering if at least song would work like she'd do underwater to amuse herself sometimes, yet that did not work any better than human speech.

"Why can't I talk?" The panic at still finding herself unable to make even a sound gave more volume to her inner speech, and she instinctively reached out, questioning and grasping for an answer from someone, anyone. She shook her head vehemently to underscore for the others that, though she tried, she couldn't. There was a path that she could feel outgoing, and so it was in that direction she poured the voices of her thoughts, mostly wordless as they were. Awareness of her surroundings dimmed as she was brought the rest of the way to the healer's wing.

Instead it was the sound of the sea that she heard, pulsing and breaking upon the shore, and the salt tang of it licked her nostrils.

There was the sense that who she had contacted pulled back for a moment in surprise while she continued to extol her terror, loudly, and perhaps deafeningly along the link. Just as quickly the feel of familiar arms closed around her as the recipient of the mental cacophony regained his balance. There were other presences, but it was the sea, the brush of a tiny bit of silver and copper, and the arms those rings were connected to that was the strongest.

She could feel his voice now, even if she couldn't think of his name or make out what he was saying. He was simply the scent of snow, fur, pine, wood smoke and assorted potions ingredients. The swells rose again in intensity, and the ship under her in this inner world creaked and thrashed in the sea. She felt the ship strike rocks and break under her, and the water washed over her. The arms tightened yet more, pulling her from there, then joined by another set, and a pair around her legs while something worked at her mouth and throat.

The panic and time that stretched and compressed for her as incomprehensibly as if she had been passing between realms of existence eventually subsided to irritation, which was far easier for her to handle. Kirsty was able to see around her again. White curtains surrounded the metal bed, serenely draping from rod to ceiling and clashing with the austerity of the atmosphere. Ally was out of the way near the foot, looking stricken.

"She kicked me!"

"Hold her tighter so we can look in her mouth." The Healer barked, and two sets of arms tightened around her, but thankfully there was no binding magic. Ally was back at her feet, literally laying on them and locking her legs around Kirsty's.

Kirsty began to struggle again, as her body had been while she had been mentally checked out.

"Kirstin! She has to look at your tongue and throat."

Kirsty turned her head to find her aunt pinning her with an icy, now a glacial green, gaze. It was suddenly cold as her aunt's will to still curled through her and took possession of muscles and sinews. She took a breath, exhaled, and forced herself to relax.

The inbreath brought not only her aunt's scent of old books, ginger, tea, and ancient forests, but the scents she had smelled while trying to communicate her earlier terror to anyone that could have any way to hear. The lingering scent of fur, the tease of the pine breeze overlaid by the assorted scents of potion ingredients pulled her gaze to her right shoulder, where she saw David's blue eyes. With that, she relaxed more.

"Let me go. I don't need to be pinned..."

Once again, Kirsty's lips moved, but no sound came. Her eyes watered a bit, the frustration coming back swiftly.

"Still can't hear me...?" The water pooling in her eyes deepened and spilled as the blue darkened.

"No. We can't." David squeezed her a bit, and she felt the warmth from the copper ring next to his Deity's silver ring. "Yet."

"Open up Makay, you'll likely go insane if you don't let me see what to do to give it back." The Matron butted in tersely, drawing Kirsty's eyes back to Laryna.

Despite looking, Kirsty didn't take in any of Laryna's black habit for the day. Kirsty opened her mouth as wide as possible to allow the Healer to shine her wand in, then nearly gagged when another wand was shoved in and started squirming and turning. The unwelcome and unexpected feeling intensified, and though she tried to remain still her body had other plans, thanks to the intrusion. Once again their arms were needed to hold her still so that Laryna could do her work.

"Seared her vocal cords right out, poor dear... Just *what* was in that salsa you mentioned?"

Kirsty gagged as the exploratory wand was withdrawn, and would have allowed her breakfast to come up to spray the Matron, if the news of why her voice wasn't working was not enough to stay the impulse.

"What do you mean my vocal chords are seared out?! How am I going to discharge my cyclic duties? I don't think Mara's ever had a Mute priestess – oh no! What if David won't want me if I'm a Mute?" She screamed in her mind as the cold spread and her stomached roiled like a butter churn at Ms. Kitsch's after Byron's lambs had been weaned from their mothers.

David winced, hearing her thoughts somewhat through the ring, but this being no time to address her fear. Indeed, Kirsty likely would have been mortified to know he'd heard. Instead, he squeezed her just a bit tighter, hoping she'd notice, trying not to feel sick himself.

"So Kirsty won't ever talk again? Because I fed her *salsa* just wanting her to pay attention better? I didn't know it was *that* spicy!" Ally wailed.

"Allison McNamara! Now is not the time to panic. Kirstin, this goes for you as well. Kirstin. *Suaimhneach*!" Professor MacLeòmhann's voice was a vice grip, inexorably pressing down on all that heard it.

"Well!" The Matron sighed as they calmed. "With that out of the way, I did not say she would never talk again, only she will go crazy if she does not get her voice back. It *is* fixable. You can let her go now, I don't need to get back in the poor girl's throat."

Kirsty sighed silently, slumping into the mattress as her muscles all released at once, joined by David's less quiet sigh.

"You couldn't have done that before! Honestly child, I'm a Healer. You're supposed to *trust* me." Laryna glowered as she went for *Sgòrnan Slàinte*, the potion usually only used when someone coughed their throat out, sometimes literally.

After drawing a large bottle from the cupboard, she carefully poured a green viscous fluid into a crystal vial. With a wave, the entire pharmacy slid safely back to the end of the hall, without so much as a drop or particle falling from place. The vial she handed to Kirsty with a curt nod.

"Drink up child. Come back after lunch and after dinner, then we'll see tomorrow if you need more doses."

Kirsty sighed down to her toes and looked at the vial. When two breaths passed, her aunt cleared her throat reproachfully. Kirsty looked up at them while the Matron puttered off to give her the space she knew Kirsty needed. Though room temperature, vapor curled off the potion in great slow clockwise spirals. Pinching her nose, she swallowed it in one long draught.

Kirsty promptly fell over to the side, reaching for her throat and shivering.

"Did. Not. Say. So. Cold..." Kirsty wheezed and scratched like a long time smoker trying their hand at operatic Mermishdian or perhaps Xhosa, yet managed to be heard. Although her potions studies had introduced her to the concept that some healing potions would be cold at room temperature those texts had also understated the fact to the point of barely mentioning it.

David sighed. Kirsty smiled sheepishly and tried not to dwell much more on the iceflow retracing its steps down her esophagus with all the certitude of a glacier.

"Well then," Professor MacLeòmhann spoke softly, "I think I shall be finding out who helped this happen." The Lilitu boy's laughter in the great hall had been far too delighted for her taste, and knowing of how long the Makay and Lilitu families had been against each other, it was far too suspicious. Perhaps if young Morvan had been responsible there would be enough proof of malicious intent to expel him, influential parents or not.

The bell tolled its first call through the castle, announcing the time for all to prepare to head to their first period classes. Kirsty slipped off the bed and scooted out the door, not fearing that they might be late, but instead that she might get roped into an impromptu exam now that her aunt was fit to rouse ancestral spirits.

Kirsty scurried past Thomas, who was already on his feet thanks to leaping up from the bench outside paying respects to the headmistress. She wanted the salt tang air of the sea and to be home, preferably playing in the surf with David, one of the seal pups, or even better to sing with her mother while preparing a batch of fish for the long snow laden winter. The sea was tantalizingly close. All she had to do was go from the loch, through the underground passage, and the fresh water would turn to salt and the whale song would sweep through her as they passed near.

Yet, the mere fact she was part human trapped her here till she was of age to decide for herself which magic would take precedence.

Chapter Twenty Four
to Artenhame

Classes were out for the remainder of the day, a consideration for those of the pagan persuasions in their school. Samhain, was it? All Hallows? Halloween? Most of those observing more than the usual 'going soul caking' in the local village – disguised and under supervision of school staff and village volunteers – made use of the time off to relax. However, there were others that met in Moots and Covens to worship their various deities, or to experiment with seasonal magic.

He did not believe in those deities. He did not even believe in the Christian god, though once he and his family would have been denounced all over the British Isles and the European continent as heretics. Now it was the believers that were the heretics, superstitious ones at that. The evidence against gods and goddesses was staggering to him, and the holdouts were either insane, like that Diana Demeter girl, dangerous half-breeds as he was positive was the case with the Makay ilk, or naïve dreamers like Nevin Buckley tended to be. After all, how could they exist, when so many religions claimed that different gods and/or goddesses had created the world? It was a sheer impossibility that all of those fairy tales could be true. There was also the fact that he had never met one, despite how hard he had tried when younger.

He had wanted to believe... Even at this 'ripe' age it made him feel empty to think how there were no gods to grant redress and only one life to live. Demons, yes. Gods? No.

Morvan remembered the day that he first laid eyes on what was left of the Makay clan, with their ever changing eyes and strange way of walking over the land, as if they could leap from the beach to a handy spar and then do a jig. He particularly remembered a five year old Kirstin, clutching her mother's hand, and the red velvet of their capes swirling with the blues and greens of their skirts. He watched, bemused and entranced, as mother and daughter floated past where he held his own mother's hand, through the Ministry Commons toward the Presentation Hall.

Neither looked dangerous. Yet, that day, that fateful day, the illustrious Lilitu family had been accused of environmental endangerment, blackmail, corruption, and abuse – because of the testimony of the selkies that had once infested their beachside and dared to try yet again to regain the homes their forebears had been evicted from and the translation the pair provided.

He hadn't understood then exactly what those charges meant, or why his parents made such large 'gifts' to the various governments around that time. Morvan had grown to understand though. Selkies were dangerous sirens that beguiled with their voices, soft manners, and pleasing forms, refusing to bow to those more evolved.

The smile and the wide placid blue eyes that Makay had fastened on him as she escorted her mother that day particularly bothered him. At the time he hadn't been sure that she even knew who he was, or why she was there. It changed to disgust later that day when the minister of the Department of Mythological creatures called on him to relate his own experiences with the selkies always disturbing his family and home. He did not care if she remembered that day that her mother and herself had made the selkies look to be the victims of eviction.

There were plenty of other places the fur-ridden shape-shifting monstrosities plaguing them could take for home. Why did they need that particular stretch of beach, so near to the secret vaults filled with treasures that had been plundered generations ago from the Makay's trading ships and other ancient, but now extinct families – which of course he never mentioned? Even worse, why did the selkie females always insist on coming ashore and stripping their skins to dance below the full moon and bathe, arms outstretched to sea and sky in that silver light, singing their siren songs?

The song from the loch filtered through the glass windows and into his consciousness, overlapping the one from his memories and those far away shores. Gradually he became aware of his housemates watching one of the fish-like female selkies. It had ceased being novel to him that they were so different in appearance from the sea-dwelling seal variety. Her rainbow striped scales flashed as she harvested the ornamental trailing purple fingered waterflowers that grew so far below the surface. As she wove a garland of those flowers, some of his male housemates tried to catch the eye of the sinuous half-human monstrosity. The loch selkie would dart away shyly whenever one did catch her eye, always coming back though so that she could finish her project – as if it were the only place those particular waterflowers grew.

Morvan wondered who among them would be the next that they tried to drown by tempting them into vanishing one of the glasses. It was something very rarely succeeded at since the founder of Spiralis House had taken this into account and placed powerful wards on those fateful panes. However, a few students through the school's history had managed it, and it had always had disastrous consequences. Not for the first time, he wondered why Spiralis had chosen to site their dorms where he had. Surely there had been a reason he had ensured that each room had a way to monitor the nearby water.

As often happened, several of the students watching her debated as to why some selkies could shift, and why some couldn't. A few others were now leaving the commons, the choir members he thought. He smiled secretly. Makay certainly would be annoyed at not being able to sing while her voice healed. It was worth detention even though Professor MacLeòmhann figured it out far sooner than he had anticipated. It had not been quite as satisfying as the day that he had knocked all of her school supplies all over the shop where Morgana had been able to see, but it mollified him enough. There were still other things that he had done and planned to do that she had not sounded out yet.

Morvan continued smiling as he got up. If Makay truly did go insane from not singing, as the lore he'd heard and read about selkies indicated she might, then it would be one more sign that he could use to unmask her and her whole family as only half-human. The time was drawing near, both for her unmasking and for the time he was supposed to meet Professor MacLeòmhann to discover what he was to do for his detention.

Morvan passed beneath the writhing snake graven archway of the vestibule and through the broad passage dragging his fingertips over the moist stones, the scent of earth and water heavy in his nostrils. This lightened as he passed through the false wall, which drew back for him, revealing the slide to the floor of the passage below. By the time he followed the winding tunnels to the main halls of the dungeon, and then out to the lowest classrooms, the smell had transformed to the odors of brewing potions and processing.

Imp followed Morvan, unable to hear or follow his quarry's thoughts. When he had told Mistress's aunt of what he'd overheard from Lilitu and his friends during his earlier stalking, it had only been further proof. He had not been aware of the Headmaster's ability to read minds and discern truth, but he would have investigated Mistress's Enemy anyway.

As it was right now, he wanted to see what the punishment was to be. He hoped to meddle and make it worse if possible, and he suspected that the *Thing* that had gotten onto the grounds was no accident either. Yet, he had no proof! Being an imp, Imp knew very well how easy it was to be summoned into an enclosed barrier, and the Lilitu family was known for dark magic of this very variety. It would not surprise Imp if he discovered that Morvan had some object that he could use as 'non school space' to provide a hole.

First, Imp just needed a little proof, then he could better protect Mistress...

Headmaster Guirmean met Morvan in the mezzanine where

he had been waiting under the Examining Lintel. Professor MacLeòmhann was nowhere in sight, although Morvan looked for her. Somehow his blue robes and glinting gaze were more intimidating than her green robes and sparking eyes would have been.

The carved representatives of the three houses glowered above the flatboard Professor Guirmean wore, notched inward at the back – unlike a mortar board – and edged tonight in beaded tassels of jet beads. Today they had color in their eyes. Deep blue sapphires sparked from the white and black ravens, while emeralds mingled with ruby shots in the eyes of his own house's snake. Finally, the lion regarded him with plain disdain and curled lip below topaz and garnet bullets. The latter actually growled.

"Good evening Headmaster, where is Professor MacLeòmhann?" He did not bow, even slightly. Instead he stood still and ordered himself, whilst looking up and smiling in what he hoped was a winning and chastened way.

"The Headmistress is somewhat busy at this time due to some issues that came up with the group. Instead I will be escorting you to your detention assignment. I hope you followed her suggestion."

The Headmaster looked down sternly into his eyes, and Morvan felt a chill. For a moment it was as if there was nothing around them, darkness swallowed the mezzanine completely save for the Headmaster and the House personifications. In a panic he threw up a mental fight again, but it failed just as it had this morning. The darkness faded, and he could see. Now that he could see the Headmaster's face again he almost preferred the darkness.

The hand settled on him lightly, slender bookish fingers now lightly gnarled with age gripping him as commandingly as if Morvan was a sword, wand, or staff. The other hand still firmly gripped his gnarled stang, topped with his family emblem of the crane. The wizened wizard guided him out the doors, through the courtyard, past the fountains, and then toward the cottage of the groundskeeper.

Morvan struggled a bit to at least go at his own pace. "Sir, remove your hand. My father will not allow me to be manhandled so. I'm sure you do not realize what you are doing."

"Oh, realize I do *Bairn* Lilitu..." the Headmaster's grip only tightened. "You Switched food at Table with magic and seriously injured another student. You'll make it up to her whether your father wills or no."

Morvan glared at him, letting go the facade of respect. The Headmaster seemed unimpressed by his lineage and did not falter in his step. Merlin himself would have likely given such a cool look to Lancelot, Guinevere, and Arthur before the Morgana that his girlfriend was named for encased him in ice and trapped him in eternal sleep in some watery underground cavern.

"The nerve!"

The only time the Headmaster let go of him was when they paused at the doorstep of the groundskeeper's cottage. It was a one room affair with a deep peat roof the during the spring and summer, and was still redolent with vivacious flowers of unbelievable hues. Vines of rose, moon blossoming jasmine, and raspberries crawled over the greystone siding that had been carved from out from local quarries while lichen sprinkled the rest of the stones in purple and green. Nearby hunkered the storage shed for the tools the groundskeeper used, and through the half open door Morvan could glimpse the glint of headlamps on the riding lawnmower that was known for chasing both students mischievous enough to try digging up the lawn's sod, and the moles that stubbornly tried to erect great hills near the gardens. Students riding stangs and brooms, according to legend, were not safe in the air either if they damaged the grounds. Reaper would catch them.

Inside the shed, an engine coughed and sputtered. Morvan suppressed a shudder. Reaper was awake.

The knocker on the oak door was a simple wrought iron ring,

and gave a resounding summons once dropped onto the matching plate below, jarring Morvan from thoughts of what the ensorcelled machine might do to him. The bays of two large dogs came from within, and there was a rumble as they charged the door. This mingled with the thuds of the groundskeeper as he followed.

"Och, dry it up ye saps! Mus' only be bein' the Headmaster now." The door swung open and a black Newfoundland wolf mix eagerly pushed its way out to greet the Headmaster with slobbering kisses and shoulder pawing.

Professor Guirmean was pressed back by this wave of dark fur and drool while Morvan attempted to dart off to the side. A hand shot out from the door and fastened onto his cloak, yanking him back to be greeted by the growls of the matching dog that Dunstan Ainsley restrained. Though the newfoundland-wolf crosses were big, the groundskeeper was bigger.

The man was kilt clad in the Ainsley way of wide stripes of red and blue chased with thin crosshatches of white and black lines, and matching Argyle to the knee. A black fur sporran hung to the front, similar to the white pouch Makay wore at her hip on the High Days, but far more masculine. A dirk lurked at the waist, the *sgian dubh* tucked itself away in his kilt hose, and a Montrose Doublet contained white lace froth at cuffs and throat, his accents twinkling. A fly plaid draped over his left shoulder.

"Yer a goin' nowhere bucky," Mr. Ainsley growled. "Save to help perform the duties o' the Guardian with me an' the Headmaster. If yer lucky ye'll nae ha' annoyed the Hooded Man."

"Guardian?! Is that what I'm to do tonight? Wait... Hooded Man?"

"Aye... Didnae the Headmaster tell ye ye'll be a'payin young Miss Makay back fer takin' 'er voice? Tha's 'er most prized possession other n' mebby 'er brain or 'er sporran."

Morvan's eyebrow twitched at the groundskeeper's dialect, attempting to decipher it. "*Why on earth would a pouch be as 'prized' as a brain?"*

"Oh most I certainly did, Ainsley, but I did not tell him what he would be *doing* to make up for it." The Headmaster had gotten the dog under control again, scratching affectionately at it. Even sitting, the head came up to his shoulder.

"An' why not Professor? Seems to me a Guardian needs to know what he's aboot. Or is there a reason ye've been a waitin' sir?"

"I want him to meet up with the others first."

"Ahhh... Righty then. Allow me ter grab me crossbow and bolts, then I'm ready."

The dog that Ainsley had been restraining sat and watched Morvan keenly while his master grabbed the weaponry. The Headmaster waited patiently, stepping back a bit more to let Ainsley out and looking toward the hill.

The mist was coming down again, bringing the greener greens and greyer greys that made one wonder exactly how close or how far the realms of the fey and deity were. Fairies were known and seen, but it had long been known that the fairies most people knew of and thought as faery, originated in other realms of reality. Many students went on to specialize in the study of the fey, and some never were heard of again once leaving their preliminary studies. Such weather reminded him of his own youth and roguishness, though never to the extent he sometimes saw pass between Kirstin and Morvan.

Guirmean closed his eyes and sighed tiredly.

It was not long before the three were off the stoop, the large dogs ranging around them as the Headmaster led the way up the hill and down the road to the front gates of the Castle's spread. There a small group awaited them in various garb, each according to the Tradition that they followed.

Young Mr. Harper wore light green breeches that were

bloused below the waist and close fitting below the knee topped with a tunic of green and blue edged in black and gold stitched roses covered over with an olive Kinsale cloak. This cloak had in turn been lovingly masked over with conjured ivy leaves interspersed with oak and mistletoe to the point that if the wearer wished to he would easily blend into the forest – despite the garish hat that was another nod to his family's bardic and troubadouric origins. The airy Demeter youth played with the purple feather in Harper's hat, clad in a white gown that mixed Grecian and Celtic attributes, likewise covered with a cloak and with her hood back.

The boy blushed at the attentions from his fellow Bertramus and shot self-conscious glances at the McNamara girl from Leomaris, where she giggled with Miss Makay, who only smiled that strangely wistful smile she wore far too often. Whether or not Miss McNamara saw young Mr. Harper's blush where it was likely leaking below the mask of faux fall ivy leaves he was not certain.

The Headmaster shook his head, glad that presently the group was occupied with the pursuits of youth before taking up the roles that their rites would ascribe. He appreciated seeing a curious non-pagan joining her friends to learn about their beliefs. To him, it spoke of hope that one day perhaps the magical community would one day fully reintegrate with the non-magical without having to fear their powers being abused for governmental gain, or that their people would relive the Burning Times. Then again, as Allison McNamara was born to a non-magical family perhaps that was too much to hope for yet. Witches were still stoned and burned in African countries after all, so perhaps it could only be achieved after the world learned religious rivalries were useless and to differentiate fact from story.

McNamara did not have anything out of the ordinary on he noticed. She was dressed in a sensible warm dress in blazing harvest colors, her nod to the beliefs of her friends and the gathered members of this Society. She too was masked, though in simple black. Beside her, Makay wore a billowing dress in her family's tartan, an eye-catching medley of blue, green, and darker forest green. Her sporran was chased with silver and worn at the hip instead of the usual place others carried them, an oddity that he had never understood, and her fly tartan was held in place with pins fashioned like silver waves. White seafoam lace took the job of providing other accents, and the white lambskin cloak stirred restlessly. Her face was not masked, but instead had been painted with blue stripes and swirls on white, her hair arrayed with shells, tiny white feathers, and bits of white fur.

Makay patted and stroked her sporran often, playing with the fur of it and gazing longingly in the direction of the unseen sea when she thought the others would not notice.

He noticed though, and he knew that her aunt noticed as well where she stood with the checklist and her bagpipes near, tallying the yet others that were part of the Moot. Each of these students were carefully costumed and either masked or painted, a total of 13 of them. They would not be recognized as students of the school, nor would anyone stumbling on them – should they get past the Guardians – be able to recognize them as individuals at any other time either.

The Headmaster turned his eyes again over Professor MacLeòmhann and her Scots variety of the Makay tartan in her robing and feline mask rimmed with white owl feathers. This robing too was green, but more clearly reflected the relationship to forests due to the absence of the sea's blue, and bore shots of red that young Kirstin's tartan lacked. Belara held an odd position in the remnants of that clan, though it shared a name with the mundane version of the MacKay line. Although she'd married in, her name had never changed due to the confusion it had been likely to cause students her first several years of teaching. That she'd never remarried after the loss of her husband even after so many years that Finnol was too young to remember him worried the professor.

On the other hand, Belara considered all the students in the manner of her own, even those she severely disliked, so it was safe to assume her married to her work.

All this was taken in quickly, then he was on them. Enough elderly introspection.

"Artair, Dunstan." Professor MacLeòmhann nodded in greeting to them. "Lilitu..." No nod this time, and the way she spoke the last caused even Mr. Ainsley's hairs to stand on end and ice to prickle his veins.

"Is this everyone that's going Belara? It's a small group this year it seems."

"Yes, Artair. Some dropped out for the night because Makay will not be able to sing." Professor MacLeòmhann gazed briefly and coolly at Morvan, no longer as relaxed as she had been before his presence was noted. "Others had to drop because their parents sent letters of request to keep them inside the school's boundaries. Professor Gerwulf was not feeling well, so we will be short a Guardian, even with Lilitu standing in."

"Then let's be off, shall we?"

"Indeed. I hope you heeded my warning young man." She stowed her clipboard.

"Now Belara...I'm sure he's not as far gone as that." The headmaster touched her arm lightly."

Belara's nose twitched. "We shall see."

Kirsty pressed her lips together and bristled when she saw that Morvan had been brought. Ally shot her a concerned look, probably hoping that she wasn't going to try to drown him again if he made a wrong move. It was a tempting thought, but so far he'd not pulled anything new on her.

Her aunt was right there anyway. It wouldn't do to be banned from Moots as well as Duels.

Thomas stopped his blushing in Ally's general direction, and Diana left "Fluffy The Floofy Feather Of Foofdom" alone. Kirsty looked at her aunt for explanation, then to Mr. Ainsley. He only held his hands out at his side and palms toward her. She looked next to the Headmaster, who smiled slightly with his blue eyes sparkling, but very firmly and silently gave her to understand that Morvan would indeed be coming – no matter what she said.

So she said nothing, even though the other students were as confused as she was. But...*why was the sodder there? Couldn't she even go to a Moot in peace?*

Morvan tried not to glare at the Makay wench. Something about the blue on white of her face irked him. It reminded him of how some of the selkies that danced on the beaches painted their faces. Not all did it, and these swirls were different than the ones they would wear. The similarity still bothered him, as did the way she held so still.

He less than half listened as the rules of the excursion were told to the gathered students. He was a Guardian for now, so the injunction to stay with the professors likely did not bear as much weight. He felt pride stretch inside himself again at being less restrained than his fellow students in their costumed cortège, as they would perform empty rituals in the honor of mere phantoms. The other students listened attentively. There was no need to hang on each word though, the fools. It was no more than a trip with mummers and soul cakers, and no more dangerous than American counterparts trick-or-treating. The self satisfied smirk began to curl his lips.

The Headmaster went to the gate and pushed the wrought iron and silver bars open. A shimmer spread out from the center of the boundary to the edges of the gate, and they slipped through. The boundary rippled shut behind them again and the gate closed with a clang, leaving only a tumbled ruin beside the loch at the end of an overgrown road. Cows grazed in the fields and wandered over the grounds, which had before held evidence of no such thing.

The Headmaster placed his stang on a round flat stone inscribed with worn linear etchings and half-dreamed scroll-work. Without being told, each of the others there placed a hand on the staff, gripping tightly.

The hair on Morvan's arms and the back of his neck rose, unfamiliar energies beginning to thrum in the ground beneath them. The Headmaster's eyes smiled at him patiently, and he gingerly laid a hand on the now shining rod.

When Morvan touched the stang, he felt a consciousness appraising him coolly, then turn its back on him. The only way he could have felt a deeper rejection in his bones would have been to be told, then booted over the nearest cliff by Maldein so she could run off with a Cowan.

There were too many hands and arms to decipher which belonged to whom, but the one next to his was cool and soft. Morvan had the impression of slightly long and well cared for nails. The hand on the other side was square and earthy, yet refined.

The air began to crackle, and a green light flowed out from the stone, formed a circle, and rose above and down below. Morvan was not sure how he knew it was below, but the ground beneath him felt more alive somehow.

"From Caer Carrick and guarded shore
To sparkling sea and stone girt door.
By Earth and Firth, Sky and Flame,
Woe and Mirth, To Artanhame."

There was still a bit of day, yet the light drained away. Morvan felt as if all of the universe pressed in on him, and a rushing filled his ears. Clouds roiled up from the ground around the edge of the circle and he could see everyone's robes billow in unfelt winds while the stone and staff entwined in blue and green light. Soon, it was full dark.

At the edge of the circle he saw something horned, more accurately someone with vast spreading antlers, almost like a man otherwise – but the silhouette seemed broken by fur and leaf!

Just as suddenly the vision was gone. He looked to the other side, shaking and trying to catch his breath.

A woman in black shrouding with a deep hood drawn over her head and shadowing her face stared at him from there, belted in the red of freshly spilled blood. Morvan thought it a woman at least; the long, scraggling death-grey hair flowing out from the hood at least gave the apparition a vaguely feminine air. His heart pounded harder. The woman reached her hands up and drew back her hood far enough to reveal...

Nothingness.

He remembered feeling dread on the train, but this was much worse that that which followed with the *Things*. It was worse yet that this nothingness was smiling at him.

"I know what you did." The Cailleach's voice came to him like church bells at midnight over a graveyard on a dark and misty night. "My children are not yours to call, mortal child. You have something of mine."

Her finger pointed at him, white as the bones of ancient battles left to bleach in the sun, and he felt a shaft of jagged trepidation piercing through his soul. The edges of the wound burned with icy fire as guilt began to run through his mind.

The light returned.

The clouds dispersed, and robes settled. When looking around there was no trace of Castle Carrick, the loch, nor even the grazing herds. Morvan heaved a sigh of relief at seeing no horned shapes or hooded women swooping down on him. All that remained was the stone and the sod.

Kirsty kept her head down after laying her hand on the headmaster's staff. Her stomach churned and knotted, but not because of the distance folding or from being slipped through the planetary matrix to another point.

No, the hand that brushed the side of hers felt slimy and dark, although she knew in her mind that it could not actually be physically slimy. Whoever it belonged to, they had more baggage than she wanted to be near – and her skin itched because of it. To cope, Kirsty allowed herself to listen to the sea and whale song that was always in the back of her mind, and the slow drip of secret caverns.

Her eyes opened a bit when she felt the presence that sometimes overshadowed David. Looking out of the side of her eye, she saw the Horned One flit by. The last chase she had been part of was too fresh, so she could not smile at Herne's presence even though knowing he was there was a relief in a way. Even though she would not object to being involved in a hunt, she was there to answer Mara and the Lady's summons. What should she do if all three of them had things they wanted her to do? Also...was he there because he was annoyed that his last Hunt had been interrupted? Or was he only here for Creighton in another aspect?

Distantly, she wondered what aspects each honored deity were going to take, since some of the ones that she guessed were going to be represented had aspects in various regional religions.

The ground beneath their feet changed from the packed road of centuries into a rolling green swath, overlaying sand. She could always tell where the sea had washed. Her feet tingled.

Looking up and around once they had fully 'realized' physicality again revealed a landscape that made obeisance to every land type imaginable. In one place there was the desert, another held high granite outcrops. The forest that swept to the sea shifted, tropical one moment, mixed the next. The forest was like waves, never fully settling into one sort out of the many. A stone circle, each stone graven with nine spirals or waves, capped a small hill, out of the side of which a spring sprung and ran to the sea.

What made her shiver was the wave-song and salt-sweet in the air, and the mist of it on her skin. This mist coagulated at the edge of their vision, demarcating the edge of worlds.

The shadow of wings passed over them. Looking up, the owner of the shadow turned out to be a strange mix of human and feline, ottering her way on the airlanes and the skirts of purple robes whipping around her legs without care. A single blue feather dropped from one of her wings and was carried by the breeze, eventually landing on the stone altar in the circle of roughly hewn stones.

A pair of sleek black boobries escorted the unidentified bird/feline/human woman. Their wings looked more suited to penguins than flight in her opinion. However, Kirsty knew them to be dangerous hunters of both land and sea. They were twice the size of the human sized flying creature they accompanied. The beaks alone were seventeen inches and hooked similar to an eagle. Midnight webbed feet would rival the spread of a red deer's antlers, though for now they clutched only air, despite the gleaming claws. These paid no attention to the humans below them, instead disappearing with the other strange apparition.

Kirsty stared at where they had vanished for a moment, trying to classify the being, wondering if it were a Grecian Sphinx, then deciding that it was likely something Professor Gerwulf had not yet covered.

As quickly as the being materialized, she was gone into some other realm, fading from sight.

Silently, several of the students checked themselves over. Kirsty saw no need, nor did Morvan remember to check himself.

Kirsty looked again to the surf, murmuring her gladness in Gaelic to be near it again. The answer washed through her, soothing seething wounds.

"Headmaster... Where are we?" Morvan found his voice to be lacking the confidence he usually felt.

Dunstan bristled and puffed. "Artenhame, boy. The Home of the Stone! Were ye nae listening? Tis only one o' the places where witches and wizards repelled the Nazi invasions from! It's in the histories it is!" He winced, shooting apologetic looks to the cocked eyebrows of the Heads. "Och, sorry 'eadmaster, 'eadmistress... You know how worked up I get..." He bowed slightly to each in deference.

Professor MacLeòmhann smiled a bit at Dunstan's indignation and nodded.

"Even so." Professor Guirmean agreed with Dunstan. Though his demeanor was gentle, there was something far older yet more vital behind his words. "This is one of the places of the Wise, a place between realms, Morvan. Some places of the planet's energy grid lend themselves well to travel. Others are... different. Surely you remember this from your first year classes?"

Morvan considered, but could not remember. Most of the first year's classes he had barely paid attention to, believing that his parents had already well prepared him; he had strained instead toward the possibility of ferreting out ancient hexes. "I must have forgotten, sir."

"I think your house head would be a little disappointed if you could have forgotten this. Why else would places like Stonehenge, Mt. Shasta, Koyasan, the Bermuda Triangle, Well of Youth on Dun I, and Auchnabreck continue to be important places of power?"

Kirsty wrinkled her nose at Morvan's idiocy and edged closer to the water, glancing now and then at her aunt and the others to make sure they did not see. Something inside was screaming to get into this water, burning and writhing. Her world was focusing into one point and one purpose. Their voices faded out just the way Ally and Nevin's had before.

"I'm not sure sir. I hadn't thought much about it. I always thought that it was some sort of Pagan superstition, like the O'Drake family's well and forge for Brigit is."

Kirsty heard her aunt sniff at Morvan's reply. "That is why the O'Drakes mingle more with the non-magical people. Those getting specialized training tend to forget their roots and loose the ability to access those roots so easily."

Down the beach Kirsty could hear the floating notes of a coral flute. The days before and after Samhain made for good hunting for the Finmen, especially along beaches that were lightly populated. Focusing and slowing her breath, she looked through the mist for the source. Her heart sped and something inside tingled. Reaching out – with something she wasn't even sure what to call it – she hoped to feel how far away this Finman was, and if he had any child enthralled.

Something warm and furry, but coated in oil and slime met her mental probe. The notes broke off.

Kirsty frowned. That had not felt like the last Finman that had tried to lure her off the Point. *"Had it been something else once?"* Even stranger, why did it feel now like she was now aware of something she'd not realized was missing?

The water was a bit less appealing. Where there was one Finman there might be others. With no voice with which to scream and use against it her first instinctual response would only cause *her* damage instead of him.

Kirsty opened her eyes, unaware that she had closed them in the first place. Her aunt's bored into her and she shrank back. Professor Guirmean's regarded her curiously, though still talking to Morvan.

"This is why guardians and a few trusted observers have to come. Those that come for their rituals and offerings run the risk of being distracted from their task, and even being lured away. Sometimes it's one of the sidhe, sometimes it is something more on our sort of existence."

"And why didn't you tell me of this *before* you brought me?" Morvan's eyes had gone wide, and he released the sour fear-stench. Despite his fear, he tried to hide it with anger as he glared at the headmaster.

"You are in very little danger compared to those that will go inside the circle, but they have responsibilities they may not shirk. You also would not have believed until you saw for yourself, or so it has seemed with how long we have been watching you."

Professor Guirmean's tone was firm, like the sound of his stang as it clicked the stone again.

"We will leave you now, gentlemen. I trust you'll Anchor us and protect us from any that might stumble here." Professor MacLeòmhann's voice slit through in measured beats, already slipping toward the otherworldly over and undertones that the Leomaris students knew from the morning chants of her own prayers which usually roused them.

Strangely enough they mingled with the pipes playing themselves.

With that, the headmistress ushered Kirsty, Thomas, Demeter, and a few of the other students toward the stone circle.

Chapter Twenty Five
The Old Ones

Morvan watched as some of the students separated from them and followed the headmistress, the Makay girl among them. He pondered the way she looked longingly to the spring after tearing her eyes from the sea, and the momentary flash of terror, then the confusion he had seen twisting and raising her brows. Stranger yet was the purpose in her step once she started moving, the dreamy hesitancy he was accustomed to seeing – gone.

That was not the Makay girl that he knew. He was not sure who this was. Even that moon-crazed Demeter girl had a more powerful and direct aspect around her instead of being lost in daydreams.

This version of Makay possessed a tangible wariness, which reminded him of how the doves watched the cats and owls. He wasn't sure if she was the cat, the dove, or the owl, nor was he sure he wanted to know. She *might* eat him.

Each of the Observers called up previously carved turnips, the predecessors to the now ubiquitous pumpkins introduced from American cousins. Purple and white, wood-hard and the size of doubled fists, some were simply scooped out glorified candle holders, while others had obviously had longer to work and steadfastly managed to scrape out recognizable faces to leer... or gaze benignly.

As one, each Observer held up their turnip lanterns, which varied in size and complexity even more as they began to take on life, and murmured their own prayers.

"I ask the Lord Of All That Is to watch over and protect my friends. Please extend your hand and bring them back to yourself, and forgive their mistakes. Don't let them get hurt." Ally whispered, dipping her head and closing her eyes, far more pale than when they had set out.

Morvan wondered what she had seen during the transit.

"May the Lord of All Flesh grant the safe return of our friends, and the safety of all of us." Nevin agreed, nodding, equally pale.

"May Enlightenment and connection to Truth be gained by all in following the Way" Enid and Devan murmured as one.

"Amen," Guirmean nodded toward Ally and Nevin. "So Mote It Be." Guirmean nodded again the end of the other prayers.

"Wait, I thought this thing was a Pagan moot. Those didn't sound Pagan." Morvan hid his smirk, but crossed his arms.

Ally and Nevin flinched. Enid and Devan sighed and shook their heads.

"What's yer row with that? 'S like guests at a church." A mostly brown student from among the Guardians hissed and sighed.

"Observers don't have to share the same faith. They just have to care about those that wander between worlds, Lilitu! Just because we're all different doesn't mean we don't get along." Creighton spat at the same time. The dark haired male from the Participants stepped forward, eyes flashing and fixed as if he were a deer.

Something dark and horned overshadowed Creighton, and for just a moment Morvan caught the scent of musk, the chase, and birch trees.

Well, more of the scent of birch than was usual for Creighton, who smelled of summer birch stands even at Christmastide.

"Be still, Creighton." MacLeòmhann's tone pinned the lad.

"Yes Professor..." He cast one last look at Morvan.

"Half-blood *ghillie dhu*..." Morvan muttered.

"The same goes for you Lilitu." MacLeòmhann growled.

"You *will* learn your lesson."

"Insinuating something about my mother, Lilitu?" Creighton continued, hand still fisted.

"I can have you serve detention together tomorrow night if you won't stop. Kirstin, don't you dare think about joining in." MacLeòmhann's gaze snapped sharply toward Kirsty at the sound of willow and selkie hair beginning to swish. "They listen even now."

"Yes Headmistress..." They grumbled together, going with the higher of her titles, all hoping for some favor points.

"Damnitall..." Kirsty blinked with what she hoped looked like innocence, then conjured her own turnip, instead of making mud swallow him. She cast a wary look to Creighton and the darker haired female. With an unobtrusive sniff she tried to identify the scents coming from them.

Battle and/or the Cailleach was not something she needed to have following her, or to be blundering into. Mara's insistent tugs were enough to deal with.

Next, the other ritual participants each conjured their own, and lit the candles of their Observers and ties back to the world of man.

"Light at the windowsill and hearth always bring us home, through darkest night and wildest storm." The five Participants chanted in unison, each touching or brandishing some mark of their deity before touching the wicks of their turnips to the flames offered.

Thomas sighed and shook a bit, touching the lump beneath his cloak again once his flame was lit from Ally, and watched Kirsty rub the twinned bracelet at her left wrist once she was lit from the same source.

Creighton winked and patted the bone spearhead strung at his neck, once done accepting fire from the dark haired one. "Let's hope Kernnunos and the Oak King grant blessings, Enid. See you with a prize hopefully." Enid smiled a bit and nodded, adjusting the mask she wore.

"Of course they will. Didn't you hear the sounds of Herne's Hunt last night? They're all riled." Stone grinned, her pale blond hair for a moment looking too white for Morvan's comfort. "I can't wait to find out directly what She wants me to do."

Gale looked into the turnip he held after Stone's had been lit. "Just be careful Ingrid... Remember last time. Come back."

"'Don't wind up like the girl that bonded too close with Brigit.' Don't worry, I won't."

"Uh huh... I wonder sometimes." He muttered.

Morvan wasn't the only one looking at how Stone's hair was closer to the shade of moonlight.

Gravely, the Observers shared their light with the Guardians... except for Morvan.

Try as he could earlier in the day, he had not carved a turnip with the other students during the preparations for the time. Nothing would form in his mind either. Now he understood somewhat why people worked for hours and days on the superstitious oddities...

No turnip, no flame, no light would he have.

None would have been offered to him anyway. Superstitious fools.

He tried one more time to conjure something, but all he managed was a gnarled stub. The looks some of the others gave him... He was unaccustomed to this feeling it brought him. Even out under the open sky he began to feel claustrophobic.

Professor Guirmean moved to light Morvan's wick for him, but Kirsty held forth her flame instead. Her gut twisted, and she fought it, but some force pulled her toward him like fish in a net.

The cold that flowed through and around her, an arctic blast over frozen seas, made her squeeze her eyes shut. Images formed before her and then were torn away too quickly to grasp.

The flame danced between them, and kindled the wick of that misshapen gnarl, and the scent of some unnamed creature (which she likely didn't want to know by how it turned her stomach and made her think of the last she'd burned her hand) coiled up from the tallow and overpowered the clean herbs in her beeswax.

With a nod, she drew back, and felt things unseen click into place. She had done Mara's or the Lady's will... and that was all she knew.

Was that pity on Makay's face? Surely not. She had said nothing, so there was no way for Morvan to verify. Neither would the others speak to him. So what was that flicker in her eyes and the hated tie he had thought he had felt?

Thomas Harper was the first behind MacLeòmhann, plucking a few strains on his lute and making his turnip do a jaunty spin above his head like a demented will o' the wisp. Makay fell in line behind him, holding her head high. A strange, barely audible warble came from her, weakened further, then fell silent as she winced and reached for her throat. Diana Demeter looked up to the moon, as if she expected that low hanging orb to speak. Indeed, it did appear to be listening attentively. She too then got into line, resting her hand momentarily on the shaking shoulder.

Morvan already disliked those three, but the other two, Ingrid Stone and Floyd Creighton he knew little of besides their names and that they were of Leomaris. They were as withdrawn as Valnarius, usually.

Creighton looked his way and pulled up an antlered hood, oak leaves clinging here and there as if the great hart they came from had last crashed through a thicket of saplings. He curled his lip in disdain, holding Morvan's eyes, but talking to the one beside him. "A Spiralis... still can't believe one came with what they say about the Old Ways."

"Floyd, the heads will hear." Stone elbowed him while hissing. "We can hope 'They' will unleash us, 'til then..."

Stone's hood came up. An eerie darkness emanated from her, an impossibility that gave Morvan a headache. Without a word, she glided to the line, followed by her housemate.

The adults continued in their preparations and gestures. Ainsley carefully placed a circle of what looked to be salt around the observers, with garlic and silver at the quarters.

The crimson sun touched the edge of the mist and slid below. A bloody path formed over the water though as far as Morvan knew the path of the sun shouldn't have been seen under such conditions. For a moment, he thought he saw a large, triangular, fin breaking the water. When he tried to focus on it, it was gone.

So why did it leave the sense of foreboding, as if a white masked closet dweller with a cleaver had just creaked the door open?

One by one the Participants wended around the tor, away from the beach and into the stone circle accompanied by Professor MacLeòmhann's chants and the wails of the floating pipes. One by one they passed through the dividing line, flares and pulses passing through the Observers.

The last of the sun's light flared, the final stab to its daily life, as if from the Morrigan's spear. At last, MacLeòmhann herself entered, and Morvan heard her no more.

"Now we wait, and guard." Guirmean answered the unasked question. "Mr. Ainsley will take half of you and guard the village side, the rest of us will be stationed here."

The moon now hung low over the stones, as if watching the forms which he could no longer see. For a moment, he thought he almost could pick out a satisfied smile in the great shining face.

Or was the moon rimmed by rows of serrated teeth?

The wind rose.

Ainsley pointed to his two to follow, singling out who he knew from the roll call would be Darcy Green from Leomaris and Corriander Comely from Bertramus, in their dark leather Hunter's garb. Ainsely gave him a fierce and haunting glare, and the Head's comment *'half'* momentarily whispered through his mind. Ainsely grinned a bit, though what it meant Morvan wasn't sure. Then they too disappeared into the fog, ostensibly to position his two young guardians where he wanted them to haunt. Morvan was now 'alone' with Bartholomew Brown, Stanley Wookey of Leomaris, and the Headmaster to 'protect' the Observers.

McNamara fiddled with the edge of her cloak, peering up at the stones. "Are you sure they're really going to be all right? Thomas really does this every High Day?"

Morvan listened partially and looked around for... he didn't know what. Some moving shape perhaps. There was breathing behind his ear, but every time he looked, he saw only the settling night.

"Every High Day." Guirmean replied, resting a hand on her shoulder.

"What about Kirsty? Are these really as dangerous as people going missing? If she does these all the time, but not always with a group..?"

"Which is why she's here for this one. I have full confidence in Professor MacLeòmhann's abilities to midwife them back and forth." His tone was final and calm as the soft thump of a thick tome closed for the last time.

Ally reached up and grasped the silver cross where it dangled from its stout chain. She bit and sucked her lip thoughtfully then sighed as if pondering a question from History, Ethics, or maybe that sparsely attended World Religions seminar.

Time stretched out further, and the dark fell faster, as if the Unseelie Court galloped across the sky drawing a tattered cloak of darkness behind. The wind called his name, but as Morvan looked around, none seemed to hear it.

"I don't think I want to know if they're real anymore..." He

thought. *"Not in a place like this..."*

Kirsty observed the shimmering energy in front of her, and the space beyond. To her this barrier smelled of the lightning over a high sea mingled with the newly mown grass after Ainsley had ridden his flying sentient lawnmower Reaper around on his acrobatic kicks to tame both unruly sod and overly bushy cloud.

Then she was through the barrier and queuing up beside Thomas. Steadily he picked out the haunting refrain the stones chimed in subsonic symphonies. The primal energy pooled in her as she instinctively drank it in and tilted her face to the moon, spreading her arms and brushing shoulders as if to shed the skin that wasn't there. With an effort, she tried her voice again, joining the toning stones, silvered strings, and haunting wails. Though still weak, it hurt less in her core to try.

She knew the music carrying in the night, as sound often does, would be making the locals believe for a night in the sidhe. For them, the hills would open once more and the fair ones might venture forth. The old magics would remain in the world in some form till the next time for the portals to open. Kirsty could feel, somehow, as each of the power points on the Isles were activated.

In brief flashes, she saw the true ancient rituals, more as touches of wind than as vision. More recent events followed as the stones around her remembered, such as the nights the local witches stood to defend German invasion attempts, and the more concerted efforts to aid distantly for D-day, only known for fact to the most obscure Cowan historians, and thought to be only folklore to most of the populace... but which was still too incendiary a topic for non-Cowans to discuss among themselves despite the passage of generations.

Perhaps, somewhere out there, someone not of magical blood would be feeling the passage of the Old Ones. Perhaps it could even be one of those that decried their existence as folktales.

For now, the stones remembered, and recorded.

A riff of laughter pulled her eyes to the one beside her, and she began to remember who she was and why she was there.

Thomas actually was beginning to look a little drunk, flushed behind the mask and beneath his hat. The way his smile spread and teeth began to glint under the emboldened stars brought a small smile to her own lips.

"I'd forgotten how good this place feels..." The hair on her arms and in her half pelt rose in response. Kirsty closed her eyes. She wanted to dance on the beach, but odder was the urge – no, need – to hunt, widening her eyes and her body lifting and falling at the realization.

Soon enough all five of them were around the stone altar, their breathing falling into creative cadence as they waited and the land thrummed. Professor MacLeòmhann circumnavigated the perimeter and scribed the appropriate sigils – Ogham that had been used by the builders.

The brush of her aunt's abyssopelagic aura against her own pulled her out of the trance she was slipping into.

"The Representatives of the Tribes shall now state their deities."

"Cerridwen," "Mara, and the Lady of the Waters," "the White Lady," "Cailleach," "Kernunnos, and the Oak King," intoned each in turn. They passed the calls around the circle, first to three, and then to the three-fold three, swifter and louder each round. Kirsty's voice was a mere wash of sound like a distant surf when her turn came, while Diana was a ripple on a midnight lake. Thomas was a riff of notes and the crackle of flame under Cerridwen's cauldron. Ingrid's evocation was landslides and the clash of battle, whilst Floyd's voice was blaring horns and the sounds of hooves on forgotten moss.

With each round the energy of the nexus grew stronger and stronger. A wind roared through the stones from five different directions, meeting over the altar and then tearing down into it and below.

If any sounds would carry to those anchoring them to the world they came from, it would be this, and the moaning of the earth as she stretched and accepted the sky.

Each of them laid their hands on the stone. Lightning came from the still cloudless sky directly above.

MacLeòmhann's cry as the power broke was drowned by the thunder. It coursed through the stone and into each of them. The student Priests and Priestesses, eyes locked on the eyes of those that had chosen them, stood transfixed by the summoned deities.

As one, the group nodded at the elderly professor. She removed her hands from the stone and stepped back.

"You have done well Belara, as usual." The Lady of the Waters smiled at MacLeòmhann, as translucent and luminescent as she remembered.

"I will ensure that you will be seeing your husband tonight when all is quiet and you are in your chambers." The Cailleach stepped down off the stone. "I will not be staying long, and will return the trainee swiftly."

"My thanks, Lady."

Cailleach laid her hands on Ingrid's shoulders, drawing her away from the group. "Come child, much awaits."

Ingrid fell down to the sod, her body sleeping and her soul, now armored, racing like a hind after the war goddess.

"We must fly as well." Kernunnos, covered with the skins from his hunts and always morphing slightly, cast a measuring look at Kirsty before he stepped off. His head was helmeted by a skull of some heavily antlered creature that had not roamed the planet in aeons – perhaps ever – and where the eyes should have been, only the starry depths of the night sky before the Industrial age looked at at any foolish enough to lock eyes with him.

The butt of his dark spear sounded on a stone. Floyd also passed into sleep.

"Aren't you missing one?" His companion asked, crossing his

arms and smelling of musk. "I'm quite certain I smell–"

"That was last night, and this is the wrong aspect. Is your nose going?" Kernnunos crackled. "Let's get going, I want as much use of this moon's phase as possible."

Kirsty couldn't help smiling at that. He did not seem as bothered as she had been afraid that Herne would be. Though this was a different aspect, there were some things that carried, and he was not looking at her accusingly or demanding time she didn't have tonight.

"Well, now that you mention it, just a few hours ago there was this coven of Cowan teenagers that called me up, and then thought I was some demon to do their bidding. Tons of sul–"

"Get hunting or I'll be hunting you next! And stop sniffing toward the water girl! Off limits!"

"Yes, yes. Just a few steps behind. You'd be less cranky if you'd hunt other things once in a while." The Oak King grabbed MacLeòmhann and stole a kiss before she could fend him off, leaving her blushing furiously when he released her struggling form and dashed off after Kernunnos and the trainee.

The debacle ensuing from the stolen kiss was enough to draw the wide eyes of those remaining to be taken.

"Oakie is right you know, Cerridwen." The White Lady grinned a bit and calmly helped MacLeòmhan to straighten herself, then gave a subtle nod toward Mara, who had already leaped off the stone and was pacing as if to stop meant the ceasing of breath. "I think something ought to be done in a couple cases."

"Here is not the place to discuss it. I come to test the Harper and see if he is worthy of his next step, not to meddle in affairs of musk glands, certain hunts, or that sort of inspiration." Cerridwen's voice was the simmering of long-forgotten and yet to be learned potions and songs yet to be sung.

Both eyed Mara warily, who glowered at them momentarily and crossed her arms. The sea water following and flowing around her feet seethed.

"Agreed... Now is not the best of times. Come my young one, I have much to share tonight." The White Lady gathered Diana to herself and discarded the body. In less than a flash, the pair swam away through the sky on a narwhal.

"Shi did that on purpose..." Mara watched them swim away, the sleeping bodies of the youths around them. "Wait a minute... Shi took *Compánach* – Come back with my narwhal, you have some of your own!

"You need a *leannán*..." The White Lady's voice sifted down like starlight and moonsugar, the source already far distant, yet carrying in the way of the Elders.

"Shi means well Mara, and just worries about the effects of... you know."

"Shi didn't prod about such things for either of us a few centuries back. Now shi mates if someone is visionary and sensitive enough." Mara stalked the perimeter, grinning and licking her lips a bit when her eyes fell on Morvan, then looked back. "I have better things to do than set myself up again."

"This also may not be the best conversation to pursue, Lady Mara... Presence of your Acolyte or not... Please forgive my intrusion." MacLeòmhann once more had her composure, flowing deosil around the circle and carefully arranging the discarded bodies more comfortably than how they had fallen. "Kirstin has some pressing matters that we hope can be taken care of..."

"Yes sister. I agree with Belara." The Lady of the Water chimed in, flowing her way to Mara and laying a hand on her arm. "We should take her soon, lest the others return before us."

"Fine. We have matters to discuss and insist on as well."

Kirsty blanched and drew back, the tone was unmistakable. Somewhere, she feared this would be the night she'd been dreading since she could first remember. She opened her mouth to give proper acknowledgment, but all that came was a hoarse squeak.

Cerridwen eyed Kirsty. "What's wrong with the child? I was hoping to have heard her gift tonight as well." A heartbeat passed and the fire haired goddess wrinkled her nose. "Mara, I'm stepping into your territory to fix my territory. Don't eat any parts of those that are mine to even the balances."

Mara snorted. "Please do."

"I mean it. Don't go nipping Harper's fingers while he's taking an after hours bath or something."

Thomas hid his hands, his eyes widening, mouth forming a small 'o,' and blushing furiously all at once, then flicking guiltily around.

Kirsty and Thomas both flinched when Cerridwen laid her hand on Kirsty's throat. Her eyes locked on his for a moment, then took on the glassy inwardness.

For a moment, the shifting seas reflecting in her eyes gave way to a banked fire, then the flames coaxed upward, before becoming the shifting seas again.

Kirsty reached for her throat tentatively, locking eyes with the deity instead.

"Thank you, Lady Cerridwen..." She curtsied in the low, grandiose way that Mara preferred her to, spreading the skirts wide and exposing the back of her neck. "How should I repay your kindness?"

"Pay better attention, young one." The elder deity smiled and nodded. "And perhaps do like you are *supposed* to do under the moon a bit more often. I miss the dancing and singing, and I'm not the only one missing it since you found a way to keep that white pup company while he's contained."

"Yes Lady Cerridwen..."

Mara snorted a bit, and an elbow in her side from her sister produced an exasperated sigh to follow it.

"Well then, it's sorted. Come young Harper, we have much to

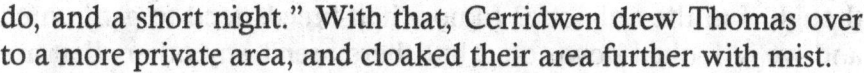

do, and a short night." With that, Cerridwen drew Thomas over to a more private area, and cloaked their area further with mist.

Mara dipped her head and resumed her prowling.

The Lady of the Well sat lightly on the ground and patted it gently. "Sit with me Kirsty. What's troubling you?"

"Where is my mother?"

"I don't know... that's something that Sister and I wanted to discuss with you. We know she's alive but–"

"She's been hidden from me. From my waters, she's been taken from me!" Mara stalked the circle again, at a pace swift enough pace to make Kirsty feel like a whirlpool would open up in the center. "That leaves you my only remaining land-based priestess that I can access."

Kirsty clenched her fists and trembled, her stomach churning... it was good that she'd not eaten as well as usual. She was cold, and she could feel the sweat beginning to form.

"She can't leave school. She's not old enough yet." Belara's hand settled on her shoulder, and she felt her settle on her left side, shielding her. "Remember the laws have changed since your race began to fade from sight."

"Aye... I remember well." Mara paused in front of Kirsty. "But it can't be helped. While there are still others of my children beached, I still have to have access to a properly trained priestess that has passed her initial examinations – skin or no, potions or no!"

"This Yule Kirstin must be home for the first test. At night, in her dreams, myself, Mara, or the White One will feed her a little more of what we desire her to know, since she cannot attend one of the Temples." The Lady patted Kirsty's thigh lightly. "She also must come visit with me in the well when she returns."

Kirsty stared at the slender, translucent, hand where it glowed blue and lit the darkening night.

"I'm supposed to test this break for registering as a shifter though. I'm the only one? I know half-breeds tend to get hunted and we're looked down on... but there aren't any others that are acceptable?"

"No. I'm afraid not, and your registration will just have to wait for the spring recess. Some candidates don't have the magic they'll need to withstand us both. There are those that abandoned one or the other of us for some other deity or no deity at all. Others don't have ancestry from the right bloodlines–"

"And a few I just plain don't like how they are deciding to be, and more that are too diluted and just simply don't see me. It's worse than if a human does not see, since even one drop of selkie blood and a child is mine 'til certain conditions are met or it shares the blood of another." Mara stalked and swirled, gills flashing at her neck. "Ever try to talk to someone that doesn't know you even exist? They walk toward you at the beach when they visit the sea, feel you, but to them you're not there. Only the seafoam on the wave and the spray on their skin. Especially if it's a marriage that brings them."

Mara shuddered, and seemed to stop short of hugging herself before that vulnerability was lost again in malice.

"Mara..." The Lady whispered and gestured to her hem. "You're showing seafloor..."

Mara drew a breath, nostrils flaring and knuckles white on the shaft of her spear. Were those tears that she saw, catching some of the light from the glowstones and her sister? Closer inspection of the goddess revealed that the dress of sea-silk indeed was showing seafloor in places. Odder yet, she trembled slightly.

"Then... I suppose I have to abide by your demand..."

Mara nodded. "Thank you."

Kirsty was not sure which of them it had been. Her stomach felt leaden though, as if she had just made a pact she would later regret. She examined her left hand and sighed. "Hidden... Why.. Who..?"

"So what do we do to find my niece?" Belara asked, before Kirsty had a chance to sink too far back into her thoughts. "Finnol certainly won't take this well."

"We call... Whoever is keeping her from me is much older and more powerful–"

"And more subtle..." The Lady brushed her skirts a bit, and a school of fish darted to the other leg.

Mara glared at her sister. "You're lucky you lost your name..."

Mara lunged at Kirsty, and on instinct she dodged. The dodge had been the wrong way though, and too hard. Her spirit separated from her body, which her aunt caught and lowered. Kirsty was unable to see the pallor and tightness of her face as she carefully lowered her physical encasement, falling through the stone altar where the lightning had struck instead.

Kirsty found herself plunging down a natural well, or at least so it seemed, the sheer rock walls rushing by her and the scent of water growing in her nose. There were passages that she could feel passing by, but she moved too quickly and it was too dark to see them.

Out of one of the tunnels poured forth an underground river, cascading down this aperture and changing its shape. She slipped into it and the coldness would have taken her breath if she truly breathed. Mingling with that roar now around her was the surge of the tide and scent of salt below. Then the crash came, the water surging up over her, literally rising to meet her as fast as she was plummeting to it.

Arms of fresh water from the underground river feeding this astral world-well drew her along one of the passages at the same time that the water deities swam beside her, and this then opened to reveal a chamber where the types of waters met in peace, instead of the war of currents she had just gone through. The cavern, strangely enough, had window-like apertures through which she could see the ebb and flow of tide through the seaweed.

Selkies – true selkies – went about their daily tasks outside, swimming and flipping past either in full seal form, or half form. None looked her way. There was no reason, despite the statues that she saw outside. Indeed, they seemed to be far too concerned with chasing fish and each other to pay her any mind.

"Well?" Mara pulled a purple sea kelp and anemone curtain over the more distracting of the openings.

Kirsty took a few more moments to process the change, and looked herself over as she realized that she could feel the water in her lungs. It took effort to remember that her real body lay in the stone circle.

Oddly, she felt a bit more complete here. She scanned the room, trying to find out why. The insides of her bones tingled as they had the first time David had told her he liked her.

Her eyes fell on a small stone chest, near a simple stone bench, both etched and worked with many of the changing creatures from the sea. This chest was heavily locked, and it was from here the magnetism seemed to be emanating.

"You could have warned her, or at least changed her so her mind would process this better," the Lady murmured, from by a silver basin near the middle of the room. She poured some water from a conch-shaped vessel into the scallop then placed a lightly glowing crystal into it.

"She knew we'd be taking her out of her body." Mara gathered Kirsty to herself and trundled her toward the basin, almost tenderly, with a few flicks of her tail. "She knows that we won't allow her to drown... for now."

Kirsty wasn't sure when the deity had shifted her form, but she settled where she was placed and gazed into the water at the crystal. "That's like the ones you showed me this summer, what you used to make it so David can swim with me while I'm preparing."

Mara nodded. "We like them, so we use them." She pulled a strand of Kirsty's hair and wrapped it around the crystal without taking it from the water.

Kirsty looked at Mara. Something was different about her here, more collected and smooth. Whale song rolled through the water, and the shark goddess closed her eyes for a moment.

Here, she was almost calm.

Almost.

Mara's eyes opened again and her gaze focused on the crystal. "Between the three of us, we should be able to lift some of that fog shrouding Etain so we can find her. Whoever it is, I doubt they'll expect a mortal calling on her own blood." Mara's gaze flicked to the Lady, "Don't say it Sister..."

The Lady sighed in exasperation. "Fine. But I'm right."

"I won't. No."

Kirsty listened, trying not to seem as if she were paying attention, but as suddenly as the door into the goddess' mind had opened, the opportunity had gone.

What had she missed that she needed to know?

"This isn't going to involve more of my blood, is it...?"

"Tears actually," The Lady answered, before Mara could. "Not just blood. The blood may come into play, but it will be later if it does."

Mara deflated slightly, but nodded in agreement. "Yes, we need both blood and tears. We will all gaze into the basin, and concentrate on your *máthair*. You will repeat our words, and you will know when to do so. The rest of the time you must be silent, or the call will go awry."

Kirsty nodded. Tears would be easy to produce, but she was not so certain that Mara would be able to. This was the softest that she could ever recall seeing her. The idea of the ever hungry, capricious, blustery goddess just did not go with the thought.

Then again, the sea wasn't always that way. More often than not, it was deceptively calm and gentle on the surface. Still, when her *seanmhuintir* died, it had been the Lady that had wailed for days after each occurrence... Mara had raged and stormed around the Point so much on the night of great grandfather's passing that she had destroyed both the lighthouse and the rock that had once lain off of it... and Mrs. Kitsch's childhood home. She remembered those nights of terror clutched by her mother by the hearth much later on the night of grandmother's passing.

"Do you understand?" Mara's voice, firm and unforgiving, cut into her thoughts, calling her back from pre-toddlerhood.

"I understand, my Ladies." Kirsty nodded.

"Good."

Mara wrapped her arms tight around Kirsty, and she stiffened at the unexpected gesture. Just as suddenly, Mara had released her and stepped back, an unreadable expression sliding over her face similar to statues she had seen in old library books of forgotten deities.

The dark hair fell around the deity's face as she hurriedly bent over the basin, sprinkles of phosphorescent starlight in the velvet of abyssal depths, and seven tears fell in quick succession. Each of those produced a percussion as strong as one of the great gongs the Director never allowed the students to use.

The Lady shook her head at Kirsty and pulled her forward, then silently shed seven tears, squeezing her right hand. The third set of seven soon joined the immortal tears, and with them memories of moonlit nights singing on the seashore and dreams of what might be when her mum returned home.

She was surprised when, after the tears landed and mingled, she had images of her mother as a laughing young child dancing before her eyes, as if she were there herself. Etain's dark hair, glinting red and black where the sun spun in it, whirled around her as the sand and spray kicked up around her. The arms in her vision that felt like her own held the laughing child up, Etain's arms wide and yearning like seal flippers for the wave. These arms holding her high to the sky were not her own though, nor the Lady's, clad instead with silver sharkskin from elbow to wrist.

The image morphed and changed, and years passed in a blink. The Lady sat on a rock where one of the underground streams burst out from the cliff to carve coves, and Etain paddled around after fish on a blazing summer day. There was laughter and clapping when Etain popped her head above water with a wiggling fish in her mouth – her first caught that way according to the knowledge that flowed to her – and the same skin flashing in her vision as the hands clapped.

Later, in that same pool, those arms were holding Etain and Finnol both. Behind the dark haired midwife, a full selkie with her skin spread waiting over the nearby rocks, the Lady stood, that ever translucent liquid hand resting on the midwife's shoulder. With a wash of pink slipped out a tiny, slick, and partly furred form which instinctively turned toward the surface before the midwife could catch it and check the child over. Here, she saw Mara fully, holding her parents – both exhausted looking – tightly and with unmistakable relief.

Mara was speaking, and she tried to listen, but the language was not one that she had ever heard before. Somehow, she understood it, and it was a long list of children, and statements of who she was.

Kirsty felt someone listening, one at first and then joined by others. The Lady took up the call next, repeating much of the same, but where her name should have been, she stopped abruptly to search.

There was nothing, and so that was what the Lady put into the call, the nagging sense of missing parts.

There was a stirring, a whispering, the clacking of looms and the shush of warp on weft with the feeling of being both everywhere and nowhere. Then Kirsty felt and heard her voice join in with this strange language welling up from within, releasing her hope and her fears for her mother like burbles of hot mud from unexplained and hitherto unexplored vents.

The story of her mother's life halted at the moment she had last seen her, and then stuttered forward. Kirsty could feel the goddesses sorting and sifting, searching for the thread forward, just as she was. The spell caught, time flowed forward.

Kirsty watched as her mother gave her life to clear a sickened and dying part of the sea, that fateful gyre draining her greedily of that strange thing they carried in their blood. Etain tried to take breath, and only got dead water devoid of life. A large shark nosed the half form back to the surface, then transformed herself and dragged the grey form onto the nearest large bit of flotsam... An aspect of Mara bent over the shell and gave that life back, driving the water from her lungs – Kirsty felt the pain that came with it – confirming some of the visions that had plagued her sleep.

She couldn't help the morbid thought that followed. *"That's one, isn't it three times the drowning man goes down?"*

Etain awoke and the *Sea Witch* brought its mistress aboard, then vanished. All that followed were blips, flashes of a strange Triton, a demolished throne room, followed by an endless sea of kelp.

They could feel Etain though in those blank places clouded over by woven mists that none of them could part for long enough.

Mara curled her lips and exposed her teeth in frustration. Her tail flicked to the side and hit Kirsty, not hard enough to do much, but it stayed curled around her.

The crystal in the basin glowed, switching rapidly from blue to purple-pink and back, faster and faster the more the power built. Kirsty had the strange intuition that similar conditions had happened in the creation of... something...

Then that intuition was gone and forgotten.

The sound of weaving intensified, attaining a maddening pace, the whooshing sound of a spinning distaff joined it, hastily producing more ammunition for whatever group of deities they now warred with.

As one, her goddesses asked the identities of those they were locked with, while Kirsty held her tongue. This language was now too ancient to understand at all, and she only had brief flashes of elderly women to go on. The number eluded her. Was it three, eight, nine? There was someone beyond them, someone that had stepped in.

Kirsty saw the flash of a pattern in the cosmic tapestry on a vast loom, if she had the time she could make out many other stories being woven – or to look ahead and see the outcome of her family's pattern.

She caught herself and redirected her focus to her mother, a single desire consuming her. Kirsty cared nothing for these balances and battles between the old ones. All she wanted was her mother safely at port, and for everything to finally be *right* and everyone to be *whole*.

"Let my Mum go."

She hadn't even been aware she'd said anything, thought that she had only thought it, but the battle of wills around her ceased. She felt little tiny threads, thicker cords and even cables fray and snap. Somewhere out there, a storm began, released by the sudden and unexpected break.

The sting was unexpected. Cords cut into her spirit as they broke around her, and she could feel the blood flow from the wounds. The goddesses had not escaped, in fact they seemed to take the brunt of it, both moving to block what they could from her without leaving their places.

For a split second she was back within the world-net. Blue eyes locked with her own, and then drove through her in confusion – dark blue as if held below the depths of the waves, and she saw her mother. Etain rested on her bed in the *Sea Witch*, still pale and haggard from the recent large uses of her magic.

Kirsty heard a shout, a deep male voice that shook the boat as surely as thunder... which followed. Etain got up hurriedly, looking toward the voice.

"So Mote It Be, then. We release her, little Changeling. She must weave her own fate home, and in exchange we take your destiny to shape instead." The Voices of the mysterious Weavers intoned, still faceless.

Kirsty felt sick, and the vision vanished. The Lady slumped and rested hands and forehead on the basin's edge. Mara pulled her close, still staring into the basin, now empty of water – odd for an underwater cavern.

"No... she wasn't supposed to speak yet..." Mara squeezed her tighter than she was likely aware, glaring into the basin, teeth bared and growling to herself. Then she lashed out at the basin with her tail, upending it.

"I have a general idea now where she was hidden... Sister! Get up and take her back. I will report when I can." Mara pushed Kirsty into her, waited for her to register and wrap her arms around the child, then tore out through one of the curtained openings, fading from sight.

Kirsty watched in confusion. "Who were they?"

"Others like us, child. With names far older than ours. At least, we think so. Ages of Old Ones are hard to calculate since we can count either from our Becoming or our finding our Names." The Lady of the Well replied.

"Older? I don't feel so well, my Lady..."

"Nor do I... But come, we must return. There will at least be news soon, and much time will have passed back on the material plane."

Kirsty could not help looking over her shoulder at the strange chest as she was drawn from the room and back to her body. Somehow, it felt as if she were losing something important all over again, before she'd fully had time to even know of it.

"I... don't think I want to go yet."

The Lady of the Wells and Waters gave her a knowing look, then pulled her along. "You will return, later."

Chapter Twenty Six
The Mark

Strange lights flickered around the stone circle, which served to attract more and more strange lights – these in the form of actual will-o-the-wisps. For the most part the night was calm and the breeze soft. The sky kept going between being cloaked in ragged clouds and clear to allow the littered sparks of stars to peer curiously at the Earth below.

Morvan's dread only deepened as he ranged and watched where he had been told. The terrain kept shifting around him, so he abided by the warnings not to stray too far without cause – if only for simplicity's sake! He was not meant for this demeaning post. His family had once whispered in the ears of rulers, and not to forget successfully taking down rival families! Here he prowled, cowering at the crunch of phantom feet on the ground, between people he didn't even like...and whatever it was that the Headmaster expected to cause the other students to even need protection...

Guirmean, for all he knew, was only blowing things out of proportion, and this Guardian business was a clever ploy to scare him for what he had done.

If so, why this knot of dread in his gut? What was that strange sensation that had passed between him and that half-blood? If this were indeed a plot simply to scare him into dropping the feud with the girl, then why use such levels of magic as was being done for this charade?

He looked again to where the Observers remained within their own protective circle. Guirmean stood watchful with his stang. His fellow students kept their gaze on the stones, faces marred by emotions he could not – would not – share.

The land directly around him shifted again, becoming lush forest heavy with the scent of rain. The wind kicked up, and he shivered.

A crash sounded to his right and he spun, brandishing his wand and flinging a rain of daggers without a second thought. They buried themselves in tree trunks, humming mockingly.

The cry came from his left. High, wild, and fierce it pierced the night and left the ribbons around his feet to trip him as he bolted. The smell of dead fish and old slime assailed his nose, but also the scent of musk and – perversely – birch.

He hadn't been aware of his own cry, but the others were. He ran past Guirmean, almost headlong into him, and would have kept going to plunge into the now glowing sphere around the Observers. However, he was yanked by the collar and spun back around to face the attackers.

At the same time Guirmean had been turning him back about, he had also been sending a pulse of energy to push the attackers back. The landscape shifted back to the seaside beach, and Morvan saw several dark and finny personages flung back, though others kept coming.

Those that dodged the blast displayed no fear. They brandished spears instead. Morvan could not be certain, but the assailants seemed to range in age from roughly eleven, to grizzled elders. Some wore armor that vaguely looked Nordic, while others wore only rags and rough-woven kelp covers. A few wore blue paint similar to the whorls Makay has slathered over her face, but somehow more sinister.

Commotion rose on the village side. Morvan knew no help would come from that quarter by the sound of Ainsley's war whoops. No, it would be up to the half he had been assigned to.

Guirmean hurled another spell, and then took a swipe with his stang at the attacker closest to him. The crane gave a raucous cry and rose off the end, flying into his face and battering with its wings, driving the green abomination back.

"Don't just cower there you lout!" Bartholomew shouted at him as he and Stanley passed by. "We're here to learn to do this!"

Darcy said nothing to him but focused on the Finmen with a snarl. The force of the fire he flung was more than was called for, damaging all of their night vision.

"Do not kill them." Guirmean called over the din, while his crane pecked and drove a Finman back. "Immobilize or drive them away, but do not kill. They are trapped as these."

Bartholomew thrust his wand, and it flared with light as he slashed. The unlucky Finman that was his target screamed as a hand separated – his right – and withdrew, clutching it to himself. Bartholomew followed, chasing and swinging his lightsword and shouting something that Morvan could not make out.

He found himself finally reacting other than to flee, using a rudimentary shield charm to deflect one of the spears flung his way.

"Why bother playing with him, this one's not worth the trouble." A deep male voice cut through the din nearby.

"He's been screaming for proof for years now and used my children. I'll warn him as gently as I will those others." The old woman from before answered, though he could not see where from.

The battle continued around him as he found time warping and the air taking on a gelatinous attribute around him. For the first time he wondered if this were all some strange dream.

The Finman now in front of him somehow had slipped into range before he noticed, so focused was he on the actions of the others and trying to piece together the nonsense he saw. Morvan's thought was that seaweed had grown fur and scales and was running toward him.

Morvan summoned a fireball from his wand. The dragon scales embedded in it complied happily, but the fire fizzled when the creature met it with a waterball of its own. The sea-eyed creature sneered at Morvan, enjoying the game of bringing down a wizard while his brethren kept the others busy.

"Didn't think non-humans had magic, boy?" The Finman

added a little more energy to his spell and the water continued onward, swamping Morvan, and he struck his head on the rock that materialized beneath.

Morvan fell through the earth into a forest of shadow where fears prowled as wolves and the snow was flung on sabered winds.

A stream of curses in the hated language Makay used followed him into this darkness, answered by equally energetic ones in yet more barbaric Finsper.

It took a few breaths to get used to the sensation of air moving in her lungs, the flow of her blood, and the beat of her heart. The ground below her was cold, and as hard as she remembered.

She could hear stirring, the other travelers settling into their bodies. Her aunt's voice sung the anchoring chants, rolling and twining, spinning the threads of body and soul together again.

Kirsty shook a bit, still too light. She had been close to some part of herself – she knew it. Her skin itched.

More than that, she awoke with the knowledge that she was still a pawn. There was little memory of what had transpired other than a terrifying fall into the waters of the realm of the Fey, and something about a loom.

Carefully, she sat up and looked around. Everyone checked each other over, the Headmistress examining them thoroughly and further anchoring those that needed it. Kirsty felt a little more normal after her aunt's hands settled on her shoulders and the solid power of earth weighed her down from her touch.

"There. All settled. It seems that some of you still have long nights ahead of yourselves though." Belara eyed Floyd and Ingrid closely. "Be sure to be careful in your dream hunts."

The pair nodded, glancing at each other and sharing secret smiles that prowled through night haunts and lonely dens.

Something tugged at the edges of Kirsty's consciousness. A frission of fear not her own buzzed along the energy line between the Participants and the Observers.

Her aunt was herding them out before she could comment, pale and her lips pressed tight. "Back now while we have the chance."

So quick were they herded that they were almost to the threshold before the first word. As the last of them stepped back to the world of the Anchor the energy field snapped closed on itself. The parallel worlds that they had accessed would be closed here until the next High Day.

Kirsty ran down the slope with the other Participants, toward the huddled Observers, toward whatever the threat to them was. At first it had been fear for her friends that stopped her heart, in case whatever had drawn the Guardians off had thought to have a silent third party attempt to break through. Then she caught sight of them.

"Finmen." Things narrowed to a point, as they did when she would work healing spells. A grin spread across her face and she broke out ahead of the descending group and blazed past the Observers. Tonight the Seelie and Unseelie would fight, and she would be part of the cosmic forces' churning.

They were hers. These she should and could hunt, and bring down whole-heartedly. Finmen were not mere fish.

It didn't matter that this emotion was out of character for herself. The part that noticed found itself shoved into the deepest recesses of her mind and stuffed under a large rock. There were enemies of her people here, her blood and bones sang of it.

The Headmaster and the Guardians here were steadily stunning and beating the Finmen back. On sight of what they were doing the darker parts of herself snarled in anticipation. Finally, some unrestrained opportunity to pay them back for the siblings she should have. Here was the chance to deal with the frustration that could not be taken out on those that kept her netted.

A burst of water caught her eye where it was overcoming the fire ball Morvan had thrown. It had to be him, the dueling styles of the others were more substance and less flash. He tended to rely on methods that impressed. The others cared more for effectiveness. Morvan was not a bad duelist and even scored many points against her during dueling club (before her aunt banned them both – her for attempting to drown him after a comment about her mother, and he for making a comment that the Headmistress insisted in both parents coming "for a *meeting*"). He lacked whatever it was that made David's fire snakes so effective.

While Stanley froze three Finmen in ice, the Headmaster dropped another large handful with a sleep spell, and Bart caused a few others to go running from the light blast he unleashed, the Finman's water blast overpowered her rival.

She screamed, unleashing the sonic weapon that Cerridwen restored on healing her throat fully. She may not like him, but he was a member of her school. In this primal state, school equated enough to clan to warrant defense against something more hated.

Kirsty leaped over where Morvan lay, not even bothering to draw her wand. She thrust her hands out while the Finman held his ears and reeled back. Instinctively she let her feelings rush along her arms and out the centers of her palms. Any water that hers met was subjugated to her own will and rushed along with hers over the creature, where it swirled.

She snarled, teeth fully bared and her eyes flared. Momentum was carrying her forward, and if she could just make contact she could let loose the poison building inside.

Wood and stone struck out at her unexpectedly, toxic energy of its own arching out to meet her. Only quick hands and a wrench of her body turned her in time to slide along the spear's staff and connect with her feet instead.

There wasn't time to ponder where a formerly unarmed Finman had gotten another spear from. She only had time to switch the polarity of the release – and hope it went out through her feet instead – without making herself ill.

She felt the shock reverberate through her, and her knees buckled. The ground met her bum not long after – too quickly to land gracefully. Kirsty rolled away as the male attempted to make use of her comparative inexperience.

She was dizzy, too dizzy, but she glared as her eyes met her adversary's. It was odd how they looked like her parents' eyes. She saw the roiling depths there and the tumultuous waves.

It only infuriated her more.

"Vile abomination!" She spat in her first tongue.

"Said the kelp to the seagrass," he hurled and grimaced. "Halfbreed harlot." With a heave he was on top of her and slashing with black poison tipped claws.

This was the last. The rising tide within broke and the shield spell she had been practicing with burst out and thrust him away as the claws contacted.

Kirsty lay gasping. She saw the flash of green that meant her aunt had passed by somewhere in her range of vision. There was the sound of the male's cry. The sounds of battle ceased. All that could be heard for three heartspans was the sound of the sea.

She got up and looked around. The Observers huddled in the circle, wands out.

"Huh... I wonder why humans are supposed to use wands..." Kirsty smiled at the absurdity of the thought.

Ainsley and his party she could see moving around through the debris, helping to drag away the felled Finmen, back to the sea. The Headmaster was bent over Morvan, but she couldn't see exactly what he was doing.

"When did they get here? Blazes, I don't care..." "I make bollocks of things..." She mused aloud, then moved closer to see what she needed to do.

If she went near those things again, she knew she would berserk again. At least with the *Things* it was accepted if one temporarily lost themselves.

Morvan's eyes were open when she got there, and fell on her.

"I had him. You interfered." He hissed at her, weakly.

"I hope you weren't getting a grade on this..." Kirsty countered. "Didn't you learn yet that large amounts of water beats weeny fireballs?"

Morvan tried to respond, but his eyes crossed and then closed. She almost laughed for getting the last word, except he *had* recently hit his head.

Guirmean pressed his eyes shut and rubbed between his eyes firmly. "Miss Makay, Detention, my office tomorrow at 21:00."

"Yes sir."

✐

"There has never been so many, Artair... Not since..." Belara broke herself off and pressed her lips together.

The Headmaster hrmed and nodded, then returned to mending the bump on the back of Morvan's head. His eyes focused on unseen vistas as he concentrated on the inner ministrations.

"Aye Headmaster. 'N they didnae head for the village like I would have expected. Like they was after sumthing, sir." Ainsley crossed his arms. "Wiped many a memory tonight."

"At least it was not the *Things*. The distraction arranged earlier at least seems to have worked."

"An' yer said my idea was a barrel o' crackers..." Ainsley huffed a bit, flashing teeth in a satisfied smirk.

"The white and red cloaks rarely lend their aid for anything not related to the water. I doubt they will do it again once the *Things* are calm again." Belara hissed, her eyes flicking to Kirsty and back – too swift for the students to catch it.

Kirsty flinched, pulling her cloak more tightly around herself and looking at the ground. If her ears could, she would droop them. As it was she had the disturbing feeling of non-existent whiskers drooping from her lips.

"Please don't argue." Guirmean interjected, finishing. "It was worse than expected, but not as bad as what could have been. We are all here, safe, and various communities will be going on as they should."

The students gathered together. While the adults conferred the Observers stepping out of their circle as soon as the Anchor was released.

Kirsty glared toward the sea, silently daring any more Finmen to materialize, even though there were likely no reinforcements. She sulked as it fully sank in that she had done yet another favor for Morvan. *"Unicorns, and now Finmen... What next?"* The left corner of her lips lifted at her thought, *"An ashray?"*

"Maybe the *bean-fionn* when it warms up enough for him to get in the loch." Imp whispered in her ear after hopping invisibly to her shoulder. "He's irritating the deities, Mistress. The Cailleach is cross with him."

Kirsty tried to step discretely away from the group, before they were finished discussing and preparing Morvan for the transport back.

"I didn't ask you to spy on him..." She frowned, speaking barely loud enough for it to reach her shoulder as he worked his way into her clothes.

"He was acting funny before you got hurt, so I went."

"Kirstin... dunnae wander off." Ainsley called, turning his head after glimpsing the movement. "While we was over village-side there were signs of *Thing* activity."

"No sir." She agreed, shifting back toward the group with a shudder. She couldn't help clutching her belly at the thought of them coming this way.

They likely would come, after such a large concentration of the Finmen, and the recent battle. Her adrenaline rush was ebbing now, leaving her sick to her stomach, and her limbs feeling strangely heavy and shaky.

The headmaster tapped on the travel-stone again once the crane alighted back on his staff and returned to its inanimate form. Ainsley clutched Morvan, curling his lip a bit in displeasure. Kirsty tried to avoid Morvan's draped hand, but was unable to do so in the press of bodies as each gripped the key for the transport through the matrix.

She snarled at his touch, even though he was unconscious for the trip. Instead she fixed her gaze stubbornly on the spot where her aunt and Guirmean's hands touched each other as they grasped the stang together.

With effort she considered the contrast between their hands, and the way the rivers ran beneath their skins through the earth bones – anything to keep her thoughts from chewing over the service she had done him, even if he were now deeper in her debt. A flapping pulled her from her thoughts. Kirsty turned her head, ignoring the nausea that came with the view change. Time began to stretch again, it should not take nearly so long to return. Then she saw the raven where it followed them, morphing into the spectral black robes of the Cailleach.

Instead of the bone pale skin she was used to glimpsing the rare times she saw this goddess, the Cailleach was more blue tonight. Her finger reached out and prodded Morvan, stabbed was a more accurate description. The cold descended, as if there were several *Things* already there and preparing to drag her soul away to rend and feast upon.

Just as quickly, she was gone again.

Morvan screamed but did not wake.

The stone outside the castle gate was below them once more. Ainsely nearly dropped Morvan at the scream. All eyes swiveled to Kirsty afterward.

"I didn't do anything! Why do you all act like I did whenever he screeches?" Kirsty glowered around at her classmates, daring them to say any different and her hair waving in the breeze like jellyfish tentacles in a current. She continued softly and looked around. "I don't like what I feel."

Ingrid smiled a bit at Kirsty. Normally it was good to see Ingrid smile, it usually came before a hand clap and an attempt to mimic her steps while people drummed out a tune. This time it made her heart pound and the ice flow. "I feel it too. *They* are close."

"Indeed." Guirmean waved a hand and the gate opened with a silver ripple, invisible curtains rolling back to expose the silver screens.

They moved quickly along the path. Kirsty was not certain whether it was the Headmaster or the Headmistress that loaned wings to their heels and the winds to their step. The distance was covered swifter than normal all the same, and she made a note to ask about that spell and the possibility of learning it at another time. It would certainly prove useful if she could talk it out of them.

The group passed through the great doors and the Examiners awoke to watch them. Kirsty could feel them prodding their minds for the results of the excursion. Each Moot at Artenhame was more than simple ritual, and although technically extracurricular for centuries their performance also affected their grades in the appropriate subjects. She could almost hear their thoughts and comments on what she had done as the group paused with their own momentary daze.

"Still only able to act defensively best when it's for others, lassie? You'd be well served fixing this." "Waterwitch. My thanks for assisting my snakelet, I will take this into account when discussing Defense scores with his head of house." "What have you learned about yourself, young lady? Come talk to us later, while the other two sleep." The voices whispered and turned in her head.

"Return to your houses, students. Remember to be working on your reports tomorrow." Professor MacLeòmhann murmured.

The three adults took Morvan to the Healer's wing. The

students paused for a bit, exchanging quiet goodnights. Ally shuffled, and then hesitantly pecked Thomas on the cheek, his eyes widening. Ally's knees nearly gave out below her at her boldness, then she dashed up the stairs before he could see her blush. The rest of her housemates followed thoughtfully, some grinning.

Kirsty eyed Ingrid as they followed Ally, Floyd, Darcy, Bartolomew, and Nevin. Ingrid darted a small smile to Floyd when he glanced back before looking back to Kirsty.

"What did she do? What's happening?" Kirsty hissed, leaning close as they took the stairs.

"Justice. What else happens when one of the dark goddesses has someone in need of correction come so close?" Ingrid said with a satisfied nod. "That is the realm of the Cailleach, after all."

"Cannae I be allowed to work out the scales for myself in my own way without her getting involved?" Kirsty's nostrils flared as they whispered. "Not that I'm not honored by the attention," she amended in a rush as her eyes darted around, in case the deity was listening and took offense. "I just would sometimes like to be a wee bit normal what with being different even among our own."

"You two coming? I'd like to get to the commons and thaw myself by the fire, especially after seeing those monsters." Nevin's voice broke in from the front of the line.

"Coming, coming. Kirsty's just being overly troubled." Ingrid replied. "Maybe we'll be lucky and someone's pinched some cider."

"We could all use some before bed." Darcy nodded, pausing in front of Mrs. Bloomsworth, who had a visitor.

An older woman with polished silver shot through faded flame hair, clad in a brown leather corset, white blouse, red velvet skirt, tooled baldric and a white cloak carelessly tossed over her shoulder leaned against the painted wall and watched the group. A bold grin flashed as she tipped a feathered tricorn hat at them, winking conspiratorially at Corriander's comment.

Kirsty blinked and flushed under the combined gaze of the two.

"Could use some what, children?" Bloomsworth eyed them, tapping fingers on opposing arms and raising brows to her blonde hairline.

"Some cocoa, Madam." Floyd slipped in. "It was a cold night and a bigger test of our skills to go with the ritual than we were prepared for."

The door guardian eyed them dubiously.

Her guest did not bother to hide her grin or her bark. "Myself would favor a bit o' grog before, or perchance a measure or two of the rum *in* the cocoa."

"Don't encourage them Kara..." Mrs. Bloomsworth glared briefly in her direction.

"Oh, we were young once. No harm in a mug of something after a night out, just to brace and get the sails brought in before going below deck."

"With your advice their 'sheets would be full to the wind' as I believe you've put it before."

Kara shrugged, then covered her ears. "Proceed to deliver thine cipher, and carry on me hearties. Live hard before the sea or fire might take ye." She gave an exaggerated wink, causing her friend to groan, and all but one of the Leomaris students to giggle.

Kirsty, however, only flushed and studied her shoes, finding the leather scuffed and already in need of replacing.

"Mizzenmast, crow's nest, and the North Star." Floyd leaned forward while whispering the phrase, and Nevin sighed in relief at not having to try remembering the phrase, more complicated than the last week's.

The entrance opened. Only after each of the students had gone inside and the door shut behind them did Kara slip away to relay her message... hoping that the recipient was at the other end of the few portals left and that she would not have to lob things at the exterior of her canvas to get his attention.

There was no one up still when they got to the common room, but somebody had left some mugs, bottles, and a pitcher on one of the tables. The fireplace flared up as they approached.

"Ally's getting bold, making advances on Thomas like that." Bartholomew waggled his eyebrows at Ally, "You'll have him all thumbs and I'll wind up turned into a toad while he's fiddling with his term project in Talismanic Magic." He poured out some of the cider from a bottle. "Oh look, Floyd gets his cocoa."

Ally colored and flumped down by the fire, next to Kirsty's slumped form. "It's... not like that Bart."

"Yeah right. He's liked you since first year. You just refused to listen to any of us." Darcy brought them over mugs of the cider while Floyd got comfortable in one of the chairs with both cider and coco.

Kirsty gazed into the flames, slipping her fingers into her pouch. They plunged past the wrapped vials, brushing them even in this state soothed her blood somewhat. She wrapped her fingers around her scrying crystal and drew it out sleepily. Her other hand accepted the mug, and she sipped with a nod to her companions.

"Told you so, didn't I? You'd have seen the way he almost fell if you hadn't run off so fast." Kirsty said quietly, trying to join the conversation so as not to worry Ally about slipping into a brood.

Ingrid settled on the arm of Floyd's chair to drain her drink. "As inevitable as battle and the winding sheet."

"That's disturbingly morose, comparing love, war, and death." Kirsty sipped after that and clutched her crystal tighter. She wasn't sure why, but she felt a little closer to David when she did, a little more anchored. "Gods and spirits help whatever man you choose to marry, Ingrid."

"Truly a terrifying thought! That could mean baby Ingrids running about – with scissors." Bartholomew clutched his chest in mock horror.

"Baby's first spear, more like." Floyd smirked before quaffing a full quarter of the mug. "You can find it on the centerfold of Warrior Times Daily, now with Accura-Flight. Good for getting you to Point Z and impaling your enemies."

Everyone stared at Floyd. "My gods... I was joking." He cried.

"I want one..." Ingrid replied.

"I don't know... I think mini Floyds are scarier. Imagine coming home from work, opening the door, and getting swamped by a pack of Creightons." Darcy swirled his mug a bit, looking into it thoughtfully. "Scarier than werewolves even."

Kirsty tensed. "I doubt all werewolves are bad."

"Rather respectable opinion." Floyd kicked his shoe off in Darcy's direction, which Darcy carelessly leaned over to let past. "I always figured that there were more types than what we learn about in class. I was looking in the Mythology stacks a week ago to find more on Herne and Kernunnos for the term paper, just to see if I could learn a bit more about the dogs. I found something about Herne that looked promising, but it was in Old German."

"Mythology...just doing your homework is an adventure..." several of the students intoned together.

Ally looked at the group. "I don't understand why you lot put yourselves through this. Why do you go to these deities and how do you get Bound?"

"Some of us don't have a choice. We're born into it and into a role." Kirsty looked at her friend. "My mum was born for this. Before that, Mara had a little more choice in who from the family line she chose for it."

"But why?" Ally asked, leaning forward and cupping her mug.

Kirsty shrugged. "Mara's got her reasons. She's always liked the family." She hedged, thinking of some of the intimations from the musty book she'd found first year. She still went back to it often, drawn by the strange fur cover.

"Others of us choose it because we want to learn a bit more about the *why* of life being the way it is. Example: Why are the different worlds kept separate?" Floyd picked up for Kirsty. "And then we have people like Ingrid, who get chosen because of their winning personality and craving for justice in the land." He struck a valiant pose for which he received a smoldering glare.

"So...why do you think Thomas Participates?" Ally mused.

Kirsty yawned and put her crystal back in her pouch. She pulled her drop spindle out instead and a bit of the hyppocampus wool she'd been working, causing Ally to doubletake when she began work. "Maybe a combination. Did you ever notice how hard it was to even hear, much less remember, his last name during the first couple years?"

The wool slipped through her fingers as the spindle span. She began humming as the cider finally began to circulate through her system. Her muscles relaxed as her eyes focused, and she could feel the gaze of the others. The others grew quieter, also relaxing and beginning to yawn.

"So... who is his deity then?" Ally pressed.

Kirsty looked up at her. "You'd have to ask him. It's not our place to tell you. Remember that not everyone can be open about their connections with the Fey *or* the Deities."

Ally nodded, eyes still fixed on the spindle and Kirsty's work. Kirsty continued humming, not paying attention to the time. She was a little leery of going to lay down, and this served a good excuse as well as helping the others settle.

Ingrid was the first to get up. "I should go. I think my body's ready, and I'm being Called."

Floyd nodded. "Same. It's been a long day." He looked at Kirsty. "I'm glad you were given your voice back. Try to get some sleep tonight...and maybe ask your bloke to come be your Observer Anchor the next High Day, or one of the Guardians."

Kirsty nodded and smiled a bit, but only slightly. "Will ask him then, but I won't be here for Yule."

"Well bugger... Maybe you could talk him into becoming a regular Guardian anyway, in case Slimy gets detention again and another lesson in whatever Lilitu was being schooled on..." Floyd grinned a bit. "Maybe he could 'slip' then, knock him down, and he'll be out of our way again."

"I don't know about a 'regular,' Floyd... He does have an awful lot on his own plate, so no promises." She finished up and stowed her spindle, causing Ally to jump and fall out of the trance she'd been lulled into.

Ally followed Kirsty to their dorm in a daze, nearly walking into the wall when the stairs curved. Kirsty frowned, keeping her ear on her friend as they walked and trailing her fingers over the old stone, absentmindedly gathering up some of the condensation.

They fell into bed readily, Ally curling up around her pillow and Kirsty checking to make sure that no one had switched out her muffle-charmed pillow. For a while Kirsty was allowed to just simply sleep, floating in a sea of solitude and silence. It was soft and silken as her mother's sealskin, like when her mother wrapped it around her while she was sick, thankfully not coarse and scratchy like Da's chest-hair—comforting though that was—and she could feel that she was not truly alone in this sea.

She paddled toward the presence, or tried to, one slow flip of her tail after another and floating between. Eventually she found a warm form and bumped into it, dissolving into comfort and the familiar scent.

An interminable time passed and the warm form was swept away by swiftly growing swells. Rain pelted her face and she turned over to her belly again, still keeping her head above water and holding her fins out to her side for some stability as she tried to take stock.

The swells continued growing and she found herself heaved skyward. She flailed when the water left her, keeping her mouth shut against the scream she would have liked to voice. While up and defenseless in the sky she could see the waves beating against rocks, and a craft being inexorably pushed in their direction.

She fell again, back into the sea, and the silver bubbles streamed around her in the depths till she fought her way back to the surface. Kirsty knew she needed to make landfall, or to wake. There was no land though, and the current was drawing her to the rocks as well.

Chapter Twenty Seven
Pyramids and Problems

Time and place hath no ken
Upon or below sea's waves when
Outside of mortal land mariners wend
And sea and sky no longer bend.

Beware sea witch upon the sea
The sirens of the briny deep
Do not all take the form of fin and cheek
For those that homeward wending seek.

Well ye fare and fare ye well
Riding sea and breasting swell
Avast, avast, and mind the cry
From under sea and sundered sky.

Etain arrowed after her quarry through the warm waters and the slippery blades of seaweed. Her whiskers would have quivered with anticipation if her speed would have let them. Once she caught up to the shiny silver fish a snap of her jaws brought half of it into her mouth. Another snap sent the rest of its sweet flesh to join the previous half in her belly, fins and all.

"Kirstin would love this. I hope that I get to be the one to teach her how to fish like this. Just not here." The thought was far below and behind the rest of her mind focused on the hunt.

As she swam in search of more sweet fish the blades slipping past her flippers grew wider but less frequent until she found herself in a clearing. The light filtered down through the blue water in bars, occasional bubbles rising to the surface like sparkling gems. In confusion she turned around and around, catching a glimpse of Mimir tailing her, before heading to the surface for another gulp of air and to decompress her lungs.

She was having to grab air far more often than normal. It had been very long since she had to surface quite as often as this.

The burning in her lungs threatened to make her breathe in the water, which she could not do in this full form. The surface drew closer, too slowly for her patience, until finally her head burst free and the breeze cooled her and tickled her now quivering whiskers.

Etain gulped the air lustily, feeling the smoothness of it filling her lungs and stilling the burn and itch. She spread herself out as much as she could to make the work of staying afloat easier, gulping until her panting ceased and her ears stopped ringing.

Filling her lungs a last time, she dove down again, back down to the clearing. She stopped beside Mimir, who looked greenish and far more fishlike in this light. Together they peered deeper, trying to spot the source of the bubbles. It was too far from where they were, and with a brief glance together they gave up their spot and followed them down, he gripping his trident and she... extending her claws slightly, all that she could do in this current form.

Finally they reached the floor of the sea, where the corals sprawled over glowing sands and tiny rainbows of fish darted in and out of the hollows. Etain snapped at one curiously, her hunter's instinct screaming at her to try one of the fleshier looking ones for sustenance.

She grimaced at Mimir, and he didn't even bother to hide his chuckle at her grimace, or the way her nose wrinkled. Her cobalt eyes glowered at him in return. He only grinned wider and showed the pearls of his teeth to her. Etain turned her nose up at him and swam on.

"Well you could have asked if they were good eating." Mimir chortled a bit longer, then let it go. "You're getting grumpier, Brinetreader."

"I know, and I don't know why." She replied.

"I hear human females get grumpy a few days every month

for bleeding..."

"Yes, they do. And it's nae that. Ah, what's that over at the end of the larger bubbles?" She pointed with her flipper to emphasize.

They swam over the reef and the sand, and as they went the glow seemed to get brighter. The corals faded back the closer they came, leaving only the sand around the polished quartz pyramid that rose up from it.

"This is certainly not one of Mara's..." Mimir observed, scanning for an opening.

"Might belong to another sea goddess. It seems to be tied in with the matrix though."

As they circumnavigated the base the quartz projected soft rainbows through its faces, rippling and swirling now and then with untold changes. Finally they found a slight imperfection on the northmost face, as if here another crystal had once grown and since been removed. Here, looking inward, they could see the ghost crystals of smaller pyramids inside, nested like a Russian doll set.

Etain's eyes clouded and the seal drifted closer to that strange indentation with its healed striations. Gently, her nose bumped against it and rested at the most indented place. A soft smile curled the lips as the eyes drifted shut, and she went limp so that her body laid against the side. Strangely, she did not slide.

The whole pyramid glowed a soft blue, sliding swiftly to indigo and then violet. A few bubbles escaped from the seal's nose.

Mimir prodded her, thinking that perhaps she had been lulled to sleep by this strange object, much the way that she had gone inward before when he had seen her manipulating energy and working deep magics. On his touch he did not find a dozing selkie, but a stream of information and consciousness.

Murmurs of voices – male and female – filled his head just as Etain's voice filled his own while she was in this form. The babble was in more languages than he knew, old and new, but there was a definite cadence as if all whispered and sang of the same secrets. They reminded each other of things that had been, plotted over what would be and what was now.

They fell through the crystal into the pyramid, then through the next.

A tendril of energy snaked around them and drew them to the centermost. Here there was no water, yet Mimir did not dry. Here there was no air, yet Etain breathed. More energy swirled and condensed, a large translucent face that morphed between the features of several races materializing before them before shrinking down to their size.

Like Mara her skirts were the seas, but she was rounder, softer, darker. Suitable to the Americas these skirts were composed of a loincloth, secured with a gold brooch set with pearl and turquoise. Her breast binding was likewise secured and her dark hair spilled long beneath the gold and feather headdress while turquoise eyes measured them. On her chest she bore a heart icon, likely the result of the conceptions of those that currently fed her combining her in their minds with Mary, and great gold bangles dangled from her ears as Calypso peeked through, further mashing together what was once separate. Mama Qoca regarded them quietly.

"Why have you come so far? Neither of you belong here. None have blundered to my home since the days of pirates seeking safe islands for treasure, save for the female aeronaut Amelia that kept me company until her end."

Etain's eyes cleared and she fixed them on the goddess. *"I do not know all of it. But I will tell you how we came to be here."* She then related all her tale, as respectfully as if she were speaking to Mara herself.

The goddess was silent and shifted her gaze upward for long moments, then her eyes rolled back in her head. Something about her stillness led both mortals to wonder if she were listening elsewhere. Around them the crystal pyramid continued flashing and rippling the rainbow array of colors, filling swiftly with mist.

"I can help in part... but I need a return gift..." Mama Qoca's voice and look shifted more toward that of Calypso and Yemaya, and her voice took more of a Jamaican lilt. "Some of his people may come take refuge in my seas, but not all. There is a suitable place a day's travel within my territorial border. In return, some of the kelps that are in this bed I require to be taken back into the mortal realm."

"This seems reasonable so far, but I must still help secure homes for those left after...I assume there will be a Choosing for the refugees." Mimir stroked his beard as he thought. "Something is missing yet though..."

"I can help with the resowing." Etain nodded emphatically. *"And if they are of use for potions and medicines, I know that my daughter is very likely to help protect them and encourage the propagation. But which way is out?"*

"Ah herein comes the rest. Getting out of my sanctuary is not so easy since I have had to close the passages. You will have to go the long way and leave by the Rock that Drowns." The voice had changed yet again, and it was becoming clear that the more they talked with this sea deity, that it was not so much several that had been mashed together by time, disbelief, and forgetfulness of magic, but instead several deities concerned with their overlapping areas that had been attracted and temporarily fused.

"What is with you deities giving the child such impossible tasks?" Mimir grabbed Etain and picked up the seal easily, yanking her back and holding her as if she were a cherished doll that godly children feuded over. "The Rock that Drowns has to ability to even drown water breathers like myself! One sea goddess eats her selkie whole, another offers hope of partial completion of one of her missions... and then sends her off to drown?"

"Mimir Merisson, shhhh! Shhhh! SHH!" Etain shrilled in his mind.

"HOLD YOUR TONGUE MORTAL, LEST I RETRACT MY OFFER OF ASYLUM TO YOUR PEOPLE AND STRIKE

YOU BOTH WHERE YOU STAND FOR TRESPASSING!"

The crystal around them flashed red and yellow like molten lava. There was a cracking sound before a low rumble, which then cut off after a moment.

Etain shivered and flailed, trying to get out of Mimir's well-meaning grip. *"Tritons! There was a reason they were so few!"* She could feel the water answering its area deity, and the seafloor shifting as that deity's ire stirred the slumbering earth below. *"There will be another earthquake sometime soon here at this rate. Tsunami! No, nonono."*

Etain had the horrible vision of a great swell rushing outward and crossing between the realms, piling onto itself, rising meters and then meters of meters before crashing over islands and devouring all those on land that it could.

"I accept it, I accept it. Just. Lady... please calm yourself. Please!" Etain could not help the tears that welled and spilled as she thought of all the people that might be hurt, wherever and whenever the tsunami would cross over.

Something in the tears gave the goddess pause, and the swelling reversed until she was once more the size of a mortal. Curiously, Mama Qoca collected the burgeoning drops as they rolled down the seal's face. They coagulated, almost becoming gems in her hand and refusing to meld together.

"You cry for those you do not even know... You are a strange creature..." The deity placed one of these in her mouth experimentally, savoring the flavor of salt and... Love? Compassion? Sacrifice?

"Ah yes... I remember these... and more... It has been so long... Perhaps this is why that Mara keeps her little experiments." Mama Qoca thought, then continued aloud, "I will accept this... offering... and forgive the insult for now. Go north, and you will find the crossing by a twilight."

Mama Qoca placed another pearled tear into her mouth, savoring its sweetness and slipping into thought. The colors of the pyramid calmed, returning to the original soft rainbow hues.

Mimir glared at the little seal-woman for caving so quickly and actually shedding tears. To think that he had begun respecting the abominable mix that she was.

"Yes Lady... Thank you." The seal dipped, as if attempting a curtsy in this form, and ended up in a graceful loop.

Mama Qoca watched, and as she consumed the tears and watched the languid antics of his companion Mimir began to notice a change in the foreign water goddess.

"Perhaps it wasn't weakness at all that had produced the tears." He mused.

The energy that had pulled them in released its hold and began pushing them back out. Etain rode the energy, slipped through it and played with it like the tendrils were her own Lady's fingers.

When far enough away that Mimir was certain he would not rouse the deity again he grabbed the seal where her armpits would be and forced her to look at him. "Just what, by Mara's Fin, do you think you are doing by accepting such a task and then making tears?"

"The tasks I was born for, helping you find refuge for at least some of your people, finding a chance to get my tail home, protecting your scaly tail, and doing a little Healing. When I get back to the *Order* I will find out who is not doing their job here. Let go! I've work to do, and I'm still hungry too."

Etain wriggled free, wrinkling her nose at him, then once out she followed the energetic prompts that she received, gathering the samples that she had been bidden. She had, after all, given her word. Was this not also part of her duties, whether it was Mara or not?

Etain gave up on trying to keep track properly of how many days had passed since that day, even though she continued to dutifully mark them off in her voyage log and to plot the locations and conditions of where her samples had been taken. According to her log she had been out for six months now *since* meeting up with Mimir. Surely that could not be accurate. Even so, her stores had run dangerously low and she had been forced more and more to rely on the sea's bounty.

Luckily the kelp bed had plenty of fish slipping though the blades. There had been plenty of the fish and kelp rolls, and simply just swallowing down raw fish while hunting. It made things stretch, and she could conjure food...but was magic worth the expense just to have a varied diet?

Hunting had its drawbacks as well. The longer she slid through the sea as a full seal the more difficult it became to remove her skin. Currently she floated on her back trying to get her claws into the seam to pull it apart. Mimir flicked his tail steadily to tread water, keeping his arms out under her in case the change went badly.

He'd already had to throw her onto the deck once this week when she got herself caught far enough out of it she could have drowned.

Her claws finally found purchase, and she dug deep into her skin, and then winced again as they slid into her tender other skin. Etain's sharp teeth caught the light as she grimaced. Even after all these years of having the skin she never fully got over the sting and burn, the spreading fire, at the sensation of ripping into herself.

Perhaps it was a side effect of still carrying human blood in her veins. She could earn her sealskin and be a selkie and had the opportunity to renounce her human heritage after, so that she could be a full selkie. Etain had chosen instead to continue bearing the bloodlines of both her parents once she had earned it. What would Kirsty's choice be?

Etain pulled, and her sealskin did not slip off. It took several tries, and several whimpers, before she was able to peel and yank enough away to wiggle out and then stow the skin in the pouch.

She needed to get home soon.

The burn continued as her human skin and the gashes in it contacted the saltwater. She hissed in order to keep from crying out, and instead hauled herself back onto the *Sea Witch* via the rope the vessel dropped over her side for her mistress. The boat rode the swells calmly, but the entire vessel listened and waited.

Etain managed to catch her breath when she finally dropped to the deck. Looking down she saw eight lines through her skin and half-pelt where the blood was welling and already beginning to run down.

"How bad is it?"

"Not good, not bad."

"Honestly Brinetreader."

"An eighth of a claw deep, eight of them. I may scar though by the way they lie. Just a flesh-wound, honestly."

"A flesh-wound that rightly shouldn't happen. You've been getting weaker since the day we met *her*." Mimir rose up on a swell and held it in place so that he could see for himself.

Etain tried to cover herself and obscure the wounds, looking down and away, and pursing her lips in a frown. "I know, the only thing I can think of is that Mara's influence is weaker here."

"Another thing that should not happen, or so logic would say." The Triton threw himself to the deck and allowed the water to fall again. "Let me look better."

She allowed him to move an arm away from where she clutched them around herself. Mimir scowled out from behind his frothy beard and brows. Etain's skin was paler than the day before, paler even than before their hunt, and her flesh had gotten spongier. Turning his attention to the wounds, he discovered that already the edges were turning red, and that lines of it were spreading.

"Poisoned claws?" He examined her nails more closely, searching for a duct or traces of venom paste below them.

"No, that would be my Finnol what has those. Or I didn't have poison the last I could have used that Gift." Etain lay down and looked toward the cabin. Her vision was getting a little hazy and speech came strangely. It almost reminded her of a long ago night of courting where the Claiming got a little too rough.

This was a lot less pleasurable though, and Finnol wasn't here to clean out the wound and administer the antidote he kept with him for his poison. Her hands weren't shaking yet, but she felt strangely dissociated from her body as she slipped a hand into the pouch and felt around for a box.

"I know it's here somewhere... Medic kit, where are you?" Etain grumbled.

Now that the thought was more firmly formed, she could find it in the layers of equipment. She sighed when she found the familiar scuffed corner and pulled it out, far larger a box than one would expect to be shoved into a waist pouch. Very quickly she flipped the latches and rifled through for the tube of pinkish *sgrios-puinnaein* that her daughter had insisted she start keeping.

Kirstin had worked long on her final project for her Potionry class the last year, refining the fast-acting fluid. More than an anti-venom, and more than an anti-poison, it was her daughter's bid to show that advanced potions could be produced solely from sea items. It was one of the few things known to neutralize even Byron's poison from frill and foam.

The vial slipped from her fingers and would have rolled away if not for Mimir's quick retrieval.

Etain sighed and laid her head down on the cool deck. Her body went between fire and ice, but always screamed where she had dug too deep. She looked at the triton through the haze over her eyes.

He quirked an eyebrow at her, and she nearly laughed at how much it looked like a true sea horse galloping over a wave crest. "So, do I pour this medicine in, or do you drink it?" Mimir growled as he uncapped it.

"Put it on the wounds... then pour a line's worth into the dose cup in the medic kit. I'll drink that just to be sure to get the infection from both ends." Her voice sounded too quiet to her own ears.

He did as asked, and lifted her up enough that she could drink.

"Line's worth indeed... as if I know what a line's worth is. The big line or those tiny ones? Females," he thought.

Chapter Twenty Eight
The Rock That Drowns

The lantern hissed where it hung from the cabin beam spraying its soft white light indiscriminately and rocking gently with each movement of the *Sea Witch*. The soft creaks and groans almost sounded like a gentle lullaby. Etain drew a long breath, filling her lungs and bringing in the scent of the blanket that was finally beginning to lose the last traces of Finnol's scent.

Etain had more than lost track of how much time had passed on this voyage. In truth, she wasn't sure how much time had passed in the human world. A day in Faer or any of the other realms might span one hundred years in her own, or even the reverse was true.

It was dark, despite her lantern, and it was cold. These things crouched eagerly outside the light's reach and waited to sneak in to claim her again. Once it claimed her she knew the cold would crouch in her bones and chip its way through. Etain was only distantly aware of this. More pressing was the state of her belly, where it twisted on itself, and that of her mouth. That remained dry and parched no matter how much liquid she managed to drink. Her fresh water stores were gone, and she was left with trusting the purifying equipment to process seawater into foul tasting artificial freshwater—or to use her magic.

The use of her magic had waxed more difficult with each passing day. Overuse was something that she'd never experienced before. Or maybe it was simply weakness from not having enough to safely drink. Why did the purification equipment refuse to work?

Etain smacked her lips and curled around her guts where she lay on her side in her bunk. She flicked her eyes toward the galley door—there would always be more of the boat on the inside than on the outside so long as she floated. Did she have the energy to drag herself that far? She burned for a sweet, long, cool draught of water from the homewell.

She was about to fall back into a fitful slumber with memories of drinking the Lady's water when she was woken by insistent and measured thumping on the hull near her head. Etain rolled out of bed and gained shaking legs with effort, then lurched her way up on deck. Each step seemed more difficult than the last and spots flitted and danced before her eyes as she used arms and legs to navigate.

At last she leaned over the railing to look down at Mimir. "What is it?"

He pointed to the horizon, which was graced by what appeared to be a green sunrise. Perhaps it was sunset by now and not sunrise. A rock jutted out of the sea, slicing this light with black knives of spires threatening the very stars.

Etain pressed her eyes closed and gripped the railing with what strength she could, to at least delay her legs giving out on her. By the time she opened them again, once her body's threats of flailing passed, the rock was even larger in the sea and sky.

"That can only be it." Mimir grumbled. "Some gate."

"We'll make it somehow Mimir. We have to. We've got Her plants she wanted repopulated, that gives us her blessing for now. There has to be a way around that still takes us through the passage." Etain's breath came much less shallowly than she would have liked...no matter how deeply she breathed her head kept spinning.

"I'd trust Her blessing much more if it were at least our goddess giving it. The only way that I feel out is through the rock... The mist around the base though..."

"Implies that if we try going through the rock we'll be dashed to fishsticks. Yes, yes." Etain finished for him, far more breezily than she felt.

If only she could think through the muzzy fuzzy brain fog. Etain focused as well as she could on the looming rock. The green light of the horizon grew brighter, flickering and wavering like a banshee keen as it spread ever higher. The wash of breakers as they dashed themselves to death began to bleed into the air.

Mimir watched the woman cautiously. She was pale as sun-bleached bone in moonlight, with a pale green tint due to the infernal light. No light reflected anymore from her eyes, which had gone all to black pupils, giving her gaze an even more seal-like look than before. The dark circles under them only made these eyes look larger, and her hair had lost the luster it had when he'd met her.

Mimir pondered yet again whether it was the selkie being sucked out of the woman, or the woman being sucked from the selkie.

"Nothing for it, it seems." Those empty eyes looked back at him, after she wrested them away from the rock, the sea, and the sky. "From here it looks like that one rock is actually two. If we try to go around I'll bet we're dashed into things that we don't see on this level."

"So, through after all?"

She nodded, expressionless, and pointed. "It's no White Whale, but the gate will be hard enough to get through even though the currents will go right through."

"Sticking close then, and doing what I can to keep you off the rocks." Mimir frowned, trying not to imagine what would happen if she were forced to swim should the craft go down.

"We appreciate it." Etain patted the railing, then wobbled back to the wheel.

Mimir shook his head and readied himself. The closer they drew, the more the winds rose. He could almost feel a storm forming, as if their mere presence awoke it. Looking again in the direction they were going he finally saw what Etain had been gazing at.

A dark light bobbed within a cleft between two of the pillar claws. As he watched, the path of the currents dimly came visible to his eyes, ghostly ribbons swirling inward. The current carried them closer, he could feel it wrapping him in warm fingers with iced claws. The hairs on his arms prickled.

A keening cry went up from the rocks, as if a whole clan had gathered at the edge of the sea to launch one of the ships of the dead. Clouds billowed up from the sea, obscuring the beacon.

The *Sea Witch* lurched as the current sucked it, nearly running over him. He hurriedly moved further away.

The ship itself fought the current, moaning loudly and attempting to slip out without success. Etain had to fight the wheel to keep her in the current. She opened her senses as much as she was able, searching for the right line and painfully battled her way to it, bending the waters to her will as much as she could. All the while the rocks drew closer and the winds fiercer. Soon those too were behind them and speeding her for the rocks. By this time the storm had gotten into full force.

Etain mumbled chants under her breath, preparing for the crossover. Her teeth bared and she winced as each word stabbed through the marrow of her bones. The last syllable came, a prayer to Mara for the strength to get through, and she felt the long bones of her forearms crack.

The witch-fire began to lick the boat and dance along the edges, intentionally called up this time. The waters threw the Triton skyward. The rocks continued to grow and stretched out for them, sprouting like spring shoots in the sod. Her friend nearly landed on a spine as it grew from the waters.

"It's alive!" Mimir bellowed once his head broke water again, directing some of the water with his trident to push the *Sea Witch* further away from that hazard.

Etain cursed.

The currents shifted. The drain on her energy grew. She could feel some fur falling out from her sealskin where it lay tied around her waist. Together they worked their way through the straits that materialized.

The darkness was beginning to fall in curtains for Etain. After what seemed to be an eternity they were close enough that she could see the beacon of the joins between reality...a strange lighthouse to navigate by indeed. The edge was mere meters away!

The rocks began to sing.

Softly at first, she almost missed the sound for the wailing of the winds that tore the foam from the waves. Then louder, a mournful sweet dirge that leached the will from her bones and the heat from her blood.

Rest weary Maiden
And Wander no more.
Lie still in the waters
Before yon glome'd door.

What good the fur
Dead at your waist,
Once silken and flashing
Now drained to waste?

Come lie in our arms
Of undying stone
Where mariners and mermen
Molder back unto bone.

Etain's head drooped momentarily. The rocks projected images of peace and nothingness, finally freedom from pain and duty. It would be so easy to pass here. The current would easily dash her craft to bits. If she did not drown, or become cut to ribbons and somehow scramble on one of the rocks then she would die of exposure, or starvation.

But who would teach Kirstin how to midwife for someone in need? Or how to birth a stuck spring? Those weren't something she could learn at the Castle, even though it was an excellent school — not unless one of the loch selkies was expecting. Would she really be able to be at peace if her last child survived to marry and have a family of her own, and she wasn't there at the ceremony? What would happen to Finnol? Would he be able to carry on, or would Byron be stuck tending her family for her?

The more she tried to think of her family and to focus on her goal of getting back to them the louder the rock's voice grew.

Etain was not the only one hearing voices. Mimir closed his earflaps beneath his snowy mane of hair, yet still he heard the rocks' siren songs. He could hear as they sang to Etain, and he hoped that she remembered the tales of Calypso and of the Sirens. Ancient though they were, perhaps there was something they could use.

More enticing for him was what they sang for him, gracing his closed flaps with tales of kingship, riches, and more powers of his own.

He could wait for the boat to be dashed to pieces, and for her to be cut by the rocks, then collect her blood. The rocks sang louder of ways he could use that ruby fluid and of how sweet her flesh would taste to lengthen his life.

Mimir could almost taste its firm sweetness, and the way blubber melted on his tongue. A little nudge was all that was needed.

A little nudge was what he gave before he even realized it.

"Mum! Mum!"

The unexpected voice broke into the spell the rocks had woven. He very nearly was claimed by a rock due to his unwariness when the voice distracted him.

"Mum! Da'?!" A little silver-white seal bobbed her way through the torrent as fast her her tiny body would carry her through.

She disappeared for a moment, and then bobbed back to the surface, slamming into the hull when the unfriendly current tried to prevent her. As clearly as she stood out, Mimir noticed that at the same time he could see through her, as if she were only a mirage of the seafoam.

"Ark! ARK!" It was a very definite command from the little female. The *Sea Witch* accordingly hauled her up.

"Just what was that?" He thought, as he regained his own thoughts. In horror, he tried to push the boat back away from the rocks, at least a bit. *"What was I going to do? I swore I'd never eat merflesh of any kind again."*

The boat swept ever closer though, and it was harder and harder to have the rocks avoided as he swam about the craft. They were mere feet away from the dark light, the portal vortex. Suddenly they were swirling, being sucked down by a secondary current that was hidden until they were within the crossing.

Even his powerful body could not keep him far enough away from the rocks. They tore through his scales and his skin, slicing muscle, nicking bone in some places.

A great groan and crash went up as the rocks rent the *Sea Witch*.

Then they were through the divide. The rocks continued scraping by, the boat breaking. Etain had left the helm, scrambling over the deck and using whichever spell presented itself first to keep the hull mended and watertight. The boat itself screamed with each new assault by the rocks and the waves as they gnashed, infuriated that something was fighting back.

All too soon the craft and its mistress could no longer fight. Etain clung. She had lost track of where her companion was. A final cry rose up from the *Sea Witch* and Etain screamed as the timbers disintegrated.

Finally the waters calmed, leaving Etain to cling to what she was fairly sure was a door. Things had been so turbulent at the last that when she had struck her head she'd not noticed that her world was reduced to sound, scent, and touch. She did the only thing then that she could do.

Etain wailed for her faithful boat that Mara had gifted and a foreign sea's rocks had taken so cruelly. Never mind that passing through had been the only way to return to where she belonged. Her beautiful boat was now only flotsam and jetsam, its equipment falling inexorably to the seafloor to the fate that all equipment would one day fall. Worse yet...

How could she bring its spirit home with her?

If she could find it, bring the spirit home, then perhaps it would be possible to rebuild and give a new body. But...where was the spirit? And where had she been cast out?

Marc frowned and adjusted his hat, pulling it low against the wind. The rise and fall of the boat, and the glances from the red-nosed and red-capped Mr. Andersen were more than enough to bring The Queasy to his innards. These glances were never cast his way when Finnol was where he might see them, but it was certainly enough to make him feel the part of the unwanted landlubber.

Marc wasn't even fully certain as to exactly why Finnol had wanted his help so much, or why he had confided earlier as to the veracity of the existence of Deities and mythological creatures. He was a researcher, and here he was now 'researching' in a far more immediate manner than digging through papers and speaking with men in the pub over a pint and nuts getting fish stories.

In short Marc was convinced that the reason he was there was having gone temporarily mad. He blamed Finnol's gift of blarney. He blamed it all the way to Ulster and back, perhaps even further —from Greenland or maybe Antarctica.

Once again, the itching came, and it wasn't from his usual tweed suit, nor the wool sweater he was currently in. It definitely was not due to the blue fishing cap that the well trained horse that used to nanny little Kirstin provided for the Makay crafts through his herding of sheep.

He'd never known that horses *could* herd sheep, but old Byron was apparently good at it. If he ever saw that horse leap up and perform a jig though, he would be in trouble. He might have to take a long walk off a short pier during a high storm. Marcus was not keen on the idea by any stretch of the imagination, but the day that horses performed jigs? That would be the only recourse left.

"Get out o' yer head landlubber. The poachers aren't in there." The bass drawl grated on his ears. "They're out here somewheres."

Marc glared his direction and resumed scanning the horizon. Inside, Finnol was likely scanning the screen, or doing the strange thing with the pendulum... Dowsing was what he'd called it, but he'd only ever seen it done with sticks, coat hangers, or hands, the way that little Kirsty favored.

"I'm looking, I'm looking." Marc grumbled.

"Then look like you're not! Here, help me with this."

"Always something I'm doing wrong..." Marc tried not to snort, and did his best when turning his hands to untangling the nets he'd been given. It made him look more as if he belonged there, but at a price. The nets seemed to take umbrage with his hands and before long they bore rashes.

Finnol shook his head and sighed. So far they'd turned up no leads besides knowing which fishery to explore. There had been a few instances where it appeared that the radar equipment was jammed, but when they had gone in the direction the jamming signal seemed likely to be in all they turned up was open sea. Finding spells were having similar luck, fizzling and petering like sparklers dropped in water. When they did manage to find ships they appeared to only be in peaceful transit. By the laws of the sea there was no way to board those vessels without due cause.

He pulled the necklace from under his robes again and watched it. The fossilized shark tooth dangled from its silver cap and cord, gleaming lightly in what light filtered in from the overcast surroundings. Carefully he held his hand steady and outward to give it room to swing and waited for it to still. Dowsing at least was seeming to have a little luck and to get past whatever was in the way.

Once it stilled he let his mind still and focused on his quarry. He let the memory of what the selkie women had told him fill himself, and the desire to catch those that had done them so much harm. *"Where are they?"*

He felt the familiar falling sensation and the rushing outward. The tooth began to swing circularly at first, one edge of the circle farther away, far farther than would be normally possible. Slowly that leading edge grew farther away from his center point and the circle squished itself into a line. There continued to be one point of the swing further away from his hand than the other.

That was the direction that he turned them once he was sure of the reading. With luck they would catch up before his quarry changed tack again. Finnol frowned as he wondered whether to pray for Mara's blessing, or to direct his request to some being that specialized more in catching quarry, or one of the deities of justice.

The black edge of a tattered cloak flashed in his mind, and he shuddered. Though justice was indeed her realm, he'd not direct a prayer to the Cailleach in any of her aspects.

Finnol made certain that autopilot was engaged, then tapped the wheel simply to recheck their course would not be altered without his say. The *Corsantóir* replied silently with an affirming pressure on his mind. Then he left the cabin to walk the decks. His companions he knew would be taking turns watching, and making them look as if all was normal, but there was nothing better than using one's own eyes.

Marc cast another look toward the horizon after getting the itching on his palms to calm enough again to think. The clouds were billowing up from the sea unnaturally fast, and were a strange green that matched the waters. The waters themselves chopped and danced in agitation, but at what he couldn't hazard.

"Strange weather!" He called, honoring the request to call someone for anything odd he saw.

Mr. Andersen looked to where Marc pointed, squinting his eyes a bit. "Aye, that truly be something this time landlubber. Go have Merrow turn out. I'll get the Cap'n."

Marc gave Andersen a hard look, but did head below. If the clouds continued to build at that rate it wouldn't matter who had spied it first.

It smelled of wood and metal below, and fish, but did not have the smell of unwashed bodies. Everything was scrupulously clean. White predominated here, broken by dark brown wood beams. Several narrow bunks lined the sleeping area, each provided with dark purple wool blankets shot here and there with streaks of blue. Merrow had joked these blankets were fifty percent hyppocampus wool and that they were the warmest things ever for something so light. Marc grabbed the one that Merrow was catnapping under and yanked it away.

Merrow yowled like a cat, his red nose going even redder. He bolted up, smashing his head loudly against the bunk above his own. He snatched the blanket back and glared at Marc. "What'cha goin' aboot doing that to a man fer, Wolcott?"

"Andersen said to wake you because I saw green clouds on the horizon, whatever those mean. He wasn't pleased."

"Should say not. Don't douse yer panties." Merrow grumbled as he rolled out.

"So what's it mean?"

"A storm." Merrow replied glibly, setting his red cap back on his head and getting his storm gear on.

"A storm...so why'd he look at me like it was my fault?"

"Mebbe it be yer fault. You are a landlubber. The sea's goddesses don't take too kindly to landfolks what don't belongs taking a stroll over their homes now, does they?" Merrow waggled his fingers and eyebrows at Marc. "Haven't spurned the advances of any shark women lately have ye?"

With that he was out, and Marc toddled along behind attempting to make sense of the odd comment. "'Spurned advances'? What woman has been here to spurn?"

"Ye'd be surprised." Merrow sighed. "Not all dreams on the sea are just dreams. If ye dream of women, better just to let 'em has their way unless ye've got a wife's ring upon yer finger. In that case, better to drown on the sea than walks into the fryin' pan either way."

"That doesn't help." Marc grumbled.

"Ye'd be surprised..." Merrow mumbled over his shoulder, then drew himself up when in hearing range of Finnol. "Reportin' for duty, Finny-boy. What kine of storm have we got?"

Finnol removed the spyglass from his eye and looked at them. "It's not one of Mara's, the color's off."

Both Andersen and Merrow sighed. Marc's brow furrowed as he processed the momentary slump and looked between the three hoping for some cues for...anything.

"So what's the plan then Cap'n? Are we skirting or staying the course?"

Finnol scowled. "I want to stay the course as we'd catch them faster. Not very keen on what might go on in the storm though. What's the sense in going in when we might wind up anywhere or anywhen."

"Aye...Not fancying another brush with lost pirates are we?" Merrow grinned a bit and tossed his head toward Marc. "I don't think your friend would either. Not till he's made a few more trips anyway."

Finnol shook his head and looked back to the storm, blushing. "That's another good reason to avoid anything I know isn't from Mara... Just be ready."

Merrow and Andersen nodded, then went on one last patrol of the decks to be certain that everything that could be battened down, was. Marc went with them, observing and helping where possible. He could feel as Finnol changed their tack a bit more so as to hopefully stay out of the storm.

It took less time than it felt like, and soon enough they were below again, near enough to the door up into the navigational cabin that they could be of assistance if needed.

"So...what was that blushing about pirates?" Marc leaned forward over a mug of black coffee.

"Oh, that." Andersen's lips twitched a bit under his red beard. "A few years ago we were out on a mission..."

"And this storm came up, bluish clouds instead of that green hue. The winds blew and blew, I swear it nearly pulled up one of the planks." Merrow burst in, his white, vaguely pointed teeth flashing with each word.

Marc took a deep swig of his coffee trying not to visualize this.

"Don't exaggerate too much or ye'll scare him off. We can use a few more Cowans on our side knowingly." Andersen leaned back with his own mug. "Mid storm we 'found' ourselves boarded." He took a long pull despite the liquid's heat.

"And?" Marcus leaned forward.

"And what?" Anderson replied after wiping his mouth.

"Well...you all seem to have magic, so... 'found?'" Marc tried to keep from moving to the edge of his seat, but it was hard to refrain from craning forward.

"They had magic too." Merrow's eyes twinkled as he watched over the rim of his own mug. "The Cap'n took a bit of a shine to Finny-boy and she looked enough like his wife that her glamoury almost succeeded in getting him to break some rather important vows."

"Etain doesn't know this one, so don't you be breathin' it to her with yer fish tales." Andersen growled. "It's one thing to tease him about it so it won't happen again. It's another to be inciting the frying pan on the lad."

"Of course." Marc nodded, then drained the rest of his mug thoughtfully.

They continued in silence for an hour, but by the way the boat pitched and rolled, and the wails outside, it was clear that Finnol had not been able to fully avoid the storm. Marc's hair stood on end. Some of those sounds sounded like a woman keening, while others sounded almost like speech.

Finnol shouted.

They left abandoned empty mugs behind them.

By the time they were up in the cabin from down below the green light that had broken out from phantom rocks and crackled up from the sea and across the sky was fading. The air smelled of sulfur and baking seaweed. Finnol had an arm flung across his eyes, which were screwed tight shut. The dials spun and whirred, some with broken glass.

The clouds parted, and the water calmed before their eyes as if the storm had never been. When their eyes adjusted flotsam and jetsam bobbed morbidly.

"Look for survivors boys." Finnol removed his arm from his eyes and blinked. "The readouts said no one was near enough to show..."

"Dunnae forget the eyedrops before you search Finnol." Anderson tossed as he made his way out, followed by the others.

The three got into one of the lifeboats after untying it, lowering it over the side with the pulleys. It touched down with a splash and together they manuevered through the wreckage. Both Andersen and Merrow created bright orbs of blue seafire to bob over the scene, giving the entire thing an ethereal air. Movies wouldn't capture this, Marc knew.

Merrow growled. "It'll go too slow this way. We can move

faster if one of us swims under and brings attention to anyone still here."

"An' I suppose yer thinkin' it'll be you, now. Go on then laddie, Wolcott 'n I will man the raft."

Merrow pulled a pendant from his shirt and kissed it. The brief glimpse Marc got of it looked like a coil of carved bone of some sort, on a dark brown braid of some kind...possibly hair. He kicked off his shoes and pulled his clothes off before slipping backwards over the side, changing form as he went.

The man's legs fused together and gained silver-green scales, ending in great spreading fins, horizontal like a mammal, not vertical like a fish. Those scales blended upward into skin that took on an avocado leather appearance, and his hands became elongated and webbed. All that remained the same was the man's facial features and shocking red hair...the red cap clinging to it stubbornly.

Marc blinked hard and rubbed his eyes after Merrow slipped below the water. "He just. He's a.."

"Yep, Merrow's a merrow. Come on now, even if this was a poacher ship we cannae leave 'em to drown in the cold. T'aint humane, is it now?"

Even with Merrow swimming through the wreckage faster than they could maneuver, and with him diving down in case anyone had already succumbed and was sinking, they found no one. Plenty of equipment, but not even busted open food stores.

"Not even a keg of ale." Merrow hauled himself back up. "Like the wreck of a ghost ship it is. I did find this though... I think Finnol ought to see...this too." He handed Andersen a longish plank with lettering, and something smooth that looked almost like it was intended to be a hidden figurehead.

Andersen conjured another blue mer-orb to float above them as the previous one dimmed too far to read, then set it down carefully. "Aye...That he will. I hope he's got the whiskey out already. We're all goin' ta need a bracing."

"Oh no... That's not–?" Marc couldn't help the coughing fit that overtook him when the plank turned enough for him to see the letters.

Merrow silently took up the oars and rowed them back to the boat silently, his red cap no longer quite as red as it had been.

Finnol was already pacing the deck again when they got back, and looking into the boat as soon as he heard Andersen's, "Ahoy!" As always fell to the last on ship, he'd already gotten everything in order for an unknown number of rescuees and watching for any that were missed. His face fell when seeing no one more than had gone out.

"No joy?" He called as they hauled themselves and the rescue craft back up.

"Worse than none, Finnol..." Andersen handed him the plank and the faux figurehead.

"Oh no...no, nonono..." He didn't even need to read what was on the plank, but did so anyway. The energy from the figurehead had already been enough to tell him what craft it had been. But he did so anyway, several times, knowing the hand too well to do otherwise. "And you didn't find her."

"No sir. Wherever she is, she's not there." Merrow answered, sitting on the nearest available surface with a dull thud. I dove down further than any bodies could be expected to have made it."

"Maybe we've got some hope." Andersen interjected, seeing Finnol's knees give way and send him to the deck as loudly as Merrow. She's a selkiewife after all, near as hard to drown as us merrows be."

Finnol didn't answer at first, only stared at the sea as if he was about to hurl himself into it.

Marc went over, just in case that was exactly what was on his friend's mind. Gingerly he laid his hand on his shoulder. Marc wanted to be able to be as soothing as Andersen was attempting to be, but what could he say to comfort a man whose wife had probably drowned in the storm? He'd seen some odd things, and knew Etain had a way of getting hurt but coming through...but this?

Finnol looked up at him, then back out. "I don't know whether to wish I still had my Da's skin or not..."

"I know boy..I know. But she's not here laddie. Ye'd ha' felt 'er. Ya heard Merrow. What would it do to go in yerself?" Andersen answered.

Marc tried to say something, any words of comfort, but they still were stuck under the lead in his heart. Finnol continued clutching the artifacts to his chest, beginning to shake. His breath shuddered like Halloween bones on a child's bracelet.

Merrow got up with effort. "Beggin' yer pardon Finnol... I... could use a warmer. Will I be bringin' you one, or will ye be a'followin'?"

Finnol continued to not answer, though he did begin rocking a bit. It was the cry that caught them all by surprise. As if from the depths of his soul it welled up in a geyser of grief. The three of them fell back to the deck with their hands over their ears. They were too deafened to hear his wild summons after that, and he ran to the side expectantly, glaring through the night as if he would rip it for taking his wife from him. His hand extended and hooked back toward himself.

When her body was not pulled from the depths he howled again. Unheeding of the other men with him he hung his head over the side and allowed the tears to come. Finnol concentrated on her, counting as each fell from his face, then pulled away before more than the magic seven could fall.

"Seven tears for my selkie love
Seven tears to call you home
Even if the nine waves us part
If ye live, return ye to this heart."

Chapter Twenty Nine
Dreams and Divination

Kirsty could not fight the current pulling her to the rocks. Even though it was just a dream, she was afraid of what those sharp teeth would do even more than Mara's teeth and wrath. Mara would throw a fit but she would also give aftercare, at least according to all she had been taught—not to mention the scars on her mother she'd seen during her short life.

Rocks, however, did not care. These rocks especially seemed to be eager to eat selkie blood and sink boats. What would they do to fish?

The boat continued toward the rocks as well. Perhaps if she could just get to it? Maybe there was some way she could help her mother still? Why was there no light warning of such a hazard in *this* day and age?

These thoughts swirled in her mind too fast to be fully conscious of. Kirsty tried to swim across the current, just as if it were a rip tide that had swept her out. Perhaps together they could avert the course fast enough to avoid disaster.

The water burned due to the frigid current bringing either Arctic or Antarctic waters. Her muscles burned from the strain of trying to go swifter than it wanted to allow. Would it be easier to dip below, as if to pass through coastal waves, like she'd heard surfers would do?

She risked it, only to find the currents of the lower layers just as tricky. After who knew how long she won her way to the surface once more. Kirsty opened her mouth and sucked the air again greedily, always swimming for the boat.

Another immeasurable pass of time came and went, and she was finally close enough to the ship to call out.

Then it shifted.

Instead of the *Sea Witch* it was the *Corsantóir* that rose before her and groaned with the effort of wresting free from the currents just enough. Her father's voice filled her ears as he bellowed something, and Mr. Andersen answered him back in the same tone.

"Aye Lads, ye heard the Cap'n! Who's got one of the Stones left? It's either that, or Finnol'll have to feed our bonnie lady again."

"NAE!" Mr. Merrow's voice called. "I used my last one on that shoal of soulfish. Wolcott better be sure to keep Finnol from the bloodlet with us out here. We's got more blood can be spared than he."

"AYE!"

"This had better be just a dream. Both Mum and Da' out?" Kirsty groaned mentally.

"Ork! Ark! ARK!" She called out.

The *Corsantóir* shivered in response to her calls.

"I think we've lost one of the moorings!" Andersen's rough voice bawled. "I don't see it bound where it was."

"We'll get new rope then if we get out of this." Merrow called back. The force of their energy pushing against the current twisted her stomach and made her bones hurt. "Now shut up and help me with this current work."

"Yer the one not pushing and feeding enough, ye great fish!"

The rope dangled in reach. Kirsty clenched it in her jaws, and the ship hauled her to the deck. She lay there, a bit of moon on the black, wet deck, and caught her breath. A knot had formed at the jaw hinges, and she worked to make it loosen enough to even try speaking.

Neither the swarthy red haired Mr. Andersen or equally red haired and red nosed Mr. Merrow spared her much of a glance. Perhaps they were used to things getting hauled on deck by her father's boat when they were out working on...gods and spirits just what would have brought them out here? They certainly were unlikely to recognize her like this.

Her muscles stopped burning long enough. She flopped and inched her way as fast as she could over the pitched deck toward the cabin. Without a skin of her own, it would be impossible to transform back unless whatever spell was on her let go. Still neither of her father's friends from the *Order* paid her any mind, concentrating more on trying to move the boat from the current's grip.

At least they seemed to be aware of the rocks they were being sucked toward. Da' was always canny about things like that, even if he couldn't see them. Da' and his usual crew also tended to be better at manipulating the currents.

If he got out of it she was giving him a cape when she got home. She'd start knitting during break after she was up, since she didn't have a big enough loom.

First though, through the door!

Which of course did not want to open because she was a seal. She reared up and fumbled at the knob with her flippers. Kirsty got her mouth around the knob and twisted her head about one way and then the other. It tasted of salt, and dust, metal, and other things that she didn't want to think about—probably seagull poop with her luck, that was about right—but it still just stayed shut instead of giving under her weight.

Kirsty howled in frustration. She still had to tell him. If she could offer to lend him the use of her human magic stores, since she was stuck in this form and unable to use anything that was not part of the selkie heritage, maybe it would help?

Finally the door crashed open, though she wasn't sure what she'd done differently.

Instead of her father, she was shocked to find her mother at the helm, pasty white as if recently drowned. Kirsty reeled back and looked outside again. Mr. Andersen and Mr. Merrow were gone. Looking back, the cabin was most certainly that of the *Sea*

Witch, not her father's boat. She looked back at her mother. If she could offer to Da', she could offer her stores to Mum, and either of them would know how to do it. They were old enough to have learned.

"I really hate dreaming."

Kirsty turned back to look at her mother, opening her mouth —surely Mum would understand seal—then screamed.

Etain still clung to the wheel, had even taken her eyes from gazing forward to looking at her. Those beautiful sea-blue eyes gaped blindly at her, fogged over. Her mother's skin was even pastier now, and decidedly puffy. Her cheek even looked like fish had been nibbling on it. What was worse was the smell...turned fish and rotting meat.

"Light the candle Kirstin and toss the line.
I'm afraid I might not get home in time."

The scream from the bed on the other side of the room broke through the muffles and spells that had been layered with increasing depth and frequency. Ally bolted up, crying for a light while grabbing her wand. A spark flitted from her hand before she touched it, landing on the wick.

The lamp between the beds flared, revealing the stone walls and heavy red velvet curtains chased with gold marelions. Kirsty's sheets were a tangled mess, but there was no one in the room. The salamanders that had been napping in the little fireplace lined up just inside the edge of the coal bank to watch, dancing in agitation at the firewitch's agitation.

The first scream was still ringing in her ears when the second scream came, throwing Ally back to her bed for a moment, which only bounced her back up. Ally stumbled to her friend's side and twitched her wand.

Kirsty was rolled out of bed, landing with a loud thud. There was a crunch...what had she landed on?

"Mary, mother of God... What did you dream this time?" Ally clutched at her chest and slipped to her knees, examining the wards she'd placed on Kirsty's bedframe just the last week. She'd been replacing them weekly since Samhain, and it was now almost time to head home for the Yule holidays.

All that remained were some charred bits of paper. Ally grimaced. She'd have to pick around for more ideas for a sound night's sleep. Making these was getting expensive in both materials and time. On the plus side, she had the process down pat!

"You dunnae want to know this time... Help me out of this cocoon?" Kirsty flopped and wriggled, trying to work her way out. She couldn't even use flippers this way.

"What was worse? Finding yourself a full seal without choice, or having arms and legs, but all wound up like in the shroud?"

Ally came around to the other side of the bed and began the surprisingly elaborate untangling procedure. "Why won't you just ask Professor Sevrin for a stronger potion? He's bloody grumpy, but I know he's got to have something since he and David were discussing some the other day."

"And what if me mum dies on voyage or needs something of me, but I miss the message because I'm drugged up? What kind of daughter would I be?" Kirsty's accent was thick with her agitation, and Ally nearly had a hard time following the waterwitch.

"And what if you make me go deaf with your screaming? These are only getting worse. At least have another talk with Professor Gerwulf then. Maybe it's just something trying to interfere with your dreams, like some Thought Form Maldein or Lilitu came up with. Or the Counselor, maybe it's just one you've made on your own with all this fear and whatnot." Ally pressed.

Kirsty sighed. "Mine aren't the only dreams getting worse. Professor Sevrin was making that potion for Lilitu, had already tried to get me to accept some, and for all I know David was just interested in the process from an academic standpoint because of our advanced studies." She did make a mental note to consider any drinks David brought her though...just in case he did try to slip her something. But that was unlike him so it wasn't much of a consideration.

"Lilitu? What's he got to have nightmares about? He's rich, gets his way almost all the time, and I highly doubt his parents do anything to get dirty, much less dangerous. And he's ok looking..." Ally grumbled the last bit, huffing a bit after. "Thomas is still much cuter though."

"I'd make sure your hair never dries if you ever develop a crush on Lilitu."

Ally made a face. "I'd burn my eyeballs out first. Don't worry. He wouldn't want me anyway. Maldien might drive him crazy later though."

Kirsty smiled briefly, then tossed her sheets and blankets back on the bed. She debated using her wand to fix them, then just crawled back in.

Some things just weren't worth using magic. Besides, she was too tired to control the human part of her magic anyway. She'd probably have made it all pretty without the ability to actually get *in* the bed.

"So, really. What's he got to have nightmares about?" Ally persisted, crawling back into her own bed.

"Don't know, don't want to know." Kirsty yawned and stretched, noticing that Imp was out again only now. "I've felt the Cailleach too much lately, and the Nightmares like her just as much as the *Things* do."

Ally mumbled as she rolled over in her own bed, pulling her pillow over herself for defense against any more nightmares. Kirsty watched her for a bit, then rolled over to face the opposite direction, curling up.

Ally's soft snores soon filled Kirsty's ears. Kirsty smiled a bit. *"At least this is normal."*

She watched the window for a while, observing the stars idly while waiting for sleep to reclaim her. Once it did she slipped below its waves gratefully, hoping the dreams were done for the night.

Morvan tossed in his own bed. As the days stretched and he complied with orders his sleep grew more and more restless. A great weight pressed down on his chest, slowly growing heavier with each passing breath. For now he did not feel it, lost in his dreams. Beside his bed stood a stallion, ink dark with ruby eyes blazing and competing with the fire for the privilege of lighting the room. Tendrils and whisps of swamp mist, burial shroud, and the requisite night of underground caverns flowed serenely to form his mane. A solid iron hoof, ever unrusted, stamped lightly on the stone floor.

Imp watched in glee, hopping up once more on the nightmare's shoulder and stroking his mane with relish.

"Pretty pretty. Thank you for coming again."

The nightmare whickered in reply and exposed his teeth, all points and serrated edges of tempered steel and sharpened bronze. Morvan moaned again and clasped his arms around himself.

"No, don't come any closer!" Morvan whimpered, sweat beginning to pin his hair down.

The nightmare watched the boy, snorting. "Of course." He replied. "I've never failed the Cailleach yet in her corrections." He sniffed. "Ah, there, he's opening back up. Do your thing while I get my feed."

With that, the nightmare laid his large head on the boy once more. The weight on Morvan's chest increased and he fell deeper into dreams. The nightmare's eyes glowed brighter as he sucked in the fear and life energy of the little speck.

It was going to be a very busy night indeed once he returned to his lovely mares and possibly bred up a few new foals for his mistress. They would be needed soon if he guessed his Lady's agitation right.

While the nightmare fed, Imp climbed up his neck and ran down his head before jumping. He made sure to land right on the boy's nose, then sat down and let loose with a long, swampy fart. As the heavy scent of rotting foliage bubbled up around him Imp grinned maliciously, his mouth splitting all the way across his face and literally ear to ear.

He bit Morvan's eyebrow heartily, being sure to draw blood and sucked hungrily. It wasn't as sweet and pure as what Mistress Kirsty sometimes fed him though. Hers tasted of honey, cold spring water filtered by clean rock, old magic—that was smooth and sweeter than watermelon—and brine and it never failed to give him a zing and tingle from top to bottom no matter how little of it she fed him. Morvan's though was copper and the tang of fear, and some slimy rotting flavor that he could not quite put his finger on. What taint did he carry in his blood?

Icky. Maybe it was excrement or the remnants of some curse.

Imp drank it anyway and took a little extra, just because of all the things he'd done and likely would do to his kind mistress. He'd be sure to steal Morvan's shoes before morning and put them under Professor Gerwulf's hat. They were maybe a little small, but they were in much better shape than his own. Maybe he would like them. Yes, that was what he would do, because the Professor was kind to Mistress.

Imp shook himself, teeth still firmly clamped in the squirming boy's face. It was time to focus or he wouldn't be able to pick his head for more information on the amulet. When he found how Morvan had been bringing *Things* on the school grounds and told mistress, then *he* might be more favorite than that drippy old waterhorse. He could get more lovings and pettings and maybe even pressies. Master David might be pleased with him too. He was much harder to please.

Imp shook himself again, pulling away from thoughts of praise. Instead he delved as fast as he could into the boy's mind while the nightmare—nightstallion might be better—had him cracked open like those coconuts some of the students clopped around with when being funny.

Nutters they was. Bored humans did strange things.

Imp poured his awareness through the crack. It felt much like running between a couple narrow rocks where the springs bubbled out of the ground onto the surface where his old stream had been fed from. The difference was that he was going against the current, and this was a mind he was worming into.

Imp found himself in a large room, perhaps as big as Kirsty's parlour, kitchen, mudroom, and Finnol's study combined. It was not as large as the dining hall of David's home though. He saw a large fireplace, easily large enough for two people to walk through at once. Curios gleamed on shelves and walls, as well as a few selkie skins mounted.

Imp bared his teeth, barely restraining himself from bouncing up to take those down and try to return them to owners or family. Those owners were likely long dead though. Some had names below them, which certainly would have made it easier to go through with the idea if this were not just the boy's dreams. There were also what looked to be bits that had belonged to boats, and in one case a figurehead of a barebreasted and rather fierce woman, with blue paint swirls slowly flaking away from her cheeks as she gazed balefully over the room.

He was unable to resist jumping up to more closely check some of the names. *"Zendra Makay, collected off the African coast... Salena Moribeth-Makay, Duestschland... Germany, really?"*

Movement caught his eye by one of the wingbacked armchairs drawn around to face the fireplace. The pale haired irritation cowered into the cushion, his face tight while gazing into the fire. Vague purple and green flames licked below the regular orange and yellow flames that strove to heat the room unsuccessfully.

Morvan took a deep breath and leaned forward toward the flames, apparently picking up where he had left off. His hands shook as he extended them, tossing another yellow handful of a powder that billowed acrid clouds into the air.

Imp gagged. *"Sulfur. Don't tell me he conjured demons for this."*

Morvan drew a breath, then extricated his gangly body from the chair. Crouching, he scratched out chalk diagrams of what Imp thought to be one of the Greater Seals of Solomon...if he remembered Mistress' book of Talismans well enough. Morvan sat himself in the center of this, then drew a pocket censor out before placing it before his crossed legs.

Dragon's blood resin dropped onto the materialized coals and let up a much sweeter and far more palatable cloud, which mingled with the nonsense syllables. Imp's body prickled, and he wished that he at least had hair to raise.

He sidled behind the nearest curio, a piece of wood that still stung of an iron ball. If the painted figurehead had been able to glower any more fiercely at the boy's fumblings then he might have burst into flame then and there. Imp half expected a bevy of demons to flame up from the fire and drag Morvan from the circle back into their world.

No such thing happened.

Morvan waited, gazing into the flames and keeping his hands extended. His breathing slowed and he could feel his eyes begin to bulge and his brow furrow while he concentrated on generating the needed energy. Some he could pull from the incense, but most he was aware was coming from him. Perhaps, this time, he could make contact with something. Anything. He was a Lilitu!

His bones were beginning to ache.

He was ready to give up, mentally chalking this up as yet another failed experiment. What good was it to specialize in dark magic if one couldn't conjure a lesser demon to bring him the sort of thing he needed? What use to channel his energy into this? He needed some way to hurt her. It didn't matter what had started the feud, only that it be ended the way it must. He'd give anything for that honor to be the one.

The flames flared finally, rising to fill the fireplace and the room was suddenly awash in light and heat. The stench of sulfur filled the room even more powerfully than what he had cast on the flames to open the gates. Black smoke rolled forward and encompassed his circle.

Imp turned to liquid and hid himself within the dry wood he'd been hiding behind. Even though it was only Morvan's dreams and memories, there was still the possibility that this was indeed an actual demon.

Morvan tensed, waiting for the demon to materialize. A form started to congeal before the circle. Morvan smiled.

The form just as suddenly dissipated, as if once observing Morvan the demon wanted absolutely nothing to do with the boy. Morvan stared as the smoke roiled back into the fireplace and the flames squatted back down, taking the heat with them.

"Why?" Morvan screamed as he jumped up, stepping forward and out of the circle.

The stones in the firebed cracked and yawned open, exposing a chasm shot with glowing globs of molten goo. The dream started to pixelate.

"You are supposed to serve my family! Come back and hear my demand." The boy screamed.

"Come back when you're older, little boy." The ground itself seemed to growl the answer.

Imp slowly extruded a bit of himself so as to better see and hear.

"Since you do exist you would be well served to remember how my forefathers bound you." Morvan stood as tall as possible for his small frame.

"You would do well to remember you're just a puffed up toad

in an expensive suit compared to me. Tell me, child, do your parents know you're here trying to get me to help you get revenge against a little girl like yourself?" Low chuckles rolled up from the depths.

"The Makay whelp is no 'little girl' and you will give me something that I can use to expose her."

"Go crawl under your blankets before you wet yourself, little girl. If you really want something you can use to hurt her with, go look in the vault for the amulet that has the purple glow. You'll find it."

Morvan clenched his fists and gritted his teeth, remembering the oppressive, dark hole. "I've scoured the vault several times already, and there is nothing there that will do it."

The demon sighed, shaking some dust from the mantle. "Are you really that dense? Astereth regains his strength for another cycle. That means that the amulet will work. If you use it, you will be rewarded well."

Morvan stared doubtfully into the chasm, but could not hide the queasiness that the name filled him with.

"And what if I don't use it? As you say, I'm still a child. It may be one of those I've already been passed, but not all of them I've learned what's required yet?"

"Astereth will collect your soooulll." The demon wailed up merrily. "And I might have a chance to finally be free of you brats and your petty demands." Laughter followed as the chasm slammed shut, bringing a load of dust down from the rafters and on top of the formerly still clean boy.

It was only then that he realized he had stepped out of the protective circle. Morvan narrowed his eyes and stepped back in, going through the motions of bringing the ritual to a proper end.

Morvan made sure to use the Lesser Banishing Ritual...even though the demon appeared to have left. Crossing himself, he intoned, "Atah Malkuth Ve-Geburba Ve-Gedulah Le-Olahm, Amen." After a pause he drew the four banishing elemental pentagrams, drawing them always widdershins, and turning widdershins as well.

The blue flames that lit the pentagrams' lines burned black at the tips, not quite able to purge all of the remaining energy. However, a vague breeze did curl though the room lazily, bringing a little fresh air and the scent of sea and bloom.

Imp hated this ritual, it always left him feeling vaguely unwelcome, though never fully dismissed. Mistress always performed it so much better when she did feel a need to use it to get rid of things bothering Mrs. Kitsch and the few other people vaguely within the Point's jurisdiction.

Vague...that pretty much summed up Imp's opinion of Morvan's whole performance.

Morvan tried to call on the Archangels next. Imp was unsurprised when said archangels completely ignored the summons. Well, perhaps not completely ignored...

A mound of sparkling sludge materialized at each quarter. It smelled of appleblossom and frankincense, but had a decidedly soft consistency suitable for manure. *"Angel excrement? I wonder what the family, or Morvan, did to annoy Archangels that badly. Mistress will never believe that one."* Imp struggled not to laugh, not to influence the dream, but he was starting to bubble with the effort.

Finally, Morvan's farce ended, and he stormed to the fireplace, then through.

Imp leaped down, returning to his regular shape, and tried to follow, only to splat against the stone backing.

"He's starting to wake." The nightmare's voice slid through Imp's mind.

"Coming back out then. Maybe next time I'll get it. Preoccupied with demons." Imp let the dream go, following the stream back out and returning to himself where he crouched on Morvan's face.

"Who's Astereth?" Imp asked as soon as he was out.

The nightmare went grey at the name. "Someone that my Mistress thought she was done with. A former student that was removed from the cycle of birth because of his penchant to take away their servants..." He made his way on silent hooves toward the window and jumped through, galloping away though the sky as the light began to turn the sky a matching shade of grey.

Kirsty leaned against David on the cushion they shared at the low table, trying not to nod off in the reddish light from the central fire and that streamed through the thinning velvet drapes. The scent of mugwort lay cloyingly heavy in her delicate nose, combined with lavender and overly strong tea. She studiously ignored the way the light danced in the quartz ball on their table and the candles set to either side. David's breath came shallowly and barely raised her as they both tried not to breathe much of the fumes.

"I don't suppose any of you have been keeping track of your dreams and divinations in your Book of Mirrors, like I told you would be required for this class?" The dark haired Professor Zeldithn trawled along the edge of the circle closest to her fire, her ebony hair a waist-length cloud that blended into the voluminous black velvet skirt studded with mirrors and silver bells. Those bells and the bangles around her wrists tinkled with every slight movement and sounded like a hard rain with any regular motion.

She dropped a bundle of belladonna on the coals to join the mugwort and lavender fumes. The silence was broken by collective shifting and rustling of robes.

"As I expected." Zeldithn sighed, settling beside her fire and shuffling a set of playing cards she drew from her pocket. "This class is required for a reason, seekers. Despite what many of you think of them the skills I teach you will serve you in good stead...if you listen to your senses. We are not only these bodies we wear."

She lay out the cards in the standard Celtic Cross pattern.

"Those of you too shy to read your dreams in front of the others may send me copies of your books and your notes on those dreams and visions. Those who have not done as asked may make up some of their points by giving me a one eighth inch thick saddle-stich manuscript of their mid term essay on why their attempts failed or their argument of why they feel they are advanced enough to not require doing the assignment. 'I don't believe in this, it is evil,' or other similar excuses will result in points deductions."

Professor Zeldithn glared around the classroom where she held court over the pictured cards. "For now, each of you will come to me and write this reading and your interpretations *based only on what you glean from the cards themselves and not from your books* on the parchment and with the quill I provide. Or if you feel like saving your hands you can murmur the reading to me."

"Understood Lady Zeldithn," droned the students as one.

David and Kirsty exchanged a look. Kirsty sighed and flashed two matching green diaries at him, nearly identical save that one had a seal on a silver anchor set into the front cover and the other a rather lifelike doodle of a tallship in full sail.

David nodded, smiling very slightly.

Kirsty lifted her eyebrow in question, and he shook his head. She tried to hide her sigh by sending it through her nose. He sighed in response and opened the blank black notebook he'd set for the class. Flipping the pages for her, each was nearly empty, although they had been carefully dated. There was a preponderance of "no dream" and "I woke feeling ill" with the occasional "Thomas was practicing all night with something and kept us all up even though we couldn't hear him. Must find out what he was working on."

"You must sleep like the dead." She whispered and poked him while they waited their turn.

"I don't know... I just don't seem to dream. The ones I do, I'd rather not share with her." David replied, closing the book and attempting to avoid her finger. "Must you do that?"

"Yes, because I like you."

He set the notebook on the table, avoiding her eyes where they were reflected in the crystal.

"Those of you waiting to take your test, please practice with something besides talking." The professor's voice pushed back down the slowly beginning drone of discussion.

"Yes Lady Zeldithn," came the measured sing-song.

David gave Kirsty a mock-glare, as if it had been solely her fault he now had to spend who knew how long staring into a ball or sipping overly brewed tea. Kirsty grinned back at him and opened a fresh page in her copy of her journal before beginning to doodle.

David shook his head and slipped one of his potion books behind their class text, holding it up so that the only thing visible from the professor's view would be the blue binding with the silver moon phases.

"I don't think 'auto-doodles' count..."

"Nah, she loves 'em."

"Don't whine when something takes over your hand then and you draw something that really happens."

Kirsty promptly switched her doodling to hearts, sparkly vampires, and clearly alpha wolves with feathers braided into the fur.

Thomas leaned a bit from the next table at the whispering to see what was being drawn without attracting attention. "Vampires don't sparkle... and wolves don't wear feathers." He mouthed at them. "If they start, David and I will be blaming you."

David nodded once briskly. Kirsty stifled a snort.

The first of the examinees took her seat, her friends queueing behind her to both hear and provide any needed support. David turned his eyes to his studies.

Every few students someone would get pulled back to their tables and a strong black tea poured into their mouths to reground them and pull them back to the present, though most only needed a nibble from a cracker to tame their queasiness. Of course there were the usual two that were overly dramatic about their 'visions.'

It took some time before David was finally called for his test. The professor leaned toward him in a cloud of patchouli and attempted to dominate him with kohl-rimmed emerald eyes.

"So, Mr. Valnarius... Tell me what you see in this spread—other than 'a lot of cards with ugly pictures.'"

David settled on the cushion, leaning a bit backward when the professor leaned in a little closer, likely what she thought would be encouragingly. He tried to hold his breath. Her scent made his nose burn and brought a dull ache in his sinuses.

"The Queen of Swords inverse, Professor. The spread is about a dark haired girl. The inverted position shows difficulty."

"Is that all?"

"Yes Professor... That's all I see."

"And this one?" Professor Zeldithn pointed to the card laid crosswise over it with one long, well-manicured amethyst nail.

He studied the black robed and white faced figure where it stood in the boat, a hand on the till to guide the craft across choppy waters. In the other hand the figure held the traditional scythe, while rusted chains pooled around a naked figure sprawled on the floor as if dead. David kept his face carefully blank.

"Death in the upright, Professor. The most maligned card in the deck. It's the ultimate loss if I remember." He kept his voice level, but to his ears he sounded very clipped. It was tempting to simply leave the test, take Kirsty by the elbow, and suggest that she probably had enough points she could forfeit her midterm.

He doubted that would work though.

"Yes, one interpretation, but that is by the book. What do you *see*?" Zeldithn asked, leaning further forward with another billow of perfume and tinkles and an uplifting of lips the color of congealed deer's blood.

"A card that is going to make Miss Makay sit up nights and loose more sleep if you don't change it before her turn, Professor." It slipped out calmly. "I forsee her father having to force her to drink something to even take a nap."

The Professor let her gaze wander back to the cards, drawing her finger over them lovingly to the last. "Then she'll have to take extra studies if a gateway card can do that to her. What about this one then?"

"That's the outcome position." He ground out between clenching jaws. "Three of swords inverted signifies loss and heartache. That's the pierced heart and the rain. Inverted makes it harder."

He wanted to rip the smile off her face and scatter those too-white teeth the professor revealed.

"You tell me that you can't read the cards, but you seem to have done very well for someone that reads potions books during my class." Professor Zeldithn made no move to change the spread, instead making a few notes in her own notebook. "Please return to your seat and send her over...*without* warning her of what's here. She may end up reading for someone else."

"As you wish, Professor." He bowed slightly before getting up, a barely perfunctory inclination more a result of getting up than an actual bow.

Kirsty watched him as he walked back toward her. Right now he prowled like the blood moon had only recently passed, tense as if he'd pounce on anything given the least reason—far more pronounced than was usual after returning from Professor Zeldithin's examinations. The ice in his eyes made her cramp, and it was not even that time of the month just yet to explain such cramps.

It was hard not to flinch when he glared into her eyes. For just a moment she was eleven again and pressed against the mail room's pillar as the wolf-boy in the heavily furred cloak he'd been using to keep his forced transformation hidden with stalked toward her. Her heart pounded painfully in her chest.

Then he was sitting beside her, leaning close to murmur in her ear. "She wants you."

"Is it that bad?" Kirsty wasn't sure if she should lean into him, or step back, pull her robes around her, and hope the temporary invisibility charm in her cloak worked long enough to get her somewhere safe—if he looked like that...

"I'm not supposed to say." His tone was softer, and he rested a hand briefly on her shoulder, glaring now toward the central fire.

Kirsty closed her eyes for a moment to collect herself, pressing her dominant fingers between her brows on either side of the third eye. Then she allowed her feet to carry her to the former gypsy.

"Lady Zeldithin," she breathed as she sank onto the cushion and cast her eyes briefly over the spread. "Who am I reading for today?"

"No one in particular child. Please only tell me what you see. If any names come to you, of course share them though."

"Of course Professor."

Ten cards peered up at her. She immediately picked out what had set David off. The woman on the Queen of Swords looked very much like herself and Etain, and paired with Death in the challenge position crossing it, his reaction only became more clear.

"The Queen of Swords must overcome the trial of rebirth, but first that which chains her must pass away. This will be painful and requires a choice and sacrifice." Kirsty's voice both fell in octave and increased in volume, far more so than had happened with previous students.

Another breath, another beat of the heart. The fumes of the herbs were far more potent here. The odd feeling of being several people at once settled onto her.

"The crowning goal is the High Priestess inverted. She stands between the two pillars and must be the balance and the join between the two. She must be the healer, and in the inverted position she must be wary to neither be overly demanding, nor not demanding enough. The goal then is successfully managing."

Kirsty was unaware of her professor leaning further forward to check her eyes, which had glazed over and reflected blue in the flames.

"In the past lies the Knight of Wands. A fight results in a flight, and the charger carries away the rider until control over reaction to environment is gained. The Tower lies inverse in recent events. The Querent has suffered the loss of foundations. Anything built at this point, until the rubble is cleared, will fail. The Nine of Swords stands on its head in the near future, bringing despair, pain, and the dark night of the soul wherein death or rebirth will occur."

Professor Zeldithin took notes gleefully. "This children, this is what I am trying to teach you so that you can call on this gift when times are dark and you are lost as to where to go in life."

Kirsty continued, unhearing. "The questioner is the Fool or Child, only just beginning their path. Inverted again, he or she is stubborn and tries to go upriver and against the current, instead of making use of it or even swimming crosswise. It ties in with the Knight, see how they point to each other. The eighth card shows the Moon and Illusion as the environmental factors that are exerting influence. There is interference here that the Querent must beware of if the goal is to be obtained."

The water in some of the scrying bowls began to bubble, and Kirsty was shaking, her hair beginning to frizz.

Ally stood up. "Make her stop, Professor! Something's wrong."

David stormed over, placing his hands on Kirsty's shoulders. "Kirsty... come back."

"She's fine seekers. Let her finish." The professor crossed her arms and smiled. "I suspect someone's been practicing more than her weekly reports mention."

Kirsty turned her head to look at David, then to Ally vacantly, drawn by the voices. "The Ten of Wands is also inverted in the ninth position, warning to be watchful for overburdening. Too many dishes at once result in a burned meal, and it only takes one more thing to cause all the flaming wands to be dropped. If these warnings aren't heeded—" Her finger landed on the final card with a light click of shortened nail on cardstock. "Then there will be heartache that will be difficult to overcome."

David squeezed her shoulders, hoping that maybe that would break her trance.

"Is the person that the reading is for in this room, Kirsty?" Professor Zeldithn asked calmly, shooting a warning glance at David.

David refused to remove his hands from Kirsty, holding her gaze in return.

"Yes, but I have no idea who. There are several." Kirsty's voice was swiftly returning to normal, the glaze leaving her eyes. "Oh I feel terrible... What happened?" Kirsty became aware of David's hands. "Why are you pinching off the nerves to my fingers..? I didn't levitate or something did I?"

The pressure left, David releasing her as if burned. The feeling began to return, and Kirsty wished that it didn't.

"You can take her now, Valnarius... perhaps some of the tea would be a good—"

Kirsty wretched loudly, her breakfast landing on the spread and gracing the divinatory fumes with the stench of half-digested pickled herring. A bit splattered, pelting those nearest with a few drops. The professor sighed and dabbed at herself, "Too late... We'll work on that more next semester."

"Do I have to?" Kirsty started to stand, then wretched again before she could finish closing or even covering her mouth from speaking, this time getting more of it on the professor and the table.

David looked down at where some of Kirsty's breakfast had splattered onto his clothes. "I hope not." He stated with as much dignity as he could muster.

Chapter Thirty
Complications

Snow lay thick on the grounds outside and the fire in the grate crackled and smoked with the scent of cinnamon and nutmeg that had been laid in for the festive odor. Earlier in the month they had hung garlands of pine, holly, tinsel, and the odd sprig of mistletoe.

Kirsty drew the line at helping Ally try out a paper poppet love spell they'd found in the library while working on a paper for one of Ally's classes. This morning she then found a strange discovery dangling from one of the posts. A white and red stocking hung at eye height. Groggy, she carefully as possible took it down and opened it, then groaned.

Inside she found two paper poppets labeled carefully with her name and David's, and some suspiciously familiar glyphs, although one or two looked a bit different than what she remembered reading. She sniffed it, her eyes widening once it registered. Rose oil curled tantalizing inside her nose, filling her with wistful sighs and roaming thoughts that she hurriedly stamped down.

"Aw, come on! Now what do I do? How am I supposed to undo that without making him avoid me. Ally!" Kirsty sighed and tucked it into one of her skirt pockets.

With luck she'd figure out a way to talk to him about it without making it look like it had been her idea. With even more luck maybe her aunt or someone would help her figure out a way to undo any spell that had been cast if this wasn't just an uncharged prank, without damaging her current relationship or her friendship with David. If anything continued on, she wanted to be sure it wasn't the result of some silly teenage love spell.

Kirsty looked one final time around the dorm to make sure that she was fully packed for break. Ally's posters were still up, as

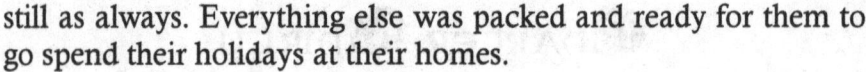

still as always. Everything else was packed and ready for them to go spend their holidays at their homes.

It looked quite empty in her opinion.

As excited as she was to be going home, she couldn't help the flipflops in her bowels. Perhaps, if she was lucky, her mother would come home while she was there and prove all of those dreams to be mere phantasms.

"What if I don't come back..?" Kirsty wondered briefly what David would do if she did die over the break. Fourteen or so days was a short time to cram any quest into, partial or not.

She pushed the thought out of her mind. If she did, David would likely just continue to carry on. The loss of one half-breed wasn't going to bring his world to an end. If she were going to die or forget about the land, better it be while young and before anyone besides her parents formed too strong an attachment.

"Riiight..." Kirsty frowned at herself for the strange path of her thoughts and her brain's insistence that everything would start crashing down around her ears. *"What if something goes wrong and suddenly he and the others won't like who I am?"*

She snorted at herself. "Grow up little girl. You didn't have friends your age before, because of who you are. You'll make do if they all change their minds."

Kirsty went to pick up her trunk, fully prepared to carry it down herself, but it was already gone from the foot of her bed. On a little plate at the foot were a few squares of kelp candies arranged in a messy smiley face, still in their green metallic wrappers. Her lips twitched upward a bit.

"Thanks Imp. I could have gotten it myself...but thanks." She murmured, placing one in her mouth and the rest in her pockets.

Kirsty scowled and nearly spat the treat out once the taste registered. It was not the toasted-salt crunch of kelp candies that greeted her tongue, but the acrid tang of the health tonic that her imp had lately taken to foisting on her at every opportunity. The water imp most likely had been looking through her notes again on what worked and what didn't, or something had riled him up again.

Breakfast in the feasting hall was a peckish affair of plain toast and unsugared mintkelp tea that had been slipped up from the kitchens. She attempted an orange, but two sections of its acidic flesh revealed it as a mistake when her stomach started cramping.

She placed the fruit back on her plate before the flurry of straggling letters arrived. A large white tern dropped a longish package in front of her, causing several cups to spill. Ally and Nevin leaned over curiously to watch as she carefully unwrapped it. The tern circled the hall querulously instead of doing as the other messengers did and refused retreating, as if awaiting some form of reply or reaction.

Kirstin, I want you to be especially careful. Remember I love you no matter what. She's got her 'lucky charm' so she could still show up.

We can pray.

When you get home, if you get there before me, make sure Mrs. Kitsch actually reads the message I sent her. She might not be out at the lighthouse anymore, but she'll remember what to do still. I think.

—Da

Kirsty frowned as she read the letter, and then turned the board over that had been revealed. She wanted to scream, sucked in a chestful of air...but the pain was too deep to let her. The world was a greyscale graphite drawing, cold and empty.

Instead she grabbed some cold cuts and bread for later, then went down to the games pitch to wait for the hour to load into the carriages. For once the water held no draw, and though she wanted to go for a good run through the forest that was not an option at the time. The games pitch was the best that she could do, and by lurking around the bushy thickets that made the edges she could almost pretend that she was shrouded in the trees. Kirsty wandered among the mazes picking over the usual bothersome paths of her mind, the pitch conforming to her needs and the hedges becoming thicker.

The memory of her latest nightmares mocked her, and that package had killed her last hope that they were not accurate visions. For a short time she wrapped her arms around herself and leaned into the bare hedge, ignoring how the twigs scratched her through her thick winter clothes.

Kirsty shuddered as the tears came. This wasn't supposed to happen. She hadn't even won her skin yet, much less gotten fully through the initiation.

"Why didn't you tell me! You're the sea goddess. We pray to you for safe passage, and you guide us home." She beat the hedge behind herself and scuffed the ground, working out her emotions in the safest way that she new how.

A whimpering broke her out of the thoughts, and she looked from her feet to the sound. The black mangy dog from before, even thinner than the last she'd seen him up close, wagged a bedraggled tail hopefully.

"Hey boy...you're still here, huh? Wish I knew something better to call you." Kirsty wiped her face, then she pulled out some of the meat and bread, making it into a rough sandwich before holding it out for the dog. "I thought you'd gone since I've not seen you since that night."

The dog's eyes brightened, and he slobbered all over her hand as he took the sandwich from her.

"What are you doing here?" She dropped down to look into his eyes, easier than continuing to bend down, and hoped it was less threatening since if animals talked they were more willing to do so when not confronted. "You look like just a regular dog now. But I'm positive I heard you talk before. You look a lot less like an Angus now, and more like just some dropped off stray."

The dog only wagged his tail harder and begged for more. There was a rustle off to her right, but not quite loud enough to attract her.

The newcomer stepped a little harder, intentionally making

more noise, but he was downwind and Kirsty was not in a state to focus on more than one thing. The dog heard him, but since the boy wasn't a threat he continued to not react, opting instead to keep eating what the strange sea-salt smelling girl continued to offer. It had been so long since the last meal he'd found. The food eased the cramping in his gut somewhat.

"You probably shouldn't talk to strange dogs Kirsty. What if it's sick or crazy?" David's rustling of the hedges to announce himself had been too soft to attract Kirsty's attention in any other way. He hung back a little, trying not to get her running again.

Kirsty shrieked and spun around to face David, drawing her wand as she turned. David jumped out of her way, drawing his own wand. When she saw it was only him the spell in her wand died and she clutched her chest.

"David! What are you doing sneaking up like that? I could have hurt you!" She pressed a bit harder at the pain in her chest, trying to ease it. Such a strange symptom had been happening more and more often when startled.

"Coming after you to make sure that you're ok. You don't have to attack me if you want to be alone. Just telling me will do." His voice was cool and still as a dead lake, and Kirsty couldn't read his eyes for once. Only after looking into his eyes for a moment did she register the wood he held.

Kirsty very gingerly reached out for the remnant of her mother's boat, and he pressed it into her hand. "No... I'm sorry. I just wish you'd not scared me is all. Don't go." To her own ears she sounded petulant and clingy, and she silently berated herself. *"Way to look the part of some melodramatic twit, Kirsty,"* she thought irritably.

David sighed and shook his head. Her fear and the salts still curled in his nose, but now it was joined with another scent he'd become far more accustomed to. Embarrassment.

He smelled that as well as she could smell his exasperation. Maybe that look of being caught unprepared was just part of what she was. He still hadn't interacted with enough of them to draw any conclusions on selkies beyond the short lesson in Professor Gerwulf's class.

"You still should be careful with strange dogs." His wand slid silently back into its sheath, as did Kirsty's into her own. "Even the friendliest can bite if too eager. Or when they get spooked."

Kirsty blushed a bit. "He's alright, just a wee hungered. This is the one that helped me that one night."

David looked the dog over again. Skin, bone, and fur, that's all he was other than some gold eyes. There was something a bit 'more' to him that he simply could not place though. "A 'wee?'" He mimicked her tone. "He's not going to be getting a lot with the castle clearing out. What's keeping him here?"

Kirsty shrugged and made the dog another sandwich. "Poor fellow."

"You're not feeding him all your breakfast I hope..."

"Maybe..."

"You're going to regret that when all you'll have access to on the way home are sweets." Despite his words, David did pull out some of the sundries he'd filled his own pockets with, and laid them out for the dog.

He wasn't going to place his hand anywhere near the strange dog's mouth though. Not after things he'd seen and tales he'd been told.

"Thank you children... As for why I'm here, neither of you would believe me anyway. Let's just say I'm keeping an eye on things that need not concern you."

Kirsty jumped backward, mostly as she'd heard the voice with her ears instead of her mind, and temporarily vanished to David's eye, regarding the dog carefully. David, however, did not notice that she'd gained temporary invisibility as she was behind him by the time it fully settled. His focus was on finding the voice...but it sounded like it had come from the busily chewing dog.

The dog continued eating calmly, tucking his tail under him

to look less threatening, and then licking his chops clean after finishing and looking where Kirsty had been. "Well, that's an odd thing."

"Quite..." David agreed. "I'm not used to hearing dogs talk."

"Well... I'm not quite a dog. Not really. I was referring to the vanishing girl."

Kirsty's instinctive spell began to wear off.

Before he had a chance to explain—the fact that these children could hear and see him was indeed a comforting thing—the familiar chill overrode the already frozen winter morning.

Kirsty moved in closer to David as their wands sprang back out. Basilisk feather and selkie hair cores both hissed and sang their separate songs as they placed their backs together...or as close as their separate energies would allow.

"In broad daylight?" Kirsty hissed, eyes darting around and scanning her half. "This is ridiculous."

"They've had a target set, they'll keep coming in until the hole's found and taken back. *Defectors.*" The dog spat and growled, mumbling worse epithets.

David glanced at the dog and then went back to scouring his half of the circle, reaching back with his non-dominant hand for Kirsty, intending to encourage her to follow him. "For more than just finding mixed bloods like we've been told?"

"Oh no boy, there's some doing that too. Also *Defectors.* But some are after whoever the current owner of the Black Gate wants to die." The dog replied. "It's here somewhere, but I've not found who's got it yet."

"Spiffing..." Kirsty grumbled low, edging the way David was guiding her. The familiar panic was warring with the calm she tried to maintain, and the suppressed memories were digging gnarled fingers into her consciousness as they tried to haul themselves back to the forefront of her mind.

Sharp green clawed fingers and matted tangles of fur, rotting seaweed, and the flash of scales surrounded glowing green eyes that stared into her window seemingly every night as a toddler. Those fingers she knew wanted to close around her throat, or to drag her from the shore under the waves.

David's hand squeezed tighter on hers as she stumbled on a rock under the snow. She was here in this time, not sleeping in her parents' room to escape the eyes and crushing fingers.

The *Things* congealed, shadows where no shadows had been before, and two of them circling with their rotting black winding sheets flapping. In the daylight their pale flesh seemed to hold a strange glow, almost hypnotic in its horror...not quite bone and not quite flesh, but very definitely more than the shadows that some texts claimed them to be.

If these were just the congealed essence of terrors, then they were the result of aeons worth.

The *Things* lunged for them with arms outstretched, but their brumal atmosphere reached them first, blasting through them. It burned their faces and nearly froze their senses.

Kirsty tried to recall the feeling of calling up the volcanic waters, and channeled it through her wand. The heat thawed her insides and she could feel the fingers of terror lessening their grip on her mind. The steam rose high and thick as it hit her attacker and drove it back. Simultaneously David summoned his fire-snake from his own wand, which struck at the attacker on David's side and coiled around the pair once the last of Kirsty's heated blast had cleared where it might fall on him. Both blows struck their targets, but not directly, leaving gaping holes in the rags which smouldered, the *Things* managing to dodge at the last and circling them again for another pass.

The screams of pain and rage shook snow from the hedges. Somewhere in the forest within their range a sleeping squirrel's heart froze over.

Kirsty's breath came in rapid pants as she tried to protect her lungs from the searing cold, David's much the same. Even though they had a buffer between them and their adversaries they were forced to keep circling. The fire-snake's presence around them did dispel the unnatural chill somewhat, but not enough for them. It settled in their chests as heavily as a nightmare's head.

The snake hissed and wove, striking at every opening that it deemed likely. Likewise the *Things* continued to dodge its blows and make strikes of their own, the battle becoming increasingly frenzied.

"Plan?" Kirsty asked.

"Live." David replied. "Kill."

"Some plan." Kirsty's eyes never left her *Thing*. When she saw her chance as it started, she tried again to bring down hers. She couldn't create a serpent, but the *Thing* certainly wailed at the superheated water she streamed at it.

David made no reply, his consciousness slipping more into the snake the longer it remained manifested. The dog growled and bristled as much as possible at the *Things*, puffing protectively but left no opening to get through between the strange children's efforts in order to rip at former fellow servants.

David started to slump, and Kirsty left off her adversary in favor of catching him. The snake grew in size and heat, the snow melting and the grass below it scorching black as a stump left over from a forest fire.

Kirsty shook a bit as she held him up. The snake lunged at the nearest adversary and caught it with full fang, then whipped around after the one that Kirsty had weakened. The fire serpent was a wall of flame and it was all Kirsty could do to keep the air around them moist enough now to breathe.

When the fire went down, and the serpent lay coiled again, the *Things* were gone, and the pitch considerably warmer. At the edges, beyond where the burn had happened, some of the plants had mistaken it for spring and begun to sprout again. Those Kirsty knew would not make the hour, if even that. David, however, took some time to recover after the considerably larger and likely fed manifestation looked down at her. She was quite certain that she saw something of him in the eyes before it all vanished back into the wand.

Kirsty kissed the lad and held him close, hoping that somehow some of her energy—as little of it as there was after pulling such hot water so far from the sea's depths—would pass to him and restore what he had just used up. She tingled as it trickled from the source of the Well, through her heart, and then past the chastely closed gates of her lips to him.

In her mind she could see the familiar glowing blue outline of the Lady and the unnaturally blue eyes. She saw a silver sword belted at the Lady's waist before the contact faded. The whole experience spanned less than a heartbeat, and somehow was outside of time all at once.

When David was awake enough he slipped his arms back around her in return, kissing back. As the flow tapered off Kirsty broke the kiss and pressed her forehead to his, squeezing him in relief.

"Are you alright?" She murmured.

"I will be." He sighed. Truthfully he was very tired and would be very glad of several hours sleep, after food if possible, but since he wouldn't be likely to get that he was not going to say anything to worry her.

"You should be heading back." The dog snuffled at where he'd seen the *Things* disappear when the snake burned them as it ate. "I wouldn't be wandering anywhere alone though until I can find and take the Black Gate back to my Mistress." He pinned them with his now glowing eyes, *"and so I can report to my mistress that two of the Defectors are no more,"* he thought.

They nodded, and went to see if the carriages were ready yet. When they got there, they found Byron waiting by one. A puddle of water was beginning to turn to slush around him.

Kirsty frowned. "I suppose this means that I'm not going home the usual way..."

David nodded. "Go on Kirsty. Be careful. I'll see you after break." He tried not to let his uncertainty show. What should he say here?

Kirsty nodded, her mouth suddenly dry and tongue thick. She shifted awkwardly. "I'll try." She then looked at Byron and put her arms around his neck. "I need to talk to auntie before we go home."

Byron glanced at David briefly, then drooped his neck down Kirsty's back, pressing the underside of his jaw lightly against her to approximate a hug. "I got here a smidge too late to take care of something, didn't I?" He asked.

"We managed, Byron. We expected to see you in London, actually." David said.

"Faster this way. Mara's in a very bad mood. I guess my letter wasn't received."

"No..." Kirsty replied. "It's not come unless it did after Da's"

Byron sighed. "Of course."

"I'd appreciate it if you could wait until after the other students have left, Byron." Professor MacLeòmhann murmured, a hand tightening on Kirsty's shoulder.

The kelpie gave her a measured look. "Of course, that gives me a little time to rest anyway."

Section Three
Tidal Activation

First Activation's Crystal by Teresa Garcia

Chapter Thirty One
RETURN TO THE BEGINNING

Kirsty spent her waiting time at the stables for her aunt, once it had been made clear she intended to accompany her home. Some of the stalls were empty, but she could feel and hear occupants. If the light were better, she knew she would see the glamoured beasts. She wasn't sure of what exactly they were, but she was aware of kelpie being part of their mix, as she heard mumbled words now and then.

Other stalls truly were empty, waiting for their occupants to return. Yet others held various other beasts...an old kelpie without the benefit of age freezing. His gnarled knees and shabby coat brought tears to her eyes. Before she curried Byron to occupy her hands she checked Mr. Ainsley's chart he had by the stall.

It was nearing time for his medicine. To help Ainsley out, who was likely busy with rounding up children and getting them to the train, Kirsty read the bottle carefully before she administered it, then checked off that it had been done. She whispered to the old lad in Irish and then massaged away what she could of his aches while he lipped at her and watched with cataract clouded eyes.

"If I were a younger lad, I'd be repayin's your gentle touches with a few of mine own..." The old one murmured as she stood up.

"If you were a younger lad, and you were giving her some gentle touches, then I'd be having a wee discussion about it." Byron grumbled, having watched carefully the entire time. "You'd not be giving rides either. She's younger than she looks."

"A pity, 'tis so hard to ken a lass's age when her mind and spirit dunnae match her body." The old one observed, still trying to hold himself in a manner fitting a young stallion. "By her smell I thought she was older."

Kirsty looked confused and glanced at Byron, but he shook his head. He would answer the questions he saw forming out of earshot of hoary old males. He sighed deeply. Byron knew that this would only get worse till she was through her puberty. The selkie blood didn't care a fig for what human 'society' thought would be a proper time to become a woman.

How many more generations would he go through before he just started trying again to eat anything male that looked the way of his female charges?

At last, Kirsty's attentions turned to him, and he accepted the currying. Byron closed his eyes as the brush made its way through his fur and Kirsty's humming wrapped around him. Finally though they were able to make their way back to the castle.

Only the children that were to stay the holidays remained, safely tucked away in the castle with their boisterous conversations or solitary wanderings. Professors MacLeòmhann and Guirmean stood beside the loch in the spot that David and Kirsty often retreated to, where the branches framed the castle and Kirsty had privacy for her lessons and changes. The two were in deep conversation when Byron and Kirsty arrived.

"Belara, for the thousandth time...I will send for you if something happens. There are few enough students to administer to that it will not harm anything for you to take a little break yourself to be there for Kirstin's first trial." Guirmean held her hand, his eyes caught somewhere between a sparkle and a somber reflection. "It's better to accompany her home anyway with how clear it is she's targeted."

"I know...I just... Oh Artair, why is it always that so much happens during the pivotal life events?"

"Belara..." Guirmean smiled and pressed a mischievous finger to her lips. "You'll scare the children."

Kirsty blinked at walking up on such an odd display, and

Byron smirked a little.

"Truly terrifying that she's not a block of marble. You should have seen when she was younger." Byron agreed, his smirk only growing wider.

Professor MacLeòmhann tossed a dirty look at Byron, and he smirked even wider.

"Well, you are human. You're allowed emotions and family." Byron snorted and kneeled down for the elder. "If everything's taken care of, shall we be off?"

"Yes..." Professor MacLeòmhann got on Byron's back, Professor Guirmean helping her get situated, and then assisted Kirsty up even though she didn't need it. "Safe travels and easy tides."

"Fair winds and may the rocks never trip you." Byron replied, then looked expectantly toward the underwater gates. With the *Things* traveling the country more, he did not want to risk the barrier not closing behind him. It had been easy to enter, the barrier had him programmed into the spell with how many other Makays he had once brought or ran errands for.

There was something to be said when a mild paranoia might protect others' children.

Byron felt the headmaster's eyes on him as he carried the headmistress and Kirsty down into the water, then through the first and second barriers and out past the mer-village. Each barrier that closed, he felt a different element move through the water and the planes realign behind. The water roiled behind him as the third barrier resolidified behind him, and there was a loud 'click' as of a lock being turned.

Byron smiled with satisfaction. He was out of the plane that the school was located in. Now what remained was his travel through the water element and its correspondence to the topography. The underground passage out to the sea loomed ahead of them, the current pushing and pulling like a child drinking and then blowing straw bubbles in his milk. The outrush blew the weeds toward them like the tangles of the Cailleach's hair on a storm's night.

Kirsty trembled with mingled excitement and trepidation. The pressure here was far more intense than nights she had snuck to this outer end of the loch the previous year, before the *Things* began to patrol more heavily. There were eyes here, she could feel them sizing her up. From inside came a growl, but she couldn't be certain if it was real, or if it was all in her mind.

Byron didn't pause, but slid into the gaping maw and past the weedy and stoney teeth, and through into the passage. The jagged walls closed in around her and the darkness consumed itself— and her. They breathed and oozed a presence that leered over her shoulder, and if she'd had whiskers they would be tingling from the movement of the giant eels that plied the magic tunnel further ahead.

Byron continued onward, his hoofs moving swiftly but placed carefully to minimize the sound and vibration. With such narrow passages and craggy sides a misstep could shred his cargo and release blood to call any hungry creature. Worse yet was the possibility that an eel would slither through anyway, investigating and hoping to win through to the loch and village for a meal. If it were only himself then he could have risked it.

Time stretched strangely for Kirsty, with her wand drawn and her phantom whiskers quivering while the rest of her reached out beyond her body listening. Her aunt pressed against her back lightly, and she knew without looking that she also had hers at the ready.

Twice Byron pressed into the side of the passage, squeezing into the ripped gaps in the stone walls from whatever force had formed it. Twice they held their breath as they felt the large forms displacing water and gliding past. The second time Byron had his teeth bared when a glowing feeler nearly slid into their hiding place, but Kirsty was able to manipulate the water to allow it to slide harmlessly past and not find any of them.

An eternity passed as more than 60 feet of serpentine muscle slid by. Yet more stretched out between their heartbeats as they waited for it to be far enough along the passage to not feel their wake.

Finally, Byron moved them back out into the passage and began his speedy exit all over again.

Then they were through the passage, and Kirsty looked around expecting to see another giant eel ready to try the entryway to the loch and through into the layer of reality they had just left. No giant toothed head or grey body greeted them for now, and the relief spread through her veins like a divination tea.

Kirsty lay down against Byron's outstretched neck, her arms wrapped around him as he galloped the miles of sea away. She tried to keep her thoughts fluid, to be less of a strain so that he could pass through at his swiftest. Her thoughts continually crystallized on the piece of her mother's boat that the tern had brought.

Her aunt's warmth pressed against her back, Belara's arms around both her and Byron, despite how Byron would never let either of them fall. If either of them had noticed the sporadic tears mixed with the salt-sea, neither mentioned it. The three rode silently, Byron changing his course whenever the edges of his awareness prickled on 'too cold.'

Byron had indeed noticed the tears. His stomach reeled, and his bones ached. At times like this he wished that he could still shift, pull the child into his arms and rock her while singing the songs from his hazy past. Instead he blazed through the water for home. The faster he got her there, the sooner she could be among the energies there, and the familiar faces and voices of forebears.

"The sooner Mara can take little Kirsty away too..." the thought rose unbidden, and he swallowed down bile and forced his frills to stay down. *"No, it's only to be Midwinter. She'll be going down the well with The Lady..."* The thought of seeing her tiny feet disappearing past the rock and dark water brought no more comfort. Byron tried to not fall into the blackness that stalked at

the back of his mind.

Kirsty tried to shift a bit, and her warmth kept him on the stable side of the brink. He sighed when her weight grew and her breathing evened out. Belara's presence on his back was much heavier. She was no sleek creature of the sea. Thin, yes. Sleek, yes. The land was just as heavy in her as it was in David, though in her case it could be described only as roots—great pine roots from the ancient forests too tired to latch onto each patch passed over—and granite. For him, it was rather like bearing the subfloor of the sea with padded feet that at least bore some of their own weight.

Or was it guilt that his searches were always futile slowing him, and that Kirsty would be stepping into too many roles far too soon? If she were Temple-bred, would things be different?

Yes and no. The hand now curling into his mane, just as it had when she was a baby, would not have been.

He almost wished for a rogue shark to attack, or for one of those nasty *Things* to feel him as he did them and to attempt to take her. Then he could have something to take his frustrations out on.

Byron was not certain whether or not he was glad when they got to Seal Point and nothing had gone amiss. He frowned a bit when he stepped out of the water and the moonlight flowed through and over him as he brought them all back to solidity.

Snow lay thick over the beach above the high tide mark, ice covering the docks and many of the rocks in hoary rims of crystalline splendor. Imp immediately went to work clearing the walkway, running along the path that Belara's wand cleared in order to get to work on the one that Byron would need to go to his barn, flock, and very small herd.

Belara slid from him as soon as he released her from his grip. Kirsty remained draped over him, her breathing even and slow. Belara sighed, clutching the charm around her neck over her chest and brushing the young head lightly.

"Poor child...she's so young." The headmistress sighed.

"Always. Always young. If she were full blood...but she's not mature with the human blood in her and the selkie latent still. She's the same age Finnol and Etain were." Byron grimaced, displaying his teeth. There was something about the moon tonight that set him on edge more than it should.

They walked up the path toward the house, the day-flowering part of the flowering vines closed for the night, while night-blooms reached blue and white petals to catch the invisible moonsugar, the spell keeping them as wards also giving them all the heat they needed. The witch's hand on his side was warm in the snowy night.

The trio passed by the front door and walked around to the side. Here too similar vines climbed the rock and wood sides to sprawl and lace around windows.

Her tenseness radiated in great waves, steady as a stiff wind. In many ways it rivaled his own. Darting a look and turning his head slightly, he caught the widow's eye. "The lad is expected home tonight. They turned to come in after sending messengers. The boys will be with him. She'll have a proper sendoff, of sorts anyway, and he will have more company than an old kelpie that should be dust."

Belara nodded. "I will stay to see her off tomorrow, then I will be heading back to the school. It's not fair to stay the whole break when other professors remain at their posts..."

"And as you are also head of house, you overstep the divide between family and student enough doing this much," he finished for her bitterly. "I cannot fault you for it, Belara."

"I can." Belara muttered to herself.

The door opened itself inward for them as they stepped to the doorstone, and the house itself listened to the conversation between the two. They knocked the snow from their feet a second time after entering, just near the door where generations had done before in the winters.

Byron let Belara pass from the mudroom first and out to the hall, then past the door to Finnol's study, where the stairs crossed down over the door, and out to the parlor.

The fire had dwindled to nearly dead coals since the last Byron had been there to stoke it. They glowed dully as a murk-choked sun.

"Byron?" Marsali drawled sleepily from her portrait above the mantle.

"Back Marsali. Hale and well." While Belara stoked the fire, he couldn't help stretching his muzzle wistfully to the essence enlivened anchor he'd painted centuries ago. *"If only I could feel your hand again,"* he thought.

"Kirstin's not on her feet, but slumped over you..." Marsali shifted, placing her hands on the border between them and straining against it, aching to sweep up her forgotten-how-many-times-great granddaughter.

"The trip, and another attack on school grounds, on top of–" he broke off, unable to finish what both already knew. His eyes locked with her own, and her lower lip trembled momentarily. No matter how many deaths and disappearances through the centuries occurred, the sting never decreased. She was too tender, too giving, too caring for it to happen.

For the zillionth time he cursed the things that had left him unable to press a suit before the damned fisherman and even before it was time to present her to the other temples as her parents sought a suitor of proper standing for their young priestess. If things had been different back then, he could have spared her all this, she'd still have her skin...and though they were dead perhaps they'd have been able to enter Mara's box together.

Her ghosted smile and wet wide eyes, that enchanting mingling of blue and brown, echoed his regrets back to him. She was not aware–or perhaps had not allowed herself to be aware–back then. She had ample opportunity to see after their death though, with the weight of station removed from herself. Carefully he rose up and touched a hoof to her hand. The anchor of the portrait sparked a bit, rippled, and they could almost touch. If only he could find even part of the ashes of Marsali's skin...

Kirsty sighed and shifted where Byron still kept her stuck to him, the comfort of home seeping into her slumber. They both looked at the sleeping girl.

"Put her to bed, Byron, before she drools in your mane. Poor dear." The way Marsali's lips slid over his name when she used that soft tone still made the blood rush to his face and his fur turn a darker shade of seaweed.

He smiled wanly. Even with her human husband long dead, and having left her soul behind in this realm, she still never called him dear directly. Those times when the 'dear' applied to more than one person though, he knew what she was really saying. He'd wait as long as needed and dance on lava if need be, just to see her at peace and whole, and her progeny safe as possible.

"Of course." He returned to all fours and dipped his head respectfully, effectively hiding the sheen on his eyes until it was back under control.

"Perhaps...stay the night as well? I..." Marsali was once more on her rock, now twisting her long hair and gazing the depths of the surf.

Belara stayed quiet, still forgoing the use of magic in favor of coaxing the wood and flame to mingle the other way. Neither the selkie's essence nor the kelpie paid her any heed. If they had looked, they would have seen her eyes had the sheen of unfallen tears and bittersweet memories.

Belara understood their situation. It was theirs to work out though. All she could do was count her blessings that she had not had anything between Blair and herself when they met late in life. He waited for her on the other side of the veil, reminded her every year after her standing Guardian over sleeping forms of initiates and trainees at Artenhame, that special subset of their society without which the deities would be more likely to forget their children. The thought of Blair's brogue as they remembered their courtship and he gave her advice on the year's trends was a balm for her.

What would have happened if Marsali's skin was found when she still lived? Would these two have met again on the other side of the divide? Belara hoped so and blew again.

"Imp went to clear my path to the barn, but as you wish, Marsali... The path will be clear for in the morning, and he will understand." Byron replied, then clip-clopped softly up the stairs with his precious cargo and his Marsali's distant issue.

As Byron went up, the fire finally deigned to accept the nonmagical processes being used upon it, and the flames spread from languid stretches to the flickers that would last through the night to warm the house. The fire provided the only sounds for a few moments, a music of its own.

"Thank you Belara, for coming...for accepting them." Marsali's voice slipped into the silence. "So few do, truly accept..." She trailed off.

"It is all I can do." Belara looked up at the portrait, removing her green pointed witch's hat and the pins from her peppered hair, letting it fall and a few years drop away now that she was not in her headmistress role. "The world would be far simpler if more people would."

"Yes, yes it would. You might want some of Finnol's whiskey before you go up to your bed. I'd serve it myself, but..." Marsali pressed her hand against the canvas that served her. "There are prices I have to pay for ensuring I can still be seen and heard by any that need me."

"That...would be a very wise idea, I think. Thank you. Has the House moved my room again?" Belara sat her hat down on an end table, and it was whisked away to the hanging nubs in the mudroom. She began her trek to Finnol's study.

"Fourth door on the left now, beyond the one it brings up for young David now."

"You mean the one Finnol used to use when he was here

visiting Etain."

"The same."

"Is that door between those rooms still there?"

"It's probably come back. You know that the House has its own ideas." Marsali smiled wistfully and shook her head.

Belara sighed deeply and shook her head in answer, and the selkie chuckled at her reaction.

"Don't worry, Belara. I doubt David and Kirsty get up to as much mischief as Finnol did." Marsali couldn't help the smile. Humans, she had observed, never seemed to be able to decide on their morals. Selkies, on the other hand, knew by instinct what was proper for themselves.

"I beg to differ. They might not do what that emotional lunkhead of a step-grand-nephew of mine instigated, but I have more than enough grey hairs from some of their adventures."

"Mmmm..." Marsali's mischievous smile continued to flicker. "Don't worry, by the time I got to my third generation, I'm sure I'd have been a grey and no longer a brown. Goodnight, Belara."

Kirsty slept through her aunt's sampling of Finnol's emergency mood restoratives, and the stomping feet of the menfolk when they arrived early in the morning. When she came down from the upstairs it was to find her father and some of his friends from the Order drinking large mugs of coffee and slumped forward in the ancient furniture. That was not exactly an unusual sight, it was seeing the Cowan professor Marc Wolcott there so early that was the unusual bit. She set that puzzlement aside for later.

Instead she flung herself onto her father with the force of a tsunami from the last step after thundering down like an entire herd of sealions. Finnol nearly spilled his coffee, but his daughter's exuberance prevented his irritation. Even if the hug he was the recipient of felt like his bones were cracking.

Finnol wrapped his arms around his treasure and rocked her, humming softly and unknowingly, the song a bittersweet mixture of love and loss. He had one remaining bit of happiness that he knew to be safe, and all too soon she was growing. For a short time he could pretend she was the precious babe lifted out of the birthing waters, or the innocent toddler trying to understand why she couldn't talk about what she was in public.

"Whoa there lassie. We know you always miss yer father, but don't kill him with love there." Andersen drawled, taking the mug from Finnol so that he could better hold the young woman beginning to enter her bloom.

Finnol nodded and hugged Kirsty a little tighter, burying his face in her dark hair and inhaling her familiar blend of scents.

"As yer 'uncles' we'd like a little love too." Merrow agreed. "How's Castle Carrick and their 'human training' been treating you?"

"Parts of it are good, parts ok–a few people that could use some time out on a rock at high tide." Kirsty replied, releasing her father and allowing him to gasp a breath, then proceeding to give her 'uncles'–more accurately godfathers–less exuberant hugs.

"Kirsty...you cannot try to put them on a rock." Belara called from the kitchen door, spatula in hand.

"Awww... Too much effort anyway." Kirsty grinned apologetically at her aunt, to the chuckles of the men. Andersen tousled her hair.

"Public Cowan schools are no better, from what I hear from Andersen's tales." Merrow assured her. "Be glad you're not homeschooled. You get to meet more people."

"Breakfast." Belara reminded them, before either Merrow or Andersen could start spinning lengthy yarns about their youth hiding among regular land dwellers. At least if they did it at table then they'd have the food in front of Kirsty and Finnol.

Marsali gave Belara a knowing smirk from her portrait, the selkie wearing her white and shell encrusted wedding and ceremonial gown this day to mark the transition point. Marc was a little slower than the others, still processing a moving and talking painting. She'd seen and been seen by Marc a few times, but never had she shown herself for being more than paint and canvas before.

Belara shook her head at Marsali. Once knowing Marsali, it was easy to see where the Makays got their mischievous streak from. She hoped if Kirsty's friendship with David progressed the way she expected it to that poor David would be up to the challenge.

Kirsty scooted into her usual seat and Byron trotted over from the stove with a cast iron fry pan and slightly soggy kitchen mitt in his mouth, then promptly dumped the fry pan full of egg, mashed potato, sea veggies and fish onto her plate. Belara busily served out for the menfolk their own portions.

"Colcanon? Not Monday already is it?" Kirsty shot an anxious look at her father and at Byron, both shaking their heads. Kirsty sighed in relief. Loosing a day or two was usually a bad sign after all.

Kirsty fell to with gusto, shoveling her breakfast and relaxing as the heavy food dropped into her belly and eased the acid and the cramps from going too long without eating.

Andersen and Merrow laughed at her focus, eating with just as much enjoyment, but more sedately–all the better to watch 'their girl' eat up. Marc shook his head at the spectacle–he knew Kirstin was an eater–while Finnol murmured him through the introductions to his aunt, the teacher.

In general, the table was a quiet din fit for any mini-reunion, even with Etain's usual seat left empty. A plate, cup, and cutlery had been set, and on that plate had been served some sea biscuits and a little of each of the dishes. From time to time someone would look wistfully where the Makay matron should have been, but then they would rap the table lightly as if to obscure a thought.

At length, and after two platefuls, Kirsty pushed back from

the table. "Thank you. I should go check on Mrs. Kitsch...before I get ready for..."

Finnol nodded and got up. "I'll go with you. I hear that even at school there are *problems*." He exchanged a quick glance with Belara.

"Yeah...a couple happened. Thanks Da'."

Belara began to clear up, but Andersen and Merrow waved her off and took over, leaving her flummoxed and having difficulty finding something to do with herself. There were no papers to grade here, no students to supervise, no extracurricular classes.

While the headmistress drifted off in confusion to perhaps find a book from the study, father and daughter tromped to the mudroom to don heavy winter boots and thick cloaks. It took a bit for Kirsty to find her riding cloak as it was buried beneath the mound of yellow rubber rain slickers. She cast a look at her dad, who grinned.

"Well, you don't get to use it much till you're here." Finnol chuckled.

"I'd use it more if you'd been able to have me home-schooled." It wasn't an accusation. Having already been at the Castle for a couple years it was simply a fact. Kirsty thought about whether or not it would be a good idea to enquire if there was something that the Groundskeeper tended to that would consent to being ridden.

Finnol's smile faltered a bit, and he patted her shoulder while guiding her out the mudroom door and around toward the barn. "If things were different, maybe that could have been."

She dragged blue gloved fingers through the snow as they walked, leaving grooves on the tops of the burms beside the path and barely having to reach down. The winters steadily increased in severity here, although Seal Point always had its own idea of what appropriate weather for the season was compared to the rest of Ireland. Still, this was not quite as extreme as the more northern reaches of Scotland or beyond.

It was cold enough though. Waist high snow was simply what they'd have here. With the snow the red barn was somehow given a more whimsical air and if she squinted she could just make out the glowing blue glyphs that helped protect from leaks and weathering.

On going in the three horses looked up from their stalls: a chestnut, a grey, and a smaller white one with a spot on the tip of her nose. They whickered softly over the quiet bleats of the sheep, watching with bright and knowing eyes. Kirsty went over to the white one and presented her hand, which got lipped affectionately. After opening the stall and going in, she ran her hands over the horse's side and pressed her forehead lightly against the horse's.

In response, the horse closed her eyes and whickered happily.

"Missed you too Seal. You been getting enough exercise?"

Seal snorted and shook her head.

"Want to go visit Mrs. Kitsch? Maybe Whiskers if he's there?"

Seal nodded and stamped her right front hoof decisively.

Kirsty giggled. "Good."

"When don't they want to go for a ride and jump fences when they can?" Finnol was already leading his tall grey, Mirror, to where he preferred being saddled.

Kirsty likewise brought Seal out, and went through blanketing and saddling properly, lavishing as much attention as she could on her horse. Seal's eyes took on a brighter sheen and she stretched the mini-frills under her mane for scratchings, then sighed loudly when her mistress granted what she'd missed so.

Kirsty blinked a little, just barely. "Her frill's getting thicker Da'. Think she'll be old enough to foal this year?

"Hard to tell with the way they age. You'd have to ask Byron. I'm not sure if he's ready for her to be that age yet though."

Finnol led Mirror out. "I think she'll be so many generations removed that he might want to reintroduce his line to keep some company."

"Would be interesting having some part-kelpie foals. I don't remember when she was one."

They closed the barn, and the horses eagerly gazed down the track to the ancient lane, waiting and stamping. After mounting, they were off, the horses first walking and warming up their muscles, then moving up into canters and trots through the snow and over the ice.

The barn, its yard, and the house fell behind. The rubble of the ancient abandoned village slumbered under the drifts as they passed through, ramshackle lines of stone fence and crumbled foundations poking up here and there, until they left that too behind. The forest enveloped them, in dense green arms and shrouding fog, and all that there was for them was the lane with its cart ruts and the frozen puddles under the snow that Mirror and Seal tried to kick up as they went.

Song and mouth music passed the time as they went, the horses holding back from a gallop in favor of savoring the trip this time. Perhaps if they weren't too mischievous there would be extra apples and grain granted them by Whiskers.

They liked Whiskers. He never visited them though, they only saw him when they made a visit.

After passing through several invisible shields around the traditional holdings like butter–which easily reinforced themselves and left their blood tingling from the reactivation–the dirt below the snow turned to asphalt. They had turned down another lane shortly before though, and down the bumpy drive where the trees thinned and the watered rays of sun once more flowed down to them. Hoofprints now mingled with the thin tracks of an older car, which had come and gone. Cows lowed in a barn behind the small two bedroom cottage, while the nearer barn lay quiet.

Deftly, the Makays dismounted and led their horses into the

barn, settling them in and making sure that there was grain and water. They spoke in low, loving tones, reminding their furred friends not to overindulge or settle too well, and to "mind your manners."

Then they left.

Once the half-humans left the barn a tiny form crept out of the mouse hole at the end of it, conjuring heaped plates of apples for the hoofed ones. With his whiskers quivering, and holding the little red cap on his head, Whiskers scurried over to hear the latest news from the horses' mouths. His tail twitched after leaping to Seal's back and began to recomb and braid her main and tail.

Chapter Thirty Two
Light Keeper

While Whiskers, Seal and Mirror exchanged the news important to horses and disguised Tomtra, Finnol rapped politely but loudly on the faded blue painted door. Kirsty scraped her boots with the bootscraper while waiting on the porch. The wind blew steadily, and in the distance they heard the soft roar of surf on the stacks. Several moments passed in silence, and he knocked again.

Still there was silence despite the light that they could see within. Kirsty shifted nervously. Finnol glanced down at her and pressed his lips. He tried the door, and the knob turned loosely, rattling when he released it. Finnol made a mental note to himself to tighten screws and fix all of the small workings inside...the sprung spring was in need of changing.

The scent of musty lonely old woman, ancient lace, ashes in need of clearing and lingering regret filled their nostrils as they stepped inside and called out for Mrs. Kitsch. A faint voice called out from the back, and they followed it to the kitchen where they found the silver haired woman crumpled in her pantry. Her lilac dress and bedraggled lace incongruously clashed with the rubble from the cans and shelf that had fallen, and she clutched her hip gingerly.

"What happened here?" Finnol kneeled down and checked her hip to make sure she was safe to move.

"My joints locked up again while I was looking for the canned hash...then I lost my balance." She looked up at him, her rheumy eyes not quite fully present while she looked into his. "I fell a wee."

"Just a wee?" He moved her hand, prodding gently. His eyes unfocused slightly as he looked more with his senses. She winced a bit "You've got quite the bruise, but I don't think anything's broken. Kirsty will probably be able to whip you up something."

Kirsty occupied herself with putting the pantry back to rights, glancing over her shoulder at her father and nodding at the mention of her name. As she picked things off the checkered floor and deftly resecured shelves she set aside herbs she knew she'd need.

"I'd appreciate it if you'd do a laying on o' the hands while our Kirsty's cleaning up my mess..." Mrs. Kitsch sighed. "Your family has always been so good at it."

"Of course. Anything for our favorite Lightkeeper." Finnol smiled, playing down the wreck for now.

"Tosh...I've not helped keep the light since before you were likely born Finnol Makay. I know you're a charmer, but really now." She admonished. "That lighthouse was gone long ago."

"A generation or two isn't so long, really."

Kirsty shook her head at the banter between the adults and grinned a bit. She could hear the pain in her grandmother's best friend lessening while her father performed the healing hands. She dusted her hands, picked up what she'd set aside – there had been a fair supply of boneset and dittany which would be good for her bones – and went to the stove to see what teas she had that could be pressed to service. Combined with the store of potion for Mrs. Kitsch's arthritis that she'd brought with her, Kirsty was certain she'd be having the old woman feeling younger and less doddery.

"Says the lad afraid of getting the dress for his daughter's coming out. I'm sure all the laddies at that silly school you packed her off to have been waiting rather eagerly for it. It really would have been so much more sensible to keep her home and send her to the local public school so she could meet a fine dockhand." Kitsch quipped.

Kirsty pressed her lips together and locked her eyes on the prickly cactus Mrs. Kitsch always kept in her kitchen window, stifling a giggle. Her father sputtered a bit. She filled the kettle, pretending not to listen to the woman needling him.

"In this age, I can't really count on a dockhand supporting my only remaining child, now can I?"

"Oh, aye... The boys at the fancy school will be having the same thoughts as a dockhand or fisherman with her looks and her singing." The needling continued.

Kirsty snorted and listened to the water heat to the proper temperature, weighing out on the scale the proper measures of herbs and teas. She only cared about what one of those 'laddies' thought of her.

"And she's getting to that age that she'll be having thoughts of fine young lads herself. Whatever happened with that boy that had been here to visit her before. The 'friend' that had her so determined to build herself up over the summer? When do I get to meet this lad and give him the Once-over?"

Kirsty groaned and blushed. Finnol's matched it.

"Don't get me on about boys. She's got David that's her best friend, then there's the Lillitu boy that I still expect Aunt Belara to write me saying Kirsty finally went and drowned for calling her a beast."

"I have to survive the Makay tests before I can think about things like *boys*." Kirsty broke in, pouring the now hot water. Despite her tone – which she hoped made it sound somewhat like she'd not ever considered David in any other light than just a very close companion that she cared for enough to disregard her safety in order to bring him some lessening of his monthly pains – she blushed. Kirsty studiously kept her head down while counting the minutes of the brew and placing Mrs. Kitsch's regular potion beside the teas for when it was time for that dose.

Mrs. Kitsch chuckled a bit as Finnol removed his hand from her hip. "I will never understand why your family does its coming of age rituals so young, or what going down the local fairy well and into whatever caverns are down there – or out on the sea for weeks at a time – has to do with becoming adult." Mrs. Kitsch breathed deeply, touching her hip gingerly. "Thank you lad. That's much better than it was. Certainly better than what those fools at the clinic can do with their pills."

"Funny you should mention that...I'm going down the Lady's Well later today. Would you mind Keeping a Light for me?" Kirsty removed the ball, then brought the tea over. She set the blue willow porcelain teacup and saucer down in front of Mrs. Kitsch with a soft clink.

"In the middle of Winter?" Her voice was sharp before she took a thoughtful sip of the tea, the usually slightly unfocused eyes sharpening to scimitar points trained on Kirsty.

"Well, it is time..." Kirsty hedged.

"All the others did their swimming and questing in the summer..." Mrs. Kitsch grumbled. "When it was warm and hypothermia wouldn't be certain."

Kirsty looked down and fiddled with her fingers, debating on how much to give away. The Lightkeepers knew some things, everyone that lived on the point still was in some way connected to its mysteries and the planes that intersected here, unless they were one of the rare ones that moved to the area looking for solitude and were kept to the areas that Cowans knew. However, of the Oldtimer bloodlines only a few still knew the tales of when the deities walked among men or that two still dwelled here.

How much did Mrs. Kitsch remember, and how much of her memories had her strange sorrows claimed? Kirsty looked up again, her eyes drawn to the portrait of a young man that seemed to be in every room of the house in some fashion. His sad eyes gazed back at her. Who was he?

"Sadly, it is important that she go down the well today, Mrs. Kistch...I'm afraid that it is something that we can't postpone without risking what's left of what the family has." Finnol broke in, his voice gentle on her ear as his hand was on her shoulder. "I don't like it myself, but I know better than to go against what has been called for."

"It's related to the sea, as always, isn't it lad?" Mrs. Kitsh sighed. "The sea always has the last word with her own..."

Finnol and Kirsty both nodded.

"Very well...I'll do it. Kirsty, I'll need a token from you to tie to the light, 'Cowan' tho' I be." Mrs. Kitsch finished her tea, then got up and moved carefully out to the parlor and to her wing-backed chair by the fire. Here too the sad man kept watch in a faded black and white portrait, though there were considerably more photos of him here. "If you'd be so kind as to fetch my lamp, some red thread, and the scissors out of my embroidery kit?"

The requested items were very quickly fetched, and Kirsty nervously kneeled down beside the old woman where she was gestured. Shaking hands lifted her hair and snipped a bit from the back, from the bottom-most layer where it would not be seen to be missing. Kirsty tried not to shiver at the sound of the snippet being shorn away. It was no different than when helping shear a sheep...much less of it being taken even.

Next, Mrs. Kitsch cut a measure of thread the length of Kirsty's forearm, and wrapped it securely around the lock of hair until it was well bound up, leaving only a tuft at each end where her dark hair could be seen. Another length of thread was cut and tied around this, then set aside while the old Lightkeeper checked the oil and wick in her ancient lantern.

"This was my father's...He passed it to me the day before we knew the Storm was coming, then sent myself, Mum, and my siblings away to your house 'to weather what was coming'. Long before your Mum and Da' were born." She said, noticing Kirsty's eyes lingering appreciatively on the way the steel twisted around the glass flute and accentuated the wick with its cage. "I think I might pass it to you when its my time to go. It's older than my Da' and supposedly was brought here by one of the ships that used to be part of your family's fleet."

"I couldn't accept it... something like that should stay in your family." Kirsty looked up at her.

"I never had children of mine own. That's why I'm so glad your grandmother did and let me play at being aunt. None of my brothers or sisters ever managed any kids either. You're like my own grandchild." Mrs. Kitsch lit the wick, and then breathed a prayer over the glass as she set the flute back in place, far too quiet for Kirsty to catch.

Carefully the old woman got up and picked her way with the lit lantern to the window, where she hung it on the hook that faced the sea. The trees were in the way now, where they hadn't been years ago. The point changed its geography on its own...but she was near enough she heard its heartbeat.

Just as carefully she tied the token about the chamber, breathing another prayer.

Kirsty felt a net around her, light as a mother's touch, and sighed as it sunk into her skin. If she closed her eyes she could see the tie between herself and the light, glowing like a silvery moon-snow reflection. Around this there was twined a slightly bluer and thinner cord.

"I daresay someone's already taken the liberty of binding you to shore, Kirstin..." Mrs. Kitsch's voice was soft, barely a whisper.

When Kirsty opened her eyes, the old woman was gazing fixedly at the space between herself and the lantern, where she had just been looking with her inner eye.

"I'm not sure who or what it is that's serving as an Anchor though." She finished, then looked at Kirsty.

"Odd that anyone would be, though I am certainly thankful to whoever it is." Finnol mused, also looking at Kirsty.

Kirsty thought for a bit. "I'm not sure who it would be. I don't think David would know how...I've not exactly asked him. Ally gave me something for Yule though..." She described the strange paper poppets she'd found and how they'd been tied, blushing deeper and deeper. "I thought it might be some silly love spell like the ones you can find in the bookshops in the occult section."

Finnol's face drained of color at the mention of a possible

love spell.

Kirsty threw up her hands. "I didn't ask! You know I wouldn't do or have someone do anything like that for me Da'! I know the disaster that comes from those, whether it's a real one or an attempt."

Finnol's face gained a little color, but he sat heavily on the settee, releasing a little puff of dust.

"Well...it might just be an instinctual response, then. Maybe your friend just felt like it would be a help. You do get a little drifty." Mrs. Kitsch looked at Finnol pointedly. "Young Mr. Makay, there's no need for that. Some day your little girl will get married and have a litter of good healthy bairns, and that's the end of it. But maybe it could use a bit of a love spell to shove her along."

Finnol gave her a woebegone look. "Subject change? I'm hoping it's just an Anchor spell."

"Fathers..." Mrs. Kitsch muttered, shaking her head. "Will there be anything else child?"

Kirsty shook her head shyly, still blushing at the thought of anyone possibly trying a love spell on her, as wary of them as she was after having seen the result in Marsali's plight.

"No ma'am. I'm sure that's all."

"Alright then. I think it may be wise to take that charm you were telling me about with you...just in case. I'm sure that between that and this Light you'll be able to find your way back from the Fae to our world."

"Yes ma'am. Thank you Mrs. Kitsch." Kirsty wrapped her arms around the old woman in a tight but careful hug, her nose filling again with the scent of old lady.

Chapter Thirty Three
Lady of the Waters

Kirsty and her father had ridden back in silence, and she didn't take long to make sure that she did have the poppets. It was perhaps slightly incongruous, but she put them in a zippered plastic baggie, before sealing that magically. The thought of anything that might be connected to David getting water damaged bothered her...especially as she was not quite certain what to expect.

She gazed into the depths of the well, the water for once reflecting no light. The Lady had not answered when she called and made greeting, which she had never known to happen before. Briefly, she wondered if perhaps the Lady was ill or hurt. Every other time she had at least made her presence known.

Worse, the adults all stood as if there was nothing wrong with this. Kirsty wished her mother was here. She would have some words of advice or an explanation. Her left wrist itched, and she scratched it, still gazing into the rather uninviting hole.

"No time like the present I guess..." She tore her gaze up, and looked over her shoulder at those gathered behind her. Her aunt was the only female. Her father, guardian, and 'uncles' all gazed back at her, none of them quite able to mask their concern. "I love you all..."

"We love you too," crashed back at her in as many ways as there were faces.

Kirsty smiled a bit, then kicked off with her feet. Twisting in the air as she fell, she brought her arms out in front of her head, diving as her instincts told her she must...headfirst as she had been born. Thankfully, not quite *exactly* as she had been born. She at least got to wear clothes. Poor Mr Wolcott probably would have died if all she'd been allowed to take was her pouch...halfpelt covering everything important or not.

The water closed over her quickly, its iciness chilling her and nearly forcing the air from her lungs. Kirsty managed to keep it though and each kick of her feet drove her deeper into the eternal night. She wasn't sure how far she had swum when her lungs began to burn, but she didn't dare use the paste to transform. She knew that this part she was expected to go as deep as possible in her birth form.

She wanted air and light, badly.

Kirsty thought of the Lady instead as she had last seen her. The translucent opalescent luminescence over her skin and dress, and the way it rippled when a breeze or one of the schools of minnows she carried moved, were some of her favorite features of the water deity. She thought harder of the way her hair flowed, and the gentleness of her voice, and the feel of those arms around her. Kirsty could even remember the feel of the sword hilt jammed into her during a particularly firm embrace when she had been a child and the Finmen attacks had been nightly.

It wasn't the first time that Kirsty wondered what her name had once been. Every time she came close to having something it flitted away. She'd looked up Arthurian legends once after reading what she could of the 'Book of Seals' and talking to David about that passage just on the off chance that perhaps they had something to go on...but the parts that referred to the one that loaned Excalibur made no mention of names.

She wasn't even sure that was Excalibur anyway since the name of the sword was different. It would be amusing though if it were, and the Lady of the Lake really lived in a simple stone well at the top of a hill far, far away from where people thought she really did.

She still couldn't feel her matron deity's presence. Her ears rang from the lack of oxygen, and the edges of reality began to feel rather fuzzy. If something didn't happen soon, then she would have to resort to the paste and change her form. Her fingers felt hazy though.

Maybe she had waited too long?

She could see a light ahead finally, and she kicked desperately for it. As she kicked, she felt reality shift. When she had been kicking down earlier, it now became kicking up, and the light grew nearer and nearer until her head broke the surface.

Kirsty gasped for air, praying the coolness of it would soothe the fires now burning in her lungs. She stroked to where she could feel the current indicating shore, then sprawled on the rock. With effort she created an orb of witchfire and set it to hang on air and light the chamber, but it was extinguished just as quickly. Kirsty simply didn't have the focus to sustain it.

Luckily the cave provided its own light, emanating from the deposits within the stone and bouncing off the drops that gathered on the ceiling and walls. Patches of blue, purple, and green winked and danced alternately. The water itself glowed vaguely, flicking between blue and green.

It wasn't the same chamber as the last time she had been here, when the Lady had pulled herself and David to have a meal and a chat in one of her fits of loneliness...when she had gifted David the crystal.

As her breathing smoothed and her lungs stopped aching she was able to take in more of the chamber. If she looked carefully she could just begin to make out some of the runes she saw in the older sections of Castle Carrick. There were others as well, and these reminded her more of the strange glyphs that she had found carefully scribed within 'The Book of Seals' shortly into her second year. She still had no way to describe them.

Finally she sat back up again. Phantom whiskers quivered as she listened and looked with her whole being, and she didn't reach to rub at them. The light seemed a little more intense through one of the passages that she was now dimly able to see, and she followed that path.

Sometimes she found herself walking in waters ankle deep and strangely warm for both a midwinter and a non-volcanic area. Other times she found herself swimming. At times the passage branched off, and here she was able to sustain light long enough to find carvings in the stone.

Several hours passed this way, and she noticed that she was lingering less and less at the forks. The more often she came across the dominant signs, the more convinced she became that one sign was for Mara...this a complicated series of knots that resembled waves. The water in those passages made her feel more buoyant and had a slightly saltier savor. The other had a more sinuously flowing quality that suggested rivers and lakes...that surely was the Lady. The waters in those passages were sweeter.

Kirsty was positive that with all of the branches, which surely doubled back on themselves, she truly had not gone very far at all. When the passage she followed split into five branches her groan echoed and magnified until she had to cover her ears while treading water.

"Now what?" She asked herself aloud, already tired of the only company being the pale glowing fishes that reminded her of moon slivers.

She made out a shelf of sorts to one side, and hauled out there to rest, casting her dim orb to hang above her. Her body was heavy and clumsy on land, and her legs would not hold her anymore so she dragged herself up a bit further with her arms...just in case something hungrier than little fishes came through. Distantly she was aware of the tide beginning to rise, and she hoped that it did not occur down here. There would be no escape if it rose too far.

The water in her clothes she knew was helping to sap her strength. Looking around another time to ensure that she really was alone did little to allay her worries that someone would see what she usually hid. Still there was no one, so she removed her clothes, leaving only the close under layer to preserve some modicum of modesty, and wrinkled her nose at herself.

"I can't believe I'm doing this..." Kirsty grumbled to herself, extracting the water from her clothes before shoving them into her pouch. She then rearranged her pouch and wandsling, running her fingers over the wand's sheath. "I wonder...was it your pups that had to start doing this, or was it the grandchildren? You always say you'll tell me when older and never do..."

Kirsty rolled to her back and closed her eyes, resting and trying to keep from feeling like someone was going to pop out of the water or a rock wall at any moment and find her in her frillies, not that they were very frilly. They actually were more modest than most bathing suits she saw the girls at school use, and at least they weren't white. That was one of the last things she needed in a blacklit underground water system.

At least she didn't have to poke anyone's eyes out. She was freezing, and it stung, but at least she wasn't carrying extra weight where she couldn't afford to.

Kirsty brightened her light with what energy she could draw from the water and stone, then examined the passages carefully. At one shone a moon with a pale silver light. Two passages held the familiar sea and river glyphs. The central passage seemed to be marked with licking flames whose lines glowed a golden-copper, and she had dim memories of seeing these on stones at the abandoned village forge. The fifth glyph, however, she was unfamiliar with. It stayed a strange green, but constantly morphed.

"Right then...only one. WHY are there five though? Mara's I understand. Who are the moon, the flame, and the...whatever that is? Imp?" Kirsty sighed when she remembered that he would not be lurking and waiting for her to call...This was her test, her further initiation.

When she was rested enough, she took the passage marked by the glyph that she thought was the Lady's, praying that she chose correctly. She could feel presences watching and weighing her actions. With the pressure of the eyes she regretting stripping down so far, but the further she went the more bogged down she was by what little cloth she continued wearing.

The water became thicker the farther down the passage she stroked, until it felt like it was not water but sand that she propelled and undulated through, despite how she could see and taste what it truly was.

Kirsty frowned, sending her consciousness further into the water and trying to find why it rejected her so. Any hint of what she could do to remedy the situation would be a vast improvement and giant step forward.

It was a puzzle.

She liked puzzles.

The water's energy slipped away like a fish and her mind followed, her body a trailing afterthought. It flashed in the light of the phosphorescence, shimmering moonbeams trapped in an eternal night, the glimpse of the Salmon of Wisdom that Taliesin became briefly. The further her mind chased, the further her body flowed.

Finally her hands closed around the flash. It struggled to burst free but she held firmer to the slippery essence, trying to use body and mind to contain it. If she could just master the water's energy, hold it a little longer then maybe she could get the water to let her through better.

The light grew brighter, exploding into a thousand swirling suns each showering the area with luminescence. Kirsty floated motionless in the water. She did not process the fact that she really had finally made her way through the watery passages to the center of the subterranean labyrinth. Instead she desperately tried to see or sense what was around her.

Her world was awash with echoes vibrating through her, tickling skin, pelt, and bone. She both saw nothing, and yet still saw every detail of the central cavern in excruciating detail. Her ears filled with the slow plink as the water filtered down, and the inexorable beat of the far distant sea.

Kirsty finally gained awareness of her body and the vast distance that she had swum. Her cells still vibrated, far more than what she would feel when Byron would become water while carrying her. The lack of a proper skin screamed from her core far louder than usual and the little pelt covering her torso suddenly was not enough, instead of an embarrassing seal-trait to hide. She ran her hands over herself as she tread the water, wishing for the change.

If she could find her way out to the sea, and play along the shoreline or let the saline waters course over her, would she then feel complete? She was really a seal, wasn't she? Not this strange body with the odd fins for the land? Just where was her fur?

A tug on her heart broke her thoughts, while she took stock of herself, and then another.

Still treading, she closed her eyes and sought for the thread binding her. One hand reached for her heart, the other falling lightly on the pouch that still clung to her waist. Her breathing slowed, falling back into a rhythm that matched the eternal water's dance.

Instead of one thread she found several threads. Some there very thin and tenuous wisps. Others were like sewing thread. Kirsty watched these dispassionately.

Who were these people? She could not remember and knew that she should. There should be names and faces, or glimpses of at least something when she touched teach of them. Yet there was nothing.

Slowly she began the work of plucking them. With every broken thread she felt less entangled, and Kirsty smiled. With each removed tie, each bit of the netting that held her she grew more eager to sever the bonds. Soon there were only a few left and she remembered less of her life on land.

Seaswimmer fingered these remaining thicker threads thoughtfully. They were more like twine or yarn, and much stronger. Idly she rolled onto her back and floated, resting.

One belonged to Byron, she remembered him well. Seaswimmer smiled when thinking of his sharp teeth and the sharper wit that he liked to use. Seaswimmer let that tie stay. Her finger moved to another, and she discovered her father at the other end, and his eyes and smell. He waited above the well, but would she return? What if she decided that she'd rather stay in this pool in the cavern. There were plenty of cave fish. Their passage licked through the water and tickled her without touching.

She liked fish.

Seaswimmer allowed that thread to stay as well, and moved to the next.

This cord was fraying as if rubbed between two rocks for a short time so that it bore little fuzzy threads stiving to bind itself back together. A wave of sorrow and worry washed over her. Her mother's face should have greeted her even fleetingly. Instead all she found here was darkness and danger.

Seaswimmer caressed that cord thoughtfully. Perhaps she should swim after it and help her mother. What if she were out there waiting for her? What if she'd lost her skin, or it had gotten cut up beyond a speedy enough healing to come home? She stroked that cord softly, as if it were one of the fox kits, then moved to the next. That cord would also stay.

The next cord she found was a complicated one. Two tied together came in close by each other, and Seaswimmer got flashes of a girl that looked very like herself, laughing and dancing with those on the other end. One held some sort of stringed instrument, and had strange robes. The other had a head of red hair and a mischievous grin. Her heart throbbed again, differently than the pangs she'd felt with her parents.

Seaswimmer frowned as other memories of land tried to push through. It was a silly thing, as if she had lived on land. She was a selkie though. Surely these were false memories then and she really belonged to the sea.

Or was it to the underground water system? How did she get here in the first place? Where did she really come from?

Seaswimmer paddled thoughtful circles, still lounging on her back, trying to remember her name. She tried to pluck the twinned cords, but a third wrapped these protectively, a shimmer of light that repelled her fingers as soon as the thought to sever the troubling cords had formed. There was the flash of an elder's face and silver hair, and the scent of a fire on a fog-shrouded day.

Why would the Light Keeper's cord protect these? As she watched it wrapped around them to form a thicker yarn, Seaswimmer turned her attention to the last cord instead.

This cord made her smile as soon as she touched it, but it made her heart ache at the same time. Recently something had been done to make it thicker and stronger. Running her fingers on it curiously, the story revealed to her fingers told of both sides feeding into the fiber...but someone else had tried to augment this, almost as if to protect it from threat.

A dull throbbing sensation came from the pouch at her waist, and her fingers played over it without diving in. A hazy memory of a set of red paper poppets and twine swam to the surface before diving back down, and she blushed. The memory of a warm voice, sandy hair, and ice-blue eyes was next, and she touched her cheeks curiously to trace the still increasing warmth as a flood soon followed.

Kirsty scowled and flipped back to her stomach and tried to sense where to go next. How could she have forgotten so easily? What had happened that she temporarily misplaced that part of herself? She had to find the Lady, talk to her and see what it was that needed to be done to complete the initiation and finally stand ready for whatever trials would be found in the sea.

After what seemed to be an eon she finally found an island in the middle of the underground lake. She hauled herself carefully onto to smooth dripstone and waited for the water to fall away and her muscles to get used to the lack of support.

"That took longer than I expected it to." The voice was soft and slightly disappointed as it welled up from the water.

Kirsty looked where she thought it centered. A light gathered and streamed together into a ball deep below the surface, then slowly rose. By the time it broke through the surface, the orb was the familiar water deity, this time clothed in a silver gown and once more with a sword at her waist.

"I'm sorry, Lady." Kirsty bowed her head. "I wasn't sure of what I was supposed to be doing to find you since you usually come to me."

"That's why you had to find me first." The Lady stepped onto the island, bringing the soft light with her. "An initiation is a rebirth, very different from the initiation that your school offers."

"Is that why I forgot who I was?"

"In part." The Lady looked into her eyes, her own eyes endless pools of eternity of undeterminable hue. "It happens to each that undergoes the Trial of the Paths."

Kirsty made a quiet inquisitive sound, only a slight squeak.

The Lady smiled, catching the thoughts that went unvoiced and half formed. "You were just tested on which of us you are most likely to follow and who is your core. I was already fairly certain that you would find my path here. The others would have eventually led you to me here as well but they also would have revealed different tests at the end."

"Mara would be the waves I guess, so it would have had something to do with the sea?" Kirsty felt her brow creasing.

"Yes. If you had followed the moon you would have had a dream or an illusion perhaps. We have overlapping areas just as shi has overlapping areas with Mara." The Lady smiled a bit. "Shi has always been a very good ally and friend."

"What about the flame?" Kirsty wanted to lean forward in her curiosity, but managed to refrain.

"Brigid left a long time ago when she consolidated her forges at *Draiganpáirc* under the care of the O'Drake family. Your test would have had to do with creativity most likely." Sorrow flitted across the Lady's face and she briefly glanced away, as if in the direction the other deity had withdrawn to.

"What about the fifth?" Kirsty pressed.

"You might yet undergo a challenge from him, or one like him. You'd have had to hunt for me more than you did, and in a different place than you would have expected me. His test would have been a very good one. I think that just having to overcome a problem similar to my own is fitting for you though." The Lady watched Kirsty with unreadable eyes.

"He who, Lady?"

She smiled. "Someone already involved and watching you. You know of whom I speak."

Kirsty frowned. What other deity would be watching? The Moon of course made sense. Selkies had their own lunar rituals, whether she shirked them or not in favor of lending David her healing touch.

Her eyes widened. "Herne?"

She paled as the Lady nodded. Kirsty's stomach roiled. It was hard enough trying to keep up with the expectations of two goddesses. She already knew he'd likely be watching and evaluating, but the thought was still terrifying, like being expected to successfully cast a complicated spell the first time without being told what it was she was supposed to be casting.

The Lady laughed. "It's not that bad, child!"

Kirsty looked at her doubtfully. "I'm still terrified I'll mess up something."

"Yet you also can't really fully think about life without him being some part of it, can you?" She pressed.

"Well...no... If I'd have fully become Seaswimmer I probably still would have found my way to him eventually. Going by migrational patterns anyway, and I think I would have done so." Kirsty wanted the dripstone to swallow her.

"I think you would," the Lady nodded. "Especially as his home is so accessible from the sea."

She lifted Kirsty's left hand and turned the palm and inner wrist toward her. Starting there she drew a small spiral before twining around the whole wrist with a vine-like line that returned to the spiral. The design, glowing a bright blue as well as inked into her skin, looked strangely incomplete. The more Kirsty studied, the more it looked like it needed another half. Once the lines met the Lady embedded a small crystal shard.

Kirsty screamed as the crystal pushed below her skin but did not pull away. She was afraid that if she so much as flinched that something major would be damaged. She knew one of the methods of suicide. While she held still she could feel the power of the lady stream in through the wound and through her blood.

Suddenly she felt dry and she found herself gasping for breath. When the Lady let go of her wrist Kirsty reached for her throat, her eyes going even wider. Her body threw itself into the water before she knew what was happening, while the crystal dissolved in her blood and began to spread through her cells.

She tried not to breathe the water, but her body had other plans. Slits along her neck opened and she could feel tissues growing that hadn't been there before. The water went deep, and then back out, some force expelling the water from her lungs with each breath and pulling the air with it. At the same time she could feel the gills working, and she inhaled and exhaled through those. The whole experience was very dizzying, and it took some time to figure out how to orient properly.

"That's one part. Now little fish-child, that part of you is activated and just as real as the selkie skin you crave so badly from my sister." Her voice was slightly bitter, but still supportive and loving as it had always been. "Just remember not to lose yourself, and to return. Now though you must run to the sea. This ability will serve you well during this summer's trials... However, be aware that after that it will not work for weeks at a time, only 'short' spans. Then you will need air."

"Wait! I had a question I needed to ask you that's been bothering me since Samhain. There was this Finman and his eyes won't leave me be."

"It would be best then to take one of the lunar tunnels before returning to my sister's path. The moon sees more than I." While Kirsty watched, the goddess dispersed, taking the light with her.

Kirsty sighed and spread her fingers, looking at the webbing that was now even more prominent between them.

"Right then..." Kirsty allowed herself to sink a bit lower, resting on the bottom of the pool and blowing bubbles out her nose. *"Of course she wouldn't know. Must have driven them nuts when people believed in them..."*

Chapter Thirty Four
Lunar Eidolon

Kirsty rested on the bottom of the pool a bit longer and then ventured tentatively down one of the paths back out. She swam much slower than possible down the one that had been marked with the moon, not sure to be relieved that it lay straight, or worried that it did not twist and turn.

The darkness here was just as bad as the other paths, but the further she went the harder it was for her to focus. If she popped her head above the water for even the briefest of times the air was laden with the scent of lavender, rose, catnip, and some rich but light scent she couldn't identify. It only made her encroaching dreaminess worse and added to the weight of her body pulling her down.

Soon enough her head was spinning and that horrid feeling of not being fully in control of her movements filled her. If she moved wrong she could surely float right out, or maybe it was slosh out. Her whole body thrummed, and she just wanted to close her eyes and sleep. Yet she pressed on. To stop was to admit defeat.

Finally a white form slipped through the water to her, silver hair streaming around in wavering rays. An aurora corona graced the being's brow, releasing the lunar light, and starlit eyes smiled while guiding with dreaming hands.

Kirsty fought to focus at least a little, noting how the figure was neither male nor female, and yet both.

"You had a question it seems?" Shi swam beside her. "I wasn't expecting to feel anyone in the overlap. You're so tightly aligned with my friend."

The casual politeness and curiosity did not fool Kirsty. Now that the White Lady was here she could barely restrain herself from the wriggles that she so often successfully stuffed away every month. The dream-like quality remained, and when her body spun itself forward there was no denying that the moon's deity had her firmly in hir grip.

"The Lady left before I could ask her about something she's been avoiding talking about with me, and directed me to you instead." Kirsty replied, desperately trying to get her body to at least move more sedately. The harder she tried to control her body, the more outlandish the swimming dance became.

The passage widened around them, and the deity perched on a submerged crystal, lighting all the others so that it seemed Kirsty was swimming in the depths of space, not the bowels of the earth.

"Is that so? Well, I do see much during the night's watch, and during my daytime roamings. Share with me what is haunting your dreams of late then." The deity rose off the crystal seat, all the others staying lit, and danced with Kirsty, kissing her cheek.

Kirsty shuddered at feeling the foreign deity so close, at the skin touching skin and brushing so that she knew the garments were just illusion. The deity wrapped an arm around her waist and took her hand, leading her through a waltz despite how Kirsty currently had a tail.

She tried not to look the lunar deity in the eyes. After all, it was well known how easily this one caused madness, and it was rumored that even Herne was wary. Not even her eyes were her own though. They were drawn as surely as the moon controlled the tides of the sea and her own blood. Kirsty howled inside, and the smile that flitted across the deity's face was just as pleased as if David had been howling after a successful hunt.

"Samhain, after leaving the Tor, we went back to our realm to find the Anchors under attack and the Guardians defending them."

"The Finmen during their part of the Great Hunt." The White One dipped Kirsty backwards, hir hair billowing and curtaining her off from all other realities but hirs. "I remember this part of it. Such a fierce little soft one you are. Your descendants will be entertaining."

Kirsty was righted and spun away, leaving her feeling almost like a bird before she was reeled back in too tightly for her comfort. The deity's eyes smiled back and pearly white teeth gleamed like a Cheshire Cat.

"Um... Thank you? There is one of the Finmen that particularly bothers me. He has eyes that are too distinctive..."

"Which of them?" Kirsty was thrown and caught easily, as if the deity thought little of the conversation and only cared for the movements. Perhaps it was true. "There were several there that night little water witch. Each has their own distinctiveness, and I have spent years examining everyone's eyes."

"Oh, that's not creepy at all... Maybe Herne's actually the sanest of them all?" She thought as she was taken from the waltz into a cinque-pace, without hearing any of the music that the lunar deity apparently did.

"Amusing thought. Perhaps he is. Then again, perhaps not. But you weren't wanting my opinion about the Huntsman and Shifter Lord, even though it might be useful for you later." The White One chuckled, as if Kirsty had spoken her thought aloud, then grasped her by the waist and tossed her in the air again.

Kirsty's head broke water and she felt a twinge that perhaps she would be out too long. How high could one of them throw her tiny mortal frame? Then the water sucked her down again, and delicate hands caught her about the waist.

She looked nervously down at the hands, not afraid of being dropped, but half expecting the deity to shift into another form or to take her from this reality to some other. "The eyes I'm thinking of are the ones that look like my parents'. The one that called me a harlot."

The White One laughed and pulled her tight and close, tipping hir head back and twirling Kirsty about, making her gorge rise. "That one. Ah yes, he is a special one... His fate and story isn't mine to tell to you, child. Now, if you were a certain young

Hound of Herne...perhaps I might tell you then. But you're not. You were so close once." The White One's eyes sparkled with merriness or madness, though Kirsty wasn't sure which. "I could tell you a different secret though."

Kirsty pressed her lips tighter as she pondered what the deity meant. Hir interest could be explained in part by what the Hounds did. Simply being bitten and turned to a werewolf would not make her one of the hounds though. She had to be claimed by Herne as one of the Hounds.

Her nose twitched and she blinked, her dance partner still burning into her eyes with hir gleaming fires and the maddening flickers. If her heart raced any swifter it would leave her behind.

"That's not the last you'll see of him. I'm sure over the years you'll get to know him very well." Shi giggled, then pressed a finger to Kirsty's lips, stopping the question. "I think you should have a name for me, I'm so much closer than 'The White Lady' to you, and I'm both and no genders."

Kirsty waited for the finger to remove itself from her lips, and instinctively licked them to try getting them to stop buzzing. This only caused the sensation to spread to her tongue as a sweet taste coated both, and some strange substance was absorbed into her bloodstream. As it did the sensation spread through her body, and it was even less her own. She now craved touch, and if it wasn't for this strange deity...which way would be up?

"What do you wish me to call you then?" Her tongue wasn't thick, but it formed the words strangely and she resisted the urge to wiggle it solely to get lost in the odd feeling. She could sit for hours watching starlight on the loch or the waves, or run for hours barefoot through the trees.

Shi brushed hir lips over Kirsty's ear and whispered as if discussing the details of a holiday gift in the presence of a toddler. "Ven'thrith will do for now, I think. Now...I want to see you out on the full moons more often, no matter what the young Hound wants for your safety. There are places where you can still meet your obligations to Mara, the Lady, and myself without interfering with his needs...and I will help you with his care when you go to do so little selkie-maid."

There was no room for argument. Kirsty merely nodded in agreement. One simply does not refuse the one that holds power over the tide and dreams. As gently as it had all been said the danger zinged through her. It would be so easy for the moon to claim her, and her gift of Sight could easily be turned into a curse.

The moon deity drew back with a smile and deposited her on the crystal shi had sat on before, leaning over Kirsty and pressing her back, allowing hir light to shine more and further forcing her gaze to rest on hir. "Prove useful enough and I'll help ensure that you're able to adapt your station to your passions instead of having to adapt to your station."

"Very well." Kirsty tried to keep herself in control, whatever substance the deity had laced her with still not quite up to a full potency.

Shi grinned wider and pressed the first two fingers of hir right hand to Kirsty's chest, scrawling first a crescent, and then finishing that with a full circle. "Good lass." Ven'thrith spun away. "I'll let you continue on to Mara now. I'm sure she's wondering if her sister decided to just keep you all for herself. I'll be checking on you often, especially in class."

The light snuffed itself save for the still twinkling crystal stars and there was an upward shift, leaving Kirsty suspended in the waters of space. She looked down where the Moon deity had laid a mark, noting vague lines there and wondering how they would translate to her fur.

The lunar sugar continued to move through her veins and Kirsty closed her eyes, searching for the pull of the sea to lead her back to somewhat more familiar realms. The pull was dim but insistent and she followed this inner knowledge through the waters, waiting to find a gate between, or the branching of the ways.

Chapter Thirty Five
TAMPERED

Kirsty could not be sure if it was hours or days that she swam. It could have easily been both since she was most definitely not in the mortal realm, or at least not the one she knew of. All she knew currently of time was that every muscle burned and ached – including ones she didn't know she had in not so very genteel places, never mind that she didn't count herself as 'genteel' – and that she was beginning to loose feeling as she moved beyond that. Her hair had long since matted from her actions, and it was scrambling the information from the water so badly that she 'heard' a constant low static.

Now and then she came upon half-formed fish, or what she assumed were meant to be fish. The fins curved and swept far more than ornamental goldfish, sweeping wide like Dactyloptena orientalis' enlarged pectoral fins, and brighter than the neon-hued Mandarinfish. These had spines as intimidating as lionfish, and she made sure to give them a wide berth in case they were poisonous. Those that she did find stationary began to wilt, and they stared at her with gaping eyes as if waiting for her to utter the word to finish their creation.

Where she had been taken there no longer was any floor to rest on, which did not help. She'd tried floating in place only to find that if she did everything spun around her and left her innards trying to escape, revealing why she so rarely found any life here stationary. After yet more aeons she finally found her way from the limitless expanse of lunar realm waters into a tunnel back to the previous reality.

A burning thought wormed its way to the surface of her consciousness. *"If this were the way deities experience time, it is a wonder that all of them aren't insane."* The thought drowned just as quickly, her mind too tired to grasp it.

The farther she passed down the passage the more she grew aware of the sense of taste returning. The effects of the moon deity's touch still rode through her, but she was glad to once again taste something other than sweet. With the passing of the taste her head cleared, but she was left with a dull throb at the center of her brain when she gained the forking of the ways once more.

Without hesitation she took the path marked with Mara's waves, never wavering from these runes. Nine times she followed the marked path, each time it being found in a different direction. The marks were not always clear, sometimes she had to both see and feel the stone walls to find them, and once she even resorted to using the sense of taste when the runes were so lightly engraven that she was doubting whether she had actually found any.

"At least Imp isn't here to tell David, 'Master...I don't think Mistress is well. She was licking walls and mumbling to herself during her secondary initiation.' Yes, just the thing he needs to be wondering about, if I'm going insane." Kirsty grumbled to herself, purely to break the silence that pressed in around her.

A flash of velvet smoothness and the intense crush of muscle around her stilled the mumbles, restoring the silence once more. She kept her hand on the wall here, resting now that the water would allow her. The pressure mounted, and she dimly became aware of the pulse of waves. The desire to move forward devoured her, but she was held still by the need to find the correct direction.

"This has to be the last one then." She thought, feeling the spectral muscles crushing around her.

The veil drew tighter around her with the familiar wisps and brushes of uncounted threads and yarns, just as surely as the muscles continued to bear down on her body. Unwelcome half-memories clawed through her of another time muscles bore down around her, and she felt smaller and just as clumsy. There was definite pain again, it had managed to get beyond the previous muscle numbness. The edges of her vision alternated between red and black.

"Such an aweful feeling and strange symptoms since she made me part fish too...or woke whatever was in me from the Creation..." She tried to think with gritted teeth. *"No, maybe not. Still so much mammalian."*

The pressure let up, then bore down again harder and faster. The spaces between were shorter. The urge to just go mounted til she trembled with it.

Kirsty tried to draw breath at the next loosening, disturbed at the shift occurring beneath her fingers. The rock continued to smooth and soften, gaining a definite, but slow, pulse. She snatched her hand away and stared with wide eyes, depending on the slight glow becoming visible from the wall. To her vision the rock looked exactly the same as before, merely simple – but smooth – rock.

The light tang of salt finally met her tongue and she turned in its direction. One kick of her tail followed another to propel her down the passage as the specter of a birth canal continued, and she hoped it was not a final trick of the deity she had recently left. The action of her tail's kicks seemed multiplied by the squeezing and the walls passed her by too quickly to notice.

All she knew was that she was crossing vast distances in more ways than one. The sea called her, Mara called her, and she focused on these so as to not somehow wind up somewhere else. The veil continued to tighten, and finally she could see it.

A mist hung thick in the ever-tightening passage before her, an extension of what held her. A half-formed phantasm moved on the other side. Was it a guardian? Would she have to fight this? There was certainly no going back the direction she had come from. The pressure was too intense. She very well might explode with it.

The mist was a wall as soon as she reached it, slamming into it just as hard as if she'd been blasted into Castle Carrick's wall during Dueling Club. Once again she was seeing stars, this time purely in her own head thanks to the headlong blow.

Kirsty grabbed her head and screamed, trying not to wretch.

The pressure from behind kept mounting and she was crushed up against the barrier. Her heart pounded, and the breath was pressed from her as if she were trapped in her own mortar and pestle. Worse, she could feel that she was being ground as she found herself sometimes being drawn against the mist-wall in a circle, and then other times pounded.

She watched in mingled horror and fascination as her body began to dissolve. She watched as molecules broke down and as atomic bonds severed. She had fallen beyond the pain by this point and could feel everything vibrating around her far more clearly than ever before. If she wanted to she could turn away from this and simply cease to be.

There was a firm tug at her heart and an insistent heat at her waist where her pouch lay against her. Simultaneously a bright light shone in her mind, and she became aware of direction. She had a home she had to return to. She had People and somewhat of a purpose, nevermind issues of species.

Kirsty clawed at the barrier and her tangled hair fanned out as her frustration mounted and began to crackle through it. Wherever her hair touched the mist it began to burn away. Her nails began to sting and burn, and she dimly became aware of a strange ooze forming and running down the grooves beside her nails. Her mind grasped the mist, in case it was made of water, trying to rend it or bend it to her will.

The sound and taste of the sea increased. So did the pressure behind her.

There was a shift, a click, a rift. Kirsty felt something fall away from herself energetically. There was movement as something came through the water and claimed that, but she could not pay attention. She needed through.

The shapes in the mist became clearer to her. The taste and smell came to her as she won her way into the mist.

Justin cautiously swam along the Irish coastline, watching for the sharks that sometimes patrolled the waters, or perhaps one of the bull selkies protecting the edges of colonies. He skirted the areas the selkies had been during his last raid on this shore. Here Mara's power was great. Here was where the greatest prizes could be taken. Care had to be taken though, or Aegir would step in and have a say about the trespass on another deity's territory.

It wasn't that that the raids were entirely bad. They kept the blood of the Finmen strong, and should have done so for the blood of those that dwelled on Seal Point. No elders remembered why these had started, only that women and children were needed to supply their number and in some cases supply their meat.

The shift in the waters had been strong since the last Turn of the season. Another portion of Mara was absent. Where he could not say. He wasn't trained in such things and the *Seidhrmenn* were not the least inclined to teach him.

He rubbed at a spot where they had recently re-instilled some of their spellwork on his flesh. It wasn't infected and pus-ridden, thankfully, but here something within him always actively tried to rid itself of...whatever had been done to him for so long.

Justin smiled in relief when he slipped onto the beach where the water from the underground stream formed the pool that spilled into the sea. He was surprised at the lack of bulls in this area today. The *Seidhrmenn* had said the last remaining female Makay was supposed to be undergoing some sort of test. Wouldn't the selkies *want* to protect the one that would be taking care of the well they had their tools blessed by, and who very likely would be midwifing those rare pregnancies that resulted in skinless babes? He might be considered a pariah among the Finmen, but those tests he had to go through were still guarded against interference lest he escape them.

Careful steps took him up the waters, and though he was now wading his contact was enough that he would not dry out fully and regain a wholly human visage. As he entered into the pool the waters flowed welcomingly and he had brief flashes of dark blue eyes and warm arms...with a little dark brown fur to nestle into.

The others avoided this pool whenever they landed for raids. For reasons he never could fathom he was the only one that never suffered any ill effects from the waters of the streams here, hence his blissful alone time.

Stealing a look around first he cupped his hands and drank of the fresh water. He wanted to close his eyes and savor the forbidden drink, he'd likely be paying for it later if one of the *Seidhrmenn* found out, but he wasn't ready to believe that *someone* wasn't going to come leaping off the cliff and blasting at him, or hurling spears, or that a sharp fanged kelpie wasn't going to attempt to eat him.

Justin shivered, remembering the time he'd tried to lure off a very young and tasty looking girl-child from near here several years ago, using his flute's melody. That kelpie had come thundering down the bluff at him already bloodied from who knew whom he'd been eating.

He calmed his breathing, allowing the water to soothe him. It went from cool to warm and pulled at him. After a moment he made his way further through the pool, past the hollow that the water seemed to try guiding him into. It made his heart hurt, as if someone had hollowed him out and placed a slow-burning cinder there to dry him out from the inside out. This was no place to tarry, and he had a mission anyway.

If successful, perhaps one of the unpartnered women in his village would consider him favorably, such as he was. Or perhaps he could finally prove that he was trustworthy enough to be taught some form of runework. Justin snorted at himself for even considering that any of their women would consider him. If he wanted a female companion, he'd have to steal one and then get her to understand he wasn't as bad as the others. As for learning the mastery of runes, they'd been far more suspicious after the 'visit' from a couple strange dragons that had freed part of his soul from their power.

Justin eyed the water that poured out in a waterfall to form this pool, pondering how he would be able to open the gate. Climbing the rocks to gain access to the physical hole the water poured from was an easy thing...but that was not all he'd have to do.

"Your flute is your key, remember well the tune you're always humming." The raspy, hoarse voice of the Eldest grated and scratched through his memory like a spearhead on the sharpening stone.

Justin bit his lip, securing his spear to the sling he wore, and patted the pouch at his waist before scaling the rockfall, then picked the least precarious perch he could find. The rock was stable, but the moss was slick and a little prickly as it objected to his presence. Looking around once more to ensure that he was truly alone he gingerly withdrew the coral pipe.

His fingers caressed the smooth surface, basking in the warmth and pulse. Justin drew a calming breath, allowing himself to settle more firmly and the soul fluttering within the flute to settle as well. Tentative notes picked out the half-remembered lullaby that haunted him, rolling out from mind, soul, and heart, the body walking fingers over the soul's prison to free those notes. The hardness of his face and body fell away for a time, leaving him looking much younger than his usual.

Justin's body warmed with the feeling of home and safety as it spread, and the rocks and waters listened. Images flitted through his mind, never long enough or clear enough to see, but as he launched into the second stanza there was a definite shift around him. The breeze picked up, blowing from land to sea, carrying sighs and the drift of voices from the top of the hill. He let these wash over his ears, secure that the breeze was carrying his sounds away from the ears of the land dwellers.

The breeze fell away as the shift finished and he found himself overhearing heated conversation.

"What are you playing at? You were only to answer her question...not give her a dose of that." Hissed a vaguely familiar voice. It bubbled as if coming from the spring.

"She's wandering and you know it." A calmer voice replied. "I was protecting the two of you as I have always done." This voice was far more familiar. He'd heard it many a moonlit night while hunting or simply playing for his own amusement on his favorite rocks. "The sugar of my inspiration will lead her fully back and she'll find a way to fit the better for it."

"We gave them free will for a reason. You drugged her."

"Yet the descendants you keep bound by blood so they stay direct."

Justin opened his eyes. The side of the cliff had opened, and where the water flowed out from the formerly small cleft was now more than large enough of a cave for him to get into, and even to have fighting room. The voices came from within though. It was only with great caution that he crept in, secreting himself behind rocks and peering around to determine the source of the voices before moving further.

"We do not keep them bound!"

"Herne would agree with me." The voice dropped and left Justin fighting weight and sadness. "We all bind those we've claimed for our own. Yes, it's best when they stay because they enjoy being ours, best that they don't become like all the others that have forgotten us...but bind them we do. Because they are ours."

A third voice, this just as familiar as the voice of the Moon, crashed in. "Be silent. He is here." The argument died and he felt a spear nudging him from behind, prodding him out of his hiding spot. "You took long enough, Boy."

He turned his head to get a glimpse of the one that had snuck behind him. The stern face and deep eyes were the only glimpse he needed. To linger on the shark-like lines and dark hair was to invite his death.

"Yes, yes it is." Mara agreed, smelling the whiff of his wariness and reading his vibrations. A smile curled her agreement and she continued walking him forward. "As I'm sure you guess, you were merely allowed to come, and you did not sneak through by luck."

"Always as the Lady wishes..." Justin stated cautiously. The few encounters he'd had with the deity the Finmen followed had led to him being distrustful of any of them. An enemy deity though? He'd sooner take his chances with a real shark, instead of the mother of them and all sea life.

"Not always..." Mara's voice trailed off, and Justin noticed that the other goddess had a strange look on her face. That one bit her lip and cast her gaze to the ground, as if his presence pained her. The moon god rested hir hand lightly on hers, as if to pass some inkling of strength against whatever caused the pain. "Go do what you came to do. Or try."

"You're not stopping me?" He could feel his face furrowing.

"Why should I? If the bloodline isn't strong enough to take on one of your kind, what guarantee do I have this one will be a fit champion?" Mara removed the spear from his back. "You have your worth, even in such a state as you are. By all means: Attack, kidnap, kill for food if you can, or see her wed to whoever will buy her from you."

The Lady's fists balled and her light and form went from pale blue to a muddy flood-roil. Justin noted the way her eyes flashed as she regarded Mara behind him. He wasn't sure why, but he understood, somewhat, the emotions the land's water goddess tried to keep in check.

"Maybe I shouldn't if she means so little to you. I'm only here because the elders say she means enough to make it worth sending me." His own fingers were curling into fists, and he could feel his hackles rising. His nose twitched and an odd clawing sensation started in his chest, as if a caged grindylow had gone rabid.

"I didn't say that she meant little, mortal." Her teeth could be heard, and Justin swore that he could feel her circling him even as she stood still. "Show me your worth."

The Lady was trembling now, and the tendrils of her hair beginning to writhe. The Moon God had a firm grip on the land sister now, pulling her back and away from Mara.

"Not now, dear Lady...not now." Shi ground out. "Lad, do as she says. Maybe you'll understand later." Shi shook hir head and then blew a strange sparkling dust toward him.

Justin tried to avoid it, eyes widening, but Mara grabbed him and held him fast. She allowed the full dose of the substance to douse him while manipulating the water of his body to absorb it faster through his skin when he refused the instinct to lick his lips. His vision sharpened and he felt almost as if he could see through his skin.

"Even footing. Now take this quest, since you already accepted it." The Moon God's comment was fading even as the deities themselves were.

The sugar coursed through his veins and into his brain, clouding his judgment while waking other parts of his brain he rather actively sought to suppress. The need for experience grew sharper in him, and his body pushed itself onward to where he could feel his quarry. As the water deepened, he swam against it like salmon. It tasted of fish, selkie, and human.

Time and distance lost meaning. All he knew was that the worst of the effects were finally beginning to wear off when he found a barrier in his way. His mind warred with his body as he tried to purge the moon's hold. It was a dangerous thing to have clouding one's mind before battle or mission, and more than one tribe had fallen prey before to how it clouded mind and perception. The rocks still wavered and danced around him, reaching for him with lover's arms.

Seaswimmer's scent continued to mount, and he could feel her energy growing closer. Justin prowled for a bit at first, searching for a way through. He wasn't sure how he knew, but if she made it through on her own then she would be a changed being. If he could prevent that, perhaps be the one that brought her through, then whatever she would become would be stillbirthed. Or perhaps any powers that would have been awakened would transfer to him instead.

His hands ran over the hardened mist and his nails scratched and dug, but he was unable to claw through. Throwing a large rock only rebounded it in an amplified form toward himself. Justin threw himself to the left when it came back and felt it scrape past him when it hadn't even touched him. After picking himself up again he examined the rock, finding where it had collided had liquified and reformed.

There was no way he was going to throw a kick or a punch at that. Likewise there was no good spot to lay in ambush. Justin continued to prowl, spear drawn and as large as he could make himself. Perhaps he could delay her by frightening her away from this...membrane.

She came faster than he was prepared for, as if she had slipped from one realm to another. A dark blot impacted the barrier and fell back, and the sonic wave she unleased pushed him back even through it. It fell away into a normal scream and wavered, not quite a violin note, and certainly less pleasant.

Justin readied himself, recovering as swiftly as possible despite how he could barely hear and his head rang. Seaswimmer was clawing at the membrane, and he could see her claws deforming it but never quite breaking through. An electrical current began to form like when the giant eels prepared to strike. It tasted of ozone. The membrane stretched more under the onslaught, and the closer she came the more the moon's effects began to return.

He readied his spear, his hackles rising again the further she deformed the barrier. Before he was aware of what he was doing, his blood carried him forward and the spear tip into the solidified but stretching mist. Instead of rebounding it punched through, and a torrent of odd tasting water rushed over him. His momentum carried him through the veil.

A piercing scream wrapped around him, even as hands roughly pushed his spear to the side. The tactic he had expected, she's seemed oddly good at that the last they had met. What he wasn't braced for were the welts and stings forming as hair tendrils wrapped around him. Some he had expected. To lose vision was not expected.

As she assailed the membrane the scent and feel of danger intensified. A sharp object was brought to it from the other side, and a black aura surrounded the blade that threatened her. The form she now knew to be male, and it bore down on her with all its weight and fury as it tore into her world from his.

Kirsty moved as fast as she could while also casting her shield spell, pressing the blade down enough that she could grasp the spearshaft and hoped to use that to springboard herself over the Finman.

He brought his head up into her own as hard as possible and she let go. Kirsty tried to hit him with her tail as she passed over. The membrane, ripped by his passage, let her through and she landed roughly on a rock before bouncing to the ground.

The water drained, leaving the passage half air and half water. Kirsty bounced from the ledge she'd landed on back into the water. Stars filled her vision and the ringing in her ears dulled the sound of his movements. She drew a breath, flopping and trying to move despite how each move further made it difficult to keep her breath.

Justin turned as swiftly as he was able after her powerful tail, and likely more than a little magic, drove him into the floor of the passage. His skin tingled and he could feel his blood moving in ways he'd not felt before. When his eyes fell on her she seemed to shine for a moment, but it was only momentary.

He grinned and advanced on her as she fought to move. Seaswimmer hissed at him and raised her hands. Her pupils were wide and didn't seem to focus on him as he moved, and he grinned wider.

She flopped her tail and moved another body length. Kirsty pulled what energy she could from the water to replenish what she'd used and prepared to channel it toward him. She operated more on feel than sight, the stars refusing to leave her vision.

He was on her as she felt the water leave her hands. The kiss of stone never came, only the power that radiated off his own hands and tried to control the flow of her blood. Her heart slowed, and more black crept across what little vision she had, leaving only the infuriatingly familiar eyes locked on hers while wills battled. Their energies tangled, snarled, and pushed even as hands tried to grapple or press away.

The unused wand in its sling crackled to life, transmuting some of the energies that passed between the pair. The selkie hair within screamed in protest. Another consciousness flowed through their blood and attempted to press both youths down, to drag them apart. In the backs of their minds a half-remembered face formed, marred by a deep frown and dark hair gaining another streak of silver. Pearl teeth glinted in these recesses the longer she stayed between them. The scent of tears went unnoticed while each fought to be the victor.

Again what saved Kirsty was more feeling-based than sight-based. She found a gap in the webbing his energy was casting, mercifully kept slightly away from herself by Marsali's hair. The knot was loose, as if he was not used to manipulating energy and only doing so on instinct. Kirsty focused her own energy through that point, visualizing a blade as she did to further widen the hole. She was already disengaging as fast as she could, and so did not notice when the same energy that gave her space placed itself between her strike and target enough to slightly deflect it. The electricity from her hair released again at the same time, only ripping away due to his movement.

The netting fell away even as the focused rush pressed him back. Unaware of the contortions of her face Kirsty managed to get over to her belly again and moved as swiftly as she could along the stream, using her arms more than her tail. Just above her back was beginning to go between fire and ice, and she tried to use the water's flow to further move herself along.

Behind her Justin landed against one of the stones, his own head contacting as hard as her own, temporarily taking his sight and breath. Electricity continued to dance over him for a moment, and where her nails had scratched were beginning to already swell and spread red roots.

Chapter Thirty Six
Messy Homecoming

Kirsty spilled into the pool, taking a deep breath of the water and trying not to whimper. There was a warm spot, and she pulled herself there, laying down in the hollowed shallows that seemed to wrap her in caring arms. Her body trembled as she reclined, and thankfully her vision began to go back to normal save for the red around the edges that throbbed with her heart.

She eyed the gap she fell out of, now that her vision was beginning to clear, and felt for something she could use as a weapon. It was a useless maneuver she recalled shortly after beginning. They kept the pool free of driftwood.

One of the larger fish nudged her tail. Its silvered scales did little to tempt her appetite due to her pain, unusual since she often nicked a fish from the birthing pool if no one was due. She shooed it away, but it kept at her, always nudging toward the sea.

Kirsty pulled herself the rest of the way, dragging away from the birthing area and back down along the stream's flow to the surge of the sea. There was a rush of energy when she got into the salt water. Far out she could feel the call and pull of one of the Temples. If she held still long enough she could feel other Temples in other directions. Kirsty contemplated how on earth she was going to be able to manage her way through the rocks of the shoreline in search of Mara in this state.

A surprised whinny held her short and turned her around, her arms holding one of the nearby rocks to manage the ebb and flow of the surf.

"When did you get out? I've been here this whole time!" Byron's hoof falls over the worn stone were a welcome sound, and when he was near enough she eased her arms from the rock to his sturdy frame.

"Just now." Kirsty buried her face in his green fur, letting her body wrap his legs while the kelpie laid the underside of his chin down her back.

Byron looked down her back, seeing where the purple bruising was showing from beneath damaged scales. He frowned. Selkies did not have scales, but fur. "What happened in there? You've been gone days now."

"So much... So many passages and gates, I think. And the Lady implanted something into my hand..." She lifted her hand and showed him where the scar had faded, the tattoos darker than when they had formed. "Turned me into a fish-thing to help this summer. Then there was the Moon God, I have to dance more... Then there was a Finman...he–"

"Finman?" Byron's right foreleg pulled Kirsty beneath him and held him to his underside. Kirsty made a sound of protest, she wasn't a pup anymore. He ignored her protests and held her tighter...as old as she could ever live she'd still be one of Marsali's pups to him. "How could that be? We've been trading watches. This has been secured since shortly after you went down."

"I don't know. Just that he was there, and I think he's crazed. I don't even know how he got in. The Pool's the one place they've never been able to set fin." Kirsty had given up on getting him to let go.

"Because they can't, not after what was done when they turned... The only way any Finmen would get in there is if they had the same ancestors or were allowed in by the Ladies." Byron continued watching the portal out of the Lady's realm warily, while also scanning around them for any others.

All that met his eyes were the same surging sea, rocks, and beach that had kept him company these several hours of his watch. Above them on the dark cliffs were the thick trees that always shifted, with no deer moving among the boles. Not even a seal had been in the waters nearby, as if everything had been ordered away. Likely it had been, which only left one possibility to his mind.

Byron tried not to shudder at what that might mean for

Kirsty. He nuzzled lightly and blew a little over her. "Well, you are out. You've made it to the sea. That's traditionally the end of this test. If you can turn so that you don't dry out I'll take you home."

"I don't know how. I've not taken any of the paste since I went down. I should've had to at some point, but." Kirsty looked back at the stream's exit point from the cliff, expecting the Finman to come after her at any minute.

Byron scowled. "Just what did she put into you?" He began to make his way through the surf along the shore to the dock and house further down, careful to keep Kirsty well covered by the water. Perhaps, if he got close enough, he could bolt with her on his back and get her to the bathtub in time for he and Finnol to look through the Log for ideas.

Kirsty tried to remember what had passed between herself and the Lady, but most of it had already hazed. "A shard of the same crystal type she gave David...and some energy. She just said it would help me."

Byron ground his teeth. *"Cryptic, of course it can never be straightforward. That would be too much to ask. Deities."*

There was a shark prowling the waters nearing the dock, seeking after the fishes that always swam there during this part of the tide. It came close to investigate, staying well out of the kelpie's range and fixing one eye on them as it slid past. He had other more pressing matters on his mind, and as it posed no thread it was soon left behind.

Then he was thundering out of the water, up the beach, and bellowing before the front door. It sprung open and he was though, into the parlour, where Marsali shrieked as she tried to rise off her rock to come out of the painting. He didn't even bother with trying to contain whatever water he was still putting off. Said water formed a puddly trail behind him and quickly soaked into rugs and carpeting over the wood floor.

Byron ran up the stairs and rattled portraits off walls before crashing into the bathroom and depositing Kirsty into the tub to the protests of both her and Mr. Merrow. Their splashing as they tried to regain some form of dignity coated walls and speckled the ancient mirror. Someone's flailing arm knocked over the row of bottles holding oils and soaps.

"Oi! Warn a mate before dropping a lass in his lap. 'Specially if she's dressed like I think! Her Da' may keelhaul me, Selkie or no." Mr. Merrow scrambled out of the tub and from under Kirsty, then snatched a towel to wrap around his waist. He turned his back to her as she further tried to adjust herself, until he was fairly certain she had important things covered.

"He'll kill us all if she dries out like that. Keep her wet till we figure this change out." Byron backed out with the intention of going to summon Finnol, his eyes not rolling and shot yet, but his red-spined frills were on full display through his seaweed mane.

Mr. Andersen was shutting the front door again while Marcus stumbled from the kitchen, still clad in Etain's white frilly apron and wielding the fork he'd been turning sausages and checking bangers with. Before he was able to fully do so Byron was back down the stairs and he had to fling it again. The pair only gazed for half a second before the door was fully shut again.

"Well...what a way to come home... Go put on another serving or three, she'll likely be hungry. I'll head up and see what's to be done." Mr. Andersen sighed, only able to make out bits and pieces of what had been shouted upstairs.

"Young lady... WHERE IS YOUR DRESS? I don't want your father jumping to any conclusions." Merrow was already across the hall and into Kirsty's room, Andersen could hear him trying and failing to open her closet.

Marc and Andersen exchanged raised glances before parting.

Chapter Thirty Seven
Interlude

Kirsty sighed. The water by now had gotten very cold, and all she wanted to do was get out and drag herself to bed...dry-outs or not. Her father had brought her dinner in for her before he and Byron went to his study to consult the Log in case any of the previous Makays had heard of anything like this in their travels and researches. He had also backed out quickly after handing it to her with his hand over his eyes and muttering something about hoping she remembered to be wearing her swimsuit nights David joined her night classes.

She was still stewing about that. Of course she kept herself covered when David was looking. She might have selkie blood, but she certainly wasn't so bold. As uncomfortable as the 1920s era suit was on her pelt at least she knew he wasn't going to get any peeks on accident. He might have died of embarrassment anyway, and his actually having class was one of his draws.

On the other hand she supposed that as a father it was a worry he'd still have even after she had carried on the family line. A knock interrupted her reverie.

"How are ye holding up in there, lass?" Mr. Merrow's voice was slightly muffled through the door, but understandable.

"I could sing a song about it. I was considering running more hot water. I may as well be comfy if I'm stuck as a fish-seal-freak-thing."

"Tha' well then? Well they think they might have some idea of what tha's aboot. Ye didnae look too bad what bit o' a flash o ye we saw though."

"Well, it's not like any of us can exactly say I'm hideous right now, it it?" Kirsty's tone dropped like bitters.

"Nae, but I'd be lying if I said you was a hideous beast."

"But I'm supposed to be able to get my skin this summer so I can become a real selkie and take a proper seal form if I don't want to be between! How is it going to look to have a white seal swimming around with random scales popping out? I'll be caught for sure."

"Ye'll be fine. Maybe it's jest temporary and the odd bits become less noticeable, or only come out on certain occasions." On his side of the door Mr. Merrow waved his hands and patted them downward, hoping to tap down her emotions. It was bad enough when his wife went through spats like this. But Kirsty, who was like a niece to him, and at such a young age saying such things? With his wife he at least knew what to say, even if he did sometimes end up getting relegated to the couch for telling her she was always gorgeous even if her skirt made her rump look fat.

Wordless grumbles were all that Kirsty could manage in reply before she pulled the plug and let out a bit of the now very cold water, then replugged the tub and ran the hot tap.

"Is she ok?" Marcus waited at the top of the stairs at the end of the hall.

Mr. Merrow looked that way and held his hands out, the indoor lighting giving his skin a vaguely greenish hue. "As well as we can expect I guess. Grumpy."

"Poor girl." Marcus leaned on the corner of the railing, his brows drawing down further. "Does she want a spot of tea?"

"Marcus wants to know if you 'want a spot of tea'?" He mimicked the accent exactly, earning a scowl from Marcus and a disbelieving giggle from the bathroom.

"Might be nice. I'm colder now than I'd expect." Kirsty called, "Tell him thank you, too."

He nodded and headed back for the stairs, going down with Marcus. Near the base of the stairs the door to Finnol's study was open, and they could hear Byron and Finnol consulting with the voices of Finnol's ancestors who had all added their contributions and knowledge in just the same way the family continued to do.

Marcus paused for a moment, still intrigued by the myriad of strange things that everyone seemed to be taking for granted such as talking books, drippy waterhorses, and shapeshifted children. He continued on to prepare the tea for little Kirsty shortly though, and hoped that if he had to take it in to her she would be covered.

By the time he was done Merrow, Andersen, Finnol, and Byron were talking in rapid-fire Gaelic. Instead of interrupting what he hoped was a plan, even though it was beginning to sound more and more like an argument, he took the cup up. It had an odd curl to the scent, some strange mix that he'd found in a green tin labeled 'Kirsty's tea: not for Byrons' that had a smooth spice and soft hush. What herbs she had mixed he'd never hope to guess. It wasn't Earl Grey, and not roobios or green tea. That was the extent of his knowledge.

He knocked lightly. "If you're decent I can bring it in."

There were the sounds of shifting and splashing. "Ok."

Marc avoided looking at Kirsty, despite the large fluffy towel and the shower curtain that she had between them, and set it carefully within her reach. She peeked around at him. "Thank you." Her hand snaked around and took the cup, pulling the aromatic steam with her. "It still seems strange that you're here."

"To me too. But I am. I admit I wish I'd known about all this a little earlier, but I can understand why it was hidden." He lingered near the door. "Would you like me to bring anything else?"

The sounds of the 'discussion' below continued to swell.

"What do you mean she's not finished yet? She made it to the sea! It should be done." Byron bellowed, falling to English now.

"Acetominophen...a big one. They're in the medical cabinet. Careful of the potions and wraps though. You should find the bottles of Cowan remedies in the door itself." Kirsty replied after the bellow.

"Not something from the potions?"

"No, it would react badly with my tea. You have to be very careful what you combine," she replied. "I want a clear head, won't be any use with a muzzy one."

Marcus hurried back down to where he'd been told and looked for what he'd been asked to bring. He sighed in relief at finding everything within the cabinet to be over-labeled. Several of the items he was less familiar with seemed to have instructions with them. It wasn't long before he'd found the requested pill and brought it up.

"So what's Mara aboot then, if li'l Kirsty's first trial isn't over yet?" Merrow queried.

"Damned if I know what she's doing to my little girl." Finnol could be heard slamming his fist on his desk. "She can't take her too. Not yet."

Marcus winced and ran back up the stairs. Patience had been short with his friend since the night of finding Etain's wreck. He knocked again.

"Kirsty, I got it, are you ready?" No answer came, so he knocked louder and repeated the question louder, and several times, each time growing louder.

He heard the others coming up the stairs behind him, felt the house shake as they pounded toward him. Marcus opened the door. "I'm coming in!"

Kirsty was sound asleep, her empty cup broken on the floor. Finnol bellowed for her, and he only barely had time to cover his ears, but she didn't wake.

Chapter Thirty Eight
What Lies Within

Kirsty sipped at her tea while waiting, chafing at still not being returned to normal. She wanted into bed and to have legs to carry herself there with. She could almost sympathize now with the tale of the little mermaid. Legs were great. She'd not been greatly sympathetic before since part of the focus was on getting the love of a prince from the land *"Setting sights that high? Disaster."* without speaking. If she'd just wanted to walk on land, she'd have understood that more.

"But nooo."

Then again, she couldn't exactly say that her plans for her life made the most sense either. Maybe someone somewhere was reading her story and mocking her.

"Perhaps some would be." Mara's voice came from inside her pouch, muffled to the ear but ringing in her head.

"Mara! Why aren't I changing back?"

"Perhaps because you've not finished yet. You've done admirably, but..." Kirsty could see Mara in her head, standing on the waves and crossing her arms. This version was younger than she was used to. Mara looked to be her own age, when the wind didn't have her dark hair covering her face. "You've not exactly found ME yet."

"I got to the sea though. Byron says that's where the traditional ending for this test is." Kirsty shifted in the water, setting her cup down on the closest available surface.

"Not everything we do is based in tradition. You're not going by tradition, why should we?"

Kirsty sighed. "How am I going to find you while I'm stuck in a bathtub? If I ask someone to take me back out to the ocean, especially at this time of night, Da' and Byron both will probably flip their lids."

"Then don't ask. Show me your creativity and see how you can find ME from where you are. Here is as good a place as any." Mara smiled enigmatically in her mind, but there was a warning curling through her blood that made Kirsty wonder what would happen if she failed.

The vision faded, leaving her in a darkness that was neither here nor there, somehow nowhere and everywhere at once. Now she missed her safe bathtub, as embarrassing as it was to sit there in it and wait.

No matter how hard she tried to see there was no light. Kirsty tried to create light through the several methods she knew of, but neither human magic nor selkie magic brought forth any result. At least when Ven'thrith had taken her into the waters of space, or that's where she thought shi'd taken her for at least part of the journey, there had been light from the star crystals.

Movement did not seem possible either. She could move her limbs and turn, but locomotion in any direction was constantly thwarted by having nothing to push against.

Dimly she was aware of an uproar, though she couldn't make out what was being said or where it was from. Struggling as hard as she could only seemed to take her farther away, even without the sense of direction.

Taking a deep breath, Kirsty stilled herself. If she couldn't search outside herself then it left only one direction. Surely this was something she could do. Right?

Kirsty's eyes drifted shut, or would have if she had them. It was becoming hard to be aware of even having a body. It faded away quickly now that she had turned herself inward and stopped wasting energy on the outside.

It took a long time of sitting in the same mindfulness that the Lady had been teaching her to use to find the water outside. After several tens of heartbeats she found a swirl of Mara's energy pumping through her body. Once she found it she was able to feel it all through her bloodstream and moving through her cells. Even in her bones she could feel the two energies, although she could also feel heavier presences there. Mara's energy presence was weak though, no where as strong as the fresher presence of the Lady through her being.

Kirsty contemplated this and watched as the veins formed beneath her consciousness. It burned and itched as if they grew new. There was a concentration of energy in her hand where the Lady's blood had entered her bloodstream earlier.

"Blood. Is that the 'find Mara' I'm supposed to do?" She tucked in further to herself and listened more intently, focusing specifically on Mara's energy. Where had been the last place she had been cut and traded blood with her?

Kirsty couldn't remember, and had to keep a tight rein on herself. Did she need to make Mara's presence within herself stronger? Could she even cut herself in this state to give herself and receive the water-blood?

"No, that can't be it. It's got to be either simpler or more difficult. I'm probably going to beat myself up for taking so long. Watch it be one of those obvious things like when Nevin's looking for his glasses and they're on top of his head."

Her mind drifted and she idly traced her left wrist in the twining pattern of her main bonds, observing how one was glowing brighter than the other in the darkness. Her mind rifled through pages of memories garnered from the Makay Log before she'd been sent to to school. The voices that it recorded soothed her while trying to recall anything that could be useful. Even long dead, they were always going to be part of her.

In her mind and heart she felt a click. Something opened and she pressed at the internal door she'd just found. It screeched further open like a crypt door's unoiled hinges. Towards the end the door seemed to get heavier, but she pushed at it more, sinking her teeth further into the task and firming her realization.

Behind that heavy stone – it had to be stone – door in her center she saw a muted grey-blue light. The sound of the surf came and caressed her, spreading through her. Kirsty stepped through the door and deeper into herself. Her feet – they had returned! – met sand and she wiggled her toes into its warmth. The surf washed over them and engulfed them in a chill but welcome embrace that lapped up to the top of her head and made her flush and rub her arms at once.

"That took you long enough to figure out... It amazes me how visual your thoughts are." Mara's voice came from her right.

Kirsty looked toward it to discover the disturbingly young Mara standing on a rock and preparing to spear a large fish caught in a tidepool with her obsidian and crystal spear. Her skirt was tied up high enough to flash white thighs that were slightly greyish and striped along the outside.

"Mara? This is what was meant by finding you?" Kirsty's heart rose to her throat at the intensity radiating off the seaside huntress.

"Yes." She speared the fish and held it aloft, inspecting it as the silver and black scales caught the light, smiling at the movements of the powerful muscles. "You feel about like this fish, don't you?"

Kirsty held her ground but contracted into herself at the warmth in the usually bitter goddess' voice. "Yes. A bit."

"You are still hungry too." Mara turned and offered the floundering fish to Kirsty with wide, dark eyes. "Eat then. I don't like seeing you that way."

Kirsty very carefully removed the offered fish and bit into its side as Mara nudged her nose toward her insistently. The flesh was moist and a strange mix of murk and sweet. Whatever unrecognizable specie it was, it ran between fresh and salt waters by its taste.

"It is extinct, but I still find it here because it lives still in the line you come from. Not directly related, of course." Mara's unnaturally toothy smile gleamed and reminded her of some of the manga that the Japanese exchange students sometimes would be seen reading.

"So...you're basically feeding me myself?" Kirsty took another bite and watched the goddess warily.

Mara threw back her head and laughed, leaning on her spear casually. "I suppose you could say that. Your mother was a little freer with her jokes at your age, but I am glad to see that you aren't so suspicious of me as to deny me a little laughter."

Kirsty finished the fish quickly, finding that the more she ate of it the more complete she felt...though not fully. There still existed that hollow ache to wear a skin of her own.

"Why are you acting so..." Kirsty paused, trying to phrase it the least offensive way possible. She found only blanks.

"Nice? Not-bitter? Normal?" Mara offered. "You're only meeting with part of me while the rest looks for Etain..." Her voice trailed off and her eyes swept out to the fog-shrouded sea. "I'm younger here too. I'm not always the terror that people think me."

Kirsty found herself pressing a hand over her heart at the pain welling inside. "You miss Mum very much, don't you?"

"I do. You're afraid of me. So is your mother, now, but she remembers that I am this too." Mara sat on her rock and dangled her feet.

"So...when do you turn me back so I can walk on land?" Kirsty itched to sit on that rock beside the goddess, even though she still didn't fully trust the deity. Her body moved without listening to her mind's counsel and she hauled herself up to join her.

"You're walking here, aren't you? It's already been done." Mara's hand settled over Kirsty's. Kirsty felt the calluses and scars, especially the one that matched the great gashes that she had seen her mother make across her own hand at times, and blinked.

"Why wouldn't I keep matching scars to what my children

wear?" Mara's voice was sadder now, fainter. "You are in me, and I am in you. Balance wouldn't be balance if I didn't bear the scars and pains too."

"Do you know when Mum will be back?" Kirsty held still as she floundered through the conversation, still unbelieving at how accessible Mara was in this form.

"No. But I'm trying to bring her home. I don't know where she is...but at the same time I do." Mara turned her head to the left and looked further down the beach.

Kirsty looked in the same direction, surprised to see that they were near the birthing pool, although it looked very different than the way she knew it. In that direction she could hear faint shouts and calls.

"I think it's time for you to go back..." Mara's hand tightened possessively and Kirsty cried out as a joint popped. Just as quickly Mara released her with a hiss and guilty glance.

The world around her faded as the fog rolled in and shrouded all. She could feel the cold wetness soaking into her skin and the salt air hydrating her sinus cavities...and the sting of it. As the fog rolled out she found herself sitting once more in a tub now chilling, inside an overcrowded bathroom.

"Why are you ALL in here...?" Kirsty grabbed the nearest thing to pull over herself. The shower curtain definitely needed washing by the stiff feel of it. She prayed that the rod wouldn't fall down on her.

"Kirstin! *Taing do Mara!*" Her father scooped her out – curtain, water, and all – and held her close forgetting about dignity and soggy clothes. He continued to exclaim in Scots Gaelic before slipping back through Irish Gaelic and then English. "Where were you little pup?"

Kirsty squawked in indignation and went red. "Daaaaaa'.... There's people in here and I'm in a shower curtain..." Despite how hard she tried to hide, she was convinced that everyone that had been staring at the tub like it had been empty and had seen everything. Half-pelt or not, it would surely have her thrashing at night for weeks. "I was with Mara. I figured out how to finish this test and she gave them back. Or I brought them back...something like that."

"She's got her land legs back!" Byron grinned from the door, Kirsty's ears still ringing from the din. "Lovely hairy legs."

Kirsty groaned and examined what was exposed, finding that they were hairier than the last she'd seen them. "I hate puberty. Weird changes. Not-even-half-pelt legs."

Andersen, Merrow, and Marc pushed their way out of the bathroom while Finnol sank to the toilet and refused to let Kirsty go. Byron snickered at the scene. "But wait, there's more."

"You've been watching too much Cowan TV somewhere." Kirsty considered picking up the nearest bottle and chucking it at Byron but heaved a deep sigh instead. The more worried he'd been or was, the heavier the sarcasm. She pushed her irritation aside and leaned into her father. "Sorry Da. I didn't mean to scare you..."

Byron left the door and made his way down to Marsali and the fireplace. With a sigh he reared up and rested his front hooves on the mantle to touch his nose lightly to the painting. His eyes pressed closed. "I don't know how much longer I can take this Marsali... Sliding back and forth too? There one minute dead to the world and then puff? Gone, then back again?"

Marsali pressed her hand on the canvas between them, stroking his muzzle the best that she could. The wind in her painting picked up some of the spray and kissed his green velveteen lips. "We have to. The pups all still need us, and we need them."

Byron snorted and pressed a little firmer against the canvas.

Chapter Thirty Nine
Shifter's Registry

Two days later Kirsty sighed and picked at the stitching of her dress, scuffing her feet on the floor. The rug was a sea blue with a slight wave pattern. She looked from there to the tiny aquarium by the desk where some little pink crabs scuttled around in rocks and a starfish slowly plied the side. Then she let them roam to the tiny hyacinth-pink conch shell on the front desk.

"Are you sure you'd rather not wait in your father's office for your aunt?" Hyacinth asked, looking up from her desk. "You're changing the tide in the aquarium and making me thirsty."

"Da' needs to concentrate on the conference with that diplomat he's lobbying. I don't think Mr. Whatsis would really appreciate a girl in weirdly old-fashioned clothes listening in." Kirsty shifted again, and the clock struck the hour from the corner.

Hyacinth leaned back in her creaky desk chair and chuckled. "Afraid you'll make him nervous and not consider what he's being told about those ejected selkie herds?"

"Very. Do you think we'll be seeing more coming to the Point this summer?" Kirsty flexed her toes in her shoes and squirmed.

"Maybe. Your father always makes it sound so safe. I wish I could live somewhere like that. Must be neat to be in a place that's there but not. Tea?"

"Shells and spines, yes. But just a little. What if it comes back up at the Department of Myths...all over some priceless knickknack." Her blood pressure rose as she imagined the look on her aunt's face, who had gone to such lengths to ensure that she could get everything done legally without raising suspicion as to why she had learned to shift.

Hyacinth nodded slightly and flowed over to the corner table.

Methodically she poured out a half cup of tea into one of the plain waxed paper cups. It took a moment to remember the proportions of sugar and cream that Kirsty liked, but Hyacinth prided herself on being able to mix a drink just perfect for the drinker. "You'll do fine. What I've seen here, you do just fine in turning into a fluffy cute kitty."

"I'm not cute." She took the cup and gave Hyacinth a wan smile when she brought it. "But thanks. What I'm worried about is the stress element that they'll add when testing for the registry. As keen as they are to quantify anything that might not be regarded 'human' and anything like the old tales of witches, I hear some of those in the Department really like when they can make someone get stuck and can shunt them off into 'Beast.'" Kirsty took a slow sip.

"I never did understand why so many ministries and departments." Hyacinth sat back down as the tea started its work on the girl. "Really, are they under the aegis of the country's government, or are they supra-governmental? Or just merely hidden? Trying to take over the world? It's more confusing than the UN."

Kirsty groaned. Even when she did grow up and immerse fully in potions, the United Nations she would still have to pay attention to while filling Mara's duties of protecting the resources she used. "I haven't the foggiest. I think its some weird combination. Maybe its some complicated plot to take over the world, like those Illuminati that the Cowan think aren't real. I'm really not looking forward to possibly dealing with all that stuff."

"I don't think most in the Order do." Hyacinth leaned forward. "We're counted on though, for all our little contributions."

"This is going to be one of your 'if you can do this, then you can do that' talks. Isn't it?" Kirsty's eyes took on a tinge of seafoam when they looked over the partially tilted cup. "I'm not a full member yet since I'm still a minor."

"But you've already got the white cape."

Kirsty snorted. "That's because of being a priestess by birth and my coloring. This one's not earned."

"But you're earning it going through the magic school, and through the training for the high magic. The combination of what each member of your family has to attempt on their own is much more stringent than the general Order requirements." Hyacinth shifted the paperwork that waited for her return to processing. "So what's one little test of whether you can transform while being confronted with your deepest fears?"

"I'd rather not see David or anyone dead... I didn't like that class even though it was only illusion." Kirsty pouted, scuffing the carpet with a black leather toe again before kicking out to lay her boot heels on it. She finished her tea while trying to think of a retort that made sense.

Hyacinth looked down and smirked behind her hair when the pause had gone on long enough, not at the idea of some boy she'd never met being dead, but instead at how firmly child-like this girl was.

"Fine. You win this one. I'll try to be confident." Kirsty got up and went to make herself a full cup of tea. "I'd like more, I'll get it though. You have things to do before someone comes in."

Hyacinth's smirk turned to a grin. Kirsty prepared her tea, carefully measuring each spoonful several times before finally adding it. She hovered by the table and drank, and by the time her cup was drained again Professor MacLeòmhann pushed the door open to set off the tinkling bell.

As usual Professor MacLeòmhann was swathed in green, though this time in the green and blue of the Highland MacKays, hiding the clan in plain sight with the association and shared tartan with the Makays, with small nods to her birth clan in gold and red. "Hyacinth, I hope I'm not late."

"No Belara, you're actually a little early. I think you came at the right time though." Hyacinth nodded her blonde head meaningfully toward Kirsty. "She's over there filling her bladder."

"Thank you." Professor MacLeòmhann nodded at the receptionist and held her arms open to Kirsty.

Kirsty dropped her empty cup in the bin and slid into her aunt's arms, resting her head against her chest and inhaling her comforting scent. The thin arms folded around her. Kirsty gripped a little tighter.

"I heard the well trial did not go smoothly?" The last of her professor role fell away for a time, leaving only Belara stroking the child's head. If only she had been able to have children in her long ago youth. But then she would have had her own children trying to earn skins if they had taken after her departed husband, not just distant nieces and nephews. She rested her nose on top of Kirsty's hair. While Hyacinth returned to her paperwork, "We can wait another year for this if you need to, I could make it happen somehow."

"It was a bit of rough water, but it's done. I'm not so sure of what to think about some things and it's too late now, if there ever was a time." Kirsty looked up at her aunt and noticed a few new lines had formed on her face since she'd last seen her. Surely those couldn't all be from worrying about her. "The faster this is done, the better so they can't harass me later and find out something more sensitive."

"Very well Kirstin." A final stroke of her hair and Belara let Kirsty go.

"I'll let Finnol know you've left, once he gets out." Hyacinth didn't look up from her papers.

"Thank you Hyacinth." Belara nodded and guided Kirsty out the door.

The docks smelled of caught sea and fish to Kirsty, and the boats all nodded together like wise old men save for her father's. The *Corsantóir* held still and heavy on the swells, just as it had handled sluggish and surly on the earlier commute to the Office. Da' had told her earlier that since they'd found the *Sea Witch* wrecked that his boat had taken to being moody and pitching things across the decks when it was just the two of them. On the other end a boom was busy transferring loads from a larger boat to the wharf. She could distantly hear workmen's shouts. The ground fell away under her feet at her aunt led her to the bus stop several blocks away.

There was enough time to sit, but though the bench was clean neither witch did so. As they came to the stop from one direction a young mother with two small children came from the other side. Her dark short hair had begun to snarl, and there were still wet patches on her shirt which had been wiped at but remained stubborn. The woman smelled of bile to Kirsty, and she wondered which of the young ones had recently spit up on her.

The woman looked between them, her breath labored from her exertion. Belara shook her head and Kirsty waved to the bench. The mother needed to sit and rest during the wait more than they did.

"Thank you." The woman sank down and held the children close. "You have such pretty dresses. I wish I could dress like that. It may be a few years before I can buy anything so pretty and flowy again. Re-enactors? Is there a Faire?"

"You could say that, we're not going to a Faire today though." Belara smiled. The eldest of the pair, possibly around three or four, fussed at his mother insistently, tugging at her top. "Do you mind if I give the children some biscuits?"

"If that's not too much trouble, we were so rushed that I forgot their snacks. I only have enough on me for the fare though." The woman's brow furrowed between the eyes, her eyes meeting Belara's and then flitting away while the color on her cheeks rose.

Belara reached into her pocket and drew out three packs of gingersnap animals, still in wrappers. She carefully opened two and handed them to the children, then handed the third to the mother. "It looks like you could use a little something to eat yourself."

"Thank you…"

Kirsty smiled, trying not to watch too much while the small family nibbled their blood sugars and stomachs back into sane states. Her aunt winked at her while no one was watching and Kirsty flashed her teeth back.

When the bus pulled up they boarded with the family, just behind, and slipped their change into the fare box. The bus driver looked down at his clipboard as they boarded and passed, double checking his next stop and checking off the current one. They sat quickly in an empty seat, and Kirsty sat a little closer to her aunt than was strictly necessary. She stifled the urge to hold her ears at all the noise and watched the scenery go by, and then the people getting on and off at the stops.

When they got to the proper stop, one that the name when called garbled incoherently to anyone except those that the spell didn't exclude, they disembarked. Once more the bus driver looked down at his clipboard and took no notice of them. Whether either Kirsty or Belara agreed with the measures that their community took to ensure some measure of intermingling for those born to the Cowan community, they could agree that the measures on the bus system worked.

Belara swept Kirsty with her in through the glass front doors, the family relationship once more retreating behind the thick mask of professionalism that her job required. A pair of young security guards kept watch inside, taking their garb into account.

"Bit odd to see your like coming in. Usually we've got the suits and skirts through our door." Slightly buck toothed, the thinner of the two had a slight lisp but a genial twinkle to his eye. "What brings you lovely lasses this time 'Ms. Greene'?"

"Walter..." Professor MacLeòmhann shook her head at him. "Mind yourself. Ms. Makay has some business of her own to conduct."

"Good luck with it then." Walter winked at Kirsty while his partner kept an eye on the doors for anyone else coming. "The lift should be clear by now."

"Thank you." Professor MacLeòmhann murmured.

Kirsty nodded in acknowledgement. A quick glance aimed at her aunt widened her eyes slightly as she tried to think where the lift they needed would be, since she had never entered the building through the front entrance. Professor MacLeòmhann led the way without missing a beat, pressing further in and through a second set of doors. A lobby lurked here, cold, stark, and efficient in dark lines of power and sweeping walls. A hall led off of this, mercifully broken with potted trees and ferns of human size. They ducked behind one of these and into the lift doors that came to life at their touch.

Kirsty shivered at the sensation of walking through thick spider webs and through the portal. The division between the concurrent spaces that shared space was sharp, not a gentle and natural phasing like what happened at the entrances to Seal Point or the school.

The ride down was swift and they stepped into the mezzanine. This 'room' was large enough to feel as if they were outside, and intentionally set up to mimic the outdoors as much as possible. Each department of the ministries had their own buildings within this space, and she followed her aunt past a fountain depicting the supposed 'order of things' toward the building that looked modeled on ancient temples of various pantheons.

The triumphant witch gazed after them, the wings of an injured tailed Angelic being 'bandaged' while other 'lost' creatures looks to the humans for help. To Kirsty it looked more as if all the evils they suffered had been imposed by the 'perfect' pair.

Kirsty bit her lip and ducked her head. There was a strange feeling that the building put off which reminded her too much of the way Morvan felt to her. The doors this time depicted a group of humans dismantling one of the old sacred wells and driving the essence from it into a box. The door burned when she touched it, but nothing else seemed to happen.

Once through the door it was no better. Orbs of palest orange fairy flame lit the walls and gave the stone walls a tomb-like feel. It was cold, and those already inside pulled heavy cloaks around themselves. Kirsty pulled her white lambskin cloak tight, grateful for the fur beneath her heavy blue dress.

"Appointments Only. Name and purpose," a clerk drawled from behind the counter, an ornate blue plume paused at the end of his sentence. His robes still bore the dust of the ancient texts that he was working with.

Kirsty glanced at her aunt briefly and then stepped to the desk. "Kirstin Makay, I am here to test and register as a Shifter."

He looked her over, raising his brows and sneering while speaking through his nose. "Age and transformation specie or ability, little girl?" Said nose rose at the end with a superior smirk.

Professor MacLeòmhann's hand closed on her shoulder, and Kirsty realized she'd begun to bristle. She closed her eyes and centered herself, visualizing how amusing it would be if when he went to wash the dust just wouldn't come off.

"Thirteen still, long-haired white cat." Kirsty breathed, not allowing the smile at the image to reach her lips.

He looked at the professor for confirmation. She nodded. His brows rose further.

"Well then, this way please. I suppose you must be the Kirstin Makay they are waiting for." He hopped down from his seat.

He was much shorter than Kirsty had expected, though still much taller than herself. He bustled down the hallway deeper into the building, and they followed. The oppressive air grew the deeper in they went, and as he turned into a stairwell the chill grew and seeped into her. The air grew heavier each step down and whispers in the dark at the edges of the light orbs swirled in various languages she only half caught.

Glancing at her aunt over her shoulder it did not look like the woman felt the presence. Ahead of her the clerk gave no sign of feeling it either. More stairs lead to another hallway. Nine doors down they arrived at their destination.

"I believe you can handle the rest from here." The clerk's voice clipped and he nodded before withdrawing with brisk steps back the way he had came from.

Kirsty watched him, then murmured once he was beyond earshot. "He seems..."

"He's that way because he either thinks us intruders or dislikes shifters or anything tied to the old myths." Belara looked down at Kirsty's darkened eyes. "Don't let it get to you."

"Why work here then?"

"To control fear, most likely."

Kirsty chewed on her lip. Professor MacLeòmhann pushed open the door and they went inside. The room here seemed smaller than it really was. Books and scrolls lay on shelves behind thick glass. One side of the room held a case with various strange contraptions, partitioned away from artefacts of stone, metal, and clay which gave off auras of power and gleamed dully. A small door lurked in the back, barred with iron and chained with silver.

"Ms MacLeòmhann... Miss Makay... nice of you to join us today. You're late by a week, but I am glad you are feeling better." A thin bespectacled woman with a beakish nose stepped out of the shadows of a corner.

"Um. Yes Ma'am, sorry ma'am." Kirsty looked her over and then looked down, feeling a sting on her cheeks.

"Ms. Henn." The woman nodded. "So, by your presence your instructor feels that you have mastered the change enough for examination. It is a strange branch of magic to be gifted in, and closely monitored as I am sure you understand. So, why?"

Kirsty was careful not to think of David, in case the Examiner was a Reader. "I like fuzzy things," she half lied. "There also have been a few times that I wish I could just have sneaked away to avoid problems that weren't worth my time." That, at least, was a full truth. "I think that being able to take on a different form also helps to give a different view of the world, which can help keep things in perspective."

"A decent enough reason. If you pass you'll be put on the registry and your form recorded for if you use this skill to do anything *illegal*. Since you are a minor though, your entry won't be publicly visible until you've reached the age of majority. This might be at 16 since that is what it is here, or it might be 18 since that is your home country's." Ms. Henn leaned down slightly, bringing her head closer to Kirsty's. "If it were me I would be braced for the lower age of the two," she whispered with a slight wink and head bob.

"I would have thought that the age standards would have been sorted by now." Professor MacLeòmhann mused, her voice sliding between Kirsty and the Examiner.

"Well, until there is a more unified government I doubt it will happen. It will some day though, I am sure, and that will make things easier for everyone." Ms. Henn smiled, her eyes dark and gleaming. "If it doesn't happen in the open community then it will start in ours and it will be the job of our next generation to spread that for a better and more stable world."

Ms. Henn turned briskly and pecked toward the door, giving it a lingering caress before undoing the chains. Kirsty wrinkled her nose and glanced up at her aunt, silently asking her if she really had just heard what she thought, or if the test was already started and it just wasn't what she had trained and braced for. The professor's eyes were trained on the door and Examiner, narrowed and emerald green sparking with gold, as if she wished to pounce.

No acknowledgement was forthcoming, so Kirsty looked harder, opening her senses past her comfort and searching for answers as to why Ms. Henn seemed so fanatic with her opinion. All that greeted her when looking in this fashion was a dark mist that tickled warnings and vague memories of discussions with the Lady. Ms. Henn turned her head toward them as the door swung open.

Kirsty slammed herself shut again.

"Ms. Makay, if you will accompany me inside the testing chamber. Professor, I am sure that you won't mind waiting here."

"Of course..." The professor nodded curtly. "I'll just conjure myself a chair then while I wait for you to finish."

"Oh, no need. I'm sure this won't take long at all." Ms. Henn smiled, though it didn't reach her eyes.

"Perhaps, but it is better to be prepared." She conjured herself a chair anyway in an out of the way corner facing the testing door. It was a simple wood affair with a deep green cushion seat near enough that she would be able to spring up if her niece returned being carried. Professor MacLeòmhann quirked her eyebrow at Kirsty.

Kirsty nodded imperceptibly. Obviously it was not who her aunt had been hoping for. Maybe later she would have time to puzzle out what the past history between the two was. It prickled her skin as badly as whatever the other thing she was sensing did.

Once ushered through the door it closed with a heavy boom, the chains rattling as they resecured themselves. Here the air weighed on her even more, and she regretted not practicing deeper sea dives to cope with the atmosphere...even though it wasn't the same sort of pressure. It pressed her lungs anyway.

"Well then, it's just you and me, isn't it?" Ms. Henn traipsed slowly behind her, running a hand over her shoulders as the darkness grew. "I'm going to have fun with this. How well can you change when everything is falling apart around you?"

Kirsty didn't answer and Ms Henn smiled. "Wise girl. Show me."

Without much thought, Kirsty let her bones slip, remembering what the body of a cat should feel like. She wrapped her puffy white tail around herself and looked up, black whiskers twitching once in question. Faint grey lines twined around her left wrist where the tattooing was on her human form, blurred from the fur. A very faint silver crescent moon lurked on her chest so pale as to be easily merely a fold in the natural fur flow and disappeared when her neck stretched up.

The transformation back was just as simple when given the order. After all, she had been working on this for quite some time now. *"It's not going to be this easy. What's she planning? No fears pulled out yet..."*

The strange creeping dread about the room began to press in on her more, wrapping unseen tendrils around her body and brain. She stiffened and tried to push them back, but they wormed in deeper and tickled mental recesses that she had been trying to avoid.

"Except this one so far." Kirsty amended to herself. She kept breathing through it, ignoring the feeling of being judged and found to be lacking.

She felt the push of a mind against her own and sharp pecks from unexpected quarters. Instinctively she tried to repel the mental invasion, but the witch was older and more experienced, and slip through the waters as she could...Ms. Henn still managed to break through.

Ms. Henn clucked and pursed her lips, scratching through the child's darkest corners eagerly for the deepest fears and eagerly casting them into the light. Around them the room began to shift while these combined to form a scenario.

The Examiner squawked and flapped mental wings at finding a tightly sealed chest in Kirsty's mind. Scratching at the seals gave her no purchase to open, nor did her unlocking spells. Around them the storm began to form. The floor became a listing deck and waves crashed over the side of a boat.

Kirsty nearly lost what little edge she managed to keep on the contents of her mental chest when the deck began to tilt. The room's magic had nearly completed the spacial shift, surely her Examiner had enough to be working with by now?

Ms. Henn narrowed her eyes and ducked her head against the spray, still trying to force open the chest. Kirsty looked at her feet and staggered to keep her balance. If this continued too long then those secret might be found, and since they weren't hers there was only one thing that she could do.

Without being told when by the Examiner she wasn't sure if this plan would fail her. She let her mind slip toward the cat that had started taking up residence within her mind, wishing that it would work for a seal transformation. If she could, then she could get away that way while showing that she could transform.

Her thoughts did not slow, but they focused. They did not simplify, oh how she wished that they would, but the constant buzz of her mind did fade when the unimportant ones were left aside. Kirsty focused as hard as she could to speed it...if she got stuck here she could wind up part cat and need assistance regaining herself. Ms. Henn's heckling and psychic pecking combined with the magically produced stimuli of the Examination chamber constantly kept her away from her center and kept away the warm feeling of freely flowing magic.

Her bones burned. She tried to hold her focus and to relax, but it simply wasn't happening. Every time she relaxed enough for the burn to ebb a bit, that infernal woman as at the lock. The winds of the sea storm raged and she heard her mother's screams.

"It's illusion." Kirsty clamped more firmly on herself, keeping her head from turning toward the source. She felt her shifting bones and grimaced.

A green suckered arm reached up over the ship and slammed down just behind Ms. Henn. Kirsty's eyes flung open at the sound to see the thick muscle curling to encompass them. Adrenaline pumped through her and she hissed, springing up. Getting away from that was now all that mattered, nevermind keeping Ms. Henn out of her deepest secrets.

She landed on the arm with all four paws, undershooting her target but unsheathing and driving her claws deep through the slimy hide. It smelled of squid and she sank her fangs as another arm wrapped around the ship. Kirsty shook her head for all she was worth to rip as big a chunk free as possible, since with this form she was unable to use her main defensive spells.

The blood and squid flesh tasted sweet to her, though she did not have the time to enjoy it. She released the squid and was leaping for the mast, climbing that as desperately as she had when David had chased her that first year. Ms. Henn's mental assaults let up unnoticed by Kirsty, so focused she was on getting up to the crow's nest of this generic and ever shifting ship.

Landing in the bottom of the basket she shifted back with slightly less difficulty, nearing the edge of how many times her stamina would likely allow her to shift. She barely remembered to pull her wand to hide the source of the spell and then unleashed a focused blast of water, trying desperately to pinpoint it enough to produce a blade to sever the arms that had materialized during her climb. Her breath was swift, her ears rang, she trembled. Bile rose in her mouth and scorched her esophagus.

The strike was partially good. Two of the three she targeted fell away with an earsplitting cry from the kraken. A shudder ran over her again and her heart felt as if it would explode.

Kirsty looked down more thoroughly. Ms. Henn was nowhere to be found. "Did it get her? Was Auntie right about being able to die during this test? What happens if the Examiner dies? I have to find her!"

She looked for her harder, hoping that perhaps Ms. Henn had just taken cover and would either end the test or help deal with the kraken...the storm was a separate issue. Against her better judgement she risked attracting the kraken's attention and called out for her.

At least when her aunt had had her practicing to be ready for this, and had had David there to help if she got lost, she knew they were likely to be safe.

"I think that I've seen all that I need to." The voice scratched and clucked irritably over the wind and wails.

The scene around her faded and the dim room returned. Kirsty landed hard, her knees buckling under her and then cracking against the floor. She curled up briefly around them, unable to stifle the initial cry of shock and pain, but managed to hold back the rest.

"You took far too long to transform. You're lucky that you were not stuck longer halfway." Ms. Henn's pointed black leather booties came to the top of Kirsty's vision, before she turned her head up. Ms. Henn's eyes bored into her own, flashing angrily, "I don't know if I should fail you on that, or pass you for the completeness of the change and swift thinking in heading for the high ground for your attack."

"I was distracted," Kirsty looked back down and admitted, not rising yet and chest still heaving. "I don't like having my mind explored and pecked at like that." She winced after realizing the word she'd used for the sensation.

"Hm... You did put up a rather good fight on that end, for a child with a long way to go." Ms. Henn crossed her arms. "Perhaps you just earned a few extra points as well."

Kirsty looked up, her eyes wide. "Why?"

Ms. Henn shook her head, unwilling to reveal what her transformation animal was. "It is just something that you said child. If you can get up, go to the book at the end of the room."

Ms. Henn did not wait, nor did she help Kirsty up. She only moved toward the large black book on the stone podium that appeared when called, and picked up an ornate red quill.

Kirsty got to her feet shakily and pushed herself that way, refusing to show how queasy each step felt and unable to recall the last time the shift had been so hard on her. She eyed the book warily, her hair on her arms raising further, or would have if it could have. An oily vibe rolled off of the ledger, and Ms. Henn stroked it lightly.

"This registry goes back centuries and records some truly excellent wizards, sorcerers, magicians, witches, healers...and of course the stray warlock or two." Ms. Henn smiled, it being just as oily. "It dates back to the first Ministry. Nearly everyone that has a shifting power is recorded here, and soon your name and passing will be as well."

"Not everyone..." Kirsty thought, *"Far too many selkies, kelpies, and faeries to record them all."*

The woman grabbed Kirsty's hand and jabbed the tip of her quill into her finger. Kirsty tried to pull back, but was still too weak to manage it. The quill sucked up enough blood to fill itself and then Ms. Henn removed it from her finger. Kirsty popped it into her mouth and sucked wide eyed before holding her tongue tightly against the wound and humming a sublingual healing tone.

"Now, now. Big girls shouldn't be sucking their booboos. You and your family are safe now, after all." Ms. Henn clucked in satisfaction. Kirsty's blood mingled with the ink that had already been loaded in the chamber and then flowed across the page with her details and the test results in a tidy but thorough summary.

"If any deities can hear me and act, please remove my blood from that infernal book. It's Tainted." Kirsty prayed, eying it. A faint ripple went through the room and a brief cool wisp of air settled onto her head, just the vaguest impression of a breeze under the moon, then was gone. She nodded her head lightly, feeling that at least she had been heard, and hoping her prayer would be granted.

"It doesn't–" She started, then removed her finger from her mouth, "It doesn't look that old. Even with preservation magic the books that are in the same age range tend to show more wear."

Kirsty wished that she knew a spell to see through illusions, just in case it was a substitute. There were only the two choices. The original roll had been Tainted, which could be dangerous for any known shifter, or it was a fake.

"Don't be silly." Ms. Henn finished the final word with a flourish and a jabbed dot of satisfaction. "The only time this is handled is when the list must be consulted for Witch Trials if a shifter gets to the highest court for crimes related. This links to copies that see more every day handling and updates them when it is updated. Your name, of course, stays sealed until you are of age."

Ms. Henn blew over the ink to dry it and then closed it. The whole affair disappeared: podium, ledger, quill, ink pot, and all. She then ushered Kirsty to the door, undid the chains, and Kirsty emerged again to the light.

A clock that had previously gone unnoticed presented itself in her peripheral vision as Professor MacLeòmhann squeezed the air from her and irritated already abused bones. It read five o'clock. "You were gone so long, I was worried. I tried to get through the door after the first several hours, but the locks..." She squdged Kirsty again.

"Yes, I made them self-healing and self-relocking after the last student of yours that was registered." I couldn't have you barging in to save someone at a crucial last moment in their Examination, now could I?" Ms. Henn smiled, showing her teeth even though no warmth touched her eyes. "That boy really did deserve to die for the things he said about our government."

"No one deserves to die for questioning logic and methods. Since Miss Makay is here and well I assume that the Examination is over, and I have total faith that she passed, so register her and we'll be on our way."

"Oh yes, she did pass, and put up a very good attempt to keep me from using her fears and keeping me out of private things while not letting the scenario she made kill her." Ms. Henn scratched at the top of her left hand, then made her way to a cabinet. She drew out a glass and poured a thick liquid from a decanter, keeping her body between them and it. After checking to make sure she had as much as she needed she quaffed it before continuing. "Miss Makay I have already taken the liberty of recording, so you are free to go. I'm sure you can show yourselves out. I must...rest now after such an ordeal."

When Ms. Henn turned around she kept her hand hidden. This time the smile was somehow toothier.

"Of course." Professor MacLeòmhann nodded her head, her own smile not reaching her eyes. "Thank you for your time, Ms. Henn."

She guided Kirsty firmly out of the room, and shushed her in the hall when Kirsty opened her mouth to ask a question. The clerk in the entry of the department was gone by the time that they got there, and they continued on. Each moment that Kirsty could not ask about the odd feeling stretched three times as long as she thought it ought. They were at least walking away from whatever was in the Department of Myths.

The bus ride was just as bad and everything crashed around like a ship in a high storm. Before Kirsty could ask about what had been off, and before Hyacinth could even finish her greeting, Professor MacLeòmhann marched to the tea nook and took the last of what was hot, quaffing it without sugar.

"I suppose things over in Myths are worse by that, or Kirsty failed. What happened, and should I get Finnol first?" Hyacinth's question barely registered on Belara, who gave a short start after a moment.

"Oh? Yes. Yes go get Finnol if he's free now." Belara sighed and looked contemplatively at the teapot before making a gesture to begin more.

Hyacinth nodded and then went down the hall toward Finnol's office.

"So...can I ask now what was wrong with that lady and that place? She was really..." Kirsty faded, trying but unable to think of a word that adequately conveyed what she needed.

"I'm not sure what happened, but Ms. Henn was more adversarial than usual. The recording is usually done in front of the sponsoring teacher," the professor tapped her fingers together thoughtfully. "I am not convinced that really was Ms. Henn, but I don't have any proof."

"Is is usual to sign with my blood?" Kirsty stepped closer, getting a cup herself while keeping track of how long until the fresh tea could be poured. "I wasn't prepared for that, especially not with the other uses of my blood."

"No." The single word dropped like a cannonball. MacLeòmhann looked sternly at her. "I hope you didn't let her. Blood is not required for the registry."

"Well, I didn't let her. It was more like she stole it with a strange quill and mixed it with ink. It was harder to stop the bloodflow than usual after she pricked me, and she seemed especially pleased about having my blood and the book."

"Hmm.." The tea poured itself while her aunt mused.

Kirsty added sugar, continuing when it became obvious the professor was giving her space to. "There was something oily about it, and her, and the book. A definite taint, but the source was from somewhere else."

"It wouldn't surprise me. There have been many taints in the whole Ministry, and not just that one. They all are." Finnol's tone was stern and cold, measured as if he was restraining himself from going straight to the Ministry Overlap and razing the place. He had been in a fine mood after finishing the earlier conference, and then getting notification from one of their contacts that the poachers he had been pursuing had been caught in the act...by the Sea Shepherd ship at that. The irony had pleased him. This latest news about the Ministry's corruption spreading caused his happiness to evaporate like summer mist. "I heard what you said down the hall about the blood as well. I think you forgot that this place is designed to carry whispers to office heads' ears as we're out and about?"

Kirsty's heart thudded and then stopped, then her head drooped. "Sorry Da'. I couldn't wait till you got here and we really needed the tea..."

Finnol shook his head and came to wrap his arms around her. "No, I'm the one that's sorry that work kept me from being able to go with you for this, even if I were relegated to wait somewhere."

"Your work's important Da'." Kirsty wrapped the arm that didn't have the tea in it around him and let his chest take the weight of her head. "How else is the Order going to have the contacts it needs, or the Fisheries Department going to get the public stuff done?"

Finnol made a frustrated sound and held her tight for a moment, resting his forehead on her head and closing his eyes. "I'd leave it if I could, you know."

"I know Da', but then Mara would be angry with you, and who would do all the things among the Cowan that you take care of?" she rephrased her statement, making sure to dig in with her point. Yes it hurt, but she had no idea what like would be like if the previous head hadn't worked so hard. She couldn't be selfish about her Da' then, since his work meant a better world for her pups...should she have any.

Finnol smiled slightly. "Anyone can do it. But I'm more worried about your blood being in potential enemy hands. Blood magic is usually dark and powerful. Few witches do with it what the Ladies have their Priestesses do." Finnol mused, "In a way, I wish your school taught more about Dark Arts than just defense courses. Then at least you would be as prepared as Schneiengert's."

"As am I." Belara reached for more tea, having drained her cup already. "You know very well why the how of those arts are not taught at Carrick though young man." The professor glared at him over her tea, brows drawn down and lips tight. "You shouldn't speak that way in front of Kirstin."

"Is it really dark if it's not taken to a dark place?" Kirsty couldn't resist asking. "Is what I do dark?"

"No, *chailín*, what you do and will do keeps things tied, even though I don't like it for either of my girls. How can it be dark unless you make it so?" Finnol reassured her, stroking lightly.

"So what do we do about Henn having my blood, and the maybe fake book?" She worried her lower lip, trying to figure out what the most dangerous use might be. "I asked any listening deities to get my blood out of there. I got a sign I was heard too, though I'm not sure who it was from."

"I can get espionage to look into the book, maybe I can pull a few strings...unless the Lilitus are involved." Finnol thought and rubbed his forehead and sank into a chair. It was rather painfully obvious to him that he wouldn't get aunt or daughter away from the tea. He wished hard for a glass of Scotch, but was not desperate enough to conjure himself one. Seeing the woman who had raised him in such a state as to suck the tea so swiftly threatened to send him mentally back to the paralysis that had come with the lost of his first child.

Hyacinth had come to a similar conclusion and locked the door. It was long past normal business hours anyway. If anyone of the Order came for some reason then they could always be let in.

"Be careful about how much faith you place in them. They act when it serves them to, Kirsty. Remember Mara can only come aground under certain circumstances, the Lady has lost much, and anyone else..." Finnol trailed off with a grimace. "As blessed as we are..." He sighed and crossed his arms. How could he continue when every way he could think of what he was trying to say would only invite wrath? He'd not traded his father's skin to preserve his youngest's life just for this.

"I understand Da'..." Kirsty put her cup down and sat on his knee carefully, trying not to rest too much weight on him. "So what should I do?"

"Pray that whatever I come up with works." He quirked his lips up and to the right bitterly, patting her knee. "And concentrate on getting through the last half of the year so you can do your sea trial."

"What *we* come up with Finnol Makay." Professor MacLeòmhann's voice pressed down on them as sharply as a ruler rapping recalcitrant knuckles. "You're a part of the Order, we've all got concerns with everyone staying alive and unBound, including those that will be its future."

Hyacinth nodded, "I think Etain might have wanted me to smack you for acting like its all on your shoulders."

Finnol sighed. "Right then. Guess we call a meeting, and sort out getting Kirsty back to the school where she'll be safe."

Kirsty snorted, wondering if there would ever come a time where it didn't come back to being seen as an object in some convoluted fashion. Did other mixed blood kids have this problem? In irritation she shifted into cat form and curled up in his lap.

The adults would want to talk. They would of course want to exclude her from these discussions even though it was her blood in question. Kirsty knew they cared and only wanted to protect her so that she could focus. David certainly would have looked at her more as a person when coming to the thought of protecting her, and not a tiny pup unable to defend herself.

As a cat these thoughts simplified somewhat. Kirsty took some satisfaction on the amount of long white hairs that were surely going to be clinging to her father's pants.

Be watching for book two

Selkies' Skins:
Temple and Skinquest

Will Etain come home? Will Kirsty survive the second part of her trials? If so will she return to land?

Also be watching for Audiobook versions of this and other THG StarDragon Publishing fantasy books.

GLOSSARY

There are several words from both of the Gaelics, as well as other languages and cultures. This glossary is provided as a resource for those that are unfamiliar with a word or tend to forget foreign words. As language is something that fascinates me, I always try to work other vocabulary than English in when there is space and it fits properly with the story flow. This is also, in part, a tribute to the countless authors that introduced me to words that I would likely have never learned if they had not done similar.

Abyssopelagic – very deep, from the word abyss.

A chailín mo chroí – My dear child.

A dhath ar bith – Irish Gaelic for 'nothing at all' or 'not much.'

Aegir – Norse god of the sea.

Aft – Nautical term for back of the ship.

Ainsley – Scottish habitational surname transferred to unisex forename use, composed of the Old English elements ansetl "hermitage" and leah "meadow, pasture," hence "hermitage meadow."

Anchor – A spell that does exactly what it sounds like. A person will form the intent to be an Anchor when another has to cross dimensional or planar boundaries. The Observers do for the members of a Moot a similar job that the Lightkeepers traditionally did for the Makays of Seal Point by the use of light and spellwork. Lighting a candle and placing in the window is a traditional spell or prayer used to help a family member or loved one return home.

Argent – Heraldic for silver.

Arten – Scots Gaelic for Stone.

Ashray – Water or sea ghosts, also known as water lovers from Scottish tales. These phantasms can be either male or female and are said to be alluring. If caught in the light of day they melt into a puddle of water. In Kirsty's world there are two types of ashrays: 1) The type that forms when a person drowns (if they don't get turned into something else or don't get to move on), and 2) a type of fae.

Aweful – Not to be confused with awful. Aweful is to be filled with awe, or to be awe inspiring (either for good or ill). This is a little used word now, awful being thought of the most when it is heard.

Bairn – Boy.

Bean-fionn – Water Woman, White Woman. She is called th Weisse Frau in Germany and is more benevolent there. A kiss from her on a child protects them, and she is very protective of children. She's not above drowning someone that makes her angry or hurts children. In Ireland though she is more known for drowning children playing alone by the water. Whether this is malicious or merely wishing to take the children into her home is a matter of debate.

The Weisse Frau is an aspect of The Lady that is coming closer to being reclaimed by her through the association of Kirsty and David, though none of the three are fully aware of this as of yet.

Boobrie – A strange looking bird-thing from Scottish tales. The boobrie is said by some to prey on ships. Descriptions vary a bit, but generally it is crane like with penguinish wings (despite being able to fly) and is black. Individual boobries vary a bit and may have color marks. They sound coarser than peacocks when they make a cry. Some can take the appearance of horses and run over the waters...making great distractions for ancient mariners. Because of the ability of some to take the shape of horses some students of folklore equate the boobrie and kelpie as the same things. These prefer salt water to fresh.

Brumal – Cold, frigid.

Cailleach – Some say she is a goddess, some say she is a fae. There is only one of her either way. She is often equated with the Blue Woman, the Washerwoman of the Ford, and sometimes the Banshee.

Carrick – Gaelic for Rock.

Colcanon – similar to Bubble and Squeak, a fry dish made of leftovers from the previous day.

Collywobble – A strange and elusive creature that few have seen. Some have trident-like arms, and it is thought that they have tails. There are both land-based and sea-based versions. These critters are responsible for the odd fluttery feelings in the stomach and love to gather on boats and around carnival rides and moving vehicles. When not there they roam in packs looking for people to give digestion problems. They draw amusement from making people nauseous. To ward them off anise gum is excellent, but it must be flavored with real anise and not synthetic flavoring.

Compánach – Companion.

Corsantóir – Defender, protector, guardian.

Cortège – A procession, usually solemn.

Cowan – Pagan and Wiccan word for outsider.

Coven – A group of witches that work together.

Deosil – Clockwise.

Draiganpáirc – Dragon Park. This is a location in Ireland that exists much the way as Seal Point does. It is part of the physical world, but only accessible though certain routes. If someone tries to access the same space but not through the proper routes then they will find only sea or unsettled land. The division between the plains here is also very thin. This is the stronghold of Brigid's Well and Forge and the seat of the O'Drake family. Some members of this family can be met in the Dragon Shaman series, which was started long, long before these stories.

Dunstan – Anglo-Saxon name composed of the elements dun "black, dark" and stan "stone," hence "black stone" or "dark stone."

Erebus – Latin form of Greek Erebos, meaning "darkness." In mythology, this is the name of the offspring of Chaos, brother of Nyx, and father of Æther. He is the personification of primordial darkness. In later legends Erebos became the name of a place in Hades, the underworld.

Finmen – A darker variation of the merfolk tales. Where the selkies were generally considered mild mannered, the finmen were feared. The stories that I found about them referred to them liking to drown children by dragging them from the beach, and sometimes stealing them from homes by the sea.

Geas – Gaelic word for curse or compellation.

Gerwulf – German name composed of the elements ger "spear" and wulf "wolf," hence "spear-wolf."

Ghillie dhu – Woodman. This is a type of fae known to be shy and protective of the woods and forests, and associated with birch. They are kind to children but cruel to those disrespecting their home. Ghillie dhu is dark haired and covers himself in foliage (good hunting camo suits are also called ghillie dhu and use ropes to mimic the silhouette of plantmatter). In England he/they is/are sometimes equated to the Green Man.

Grundylows – These are the British Isles' version of Kappa. Instead of being turtle-like with a bowl in the head grundylows are lanky and spindly with exceptionally long, strong fingers that they choke and drown their (often human) prey with.

Guirmean – Scots. Blue.

Hame – Home.

Hemming – Scandinavian name derived from Old Norse hamr, meaning "shape." The name may have originated as a byname for a "shape-shifter" or "werewolf."

Hir – This is not a typo, but intentional as a combination of his and her for use with the gender-strange deity.

Hyppocampus – This is alternatively spelled hippocampus,

but I decided to use hyppocampus. The hyppocampus is a fishtailed horse. They would vary based on the region. Those in the colder climates would have heavier fur than those in warmer climes.

Intervening – A non-species specific spell, geas, or binding wherein a party takes on the debt of another or steps between a person and a consequence or deity. This can also be done if the original terms of a binding or geas need to be changed as observed by an outside party, but it comes with a price that will vary.

Ken – Know, understand, grasp.

Kürsch – One of the heraldic furs, it looks rather like fluffy breast feathers.

Leannán – Lover.

Leòmhann – Scots Gaelic for Lion.

Máthair – Irish Gaelic for Mother.

Marelion – female fishtailed lion, the feminine companion to the SeaLion (different from the mundane sea lion). Both males and females have manes, but the male's manes are wilder.

Meidh – Irish Gaelic for Balance. (used in Pearls of Sea and Stone)

Mermishdian – One of several undersea languages.

Merrow – This is the Irish answer for the standard fish merfolk. The ladies are said to be gorgeous and often seek sailors for husbands. The males wear red caps, have complexions that are generally ruddy from consumption of alcohol, are much less comely and attractive, and spend their days searching for rum barrels from shipwrecks. Some tales say that they cause storms which in turn cause wrecks to fuel their habit of imbibing drink.

Mizzenmast – If the vessel has two masts and the aft (back) mast is smaller than the fore (front) mast, then the back mast is called a mizzenmast. If it is a three masted vessel then the very aft mast is always a mizzenmast.

Moot – Archaic term for meeting.

Naga – Snake people. These are found in Buddhist and Hindu stories, and they have a possible connection to the dragon people. There are several sub-breeds of naga, some are land dwelling, some prefer fresh water, and some are from the seasnake.

Octopid – A type of merperson descended from and caretaking octopus. Squid merfolk are similar, and also are in this category as the original beings that Mara and the Lady created them from existed before evolution took the octopus and squid down separate paths.

Ogham – A ancient Celtic method of writing that involved the use of carved lines. This existed around the time of runes, but fell into disuse through the course of history.

Óinseach – Irish (and sometimes Scots) Gaelic for fool in the feminine case. The masculine word is amadán. (used in Pearls of Sea and Stone)

Pagan – Originally meant country dweller. Today it is more commonly used to refer to people following a non-Judeo-Christian faith. Within this though there are a vast array if different religions, some similar and others not, and from all around the world with its various pantheons. Castle Carrick chooses based on ability and talent, not religion, so it's halls are filled with a sampling of all religions including the odd Jedi.

Poop or poopdeck – The nautical term for the back deck of a boat or ship.

Port – A safe harbour for shipping and other vessels. Also it is used for the left side of the boat when facing the prow.

Prow – The front of a ship or boat.

Purpure – Heraldic for purple.

Rapscallion – An archaic word for rascal.

Revive – A spell. When the verb refers to the effect of a spell it is capitalized. This can be cast in any language, but some work better than others.

Rok – Old Danish form of Old Norse Hrókr, meaning "crow, rook."

Ryujin – Japanese word for dragon people. Ryujin is also the name of a dragon king of the sea, as well as the name of the capital city that he rules over. Yes, this is a tie in point with "Dragon Shaman" novels.

Sain – British for bless. (used in Pearls of Sea and Stone)

Samebito – The Japanese word for shark people.

Sapphire – A blue stone. When mentioned for a heraldic crest the stone is used to symbolize azure (blue).

Schneiengert – Germanic. strong spear.

Seanmhuintir – Irish Gaelic for Grandparents.

Seelie – The good (but not always kind nor benevolent) fae.

Seidhrmenn – Norse. Wise men, magic users.

Sevrin – Severe, strict.

Sgian dubh – A small, often black handled single-bladed knife. Originally used for eating, it is also part of formal scottish dress.

Sgòrnan – Throat, Gaelic.

Sgrios-puinnaein – antivenom, anti-poison.

Shi – This is not a typo but is intentional to denote a combination of he and she. The i was used to make it more obviously different than she.

Sidhe – The fae.

Skinquest – The term used for the quest a half selkie must undergo to earn his or her own skin. Some full-blooded selkies also have to undergo this if they are born without a skin (rare, but does happen).

Slàinte – Health.

Soulfish – Infernal undead fish produced from the souls of

those who drowned on the sea and carried great wrongs or sins within their hearts, or deep regrets. Left to fester they then seek to create others like themselves. Mara places these souls into their own pockets of reality for them to work through these burdens, but sometimes they manage to win through to the normal world where the borders are weak. They were seen more often when ships were smaller, and now that ships are larger are seen less often. There is a greater likelihood of encountering soulfish in areas like the Bermuda Triangle or near the sites of wrecks.

Spar – The cross timbers to a mast, which hold the sails and rigging (ropes and pulleys). The size of these depend on the size of the vessel and sails.

Sporran – Waist pouch.

Squdged – Squished or oozed up between, like mud in toes.

Starboard – Right side of a vessel when facing the prow.

Stern – Another nautical term for the aft or back of a sailing vessel.

Stunned – The spell is referred to with a capital letter to differentiate between magically induced and mundanely induced types of stunning. This spell varies in efficacy based on the specific language used, but can be cast nonverbally.

Suaimhneach – Be silent, Gaelic.

Taddywafer – a sweet mentioned in *"Pearls of Sea and Stone"* consisting of caramel, chocolate, berries, and specially prepared seaweed wafers.

Taing do Mara – Thank Mara in Scots Gaelic.

Things – There are some creatures that are so terrible that they can be given no name. No matter the language used to speak of them, the word for these creatures is always that languages word meaning "thing."

Thought Form – In some instances thoughts can take on form and substance. This may vary from a being with a body all the way to a formless force that influences a person or place.

Tomtra – a type of fairy that takes care of horses. Mine like to disguise themselves as small animals such as mice. Whiskers, for example, has a red cap. Traditionally they like green caps.

Triton – A particular type of merperson, and these are the royals. They are called so in honor of the god Triton, and the high kings among them are referred to as Neptunes. They generally are the classical merfolk with fish tails, though at times another type of merperson will also earn the right to be referred to as a Triton.

UnBound – Free and not constrained to one form, or not otherwise placed under a *geas* by any of the competing and overlapping ministries.

Undine – Generally these are seen as comely merfolk with fish tails. They have beautiful voices, similar to sirens, but are generally kinder and gentler than their cousins. They are also elemental keepers of the West and Water in some elemental systems.

Unseelie – The fae traditionally thought of as more dangerous and evil. Some fae are counted in different courts by different people.

Waterdogs – These are similar to the dogs that live on land, but are specially adapted to underwater life. Some have aquatic tails. Others look like regular dogs other than the weeds and dripping water when they go on land, making them similar in some ways to kelpies.

Widdershins – Counterclockwise.

Word – When capitalized it refers to a spell word, which is different from a regular word. A spell word is triggered by intent and a caster must have magic within them or know how to tap magic in other fashions, thus why human magic is often wand heavy. The various magical ministries have placed watchspells on particular heavily used magical languages such as Latin, although some other languages have weaker or non-existant watch spells and traces. This is due to the bias of the founders of particular ministries and their beliefs of certain heritages being superior to others. As druidry was suppressed and Gaelic started fading, watch over the magical use of such languages declined.

Xhosa – An African language known for a lot of throat clicks.

About the Author

Teresa Garcia (once Teresa Huddleston-Garcia) is a 30-something mother of two children with special needs, raising them "alone" in the small mountain town of McCloud, CA. Just because she is on her own though, does not mean that she is "alone." Many thanks are due to the McCloud Community Resource Center, to her brother and his family, and her mother, for all their help.

When not drowning in university coursework for her International Relations degree, and chained to the computer, she loves to text role play with her long distance mate Vadise, write stories, hike, paint, meditate, and play games or read with her kids. She also writes quests for, and helps to maintain, the online browser-based RPG Dragon Hearts.

She was raised in another rural mountain community, which she visits as often as she can spare time and gas, though not nearly often enough for her wishes. Her parents always encouraged her writing and artistic talents. In 2005, she decided to pick up the dream of writing and publishing a novel once more, having shelved that (and the "Shadow Chronicles" manuscript) in her early college years due to the time constraints of motherhood at the time. In 2006 she released to the public her first novel in the "Dragon Shaman" series, "Taming the Blowing Wind," and has since published a second book in the series and a poetry book, among other books. She likes to deal with multicultural themes because of her own background.

Currently Teresa has several manuscripts to work on, such as her "Dragon Shaman" series of novels and her current favorite serialized story, "Selkies' Skins." Teresa writes short stories for children in the Adventures of Lightning the Cat series, the second collection of which is to be coauthored with her daughter. Her other titles are intended for more advanced readers.

Where to find Teresa

Deviant Art: AmehanaRainStarDrago

Dragon Shaman series:
http://thedragonshamanseries.weebly.com/

Facebook (THG StarDragon Publishing):
https://www.facebook.com/THGStarDragonPublishing

Goodreads: http://www.goodreads.com/author/show/2908379.
Teresa_Garcia

Personal blog: http://rainstardragon.livejournal.com

Publishing blog: http://thgstardragonpublishing.blogspot.com

Secondary blog: http://rainstardragon.dreamwidth.org/

Selkies Skins extras: http://teresagarciaserials.weebly.com/

THG StarDragon Publishing website: http://thgstardragon.com

Twitter: AmehanaArashi